碧血丹心

——辛亥革命在广东影像实录

广东省立中山图书馆 编

倪俊明 执行编纂

廣東省出版集團

广东科技出版社

·广州·

图书在版编目（CIP）数据

碧血丹心：辛亥革命在广东影像实录/广东省立中山图书馆编.—广州：广东科技出版社，2011.8
（广州史志丛书）
ISBN 978-7-5359-5566-1

Ⅰ.①碧… Ⅱ.①广… Ⅲ.①辛亥革命—史料—广东省 Ⅳ.①K257.06

中国版本图书馆CIP数据核字（2011）第137472号

责任编辑：吕　健　邓　彦
封面设计：林小玲
责任校对：吴丽霞
责任印制：罗华之
出版发行：广东科技出版社
（广州市环市东路水荫路11号　邮政编码：510075）
E-mail：gdkjzbb@21cn.com
http：//www.gdstp.com.cn
经　　销：广东新华发行集团股份有限公司
印　　刷：广州伟龙印刷制版有限公司
（广州市沙太路银利工业大厦1幢　邮政编码：510507）
规　　格：787mm×1 092mm　1/16　印张18.5　字数360千
版　　次：2011年8月第1版
2011年8月第1次印刷
印　　数：1~3 000册
定　　价：49.00元

如发现因印装质量问题影响阅读，请与承印厂联系调换。

《广州史志丛书》出版说明

当代的地方志工作，是一项具有延续性的长期事业，是一项巨大的文化建设系统工程。它不仅仅是编纂一部志书，更需要多方位地开展地情调查、地情研究和地情服务。只有这样，地方志的资政、存史、教化功能才能得到更好的发挥。广州市地方志办公室在编纂广州市志的同时，还积极发动修志人员和社会力量广泛开展地情调查、积累地情资料、开展地情研究、提供地情咨询服务、编写地情丛书、整理旧志、进行方志理论研究等，取得了不少成果。但是，由于志书体例的局限性以及一部市志篇幅的限制，许多地情资料和地情研究成果不能入志。有鉴于此，我们决定将有关的资料和研究成果以《广州史志丛书》的形式公开出版，为广州市的物质文明和精神文明建设服务。

《广州史志丛书》的内容，主要包括以下三个方面：

一、有关广州历史情况的旧方志和其他古文献的整理；

二、今人有关广州地情的著述、研究成果；

三、史志理论研究成果。

本套丛书的编审工作由《广州史志丛书》编审委员会负责，并由广州市地方志编纂委员会办公室组织实施。

《广州史志丛书》将陆续出版，恳请广大读者对本丛书的内容、形式及编辑出版工作提出宝贵意见。

《广州史志丛书》编审委员会

《广州史志丛书》编审委员会

主　任　杨资元

副主任　王林生　胡巧利

委　员　（按姓氏笔画排列）

王　杰　李　扬　杨长明　张晓辉

张影华　陈文敏　冷　东　钟永宁

倪俊明　倪根金　曾　新

《广州史志丛书》编审委员会委托编审委员会副主任、管理学博士王林生和研究员胡巧利审定本书。

序

■ 段云章

在绚丽多姿的中国辛亥革命画卷中，广东的革命无疑是历时最长、内容最丰富、场面最壮烈而又具有鲜明特色的画面。

壹

中国伟大的民主革命先行者孙中山及其最早一批战友陆皓东、史坚如、郑士良、陈少白等人，都出生于广东，并以广东为其最早活动舞台，这就使广东很自然地成为辛亥革命的策源地。

这种情况绝非偶然。鸦片战争以来，广东一直风雷滚滚，反帝反封建斗争连绵不断，具有反清传统的“三合会”等秘密结社，在这里有着广阔而深厚的基础。广东面临海洋，并和沦为殖民地的香港、澳门相毗邻；又是著名的侨乡，对外交往历来频繁，所以，当西方资产阶级紧叩中国大门，迫使封建中国从属于它们并按照它们的面貌来改造中国之时，广东人民在反侵略过程中，最早睁开眼睛看西方，注意学习西方的长处。于是，在广东，最早出现了民族资本主义企业，出现了先进生产力发展的趋势，涌进了先进的思想文化，造就了一批较早的新型知识分子。通过对西方的了解和中西对比，先进人士加紧探索改变落后挨打局面、迅速振兴中国的新的道路，以广东为思想孕育土壤和早期活动基地的洪秀全、洪仁玕、郑观应、康有为、梁启超等人，就是上述先进人士的翘楚。孙中山于1895年深有感触地写道：“伏念我粤东一省，于泰西各种新学闻之最先，缙绅先生不少留心当世之务，同志者定不乏人。”

孙中山出生于贫苦农民家庭，“早知稼穑之艰难”，对农民的困苦及其斗争深抱同情，对太平天国反清事业早已心怀仰慕。不过，当孙中山逐渐成长的时候，农民斗争高潮已经过去，新的阶级、人物和思想已引人注目。其兄孙眉于19世纪70年代后在檀香山垦殖致富，成了华侨资本家，使孙中山有机缘从农村走向广阔的世界。他在檀香山、广州、香港接受了系统的资产阶级教育和现代政治、经济、科学文化知识。经过一段时间的陶冶、思索、选择，他终于接受了太平天国运动的反清思想，但摒除了他们的皇权主义；他以当时一些维新志士（如何启、郑观应、王韬等）为师友，却要对西方“取法乎上”，越过君主立宪，趋向英、法的共和革命。他的这种取向，得到陆皓东等人的赞同，形成了虽然人数不多却极富生机的最早的民主革命派。诚然，历史道路的选择常有曲折，孙中山也曾有过上书李鸿章以求和平改革时政的尝试，但此举遇挫，而中日甲午战争又进一步暴露了清王朝的颟顸腐朽，于是，他毅然走上了反清共和革命的道路。1894—1895年，他在檀香山、香港相继建立了以“驱除鞑虏，恢复中华，创立合众政府”为宗旨的兴中会，并于1895年10月发动了广州起义（未遂），揭开了辛亥革命的序幕。

辛亥革命义帜之首先在广东擎举与民主革命派之最早在广东组成，是一件石破天惊的大事。1902年著名的革命志士秦力山曾如此赞扬：“大盗移国，公私涂炭，丧乱弘多。而孙君乃于吾国腐败尚未暴露之甲午乙未以前，不惜其头颅性命，而虎啸于东南重立之都会广州府，在当时莫不以为狂。而自今思之，举国熙熙皞皞，醉生梦死，彼独以一人图祖国之光复，担人种之竞争，且欲发现人权公理于东洋专制世界，得非天诱其衷而锡之勇者乎！”

辛亥革命浪潮兴起于广东后，逐渐推向全国各地，到1911年武昌起义，终于推翻了清王朝，在中国建立了第一个资产阶级共和国。在这期间，广东始终是中国民主革命派领导的反清斗争的中心地区之一和武装反清起义的主要场所。

1900年10月，孙中山乘义和团运动飙起于中国北部、清王朝摇摇欲坠之机，命郑士良举义于广东惠州，并图由台湾内渡指挥作战。起义军一度获胜，发展至2万余人，后因饷械不继，被迫解散。此次起义虽然失败，却起了振聋发聩的作用。此前，孙中山被视为“乱臣贼子，大逆不道”、“毒蛇猛兽”，人们不敢与之交游；此后，“则鲜闻一般人之恶声相加，而有识之士，且多为吾人扼腕叹息，恨其事之不成矣！前后相较，差若天渊”。从此，“有志之士，多起救国之思，而革命风潮自此萌芽矣”。在20世纪革命风潮初发时期，1903年1月，在广州又爆发了洪全福、谢缵泰等人策划的起义，它虽以建立“大明顺天国”为旗号，实以实行“由民人公举贤能为总统，以理国事”的民主共和政体为目的，具有民主主义的性质。在东京留学界，广东留学生特别活跃，成立了广东独立协会，积极参与谋求国家独立和革命宣传工作，冯自由、廖仲恺、何香凝等广东志士还秉承孙中山意旨，在东京联络有志学生，结为团体，以推进民主革命。1905年，中国同盟会在东京成立。从此革命风潮鼓荡全国，发展甚速。

较之兴中会，同盟会已大大越出以广东和华侨志士为主的状况，其分支机构几乎遍及各省。但广东仍是同盟会的重点地区。在广东及毗邻的香港、澳门，设有香港分会、南方支部、广州分会、海口支部、番花分会、化州同盟会、肇庆支部、澳门支部等，还设有香山联志社、梅县松口体育会、韩江诗社、化州拜兰社、香港武峰阅报社、澳门濠镜阅书报社、澳门锄异社等一批革命社团，这些不仅位居全国前列，而且实际影响面较宽。设在香港的南方支部，管辖广东、广西、云南、福建四地，在一段时期，是策划国内斗争的一个重心机构。

武装反清斗争，在同盟会成立后出现新的高涨。在广东，更可谓连绵不断，如火如荼。1907年有许雪秋、谢良牧等策动的潮城之役，陈涌波、许雪秋发动的潮州黄冈起义，邓子瑜等发动的惠州七女湖起义，许雪秋、萱野长知等策划的汕尾之役，黄兴、王和顺等发动的防城起义。1908年有葛谦、赵声等策划的广州防营、新军之役。1910年有倪映典等发动的广州新军起义。1911年有黄兴、赵声领导的广州“三二九”（公历4月27日）起义（即黄花岗起义）。这些起义具有以下三个特点：第一，与兴中会时期三次起义相接应，广东是革命党人发动起义最频繁、最多的省份。第二，上述起义体现了孙中山的既定战略方针，即发动起义应“不拘形势，总求急于聚人，利于接济，快于进取”，而以聚人为第一着。根据他们的观察，广东成为发动起义的首选地点，于此取胜后，即由南向北，直捣北京。第三，在如何聚人的问题上，革命党人显然是在不断总结经验教训，有所前进。最初，他们着力于运动会党、防营；到1908年后，他们逐渐重视新军的发动，成效卓著；到策动广州“三二九”起义时，则拟以同盟会内留学生精英为主导，会合新军、防营、绿林、会党等多种力量，共襄大举。由于上述起义都没有充分发动群众，特别是农民群众；没有在农村积蓄力量再进而包围和攻取城市，而主要是寄望从外面输进武器，且多具军事冒险性质，故均旋起旋蹶，迅归失败。尽管如此，它体现了革命党人决意推翻帝制、建立共和国、谋求中国人民解放的坚强意志和决心，以及中国人民斗争、失败、再斗争直至胜利的逻辑。广大群众在斗争中日趋觉醒。尤其是广州“三二九”起义，虽牺牲惨重，但影响深远，正如孙中山后来所写：“是役也，碧血横飞，浩气四塞，草木为之含悲，风云因而变色。全国久蛰之人心，乃大兴奋，悲愤所积，如怒涛排壑，不可遏抑，不半载而武昌之大革命以成。则斯役之价值，直可惊天地，泣鬼神，与武昌革命之役并寿。”可以说，上述广东历次起义，是武昌起义的重要前导。

在对清王朝武器的批判方面，广东固占先筹，在批判武器的运用方面，广东也一马当先。1900年1月，兴中会机关报《中国报》（后改为《中国日报》）在香港问世，是中国民主革命言论机关的元祖。1902

年，广东民主革命宣传家黄世仲在该报发表《辩康有为政见书》，用事实驳斥了康有为攻击革命的《答南北美洲诸华商论中国只可行立宪不可行革命书》，它比章炳麟的《驳康有为论革命书》还早几个月，成为批判康有为保皇论的先声。辛亥革命时期，广东由革命党人开办或参与创办的报刊近30种，为各省之冠。它们和保皇派的论战，延续时间也最长。在东京《民报》与《新民丛报》论战的前三年，省港革命派与保皇派论战的战鼓就已擂响。香港革命党人通过《中国日报》和广东保皇报纸《岭海报》笔战逾月，随后又出现了以《中国日报》和《广东日报》为双方主阵地的激烈大论战。它虽不及东京论战的水平，但也扩大了革命派的思想影响。

在广东大力开展的上述两种批判，壮大了革命势力，打击和孤立了顽固势力，争取了中间势力。所以，当武昌起义的枪声传来，广东各地民军纷纷揭竿而起，兵逼广州；以两广总督张鸣岐为代表的封建顽固派顿时惶惶不可终日。曾经镇压过广州"三二九"起义的广东水师提督李准和拥有重兵的陆路提督秦炳直都震慑于革命军威力，而向革命方面投诚。士绅巨贾和立宪派则谋广东和平独立以自保。经过短期较量，广东终于兵不血刃，宣告和平独立，在全国较早地奏起了辛亥革命胜利的凯歌。

1911年11月10日，广东终于挣脱了延续两千余年的封建帝制的统治，建立了民主共和体制内的广东军政府。就其组成来看，同盟会南方支部长胡汉民担任都督，陈炯明任副都督，在军政府各部领导人中，同盟会会员占多数，它确是以革命派占主导地位的资产阶级革命政权。不久，胡汉民随孙中山北上，陈炯明代理都督。到1912年4月27日，胡汉民回粤复任都督，陈炯明转任广东军统兼绥靖处经略、广东警卫军总司令，后又接受北京政府委任的广东护军使职务。直到1913年6月，袁世凯下令以陈炯明代胡汉民为广东都督。在这期间，广东的主要领导人虽迭有变动，但总的来看，广东政权始终为民主革命派所掌握。它基本上按照孙中山在南京临时政府的施政方针和把广东建设为模范省的要求，实行了一系列有利于资产阶级民主的革命政策、法令和措施，取得了斐然可观的统一和建设广东的成果。

政治方面：以资产阶级民主政权取代原清朝地方政府机构，改元剪发；宣布官吏为人民公仆，不得称"大人"、"老爷"，废止跪拜；注意铨选官员，清明吏治，实行任人唯贤，讲求廉正，严惩营私贪贿；改革司法制度，实行司法独立，废除清朝刑律刑具，改革狱政；改革旧风陋俗，禁止纳妾，严禁烟赌，禁止买卖妇女，废止娼妓、蓄奴，杜绝拐卖华人出口，保护华侨生命财产安全；等等。

经济方面：废除前清苛捐杂税，整顿财政制度；重视发展农业生产，颁布多项振兴实业、交通法令，特别着力贯彻孙中山当时极力推行的社会革命政策。广东省议会通过了廖仲恺主持制定的广东地价税契法案——《广东税契简章》，这是其时各省以法令来实行“平均地权”纲领的最早的也是唯一的可贵尝试。

军事方面：裁编民军，整顿军纪，加强社会治安，改善广东建设环境；建立正式陆军，成立军务处以管理旧军，将势成心腹大患的龙济光军外调钦廉地区，为支援南京临时政府北伐，特抽调一支精干部队由姚雨平率领北上，并取得卓著战绩。

文化教育方面：注重兴办文化教育事业，军政府成立了教育司，各县设督学署，各地广兴学校，学风取美国，学制取法国。到1912年12月，计有公立广东高等学校1所，私立各种专门学校10余所，省立中学12所，县立中学14所，小学更骤增至3 000所，学生达11.1万人，随后又各有增加。这些学校力求用新人办新事。此外，还广设阅书报社390余所。在教学和宣传内容上，反对尊孔，废止“闭塞民智，蛊惑人心”的“坊刻通书”，改良年画、剧本、歌曲，刊印并奖励有利社会改革的各种图书。同时，设立体育会、音乐会，改良风俗会等，还召开了两次全省教育大会。上述法令、计划虽因形格势禁而未能全部实施，但无疑起到了开创新风气、冲击旧传统势力的积极作用。

外交方面：广东军政府在捍卫国家主权、独立与民族尊严方面，坚持了原则立场。比如，派兵监视驶入西江的英舰，与英、德领事严正交涉殴打拘捕中国工人事件，禁阻葡舰擅入琴山马尿河测量等。1911年12月，外蒙古活佛哲布尊丹巴在沙俄唆使下宣布“独立”，举国哗然，纷纷要求出兵抗俄。广东抗俄声浪尤为高亢。广东临时省议会、商会及各政党团体频频集会，支援抗俄义举。1912年8月，广东成立了抗俄会，佛山、香山等地成立了抗俄分会。各界人士还组织了“征蒙先锋队”、“敢死军团”、“征蒙助饷会”、国民军等，表示枕戈以待。时任代都督的陈炯明多次表示要亲率二师一旅，由广东自备饷需，北上抗俄保蒙。

肆

然而，正当广东革命党人统一和建设广东初著成效之时，窃夺了中央政权的袁世凯却在磨刀霍霍，企图腰斩辛亥革命。1913年3月20日，国民党代理理事长宋教仁在上海遇刺，在广东激起了强烈反响。可是，这时敌强我弱的态势已成，广东辛亥革命的固有弱点、革命阵营内部的矛盾、广东军政府施政不当所形成的恶果，都一起暴露，并为敌所用，造成广东辛亥革命迅速逆转的形势。

广东军政府虽以革命党人占主导地位，但县市以下地方机构多为封建买办势力或旧军官所把持；凶悍能战的龙济光部虽调往钦廉，但龙济光仍然野心勃勃，伺机反扑。作为民主革命派社会基础和主要支柱的广东工商阶层，因期盼和平发展，思定厌乱，反对再起反袁战争。正在演进中的广东军政府的内部矛盾，在反袁准备过程中，又有"法律制袁"与"武力讨袁"之争。陈炯明较长时期持缓进态度，直到袁军南逼形势不容犹豫之时，才仓促举兵讨袁。而这时局势已益发失控。陈炯明一直重视对军队的掌握，而广东军队干部本来有士官生与本土生之争；军队本身又缺乏民主教育，更因陈炯明高唱军队"不党主义"，使革命党在军队的影响力很微弱。袁世凯因而乘机派人挑拨离间，把粤军主要将领钟鼎基、苏慎初、张我权等贿买过去，使陈炯明成为光杆司令。原被解散的民军因无妥善安置，不少流落为"匪"，成为陈炯明"绥靖"的对象；当龙济光兵逼广东时，他们更成为附龙驱陈的前导。最终，因陈炯明勒令解散的原北伐军炮兵营余众组成的炮兵团首先哗变，迫陈仓皇出逃，广东二次革命仅历时18天即告结束。随后，袁世凯的爪牙龙济光在广东建立了残暴的军阀统治。

广东的革命虽以失败告终，但它以改帝制为民主共和的划时代事件彪炳于广东史册。它把广东人民的斗争推进到较正规的资产阶级民主革命阶段，提高了人民的民主觉悟。在广东这块富于光荣斗争传统的土地上，不仅涌现出从革命领袖到忠诚民主战士的一大批英雄人物，而且有不少外省志士在此英勇献身，他们谱写了迄今犹为人传诵的许多革命英雄主义和爱国主义的动人诗篇。他们创建了其时最先进的民主革命政权，并为广东建设成模范省进行了最初实验。同时，这场革命的胜利与失败，都给后人留下了许多宝贵的经验教训。基于此，尽管随后的广东历史仍然充满风风雨雨，但广东人民始终斗志昂扬，不屈不挠，沿着辛亥革命已开辟的新道路奋勇前进。辛亥革命后的广东不仅是革命党人反袁的重要场所，而且是孙中山等倚以进行护法斗争，国共合作，掀起大革命高潮的主要基地。

当兹纪念辛亥革命100周年之际，广东省立中山图书馆倪俊明研究馆员在其旧作《辛亥革命在广东》的基础上，继续搜罗史料，弥缝补阙，编成《碧血丹心——辛亥革命在广东影像实录》一书，内容丰富新颖，取材适当，图文并茂，从又一个方面较好地反映了广东辛亥革命的面貌。这是一件很有意义的事，人们将从兹册中获取历史知识和启示，故喜而为之序。

（本文作者为中山大学历史系教授）

PREFACE

■ *Duan Yunzhang*

In the gorgeous picture scroll of the Revolution of 1911, undoubtedly the Revolution of 1911 in Guangdong lasted the longest, its contents were the most abundant, its fighting scenes were the most violent and cruel, which was full of distinct characteristics.

ONE

Dr. Sun Yat-sen (Sun Zhongshan), the great forerunner of China's democratic revolution, and his earliest followers, such as Lu Haodong, Shi Jianru, Zheng Shiliang, Chen Shaobai, were all born in Guangdong, and took Guangdong as the first arena of their revolution activities. Naturally, Guangdong became the original place of the Revolution of 1911.

This situation was by no means fortuitous. Since the Opium War(1840-1842), storms and thunders of revolution and struggles of anti-imperialism and anti-feudalism billowed Guangdong incessantly. The secret societies, such as The Triad Society with anti-Qing Dynasty tradition, had a wide and deep foundation here. Guangdong faces the Pacific Ocean, and is adjacent to Hong Kong and Macao. It was also a famous native land of overseas Chinese, and had frequent contacts with foreign countries. So, when the foreign powers shelled the gate of China with battleship, forced the feudal rulers to subordinate to them and change China according to their system. During the course of anti-aggression, the Guangdong people opened wide their eyes the earliest to see the west world and to study the merits of the west. As a result, in Guangdong, there appeared the first national capitalist enterprises in China, and a trend of advanced productive force. New-type intellectuals were brought up by introducing western cultures. Through exploring the west and making a comparison between the west and China, the advanced personages stepped up to probe the new path to change China's backwardness and the situation of being passive and vulnerable , to rejuvenate China rapidly. For instance, Hong Xiuquan, Hong Rengan, Zheng Guanying, Kang Youwei, and Liang Qichao were the representatives among the advance personages, who took Guangdong as the breeding ground of new thoughts and the early activity base. In 1895, Dr. Sun Yat-sen wrote with deep feeling, "Guangdong is the only province which studies the new ideas of the west the earliest. Many outstanding persons showed great concern over the current affairs at home and abroad. Among them there must be our comrades."

Sun Yat-sen was born in a poor peasant family. He "knew the hardship of farming in his childhood". He showed deep sympathy over the difficulties, hardship and the struggles of the Chinese peasants. He admired the anti-Qing cause of the Taiping Heavenly Kingdom. Nevertheless, when he grew up, the climax of the peasant movement had passed. New classes, new personages and new ideas attracted him. His elder brother, Sun Mei, became an overseas capitalist and got rich after 1870s by cultivation in Honolulu, which gave Sun Yat-sen the good luck to step out into the vast world from Chinese countryside. He received systematic bourgeois education and learned the knowledge of modern politics, economy, science and cultures in Honolulu,Guangzhou and Hong Kong. After a period of study, thinking and selection, at last he accepted the anti-Qing thought of the Taiping Heavenly Kingdom. But he got rid of their doctrine of imperial power. He made friends with reformers then, such as He Qi, Zheng Guanying, Wang Tao, and learned from them. He insisted to"learn the most advanced", to desert the constitutional Monarchy ideas, to pursue for republic revolution like that had happened in Britain and France. Lu Haodong and other advance personages agreed with him. They became the earliest democratic revolutionaries, though they were small in number, but extremely energetic. However, the choice of the historical road was always winding. Dr. Sun Yat-sen once tried to write to Li Hongzhang to persuade him to make a peaceful reform of the feudal system. But he failed. The Sino-Japanese War of 1894-1895 once again exposed the stupidity and political corruption of Qing Dynasty. He resolutely stepped onto the road of anti-Qing republic revolution. During 1894-1895, in Honolulu and Hong Kong he established Revive China Society, which took it as their aim "Driving the Qing rulers out, reviving the Chinese nation, founding a republic government".In October 1895, they organized Guangzhou Uprising (abortive), which had opened the prelude of the Revolution of 1911.

That the flag of Revolution of 1911 was first hold up and that democratic revolutionaries were first formed in Guangdong were a heaven-shaking event. In 1902, Qin Lishan, a famous revolutionary, praised so, "Qing rulers stole our country, which made Chinese nation and people suffer greatly, miserable and in chaos. Before the Sino-Japanese War of 1894-1895, which completely revealed the stupidity and political corruption of Qing Dynasty, Sun Yat-sen did not hesitate to sacrifice his life to start the revolution in Guangzhou, an important city in the southeast of China. At that time, it was regarded as crazy by all. But at the second thought nowadays, all were leading a befuddled life, thinking that the country was in peace reigns under heaven. Only he alone attempted to revive our motherland and shouldered the burden of racial competition,to find human rights and general-acknowledged truth in autocratic world of the Far East Asia. Isn't that like the Heaven guide and give him the courage to do so?"

TWO

The Revolution of 1911 started in Guangdong, gradually spread to other parts of China, until the Wuchang Uprising in 1911. At last Qing Dynasty was overthrown and the first bourgeois republic was founded in China. During this period through, Guangdong was one of the central regions of anti-Qing Dynasty movement led by Chinese democratic revolutionary group and the main place of the armed struggle against Qing Dynasty.

In October 1900, Dr. Sun Yat-sen seized the opportunity of Boxers Uprising in the north, which shook the rule of the Qing Dynasty, ordered Zheng Shiliang to launch the uprising in Huizhou,Guangdong. And Sun tried to cross Taiwan Straits to take command of the uprising. The uprising troop once won and developed to 20,000 people. Later the troop had to be dismissed for short of food and ammunition. Though the uprising failed, the impact was enough to enlighten the benighted. Before, Dr. Sun Yat-sen was regarded as "a disloyal follower, treason and heresy", "a venomous snake and beast of prey". No one dared to make contact with him. After that he "seldom heard scold from the common people and most persons with ideals regretted their failure of the uprising. The situations were a world of difference". Since then, "most persons of ideals wanted to rise up to save China, revolution storms were born." At the beginning of 20th century, uprisings organized by Hong Quanfu and Xie Zuantai broke out in Guangzhou in January 1903. Though they set up the banner of "Great Ming Heaven Kingdom". Actually, they carried out the democratic republic policy of "citizens publicly selecting virtuous and talented persons to rule the country", which had a characteristic of democratism. In Tokyo, the Chinese students from Guangdong were especially active. They established independent societies, took an active part in winning nation's independence and in revolutionary propaganda work. Feng Ziyou, Liao Zhongkai and He Xiangning, persons of ideals from Guangdong, followed Dr. Sun Yat-sen's advice, united the Chinese students in Tokyo so as to boost the democratic revolution. In 1905, the Chinese Revolutionary Alliance was founded in Tokyo. Since then the revolutionary storms thundered throughout China and developed very quickly.

Compared with Revive China Society, the Chinese Revolutionary Alliance had members not only from Guangdong and overseas, but its branches spread to nearly every province in China. Guangdong was still an important region of the Chinese Revolutionary Alliance. In Guangdong and the neighbouring Hong Kong and Macao, there were Hong Kong Branch, South Branch, Guangzhou Branch, Haikou Branch, Panyu-Huaxian Branch, Huazhou Branch, Zhaoqing Branch, Macao Branch,etc. There were some revolutionary mass organizations, such as Xiangshan Lianzhi Club, Meixian Songkou Sport Club, Hanjiang Poem Club, Huazhou Orchid Club, Hong Kong Wufeng Newspaper-Reading Club, Macao Haojing Reading Club, Macao Chuyi Club,etc. They stood ahead not only in number, but also had wide influence nationwide. The South Branch in Hong Kong administered the branches of Guangdong Province,Guangxi Province,Yunnan Province , Fujian Province, and was once a central organization planning the national struggles.

The armed struggles against the Qing Dynasty was on a new upsurge after the founding of the Chinese Revolutionary Alliance. In Guangdong, the struggles broke out continually here and there, like a raging fire. In 1907, Xu Xueqiu and Xie Liangmu planned and organized Chaocheng Battle. Chen Yongbo and Xu Xueqiu's Chaozhou Huanggang Uprising, Deng Ziyu's Seven-lady Lake Uprising in Huizhou, Xu Xueqiu and Xuanye Changzhi's Shanwei Battle, Huang Xing and Wang Heshun's Fangcheng Uprising. In 1908, Ge Qian and Zhao Sheng planned and organized Guangzhou Guarding Troops and New Army Battle. In 1910 Ni Yingdian launched New Army Uprising in Guangzhou. In 1911 Huang Xing and Zhao Sheng led the April 27 Uprising in Guangzhou(Yellow Flower Hill Uprising). All these uprisings had the following three characteristics: Firstly, they coordinated with three uprisings led by Revive China Society. Guangdong was the province where the revolutionaries launched uprisings most frequently. Secondly, the above-mentioned uprisings embodied Dr.Sun Yat-sen's already-set strategic policy, "regardless of situation, uprisings should focus on gathering forces,be easy to gain supports and be quick to attack." And gathering forces was of first importance. According to their observation, they took Guangdong as the first-selected place for uprisings so that they could drive straight on to Peking(today's Beijing) from south to north after success. Thirdly, it was obvious that the revolutionaries had summarized the experiences in how to gather forces and learnt from the former lessons. They were making progress. At first, they focused on the secret societies and the Guarding troops. After 1908, they gradually attached great importance to mobilization of New Army and had an excellent result. In Yellow Flower Hill Uprising, they took the returned overseas students within the Chinese Revolutionary Alliance as their backbones, and united many forces, such as New Army, the Guarding Troops, greenwood outlaws and the secret societies. The Uprising failed because they didn't fully mobilize masses, especially the peasant masses. They didn't gather forces in the countryside, then surround the cities, and at last attack and capture them. They mainly relied on transferring armament from outside, and took the military adventures. So they rose up hurriedly and suffered setbacks quickly, then failed quickly. Nevertheless, they embodied the strong will and determination of the revolutionary partisans to overthrow the autocratic monarchy and to establish a republic and to liberate the Chinese people. Their struggles also reflected the logical road of the Chinese people fighting, then failing, then fighting again, until victory. A large number of masses gradually woke up in the struggle. Especially in Yellow Flower Hill Uprising, there were heavy casualties and great loss in lives. But the influence was also enormous and profound. As Dr. Sun Yat-sen put it later, "In this battle, the heroic blood was flying everywhere, the fighters were full of noble spirits. The grass and trees cried for them sorrowfully and the sky changed its colour. The Chinese people were greatly excited by the uprising. Their grieves and indignation pressed in their mind burst out like huge angry waves, destroying everything in the way. Nothing could stop them. In no more than half a year the Wuchang Uprising broke out and succeeded. Yellow Flower Hill Uprising shook the heaven and the earth, made ghosts and gods cry. It had the same significance as the Wuchang Uprising." The uprisings in Guangdong were the important rehearsals for the Wuchang Uprising in 1911.

In condemning the Qing Dynasty, Guangdong took the lead in China. In January 1900, the *China Press* (later the *China Daily*),the organ of Revive China Society, was issued in Hong Kong. It was the originator of speech of China's democratic revolutionary. In 1902, Huang Shizhong, a Guangdong democratic revolution propagandist, published *Argument on Kang Youwei's Political Views* in the paper. He retorted Kang Youwei's *Reply to North and South American Overseas Chinese Merchants' Views and on China Can Only Practise the Constitutional Monarchy, but no Revolution*, in which Kang attacked the revolutionary cause. It was a few months earlier than Zhang Binglin's *Rebut Kang Youwei's essay on Revolution.*

It was the first sign of criticizing Kang Youwei, a loyalist of Qing rulers. During the revolution movement, there were nearly 30 newspapers and periodicals founded by revolutionary partisans in Guangdong, which was top in number all over China. They debated with the loyalists of the Qing Dynasty, lasting the longest. In the early 3 years in Tokyo, *Minbao* and *Xinmincongbao's* debate, marked the start of the struggle between Guangdong revolutionary partisans and the loyalists. Hong Kong revolutionaries took up written polemics in *the China Daily* with Guangdong Loyalists' *Linghai Paper* for more than a month. After that there appeared an intense debate between the *China Daily* and the *Canton Times* as both sides' main position respectively. Though the level of the debate was not so high as Tokyo's, it expanded the impact of the revolutionary thoughts.

The above-mentioned two kinds of criticisms toward the Qing Dynasty in Guangdong strengthened the revolutionary forces, stroke relentless blow at and isolated the diehards, won over the intermediary forces. As a result, when the gunshot of the Wuchang Uprising came, the troops and people of Guangdong here and there took up arms to march to Guangzhou. The feudal diehards represented by Zhang Mingqi, governor general of Guangdong and Guangxi Provinces, were in a desperate situation. Li Zhun, the Provincial Navy Commander, who once suppressed the Yellow Flower Hill Uprising, surrendered at the awe of the revolutionary might. So did Qin Bingzhi, the provincial military commander, who had a large number of troops. The esquires, rich merchants and those who advocated the constitutional monarchy tried to win independence so as to protect themselves. After a short time contest, Guangdong declared peaceful independence without firing a shot, earlier than many provinces of the country.

THREE

On November 10, 1911, Guangdong at last put an end to the feudal autocratic monarchy which ruled China for over 2 thousand years in succession, and established Guangdong Military Government in the democratic republic system. Hu Hanmin, director of the South Branch of the Chinese Revolutionary Alliance, took office of provincial military governor, Chen Jiongming, deputy provincial military governor. Among the leaders in the military government, most of them were members of the Chinese Revolutionary Alliance. It was indeed a bourgeois revolutionary government where the revolutionary partisans took the leading positions. Soon Hu Hanmin followed Dr. Sun Yat-sen to march north. Chen Jiongming acted as governor. Until April 27, 1912, Hu Hanmin returned and resumed the post of governor. Chen Jiongming was appointed Guangdong military commissioner, commander-in-chief of Guangdong garrison. Later he was promoted to Guangdong military protector by Beijing government. In January 1913, Yuan Shikai ordered Chen to take the place of Hu Hanmin as Guangdong governor. During that period, though the leaders of Guangdong government changed, the power was grasped in the hands of democratic revolutionaries. It basically followed Dr. Sun Yat-sen's administrative policy of Nanjing Provisional Government and built Guangdong into a model province, carrying out a series of revolutionary policies, laws and measures which were favorable to bourgeois democracy, resulting in excellent unification and construction of Guangdong.

In the field of politics: The bourgeois democratic power replaced the former Qing Dynasty local government organs. People cut their pigtails. Officials were called people's civil servants, not addressed as "lord" or "master". Worship on bended kneel was given up. Great efforts were made to select officials who must be honest and incorruptible, persons with abilities were promoted; those who feathered their nests and received bribe seriously punished. Judiciary system was reformed, judicial independence practiced. The legal system and instruments of torture in Qing Dynasty were abandoned, the prison policy reformed. Old, bad customs and habits were transformed, concubines forbidden, smoking opium and gambling prohibited, women traffic and slavery banned, Chinese labourers abducted abroad ended, overseas Chinese's lives and properties protected, etc.

In the field of economy: The system of exorbitant taxes and levies in Qing Dynasty were abrogated and the financial system was rectified. Agricultural production was developed. The decrees for promoting industries and transportation were promulgated. The social reform policies, which Dr. Sun Yat-sen then did his utmost to pursue, were carried through earnestly. The Guangdong Provisional Congress passed Guangdong land tax and contract bill—*A Brief Charter of Guangdong Tax and Contract*, mapped out by Liao Zhongkai. It was the only and first valuable trial for practicing the creed "equal land right" by laws in China.

In the field of military affairs: Militia were dismissed and reorganized. Military disciplines were rectified. Social order was restored. The construction environments were improved. Regular army was founded. Military affair section was set up to control the former troop. Long Jiguang's troop, which was serious hidden trouble and danger to revolution, was transferred to Qin-Lian region. A troop with well-trained soldiers led by Yao Yuping was sent north in support of the north military expedition by Nanjing Provisional Government. Distinguished military success was achieved.

In the field of culture and education: The government attached importance to setting up cultural and educational undertakings, adding education department to the government, and education inspecting section to every county, advocating American style of study and French style of education system. Schools were built up everywhere. By December 1912, there were one higher learning institute funded by the government, 10 more private special training schools, 12 provincial high schools, 14 county middle schools. Primary schools increased to 3,000, with 111,000 pupils. The number arised later. These schools made every effort to practise new system. Besides, 390 reading clubs were erected. In the contents of teaching and propaganda, worship of confucius was criticized. The old almanac, which obstructed the development of people's intelligence and confused people's minds, was not allowed to circulate. New Year's paintings, dramas and songs were improved. Various kinds of books beneficial to social reform were printed and rewarded. At the same time, various sport clubs, music clubs and custom reform clubs were founded. Two provincial education conferences had been held. Although the above-mentioned decrees and projects were not completely carried through because of the situation, they, no doubt, played an active part in creating new vogue and lashing the feudal forces.

In the field of diplomacy: Guangdong stood firm in safeguarding the nation's sovereignty, independence and national dignity. For example, troops were dispatched to monitor the British warships' sailing into the Xijiang River. British consulate and German consulate were seriously negotiated about the incidents of Chinese workers being beaten up and arrested. Portuguese warship was stopped sailing up Qinshan Maniao River for a survey without permission, etc. In December 1911, when a living Buddha, declared "independence of Outer Mongolia" under the suborn of Russia Tsar, the whole nation was in an uproar. The Chinese people everywhere required to fight against Russia. The roar of anti-Russia in Guangdong was louder and more sonorous. Guangdong Provisional Congress, Commerce Chamber and other political parties frequently held rallies to support action. In August 1912, Anti-Russia Society was founded in Guangdong. Branches were also set up in Foshan and Xiangshan. Vanguard of Punitive Expedition, Dare-To-Die Legion, Expedition Financial Support Club, National Army were came into being and prepared to march. Chen Jiongming, then acting governor, expressed again and again that he would personally lead No.2 Division and No.1 Battalion,with Guangdong's military supplies and provisions, for the expedition against Russia to protect Outer Mongolia.

FOUR

When Guangdong revolutionary partisans made initial achievements in unifying and building Guangdong, Yuan Shikai seized the power of the central government and attempted to extinguish the revolution. On March 20, 1913, Song Jiaoren, Acting President of the Kuomintang(the National Party) was assassinated in Shanghai, which evoked a strong response in Guangdong. At that time, at the situation that the enemy were strong and the revolutionary forces were weak, intrinsic weakness of Guangdong revolutionary forces, the contradictions within the revolutionary camp, the evil consequences of Guangdong military government's improper administration, were exposed at the same time. All these were taken advantage of by the enemy. The situation in Guangdong took a turn for the worse rapidly.

The revolutionaries occupied the leading positions in Guangdong military government, but the local governments of counties and cities were under the control of the feudal forces and the former officers. Although Long Jiguang's troop, fierce and quite able to battle, was transferred to Qin-Lian region, Long was waiting for his chance to kick back. The industrial and commercial class, as the social basis and chief pillar of democratic revolutionary forces, were yearn for peace and were fearful of chaos, deviated from their original objects and opposed to waging a struggle against Yuan Shikai. Within the military government, in the opinion of Anti-Yuan, there occurred a dispute of "restrict Yuan by law" or "restrict Yuan by forces". Chen Jiongming held a negative attitude for a long time. He had to fight against Yuan's army only until it was very urgent. The situation was out of control then. He had paid close attention to controlling the army. But the local officers had conflict with those from outside Guangdong. The army lacked democracy education. Chen persisted non-party policy in the army, so the influence of revolutionary party was very weak. Yuan Shikai took the chance to send his men to sow discord and bought over by bribe Zhong Dingji, Su Shenchu and Zhang Woquan, the chief generals in Guangdong army. As a result, Chen Jiongming became a leader without followers. The former militia soldiers who were dismissed were not resettled down properly. Quite a lot became bandits, who were "pacified" by Chen Jiongming. When Long Jiguang's troop pressed on Guangdong, they joined them and fought against Chen. What was more, Chen ordered to dismiss the artillery battalion which comprised of the former artillerymen in North Military Expedition, they turned traitors at first and forced Chen to flee in a hurry. The Second Revolution in Guangdong lasted only 18 days. Afterwards, Long Jiguang, Yuan Shikai's close follower, imposed a cruel warlord ruling on Guangdong.

Though the Revolution of 1911 in Guangdong ended in failure, its splendid achievements of changing autocratic monarchy into democratic republic, an epoch-making event, were written in Guangdong history. It pushed the people's struggle in Guangdong into the stage of bourgeois democratic revolution, raising the people's democratic consciousness. In the land of Guangdong with glorious struggle tradition, there emerged not only a large number of heroic figures, from revolutionary leaders to loyal democratic fighters, but also quite a lot of persons of ideals from other provinces, who laid down their lives historically here. They have composed many moving poems of revolutionary heroism and patriotism still on people's lips so far. They eventually established the most advanced democratic republic then, and made the initial experiment of building Guangdong into a model province. In the meantime, the victory and failure of the revolution left many valuable experiences and lessons for the later generations. Though in the later years the struggles were full of difficulties and hardship, the Guangdong people fought in high spirit and perseveringly. They marched along the path opened by the Revolution of 1911 and struggled on. After the Revolution of 1911, Guangdong still was the important battlefield for revolutionaries to fight against Yuan, also the chief base for Dr.Sun Yat-sen to wage the struggle of Protecting Provisional Constitution, the cooperation between Kuomintang and the Communist Party, which pushed up the surge of the great revolution.

Before the 100th anniversary of the Revolution of 1911, Ni Junming, professorial librarian of Sun Yat-sen Library of Guangdong Province, compiled the photo album: *Righteous Blood and Red Heart—Recording The Revolution of 1911 in Guangdong Through Camera Lens*, at the basis of his previous work, *The Revolution of 1911 in Guangdong*, after his continuous search for historical pictures to cover up omissions. The album covers wide and abundant materials, with text, which reflects the visage of the Revolution of 1911 in a better way. It is very significant for people to gain history knowledge and inspiration from it. It is a pleasure to write this preface.

(The writer is a professor of History Department, Sun Yat-sen University)

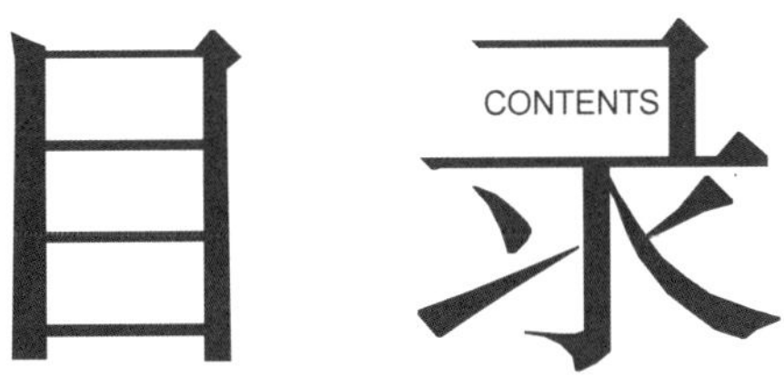

目录 CONTENTS

壹 ONE

辛亥革命前的广东

Guangdong Before the Revolution of 1911

广东地处中国大陆南端，是近代中国人民反抗外来侵略的前沿和民主革命的策源地。1840年，英国发动了鸦片战争，胁迫清政府签订中国近代史上第一个不平等条约——《南京条约》，割让香港给英国，开放广州为通商口岸。古老的中国大门洞开，广东成为近代最早向半殖民地半封建社会转化的地区。1856年，英国、法国发动第二次鸦片战争，清政府被迫开放潮州（后改为汕头）、琼州为通商口岸，英国割占九龙司，广州沙面被划为租界。此后，葡萄牙、法国、英国又分别先后侵占澳门、广州湾和新界。

为反抗帝国主义的侵略和封建专制统治，广东人民进行英勇的抗争。广州三元里人民抗英斗争、太平天国起义、广东天地会“洪兵”起义、遂溪人民抗法斗争、戊戌维新运动……给予腐朽的清政府和外国侵略者以沉重的打击，在近代反帝反封建历史上写下光辉的一页。但是，面对帝国主义和封建主义的强大势力，无论是旧式的农民战争，还是资产阶级的维新运动，均未能避免失败的结局。挽救民族危亡，寻求国家独立和社会进步的领导责任，落在了以孙中山为代表的资产阶级革命派的肩上。

西方资本主义列强在用大炮轰开广东大门之后，也开始把经济侵略的触角伸入到广东各地。1845年，英国人柯拜在广州黄埔设立了外国人在中国境内经营的第一家企业——柯拜船坞。此后他们通过开办工厂、垄断航运、控制海关以及设立银行和洋行等方式，倾销商品，掠夺原料，企图控制广东的经济命脉。为抵御西方列强的经济侵略，广东的民族资本和官僚资本也相继创办一批近代企业。1872年，华侨陈启沅在南海创办中国第二家民族资本主义近代工业企业——继昌隆机器缫丝厂；1879年，肇庆旅日华侨卫省轩在佛山创办中国最早的民族资本火柴厂之一——佛山巧明火柴厂。此外张之洞等洋务派，也在广东创办广东钱局、石井枪弹厂等一批近代企业。近代资本主义经济在广东的滋生与发展，为资产阶级革命派在广东进行反清革命，提供了有利的物质基础。

Guangdong is located in the south frontier of China. It was the front of the modern Chinese people fighting against outside invasion and the original place of the democratic revolution. In 1840, Britain launched the Opium War, and forced the Qing Government to sign the first unequal treaty in China's modern history—*Treaty of Nanjing*, which stipulated to cede Hong Kong to Britain, to open Guangzhou as the trading port. So the old China's gate was wide open. Guangdong became the earliest area that transformed into semi-colonial and semi-feudal society in modern time. In 1856, Britain and France started the Second Opium War. Qing Government was forced to open Chaozhou(later called Shantou) and Qiongzhou as trading ports. Britain occupied Kowloon and took Shamian of Canton as its concession. After that, Portugal, France and Britain occupied Macao, Canton Bay, New Territory respectively.

In order to resist the invasion of imperialism and feudal autocratic ruling, the people in Guangdong carried on the brave struggles. The anti-Great Britain struggle of people at

Sanyuanli, Guangzhou, Taiping Heavenly Kingdom Uprising, "Hong's soldier" uprising of Guangdong Society of Heaven and Earth, the anti-France struggle of people in Suixi, the Reform Movement of 1898..., punctured Qing Government and foreign invaders, which wrote a brilliant chapter in modern history of anti-imperialism and anti-feudalism. However, in the face of the strong force of the imperialism and feudalism, neither traditional peasant's wars nor the Reform Movement of the bourgeois class, could avoid the final result of failure. The leadership responsibility of saving the national crisis, of seeking national independence and social progress, historically fell on the shoulders of the revolutionary group of bourgeois class represented by Sun Yat-sen.

After the western capitalist big powers heavily bombarded the gate of Guangdong, they began to stretch their feelers of economic aggression into all parts of Guangdong. In 1845, Englishman Obye set up the first enterprise—Obye Dock Co.in Huangpu, Guangzhou, managed by the foreigner within the boundaries of China. After that, they attempted to control the economic lifeline of Guangdong, through running factories, monopolizing shipping, controling customs and setting up banks and firms, etc., dumping industrial products, robbing raw materials. In order to resist the economic aggression of western big powers, the national capitalists and bureaucratic capitalists of Guangdong founded a batch of modern enterprises in succession. In 1872, Chen Qiyuan, in Nanhai County, built up China's first national capitalist modern industrial enterprise—Jichanglong Machine Reeling Silk Mill. In 1879, Wei Xingxuan, a Japanese overseas Chinese from Zhaoqing, in Foshan set up one of China's earliest match factories with national capital—Foshan Qiao Ming Match Factory. In addition, advocates of the westemization movement, headed by Zhang Zhidong, founded some modern enterprises in Guangdong, too—Guangdong Mint and Shijing Cartridge Factory. Modern capitalist economy breeding and development in Guangdong provided the revolutionary groups of bourgeois class's anti-Qing Dynasty revolution in Guangdong with the favourable material basis.

1

1. 广东是近代中国最早遭受帝国主义侵略和被迫开放通商口岸的地区。1840年，英国发动了侵略中国的鸦片战争；1842年，英国迫使清政府签订了中国近代史上第一个不平等条约——《南京条约》。条约规定中国向英国赔款2 100万银元，割让香港，开放广州、厦门、福州、宁波、上海五个通商口岸，协定关税等。图为1841年1月26日，英军占领港岛时的登陆地——香港大笪地。

In modern China, Guangdong was first invaded by imperialists and was the region which was forced to open as trading port. In 1840, Britain launched the Opium War against China. In 1842, They forced Qing Government to sign the first unequal treaty in China's modern history—Treaty of Nanjing, stipulating China to pay an indemnity of 21 million silver dollars to Britain, and to cede Hong Kong, to open Guangzhou, Xiamen, Fuzhou, Ningbo, Shanghai as trading ports, and to fix tariff. This was The Bazaar(The Open Space Market), Hong Kong, where on January 26, 1841, the Britain army landed on Hong Kong Island.

2

2. 鸦片战争后成为通商口岸的广州。

Guangzhou became a trading port after the Opium War.

3. 1856年，英国、法国发动了第二次鸦片战争。次年底，英、法联军攻陷广州。图为英、法联军占领的广州五层楼。

In 1856, Britain and France launched the Second Opium War and captured Guangzhou the next year. The picture was Five-Story (Zhenhai) Tower, when Guangzhou was occupied by the British and French Allied Army.

3

4

4. 第二次鸦片战争后，英、法依据不平等条约，强行租占广州沙面。图为1865年的沙面租界。

After the Second Opium War, Britain and France occupied and rented Guangzhou by force according to an unequal treaty. The picture shows Shamian Concession in 1865.

5. 1858年，中、英签订《天津条约》，辟潮州（后改汕头）为通商口岸。图为1860年英国在汕头设立的大英驻潮州领事署。

In 1858, China and Britain signed *Tianjin Treaty*, Chaozhou (later it was named Shantou) was forced to open as a trading port. The picture of the consulate of the Great Britain, set up in Shantou in 1860.

5

6. 1898年4月，法国强迫清政府租借广州湾。次年11月，中、法签订《广州湾租界条约》。图为法军在湛江的兵营。

In April 1898, France forced Qing Government to rent Guangzhou Bay to it. In November next year, France signed *Guangzhou Bay Concession Treaty* with Qing Government. This is the military camp of French troop in Zhanjiang.

▲7

8

7. 1898年6月9日，英国强迫清政府签订《展拓香港界址专条》，租借“新界”给英国，租期99年。翌年，中、英签订《香港英新租界合同》，拟定“新界”界址走向。图为中英官员在标定粤港边界。

On June 9, 1898, Britain forced Qing Government to sign *The Convention Between the United Kingdom and China Respecting an Extension of Hong Kong Territory* to lease New Territories to Britain, with a rental period of 99 years. Next year, China and Britain signed, drafting the border tend of New Territory. The photo shows that the Britain officials and Qing officials are demarcating the borders of Guangdong and Hong Kong.

▶8

8. 1898年7月，香港兴中会会员谢缵泰（开平人）感慨时事，在香港绘制《时局全图》，并题词：“沉沉酣睡我中华，那知爱国即爱家！国民知醒宜今醒，莫待土分裂似瓜。”以此警示世人。

In July 1898, when Xie Zuantai (from Kaiping County), a member of Revive China Society, was drafting *The Situation in the Far East* in Hong Kong, he sighed with deep feeling and wrote the following inscription to warn the common people: “My China sleep like a log, who knows to love country is to love family! My folks should wake up immediately, not wait till our soil splited like a broken water melon.”

9. 1910年《香山旬报》登载的揭露帝国主义企图瓜分中国的漫画。

In 1910, *Xiangshan Xunbao* (a ten-day publication) published a caricature, which disclosed imperialists’ attempt to partition China.

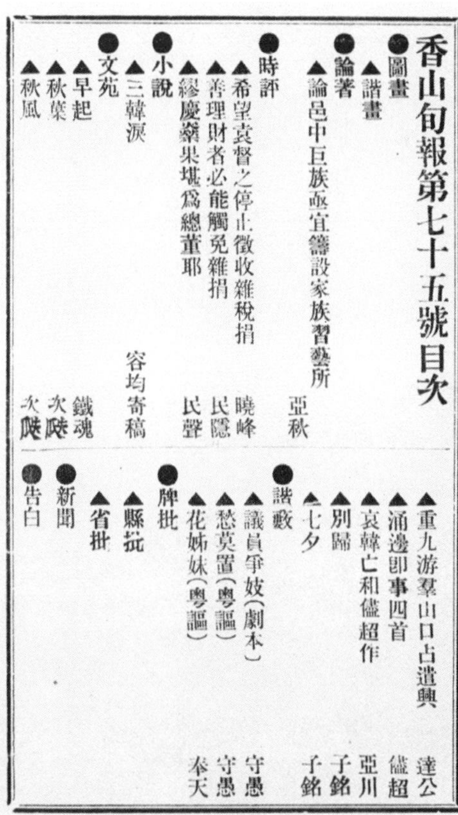

香山旬報第七十五號目次

10

10. 帝国主义在对广东进行政治、军事侵略的同时，也进行经济的掠夺。图为1845年英国人约翰·柯拜在广州黄埔设立的柯拜船坞。

While the imperialists carried on political and military invasion of Guangdong, they also plundered China economically. In 1845, John Obye rented a piece of land in Huangpu, Guangzhou and set up Obye Dock Co.

11

12

11. 鸦片战争后，外国商船不断驶进广州。图为约1850—1855年航行在珠江上的美国、法国和丹麦的商船。

After the Opium War, foreign ships sailed into Guangzhou constantly. The picture shows ships of USA, France and Denmark sailing on the Pearl River about 1850-1855.

12. 第二次鸦片战争后，外国列强攫取了粤海关管理权。1860年，设立新的粤海关，由美国人吉罗福任税务司，英国人赫德、马察尔任副税务司。图为1916年重建的粤海关大楼。

After the Second Opium War, the foreign powers seized the rights of managing Guangdong Customs. In 1860 the new customs of Guangdong was founded, with American G.B.Glover as commissioner, Englishmen Robert Hert and Mathesen as deputy commissioner. The picture shows the Customs Tower of Guangdong rebuilt in 1916.

▲13

▲14

15

13. 鸦片战争前，英国在广州成立怡和洋行。1841年，将总部从广州迁至香港。在其后约一个世纪间，曾将势力扩张到中国各大城市，成为英国对华经济侵略的重要工具。图为1868年的香港怡和公司。

Before the Opium War, the Jordine & Co. was established in Guangzhou by Britain. In 1841, its headquarters moved to Hong Kong. During about one century thereafter, it once expanded to every big city in China and became British important tool of economic aggression in China. The photo shows the Firm in Hong Kong in 1868.

14. 1865年，英国在香港设立的汇丰银行。

In 1865, the British set up Hong Kong & Shanghai Banking Corporation in Hong Kong.

15. 汇丰银行广州沙面支行旧址。

The old site of the branch of Hong Kong & Shanghai Banking Corporation in Shamian, Guangzhou.

▲ 16

▲ 17

16. 1870年，英国在香港开设以经营航运及贸易为主的太古洋行。

In 1870, in Hong Kong the Britain set up Swire Co.Ltd., which took shipping and trade as main business.

17. 太古洋行广州沙面分行旧址。

The old site of the branch of Swire Co.Ltd. in Shamian, Guangzhou.

18

18. 1895年，法国在香港设立的东方汇理银行分行。

The branch of the Chartered Bank of India, Australia and China was founded by France in Hong Kong in 1895.

▲19

19. 为反抗帝国主义的侵略和封建主义的压迫，广东人民进行英勇的抗争。1841年5月30日，广州城郊三元里一带103乡居民奋起抗击滋扰抢掠的英军。图为三元里人民抗英誓师地——三元古庙。

The Guangdong people carried out brave struggles to oppose the invasion of the imperialism and the oppression of feudalism. On May 30, 1841, residents from 103 village at Sanyuanli in the outskirts of Guangzhou, rose up to oppose British soldiers harassment and robbery. This is the place where Sanyuanli people pledged resolution to fight against British soldiers, Sanyuanli Ancient Temple.

20. 1851年1月11日，洪秀全发动著名的太平天国武装起义，有力地动摇了清王朝的统治。图为洪秀全（花县人）画像。

On January 11, 1851, Hong Xiuquan launched the famous uprising and established the Taiping Heavenly Kingdom, which effectively shook the rule of Qing Dynasty. This is a portrait of Hong Xiuquan (from Huaxian County).

此像摹自 A·F·Lindley (Lin-li 呤唎) 的"太平天国"

▶20

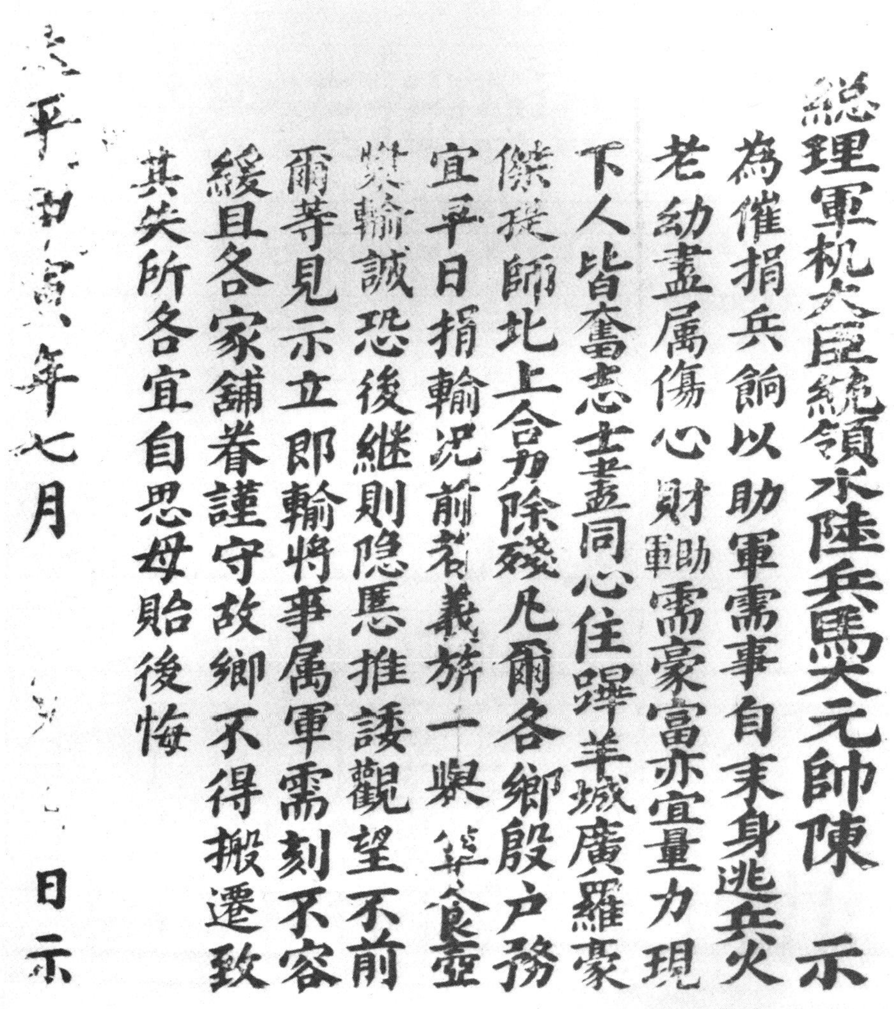

總理軍机大臣統領水陸兵馬大元帥陳 示
為催捐兵餉以助軍需事自來身逃兵火
老幼盡屬傷心財軍助需豪富亦宜量力現
下人皆奮志士盡同心住踞羊城廣羅豪
傑提師北上合力除殘凡爾各鄉殷户務
宜平日捐輸況前者義旂一舉簞食壺
漿輸誠恐後繼則隱匿推諉觀望不前
爾等見示立即輸將事屬軍需刻不容
緩且各家鋪眷謹守故鄉不得搬遷致
其失所各宜自思毋貽後悔
太平甲寅年七月 日示

21

21．1854年，陈开、李文茂领导广东天地会“洪兵”起义，支援太平天国革命。图为起义军发布的告示。

In 1854, Chen Kai and Li Wenmao led “Hong’s soldiers” uprising of Heaven and Earth Society in Guangdong and supported the Taiping Heavenly Kingdom revolution. This is the notice that the insurrectionary army issued.

▲22

22. 1898年6月至1899年11月，遂溪人民举行反抗法国侵略的武装斗争。图为南柳抗法誓师会场——上林寺。

From June of 1898 to November of 1899, the people in Suixi took up arms to oppose French invasion. This is the place of the Nanliu Rally to pledge resolution to fight against French invaders—Shanglin Temple.

▲23

23. 19世纪末，面对日益深重的民族危机，广东涌现出郑观应（左，香山人）、康有为（中，南海人）、梁启超（右，新会人）等为代表的资产阶级维新派，他们为挽救民族危亡奔走呼号，但最终因清朝统治者的压制与镇压而归于失败。

At the end of 19th century, in the face of the extremely serious national crisis, Zheng Guanying (on the left, from Xiangshan County), Kang Youwei (middle, from Nanhai County) and Liang Qichao (on the right, from Xinhui County), who were bourgeois reformers, went around crying for saving the national crisis. But in the end they failed under the suppression of Qing rulers.

24. 在帝国主义经济侵略的刺激下，广东的民族资本主义企业也开始了艰难的抗争。1872年，南海人陈启沅在家乡创办了中国第二家民族资本主义近代工业企业——继昌隆机器缫丝厂。图为陈启沅。

With the stimulus of imperialist economic aggression, the national capitalist enterprises of Guangdong began the difficult fight,too. In 1872, Chen Qiyuan, who was from Nanhai County, in hometown, set up China's second national capitalist industrial enterprise, Jichanglong Machine Reeling Silk Mill. This picture is Chen Qiyuan.

◀ 24

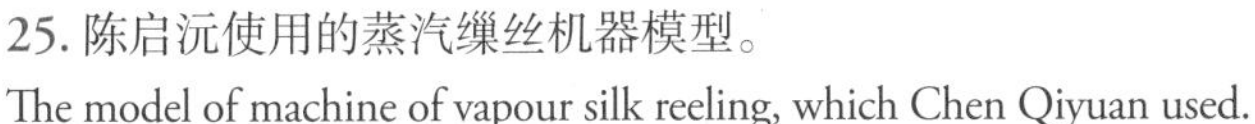

25. 陈启沅使用的蒸汽缫丝机器模型。
The model of machine of vapour silk reeling, which Chen Qiyuan used.

▼ 25

26

26. 1879年，肇庆旅日华侨卫省轩在佛山创办中国最早的民族资本火柴厂之一——佛山巧明火柴厂。图为该厂生产的火花。

In 1879, Wei Xingxuan, a Japanese overseas Chinese from Zhaoqing, established one of China's earliest match factories with national capital—Foshan Qiao Ming Match Factory in Foshan. This is a sign of a match-box produced by it.

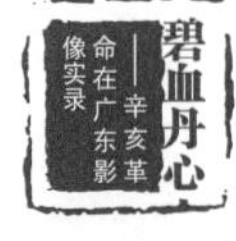

27. 19世纪80年代，洋务派也在广东创办了一些资本主义近代企业。1886年，张之洞在广州创办了中国首间生产机制银元、铜钱的工厂——广东钱局。

In 1880's, the Qing officials of westernization group set up some capitalist modern-time enterprises in Guangdong, too. In 1886, Zhang Zhidong established in Guangzhou China's first machine-make silver and copper dollar factory--Guangdong Mint.

27

 28

28. 1887年，张之洞在广州创办的石井枪弹厂。

In 1887, Zhang Zhidong founded Shijing Cartridge Factory.

29. 辛亥革命前，外债赔款及繁杂的捐税成了压在劳动人民身上沉重的负担，国内阶级矛盾和民族矛盾极其尖锐。图为上海《民呼日报》刊登的一幅漫画。

Before the Revolution of 1911, the foreign debt and indemnity, miscellaneous taxes and levies had become the heavy burdens on the working people, domestic class contradiction and national conflicts were extremely sharp. This is caricature published in Shanghai's *Minhu Ribao* (*Peoples Call Daily*).

29

▲30

30. 清末广州城郊贫困不堪的百姓。

The impoverished people at the outskirts of Guangzhou in late Qing Dynasty.

31

32

31. 清末广州街景。
Streetscape of Guangzhou in late Qing Dynasty.

32. 清末广东地方官吏。
The local officials of Guangdong in late Qing Dynasty.

▲33

33. 清末广州城。

The City of Guangzhou in late Qing Dynasty.

贰 TWO

孙中山在广东的早期革命活动与兴中会的创立

The Early Revolutionary Activities of Sun Yat-sen in Guangdong and the Establishment of Revive China Society

广东是孙中山的故乡，也是辛亥革命的重要策源地。1866年11月12日，孙中山诞生于广东省香山县（今中山市）翠亨村。1879年，孙中山在长兄孙眉的资助下，先后在檀香山、香港、广州等地学校读书，接受西方资产阶级的自然科学和社会政治学说，萌发改革社会的思想，并结识一些爱国青年，经常聚谈时事政治。1894年6月，孙中山北上天津，上书清廷重臣李鸿章，提出改革弊政、富民强国的主张，但未被采纳。上书的失败，使孙中山放弃了对清廷的幻想，走上反清的革命道路。1894年11月，孙中山在檀香山创建中国第一个资产阶级革命团体——兴中会，首次提出推翻清政府、建立资产阶级共和国的主张。旋即在香港、广州设立兴中会。1895年和1900年，孙中山领导兴中会会员并联络会党、绿林，先后发动广州起义和惠州起义，从而拉开辛亥革命的序幕。

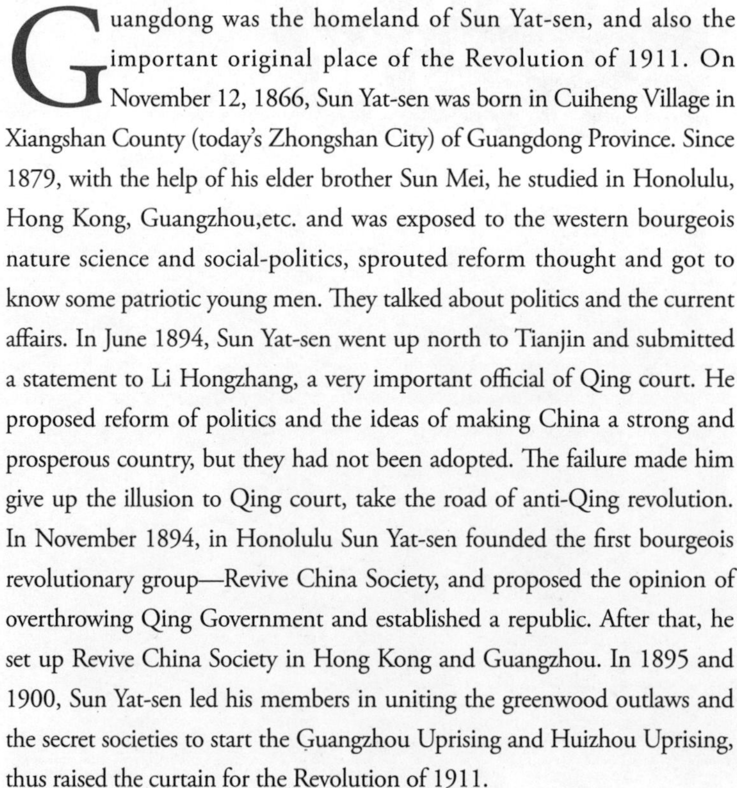

Guangdong was the homeland of Sun Yat-sen, and also the important original place of the Revolution of 1911. On November 12, 1866, Sun Yat-sen was born in Cuiheng Village in Xiangshan County (today's Zhongshan City) of Guangdong Province. Since 1879, with the help of his elder brother Sun Mei, he studied in Honolulu, Hong Kong, Guangzhou,etc. and was exposed to the western bourgeois nature science and social-politics, sprouted reform thought and got to know some patriotic young men. They talked about politics and the current affairs. In June 1894, Sun Yat-sen went up north to Tianjin and submitted a statement to Li Hongzhang, a very important official of Qing court. He proposed reform of politics and the ideas of making China a strong and prosperous country, but they had not been adopted. The failure made him give up the illusion to Qing court, take the road of anti-Qing revolution. In November 1894, in Honolulu Sun Yat-sen founded the first bourgeois revolutionary group—Revive China Society, and proposed the opinion of overthrowing Qing Government and established a republic. After that, he set up Revive China Society in Hong Kong and Guangzhou. In 1895 and 1900, Sun Yat-sen led his members in uniting the greenwood outlaws and the secret societies to start the Guangzhou Uprising and Huizhou Uprising, thus raised the curtain for the Revolution of 1911.

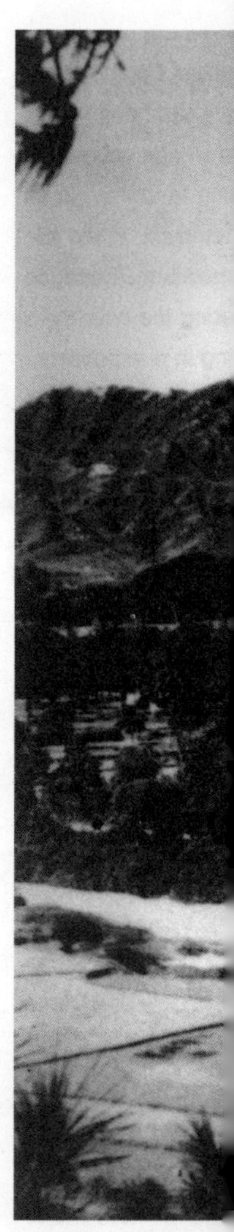

▲34

34. 1866年11月12日，辛亥革命的领导者孙中山诞生于广东省香山县翠亨村。图为翠亨村全景。

On November 12, 1866, Sun Yat-sen, leader of the Revolution of 1911, was born in Cuiheng Village in Xiangshan County (today's Zhongshan City) of Guangdong Province. This is the panorama of Cuiheng Village.

35. 翠亨村孙中山故居。

Sun Yat-sen's former residence in Cuiheng Village.

36. 1879年6月，孙中山随母赴檀香山，投奔哥哥孙眉。同年秋至1883年夏，孙中山先后在檀香山意奥兰尼书院和奥阿厚书院读书，接受西方教育，初萌改造祖国的愿望。图为意奥兰尼书院旧址。

In June 1879, Sun Yat-sen, with his mother, went to Honolulu to join his elder brother—Sun Mei. From the autumn of 1879 to the summer of 1883, Sun Yat-sen studied in Iolani School and Oahu College in Honolulu, where he received western education, and first had the desire of reconstruct his motherland. This is the old site of Iolani School.

35

▲ 36

37. 1883年夏，17岁的孙中山从檀香山辍学返乡。

In the summer of 1883, Sun Yat-sen, 17 years old, discontinued his study and returned to China from Honolulu.

◀ 37

38. 1883年秋，孙中山与好友陆皓东见到村民用北极殿内的香炉灰治病，即奉劝村民不要崇拜偶像，并毁坏北极殿的神像。图为北极殿原址。

In autumn of 1883, when Sun Yat-sen and his good friend Lu Haodong saw the villagers using incense ashes from Beiji Temple to cure diseases, they immediately persuaded the villagers not to worship idols. They also broke statues of the god and goddess in the temple. It is the original site of Beiji Temple.

39. 1883年11月至12月，孙中山赴香港拔萃书院读书。年底，孙中山与陆皓东一起接受基督教的洗礼。此为受洗名单。孙日新即孙中山，陆中桂即陆皓东。

From November to December in 1883, Sun Yat-sen studied in Diocesan School in Hong Kong. At the end of the year, Sun Yat-sen and Lu Haodong were baptized together. This is the register of them. Sun Rixin is Sun Yat-sen. Lu Zhonggui is Lu Haodong.

40. 1884年4月15日，孙中山转学香港中央书院。图为孙中山入学的注册记录。孙帝象为孙中山入学名字。

On April 15, 1884, Sun Yat-sen transferred to the Government Central School in Hong Kong. The picture shows the registration record when Sun Yat-sen was enrolled in as Sun Dixiang.

▼38

1 陳毓林	香港	Removed
2 孫日新	香山翠亨鄉	
3 八嫣	省城	Removed
4 陸中桂	香山翠亨鄉	Deceased
5 唐雄	" "唐家"	
6 任顯德	香港	
7 宋連好 小	" "	Removed
8 宋江嬌 小	" "	Deceased
9 周慈愛 小	" "	"
10 任顯日 小	" "	"
11 陳神重	恩平長灣村	

39

can be ascertained he spent about a year in the school, and then proceeded to the Hong Kong School of Medicine (this later became the Medical School of the Hong Kong University), where he graduated in July 1892.

The entry in the school register reads—

Admission Number	Name	Residence	Age	Date of Admission	Remarks
2746	Sun Tai Tseung (孫帝象)	2, Bridges Street	18	15.4.84	Parents in Heung Shan (香山)

The last entry in the school register in 1936 is number 19,817, so that some 17,000 boys have entered Queen's since Dr. Sun.

40

▲41

▼42

▲43

41. 1886年秋，孙中山入广州博济医院学医。图为博济医院校舍。

In the autumn of 1886, Sun Yat-sen began to study medicine in Guangzhou (Boji) Hospital Medical College. This is the campus.

42. 孙中山在广州博济医院读书时住宿的哥利支堂宿舍。

The dorm where Sun Yat-sen once stayed when he studied in Guangzhou (Boji) Hospital Medical College.

43. 1887年9月，孙中山转学香港西医书院，修读5年，至1892年毕业。图为香港西医书院校舍。

In September 1887, Sun Yat-sen transferred to Hong Kong Western Medicine College and studied for 5 years and graduated in 1892. This is the campus of the college.

A DICTIONARY

OF

MEDICINE

INCLUDING

GENERAL PATHOLOGY, GENERAL THERAPEUTICS, HYGIENE, AND THE DISEASES PECULIAR TO WOMEN AND CHILDREN

BY VARIOUS WRITERS

EDITED BY

RICHARD QUAIN, M.D., F.R.S.

THOUSAND

LONDON

MANS, GREEN, AND CO

44

44. 孙中山在香港西医书院读书时用过的词典。

The dictionary used by Sun Yat-sen while he studied in the College of Medicine for Chinese in Hong Kong.

Name.	Date of Commencement of Study.	Botany.	Chemistry.	Anatomy. Osteology.	Anatomy. General.	Physiology.	Materia Medica.	Pathology.	Medical Jurisprudence.	Public Health.	Midwifery.	Medicine.	Surgery.	Date of Diploma.	Remarks.
1. [illegible]	Jan. 1887	H	H		H	P	H							[illegible]	[illegible]
2. [illegible]	Jan. 1887	P	H			H	P							[illegible]	[illegible]
3. [illegible]	Jan. 1887	H	H	H	H	H	H	H	H	H	H	P	P	July 1892	[illegible]
4. [illegible]	1887		P	P	P	P	P	P	H	P	P	P	P	March 1895	[illegible]
5. [illegible]	1887													[illegible]	[illegible]
6. [illegible]	1887				P									[illegible]	[illegible]
7. [illegible]	1887													[illegible]	[illegible]
8. [illegible]	1887					P								[illegible]	[illegible]
9. [illegible]	Oct. 1887	P	P	P	P	P	P	P	H	P	P	P	P	July 1893	[illegible]
10. [illegible]	Oct. 1887	P	P	P	P	H	P	P	P	P	P	H	P	March 1895	[illegible]
11. [illegible]	Oct. 1887	P	P	P	P	P	H	P	P	P	P	P	P	March 1895	
12. [illegible]	Nov. 1887	P	P	H	H	H	P	H	H	P	P	P	H	July 1892	

45

45. 孙中山在香港西医书院的成绩单。

Sun Yat-sen's transcript when he studied at the Western Medicine College for Chinese. in Hong Kong.

46. 孙中山在香港西医书院读书时，常与陈少白（左三，新会人）、尢列（左四，顺德人）、杨鹤龄（ 左一，香山人）聚谈反清抱负，抨击时政，被称为“四大寇”。这是他们1892年的合影。后站者为同学关景良。

When Sun Yat-sen studied in Hong Kong Western Medicine College for Chinese, he talked about ambition of anti-Qing Dynasty and commented the political situation of the time with Chen Shaobai (the third from the left, from Xinhui County), You Lie (the fourth from the left, from Shunde County), Yang Heling (the first from the left, from Xiangshan County), who were called Four Big Bandits. This was their group photo in 1892. The man standing at the back was Guan Jingliang, their schoolmate.

46

47

47. 1892年，孙中山与香港西医书院同学的毕业合照。前排右二为孙中山。

The graduation group photo of Sun Yat-sen (the second from the right at the front row)and his schoolmates in Hong Kong Western Medicine College for Chinese, taken in 1892.

僕姓孫名文字載之號逸仙籍隸廣
廣州府香山縣生於一千八百六十六年
歷十月十六日幼讀儒書十二歲畢經
十三歲隨母往夏威仁島始見輪舟之
滄海之闊自是有慕西學之心窮天地
想是年母復回華文遂留島依兄入英
督所掌之書院肄業英文三年後再
美人所設之書院肄業此為島中最
之書院初擬在此滿業即往美國入
書院肄習專門之學僕兄因其切慕
耶穌之道恐文進教為親督責着
回華是十八歲時也抵家後親亦無所
責隨其所慕居鄉數月即往香港
習英文先入拔粹書室數月之後轉
香港書院又數月因家事離院再往
數月而回自是停習英文復治中國經
學二十歲始習西醫先入廣東省城美
士所設之博濟醫院肄業次年轉入
港新創之西醫書院五年滿業考
前茅時二十六歲矣此從師游學之大
文早歲志窺遠大性慕新奇故所
多博雜不純於中學則獨好三代兩
之文於西學則雅癖達文之道而格
事亦常流覽至於教則崇 耶穌於
則仰中華之湯武暨美國華盛頓

48

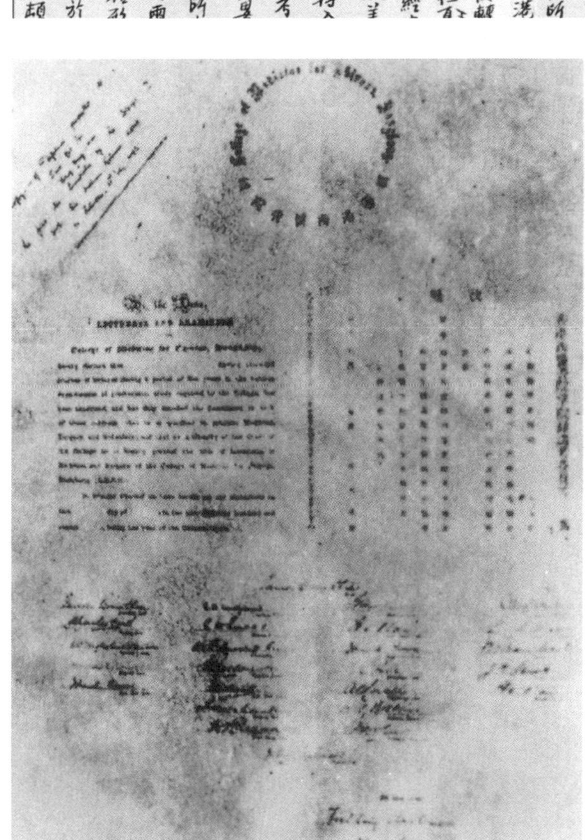

49

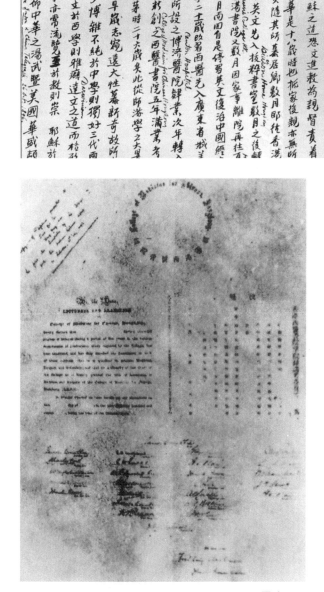

48. 孙中山写于1896年的自传手迹。文中叙述他早年求学的经历。

The autobiography scripts written by Sun Yat-sen in 1896. His studying experience in early years was narrated.

49. 香港西医书院教务长康德黎发给孙中山的行医执照。

The practice medicine license issued to Sun Yat-sen by Kang Deli, dean of the Western Medicine College for Chinese in Hong Kong.

50

50. 孙中山从香港西医书院毕业后，于1892年9月到澳门镜湖医院担任义务医席。12月，在澳门开设中西药局。图为澳门镜湖医院旧址。

After graduation from Hong Kong Western Medicine College for Chinese, Sun Yat-sen practised medicine free of charge at Jinghu Hospital in Macao from September to December, 1892. In December he set up the Western-Orient Pharmacy in Macao. This is old site of Jinghu Hospital.

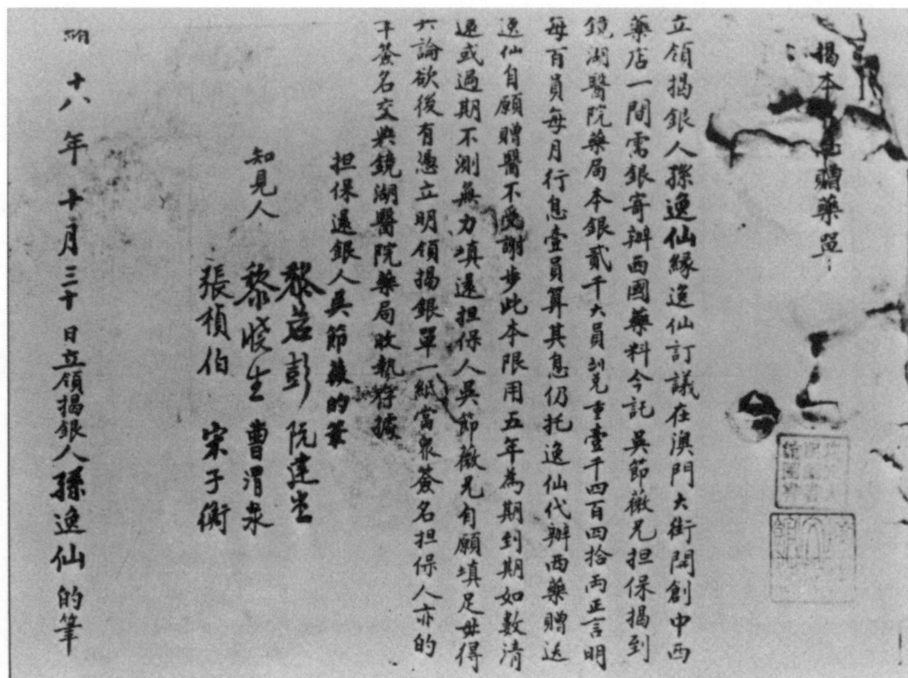

立領揭銀人孫逸仙緣逸仙訂議在澳門大街開創中西
藥店一間需銀寄辦西國藥料今託吳節薇兄担保揭到
鏡湖醫院藥局本銀貳千大員訓兑重壹千四百四拾兩正言明
每百員每月行息壹員算其息仍托逸仙代辦西藥贈送
逸仙自願贈醫不受謝步此本限用五年為期到期如數清
還或過期不測無力填還担保人吳節薇兄自願填足毋得
異論欲後有憑立明領揭銀單一紙當眾簽名担保人亦的
筆簽名交與鏡湖醫院藥局收執存據
担保還銀人吳節薇的筆
知見人 黎若彭 阮建堂
黎曉生 曹渭泉
張楨伯 宋子衡
緒十八年十月三十日立領揭銀人孫逸仙的筆

51

春滿鏡湖

大國手孫逸仙先生我華人而業西醫者也性情和厚學識精明向從英美名師游洞窺秘奧現在鏡湖醫院贈醫數月甚著功效但每日除贈醫外尚有診症餘閒在

先生原不欲酌定醫金過爲計較然而稱情致送義所應然今我同人爲之釐訂規條著明刻候每日由十點鐘起至十二點鐘止在鏡湖醫院贈醫不受分文以惠貧乏復由一點鐘至三點鐘止在寫字樓候診三點鐘以後出門就診其所訂醫金俱係減贈他如未訂各款要必審視其人其症不事奢求務祈相與有成俾盡利物濟人之初志而已下列條目于左

一凡到草堆街中西藥局診症者無論男女送醫金貳毫晨早七點鐘起至九點鐘止

一凡親自到仁慈堂右鄰寫字樓診症者送醫金壹員

一凡延往外診者本澳街道送醫金弍員各鄉市鎮遠近隨酌

一凡難產及吞服毒藥延往救治者按人之貧富酌議

一凡成年包訂每人歲送醫金五十員全家眷口不逾五人者歲送醫金百員

一凡遇禮拜日十點鐘至十二點鐘在寫字樓種牛痘每人收銀壹員上門種者每人收銀三員

一凡補崩口崩耳割眼膜癰瘡瘰瘤淋結等症屆時酌議

一凡奇難怪症延請包醫者見症再酌

一凡外間延請報明急症隨時速往決無遷延

一凡延往別處診症每日送醫金三拾員從動身之日起計

鄉愚弟 盧焯之 陳席儒 吳節薇 宋子衡 何穗田 曹子基仝啟

52

51. 1892年12月，孙中山向澳门镜湖医院借款开办中西药局的借款单。

In December 1892, Sun Yat-sen borrowed money from Jinghu Hospital in Macao and opened up the Chinese and Western Pharmacy. This is the loan bill.

52. 1893年9月26日，澳门《镜海丛报》刊登孙中山在澳门行医的广告。

On September 26, 1893, Sun Yat-sen's medical advertisement published in *Jinghai Series* in Macao on September 26, 1893.

法國刀仔發售○啟者茲有法國各樣刀仔在沙面東橋內大路萬福洋行發售欵式太多不能盡錄此刀或鑲有界玻璃之用或鑲有西洋[illegible]一幅或大或細各適其用目睹方知或發行或零沽各隨其便價甚相宜如欲 光顧請至面議特此遇知 沙面萬福洋行啟

春盎從城 敬啟者本局敦請 大醫生孫君逸仙來省濟世客歲底因事返澳度年今已由澳回省謹擇於月之初十日開辦所有贈醫出轎規矩一律如前每日十點鐘至十二點鐘在局贈診不受分文以惠貧乏求醫者須在[illegible]點鐘以前來局掛號午後出外診症西關收轎金一員城內雙門底西門河南等處轎金二員早轎加倍謝步隨意致送凡延診者須早到局掛號先生素以濟人利物爲心若有意外與夫難產服毒等症經關危急無論貧富俱可立時邀致設法施救幸毋觀望以免貽誤此佈 洗基東西藥局謹啟

53. 1893年，孙中山迁中西药局到广州冼基，并在城内双门底圣教书楼开办医务分所。图为中西药局刊登在1894年2月27日广州《中西日报》上的启事。

In 1893, Sun Yat-sen moved the Western-Orient Pharmacy to Xianji of Guangzhou, and ran a clinic in Shuangmendi teaching building. This photo is the notice published in Guangzhou's *Chinese and Western Daily* for the Western-Orient Pharmacy on February 27, 1894.

54. 孙中山在学医的同时，也积极关注社会的改革。1890年，他致书香山籍退职官员郑藻如，就农业、禁烟、教育等问题，提出改革的建议。此文为目前可见的最早的孙中山论著。图为转载于《濠头月刊》上的《孙总理致藻如书》。

While Sun Yat-sen studied medicine, he paid an active attention to social reform. In 1890, he wrote to Zheng Zaoru, an ex-official from Xiangshan County and put forward suggestions regarding reforming agriculture, opium prohibition and education. It is Sun Yat-sen's first works which can be found so far. This is *A Letter to Zaoru from Premier Sun* reprinted in *Haotou Monthly*.

55. 孙中山在关注社会改良的同时，也开始寻求革命反清的道路。1893年，孙中山与尢列、陆皓东、郑士良、程耀宸、程璧光、魏友琴等，在广州城南广雅书局抗风轩集会，策划组织反清革命团体，但后来未能实现。这是孙中山筹组革命团体的第一次尝试。图为1924年的抗风轩。

While Sun Yat-sen was paying attention to social reform, he started to search for a revolutionary road of anti-Qing Dynasty. In 1893, Sun Yat-sen, together with You Lie, Lu Haodong, Zheng Shiliang, Cheng Yaochen, Cheng Biguang and Wei Youqin held a meeting at Kangfeng Veranda of Guangya Press in the southern part of Guangzhou and planned to establish an anti-Qing revolutionary organization, but later failed to carry it through. This was Sun Yat-sen's first attempt to plan and organize a revolutionary group. The photo is Kangfeng Veranda in 1924.

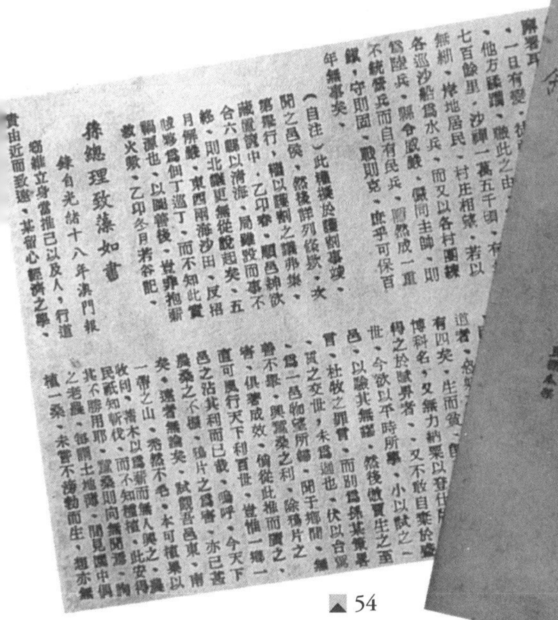

孫總理致藻如書

錄自光緒十八年澳門報

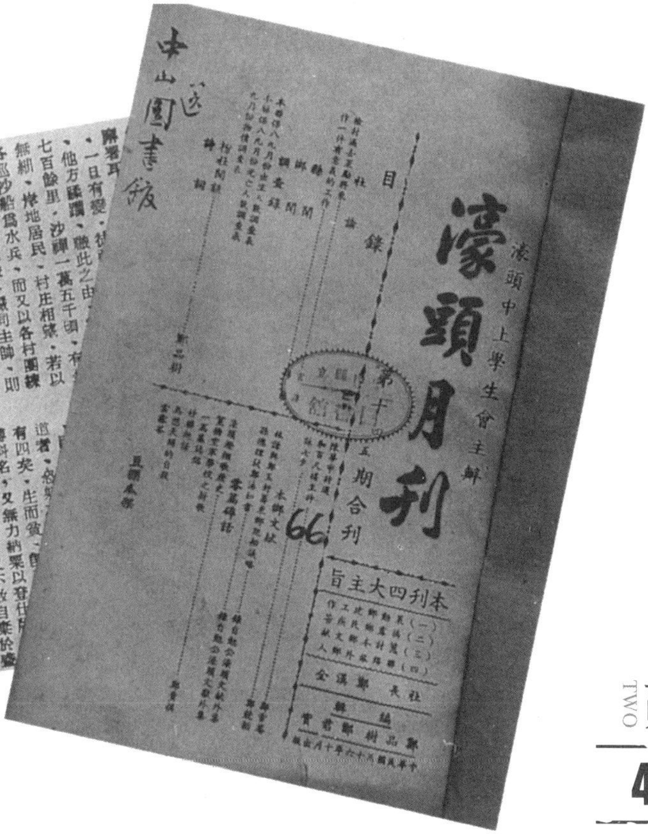

▲54

濠頭月刊

濠頭中上學生會主辦

第十 五期合刊

目錄

本刊四大主旨

中山圖書館

▼55

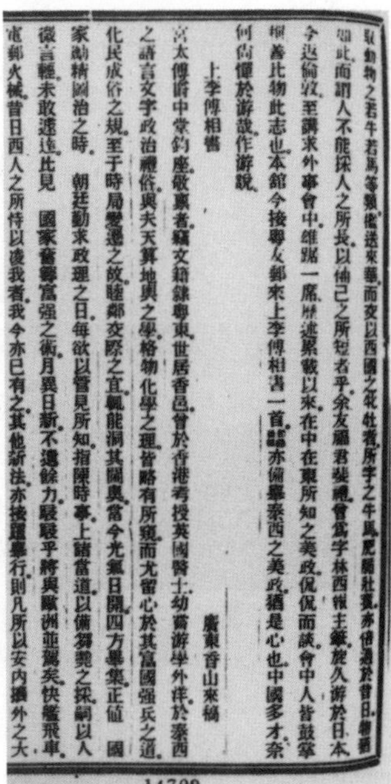

馭動物之若牛若馬等類，俾送來華，而交以西國之牧牲者，所字之牛馬肥碩壯實，亦俾遇於曾日。朝鮮嚮此，而謂人不能採人之所長，以補己之所短者乎。余友福君斐禮，曾爲字林西報主筆，旋久游於日本，今返倫敦，至講求外事會中，維踞一席，歷述累載以來，在中在東所知之美政，侃侃而談，令中人皆鼓掌稱善。此物此志也。本館今接粵友郵來上李傅相書一首，亦備舉泰西之美政，猶是心也。中國多才，奈何尚僅於游說作游說。

上李傅相書

廣東香山來稿

宮太傅爵中堂鈞座：敬稟者，竊文籍隸粵東，世居香邑，曾於香港考授英國醫士，幼嘗游學外洋，於泰西之語言文字、政治禮俗，與夫天算地輿之學，格物化學之理，皆略有所窺，而尤留心於其富國強兵之道，化民成俗之規；至於時局變遷之故，睦鄰交際之宜，輒能洞其閫奧。當今光氣日開，四方畢集，正值 國家勵精圖治之時， 朝廷勤求政理之日，每欲以管見所知，指陳時事，上諸當道，以備芻蕘之採，嗣以人微言輕，未敢遽達。比見 國家奮籌富強之術，月異日新，不遺餘力，駸駸乎將與歐洲並駕矣。快艦、飛車、電郵、火械，昔日西人之所恃以凌我者，我今亦已有之，其他新法，亦接踵舉行。則凡所以安內攘外之大

14709

中歷光緒二十年 九月

萬國公報

西歷一千八百九十四年 十月

14701

56

56. 1894年6月，经郑观应推荐，孙中山偕陆皓东北上天津，上书李鸿章，提出改革弊政、富民强国的主张，但未被采纳。图为刊于《万国公报》的上书。

In June 1894, Sun Yat-sen went to Tianjin with Lu Haodong, and presented a letter to Li Hongzhang, with the recommendation of Zheng Guanying, put forward his ideas of reform, but he was turned down. This is his letter published in the *Globe Magazine*.

57

58

57. 上书李鸿章的失败，使孙中山放弃了改良的幻想，立定革命的决心。1894年11月，孙中山在檀香山组建中国第一个资产阶级革命团体兴中会，提出“驱除鞑虏，恢复中华，创立合众政府”的纲领。图为第一批兴中会会员宣誓地——檀香山华侨李昌住宅。

The failure of persuading Li Hongzhang forced Sun Yat-sen to give up the illusion of reform and to made up his mind to make revolution. In November 1894, Sun Yat-sen organized in Honolulu China's first bourgeois revolutionary group—Revive China Society, with "Driving the Qing rulers out, reviving the Chinese nation, founding a republic" as their guiding principle. This is the place where the first group of members of Society to Restore China' s Prosperity took oaths—the overseas Chinese Li Chang's house in Honolulu.

58. 出席兴中会第一次成立会议的广东籍檀香山华侨何宽（香山人，上左）、邓松盛（即邓荫南，开平人，上中）、许直臣（香山人，上右）、钟宇（即钟工宇，香山人，下左）、宋居仁（花县人，下中）、夏百子（新会人，下右）。

The overseas Chinese in Honolulu attending the first meeting of establishment of Revive China Society: He Kuan (from Xiangshan County, upper left), Deng Songsheng (another name: Deng Yinnan, from Kaiping County, upper middle), Xu Zhichen (from Xiangshan County, upper right), Zhong Yu (another name: Zhong Gongyu, from Xiangshan County, lower left), Song Juren (from Huaxian County, lower middle) and Xia Baizi (from Xinhui County, lower right).

59

59. 早期广东籍檀香山兴中会会员孙眉（左,香山人）、陆灿（中,香山人）、李安邦（右,香山人）。

The earliest Guangdong members of Revive China Society in Honolulu: Sun Mei (left, from Xiangshan County), Lu Can (middle, from Xiangshan County), Li Anbang (right, from Xiangshan County).

60. 1895年，孙中山为筹集革命经费，以中国商务公会名义发行的股单。

Stock notes issued in 1895 by Sun Yat-sen to raise revolutionary funds, in the name of the Chinese Commerce Trade Union.

60

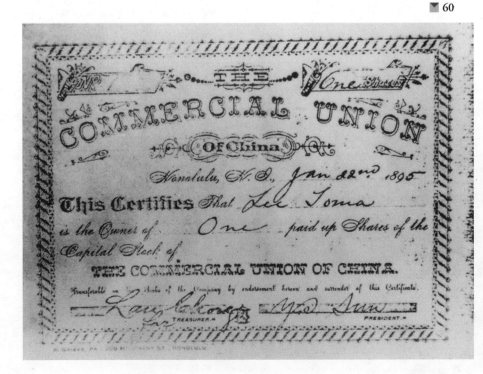

No. One Shares

THE COMMERCIAL UNION Of China

Honolulu, H. I., Jan 22nd 1895

This Certifies That Lee Toma is the Owner of One paid up Shares of the Capital Stock of THE COMMERCIAL UNION OF CHINA.

Transferable on the Books of the Company by endorsement hereon and surrender of this Certificate.

TREASURER.

PRESIDENT.

◀ 61

61. 为便于领导国内的革命运动，1895年2月21日，孙中山召集陆皓东、陈少白、郑士良、杨鹤龄、区凤墀等与杨衢云、谢缵泰等辅仁文社成员，在香港中环士丹顿街13号成立香港兴中会。会址机关用“乾亨行”名义作掩护。图为乾亨行旧址。

On February 21, 1895, in order to lead the revolutionary movement in China, Sun Yat-sen, together with Lu Haodong, Chen Shaobai, Zheng Shiliang, Yang Heling, Ou Fengchi and the members of China Patriotic Reform Association: Yang Quyun, Xie Zuantai, established Hong Kong branch of Revive China Society in No. 13 Stanton Street,Central, Hong Kong. The name of the leading office took The Tsien as a cover. This is the old site of the firm.

62. 原辅仁文社社长、香港兴中会会长杨衢云（福建海澄人）。

Yang Quyun (from Haicheng County,Fujian province), former director of Hong Kong branch of Revive China Society.

◀ 62

▲63

63. 加入香港兴中会的香港辅仁文社部分成员。该社1890年发起筹办，1892年正式成立，以开通民智、关心时事为宗旨，是香港知识青年组成的第一个团体。

Some members of China Patriotic Reform Association, who joined Hong Kong Branch of Revive China Society. China Patriotic Reform Association was founded formally in 1892, for the purpose of educating people and caring about current affairs, and was the first group of Hong Kong young intellectuals.

64. 香港兴中会骨干尢列（左）、杨鹤龄（右）。

The backbones of Hong Kong Branch of Revive China Society: You Lie (left) and Yang Heling (right).

▲64

65. 1897年，香港兴中会会员与日本友人宫崎寅藏（右四）在香港的合影。

The group photo of members of Hong Kong Branch of Revive China Society and Japanese friend—Miyazaki Torazou (the fourth from right) in 1897.

65

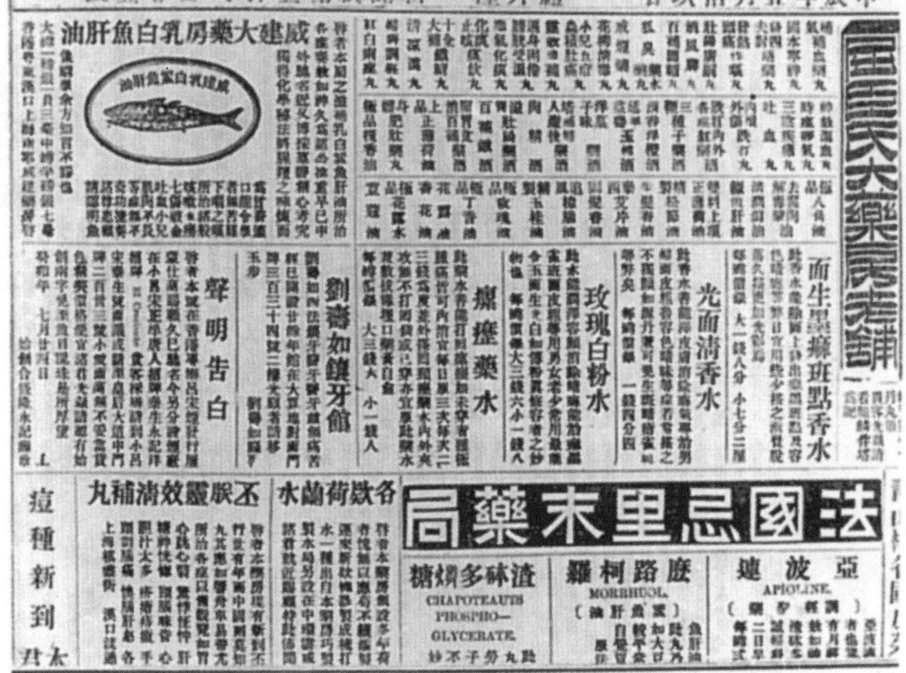

中國日報
"China"

No 1831 Saturday, 5th MARCH 1904, Nos. 92 & 94, Hollywood Road, Hongkong.

甲辰年正月拾玖日 禮拜陸

成建大藥房乳白魚肝油

面生黑癍斑點香水

光面清香水

玫瑰白粉水

癧瘡藥水

劉壽如鑲牙館

聲明告白

法國忌里末藥局

渣林多燐糖 CHAPOTEAUTS PHOSPHO-GLYCERATE

鹿路柯羅 MORRHUOL

亞波建 APIOLINE

各款荷蘭水

丕眠靈效清補丸

痘種新到

66

66. 1900年1月25日，号称“中国革命提倡者之元祖”的兴中会机关报《中国日报》在香港创刊。该报成为革命派进行舆论宣传的重要阵地。

On January 25, 1900, the *China Daily* known as “Chinese forefather who advocated revolution” and the organ of Revive China Society issued publication in Hong Kong. This newspaper became the important position where the revolutionary group propagated public opinions.

67. 香港兴中会骨干、《中国日报》创办人、首任社长兼总编辑陈少白。

Chen Shaobai, a backbone of Hong Kong Branch of Revive China Society and founder, the first director and editor-in-chief of the *China Daily*.

▲ 67

68. 香港兴中会成立后，孙中山决定筹划广州起义。1895年3月下旬，孙中山偕陆皓东、郑士良等到广州成立兴中会分会，以联络会党、绿林、游勇、防营、水师等。图为位于广州城内双门底的兴中会广州分会会址、广州起义秘密总机关——王氏书舍。

After Hong Kong Branch of Revive China Society was founded, Sun Yat-sen decided to prepare the Guangzhou Uprising. In the last ten days of March 1895, Sun Yat-sen, together with Lu Haodong and Zheng Shiliang, set up branch in Guangzhou in order to liaison with secret societies, greenwood outlaws and stragglers, garrison troops and navy division,etc. This is Guangzhou Branch site at Shuangmendi inside the city of Guangzhou and secret headquarters of Guangzhou Uprising—Wang Clan's Study.

▼ 68

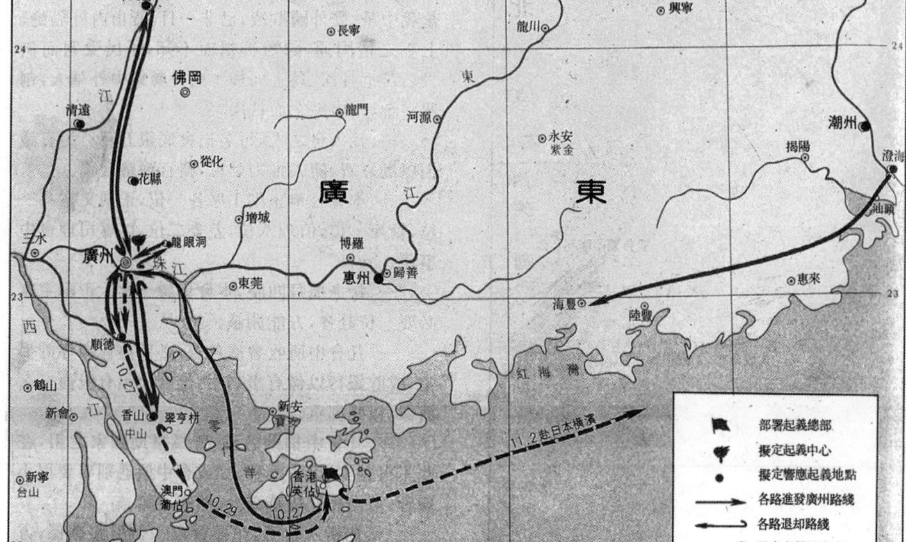

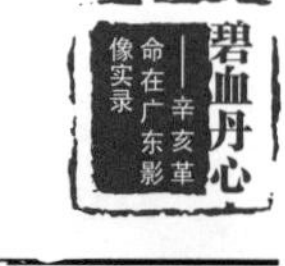

69

69. 1895年8月29日，孙中山等在香港召开紧急会议，决定10月26日（农历九月九日）重阳节起义。起义采取数路进攻的策略，以杨衢云率香港一路为主攻；同时，刘裕率北江一路，李杞、侯艾泉率香山一路，陈锦顺率顺德一路，麦某率龙眼洞一路，吴子才率汕头一路，以为策应。孙中山坐镇广州指挥。图为广州起义部署形势图（据《辛亥革命史地图集》）。

On August 29, 1895, Sun Yat-sen, etc. in Hong Kong held an emergency meeting to discuss important matters of uprising and decided to launch Chong Yang Festival Uprising on October 26 (the Chinese lunar calendar September 9). It took several tactics of attack, with Yang Quyun leading Hong Kong team as one troop for the main attack. At the same time, Liu Yu led rebels from Beijiang as another; Li Qi and Hou Aiquan led Xiangshan rebels. Chen Jinshun led Shunde rebels; Mr. Mai, rebels from Longyandong; Wu Zicai, rebels from Shantou to make supporting movement to cut off enemy. Sun Yat-sen commanded personally in Guangzhou. This is the dispatch situation map of Guangzhou Uprising (from *The Revolution of 1911 History Atlas*).

70. 由于组织不周，起义事泄，10月26日，广州清军大肆搜捕革命党人和查封革命党机关。兴中会领导的第一次反清武装起义未及发难即告流产。起义领导人陆皓东、朱贵全、丘四、程奎光等英勇牺牲。孙中山、郑士良、陈少白等出逃。图为香山籍烈士陆皓东。

Because organization was weak, the news of uprising was let out. On October 26, Guangzhou Qing army hunted revolutionary partisans and closed down revolutionary party's leading body. The first-time anti-Qing Dynasty armed uprising was abortive before launching. Lu Haodong, Zhu Guiquan, Qiu Si, Cheng Kuiguang, etc. leaders of the uprising, died a heroic death. Sun Yat-sen, Zheng Shiliang, Chen Shaobai,etc. fleed. This was Lu Haodong, a martyr from Xiangshan County.

▲70

71. 陆皓东设计、孙中山手绘的青天白日旗。

The Blue Sky with a White Sun Flag designed by Lu Haodong and painted by Sun Yat-sen.

▼71

POST CARD

This space may be used for printed or written matter.

The address only to be written here.

STAMP ... BE PLAC... HERE

▲72

◀73

◀74

72. 陆皓东设计、孙中山手绘的青天白日旗说明文。

This is an exposition for the Blue Sky with a White Sun Flag, which was designed by Lu Haodong and painted by Sun Yat-sen.

73. 香山籍烈士程奎光。当时任广东水师镇涛舰管带，被捕后受笞军棍六百而死。

Cheng Kuiguang, martyr from Xiangshan County, brigade commander of Zhentao battleship in then Guangdong navy division, was arrested and was beaten to death with 600 beats.

74. 参与筹划广州起义的香港立法局华人成员何启（南海人）。

He Qi (from Nanhai County), a Chinese member in Hong Kong Legislative Council, who participated in planning the Guangzhou uprising.

75

75. 香山籍香港兴中会骨干黄咏商。参与策划广州起义，变卖祖产洋楼一栋，供起义军费。

Huang Yongshang, a backbone of Hong Kong Branch of Revive China Society, participated in planning Guangzhou Uprising, who sold off one western-style building handed down from his ancestors, in order to support the uprising as military spending.

76

76. 参与广州起义筹备工作并变卖家产充起义经费的香山籍兴中会会员杨心如。

Yang Xinru (from Xiangshan County), a member of Revive China Society, participated in Guangzhou Uprising's preparatory work, and sold off family property as fund for uprising.

77

77. 负责运动绿林，策划广州起义，并助孙中山脱险的清远籍兴中会会员刘秉祥。

Liu Bingxiang (from Qingyuan County), a member of Revive China Society, responsible for liaison of the greenwood outlaws, planned Guangzhou Uprising and helped Sun Yat-sen escape danger.

78

78. 清两广总督署卫队长、湖南籍兴中会会员胡凤璋。参与筹划起义，预作内应，起义事泄后，即将清兵缉人消息走报刘秉祥，助孙中山脱险。

Hu Fengzhang (from Hunan Province), commander of Guard of Guangdong and Guangxi Provinces governor and member of Revive China Society, participated in preparation of the uprising, who acted as a planted agent in advance . After the news let out, he passed the news to Liu Bingxiang that Qing soldiers would capture the rebels, so as to help Sun Yat-sen to escape danger.

79

79. 广州起义失败后，孙中山和部分同志先赴香港再转往日本，伺机再举。图为孙中山在香港时的居所。

After the Guangzhou Uprising failed, Sun Yat-sen and some comrades went to Hong Kong first and then transfered to Japan, waiting for an opportunity to rise in revolt again. This is Sun's residence in Hong Kong.

80. 广州起义失败后，在澳门的葡籍友人飞南第不仅帮助孙中山脱险，还将广州起义的消息刊登在他主办的澳门《镜海丛报》上。

After failure of the Guangzhou Uprising, Francisco H.Fernanders, a Portuguese friend of Sun Yat-sen in Macau, help Sun Yat-sen to escape. He also published news on the Guangzhou Uprising in his newspaper *Ching-hai Tsung-Pao*.

81. 1897年，孙中山在日本与宫崎寅藏初晤时笔谈广州起义经过的手迹。

A letter written by Sun Yat-sen when he met Miyazaki Torzou for the first time in 1897 and discussed the course of Guangzhou Uprising.

CHING-HAI TSUNG-PAO.

每月收銀三毫

鏡海叢報

按月繳銀清收

禮拜三日　第十六號

大清光緒廿一年乙未九月二十日　新聞紙第三年　西紀壹千八百九十五年十一月初六日

目錄

80

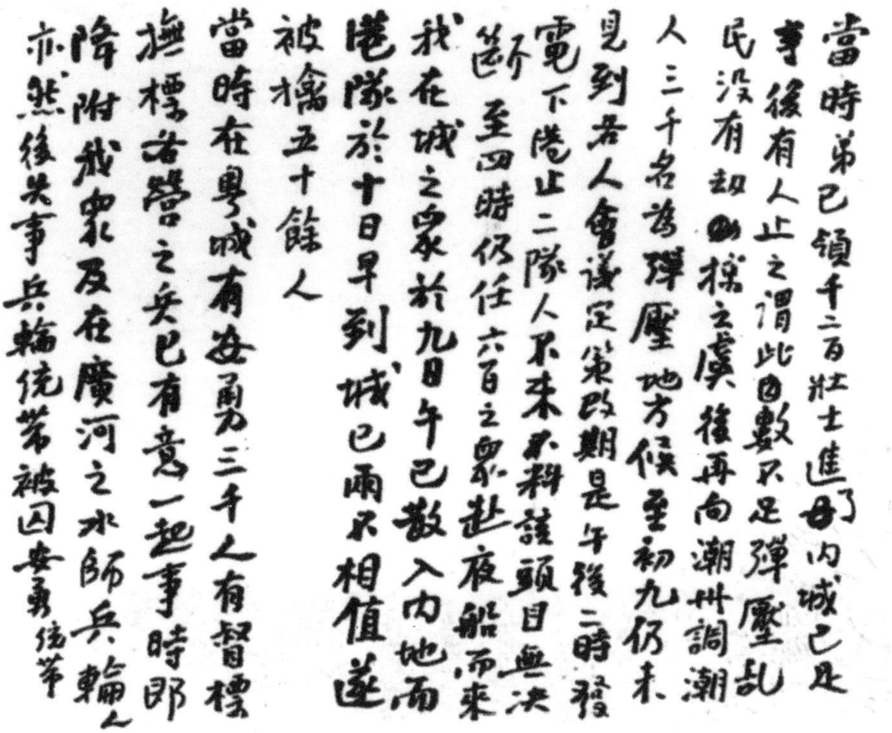

當時弟已領千二百壯士進了內城已是
事後有人止之謂此回數不足彈壓亂
民沒有劫掠之虞後再向潮州調潮
人三千名為彈壓地方候至初九仍未
見到吾人會議定策改期是午後二時發
電下港止二隊人不來不料該頭目無決
斷至四時仍任六百之衆趁夜船而來
我在城之衆於九日午已散入內地而
港隊於十日早到城已兩不相值遂
被擒五十餘人
當時在粵城有安勇三千人有督標
撫標各營之兵已有意一起事時即
降附我衆及在廣河之水師兵輪人
亦然後失事兵輪統帶被囚安勇統帶

81

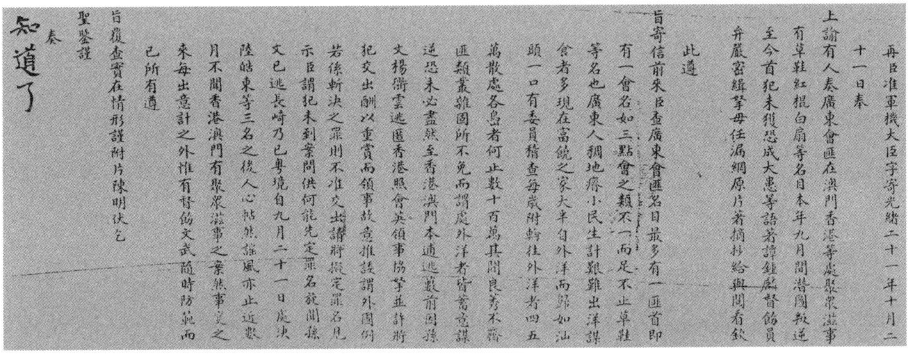

再臣准軍機大臣字寄光緒二十一年十月二
十一日奉
上諭有人奏廣東會匪在澳門香港等處聚衆滋事
有草鞋紅棍白扇等名目本年九月間潛圖叛逆
至今首犯未獲恐成大患等語著譚鍾麟督飭員
弁嚴密緝拏毋任漏網原片著摘抄給與閱看欽
此遵
旨寄信前來臣查廣東會匪名目最多有一匪首即
有一會名如三點會之類不一而足不止草鞋
等名也廣東人稠地瘠小民生計艱難出洋謀
食者多現在富饒之家大半自外洋而歸如汕
頭一口有委員稽查每歲附輪往外洋者四五
萬散處各島者何止數十百萬其間良莠不齊
匪類叢雜固所不免而謂處外洋者皆蓄意謀
逆恐未必盡然至香港澳門本逋逃藪前因孫
文楊衢雲逃匿香港照會英領事協拏並許將
犯交出酬以重賞而領事故意推諉謂外國例
若係斬決之罪則不准交出請將擬定罪名見
示臣謂犯未到案問供何能先定罪名旋聞孫
文已逃長崎乃已粵境自九月二十一日處決
陸皓東等三名之後人心帖然謠風亦止近數
月不聞香港澳門有聚衆滋事之案然事變之
來每出意計之外惟有督飭文武隨時防範而
已所有遵
旨覆查實在情形謹附片陳明伏乞
聖鑒謹
奏
知道了

82

82. 广州起义失败后，两广总督谭钟麟企图用重金诱使港英当局协缉孙中山。图为谭钟麟给清廷的奏折。

After Guangzhou Uprising failed, governor general of Guangdong and Guangxi Provinces Tan Zhonglin attempted to lure British authorities in Hong Kong with huge sum of money into arresting Sun Yat-sen. The picture shows the memorial to Qing court submitted and written by Tan Zhonglin.

ENCLOSURE 3. 138

In C.O.D.No.5 of 1896.

COPY.

Order made by the Governor in Council, under the provisions of The Banishment and Conditional Pardons Ordinance 1882 as amended by Ordinance No. 4 of 1885.

Council Chamber, Victoria, in the Colony of Hongkong, the 4th. day of March, 1896.

Whereas it is deemed desirable by the Governor in Council that Sun Yat Sin alias Sun Man

(the Governor in Council being satisfied that such person is not a natural born or naturalized subject of Her Majesty) should be prohibited under the provisions of The Banishment and Conditional Pardons Ordinance 1882 Section 3 as amended by Ordinance No. 4 of 1885 from residing or being within the Colony for the space of five years from the date hereof upon the grounds hereinafter appearing.

The Governor in Council doth hereby by virtue of the said Ordinances order that the said Sun Yat Sin be prohibited and the said Sun Yat Sin is hereby prohibited from residing or being in the Colony for the space of time aforesaid from the said date: and that the period of one month from the date hereof be fixed as the time within which the said Sun Yat Sin shall depart from the Colony aforesaid.

And the Governor in Council doth, hereby, under the provisions of Ordinance No. 4 of 1885, further order that the said Sun Yat Sin be detained in custody of the Police until he leaves the Colony.

Statement of the grounds upon which this order is made:

That the said Sun Yat Sin is, in the opinion of the Governor in Council, dangerous to the peace and good order of the Colony.

(Sd.) F.J.Badeley.
Acting *Clerk of Councils.*

附清按察使告示及賞格

欽命廣東等處提刑司按察使兼管全省驛傳事務加三級紀錄十次張

為懸賞購匪事照得土匪糾結數黨暗運軍火約期在省城滋事一案

當經拿獲匪犯陸皓東等各名當辦惟尚有首要各匪孫汶等在逃未獲

亟應懸賞緝拿合行出示曉諭為此示諭闔屬軍民人等知悉有等如

能拿獲後開賞格之各匪解案一經訊明足事即當如數給與花紅銀

兩並封存庫挹到即給慎勿懷疑觀望至此外案內被誘匪徒准其改

過自新免予深究如能拿獲後開各匪解案仍一律給賞各宜懔遵毋違特示

計開

孫汶即逸仙香山縣東鄉翠微村人頭耳不寬年約二十九歲花紅銀一千元

[illegible]

夏亞伯新會人肥矮面微黃年約四十歲花紅銀一百元

李亞聚香山縣隆都鄉蓝下村人身高眼大髮多白年約五十歲花紅銀二百元

李芝南南海縣佛山人年約三四十歲花紅銀二百元

楊衢雲香山縣人本籍福建右手共缺三指年三十九歲花紅銀一百元

[illegible]

劉裕祥清遠縣人身高年約三十歲花紅銀二百元

朱浩清清遠縣人年約三十七八歲花紅銀二百元

陳少白即變石新會縣外海人年約二十八九歲花紅銀一百元

王質甫江西人身中面白年約三十七八歲花紅銀三百元

湯亞才花縣人身高微麻年約四十歲花紅銀三百元

吳子才潮州人身高頸窄年約四十歲花紅銀二百元

[illegible]順德人身矮年約二十五六歲花紅銀一百元

陳[illegible]南海縣西樵鄉人身胖微麻年約三十二三歲花紅銀二百元

侯艾泉香山縣隆都鄉人身高瘦髮光年約五十歲花紅銀二百元

[illegible]番禺縣南[illegible]村人面圓有鬚年約三十七八歲花紅銀二百元

[illegible]清遠縣人矮瘦年約二十四五歲花紅銀一百元

84

羊城新聞

督[illegible]牌示 碣石鎮左營守備缺以海門營左哨千總[illegible]其光升補（）潘憲牌示 [illegible]春

縣缺委即用縣劉能太爺署 海陽縣洋司梅濟鈞仍赴新任（）南番兩縣正堂示

現有匪首 名曰孫文 結有匪黨 曰楊衢雲 起意謀叛 擾亂省城 分遣黨與

到處誘人 借會招勇 煽惑愚氓 每人每月 十塊洋銀 鄉愚貪利 踴躍紛紛

數日之前 聽得風聲 嚴密查訪 派勇防營 果獲匪犯 朱邱陸程 經衆指証

供出反情 紅帶為記 口號分明 給械旗幟 搜出為憑 盡反叛逆 律有明刑

甘心從賊 厥罪維均 嚴拿重辦 決不從輕 城廂內外 兵勇如林 [illegible]捕亂黨

決不饒人 惟彼鄉愚 想充勇丁 不知禍害 貪利忘身 一時迷惑 [illegible]

丟棄紅帶 急早逃奔 回歸鄉里 安分偷生 免遭擒獲 身首兩分 特此告示

剴切簡明 去逆效順 其各凜遵 毋違特示 九月十三日示

85

83\. 1896年3月4日，香港政府发布驱逐孙中山出境的命令，以5年为限，禁止孙中山在港居住或停留。此时，孙中山已离开香港远赴日本、檀香山。

On March 4, 1896, an order of banishment issued by the Hong Kong Government, prohibiting Sun Yat-sen from residing or being in Hong Kong for a period of five years. At the time the order was issued, Sun Yat-sen had already left Hong Kong for Japan and Honolulu.

84\. 清政府悬赏缉拿孙中山及党人的告示和赏格。

The notice posted to the public for capture of Sun Yat-sen and his partisans, and the award by the Qing Government.

85\. 1895年11月1日，《香港华字日报》刊登南海、番禺两县署镇压广州起义的告示。

On November 1, 1895, an announcement published in *Hong Kong Chinese Mail* that Guangzhou Uprising was suppressed by offices of Nanhai County and Panyu County.

86

86. 1895年11月10日，孙中山与陈少白、郑士良从香港抵达日本神户。图为当天报道广州起义的《神户又新日报》。

On November 10, 1895, Sun Yat-sen, together with Chen Shaobai, Zheng Shiliang reached Kobe, Japan, from Hong Kong. The photo of *Kobe New Daily* which reported Guangzhou Uprising on that day.

87. 居留广州的兴中会会员积蓄力量，密谋再起。图为1899年兴中会会员史坚如（番禺人）、崔通约（高明人）、黎俊民（东莞人）和张后臣（四川人）（从右至左）在广州的合影。

Members of Revive China Society staying in Guangzhou gathered to strength for another uprising. From right to left in the picture taken in 1899 in Guangzhou, they were Shi Jianru (from Panyu County), Cui Tongyue (from Gaoming County), Li Junmin (from Dongguan County) and Zhang Houchen (from Sichuan Province).

88. 为表示推翻清朝统治的决心，流亡至日本的孙中山、陈少白（右）、郑士良（左）毅然把作为清朝臣民标志的辫子剪去。图为三人断发改装后的合照。

For showing the resolution to overthrow the ruling of Qing Dynasty, Sun Yat-sen, Chen Shaobai(right) and Zheng Shiliang(left), who went into exile in Japan, resolutely cut their pigtails, which were the signs as Qing Dynasty subjects. This is a group photo after they cut their hair.

88

▲ 89

89. 1900年夏秋间，孙中山决定利用北方义和团反帝运动之机，以兴中会成员为骨干，联合会党和绿林，在惠州组织反清起义，由郑士良全权指挥，史坚如、邓荫南在广州策谋响应，杨衢云、陈少白留港接济饷械，计划起义成功后，在华南建立一个新的民主共和国。图为1900年前后的孙中山。

During the autumn and summer of 1900, Sun Yat-sen determined to utilize the chance of the Boxer's Movement against imperialists in North China, taking the members of Revive China Society as backbones, uniting the greenwood outlaws and the secret societies to organize anti-Qing uprising in Huizhou commanded by Zheng Shiliang with full authority. Shi Jianru and Deng Yinnan responded in Guangzhou. Yang Quyun and Chen Shaobai stayed in Hong Kong to give materials and ammunition assistance. After the uprising succeeded, they would set up a new democratic republic in South China. The photo shows Sun Yat-sen around 1900.

90. 惠州起义领导人郑士良（归善人）。

Zheng Shiliang (from Guishan County), the leader of Huizhou Uprising.

▶ 90

▲ 91

91. 1900年10月6日，郑士良率会党600余人在惠州三洲田起义。图为起义发难地惠州三洲田。

On October 6, 1900, Zheng Shiliang led 600 members of secret societies in rise in revolt at Sanzhoutian in Huizhou. This is the uprising site at Sanzhoutian in Huizhou.

92. 三洲田起义后，不到半个月，起义军连克沙湾、佛子凹、永湖、白芒花、崩岗、三多祝等地，重创清军。10月22日，由于粮械失继，起义军被迫解散。惠州起义是中国资产阶级革命党人正式举行的第一次反清武装起义。图为惠州起义形势图（据《辛亥革命史地图集》）。

In less than half a month after Sanzhoutian Uprising, the insurrectionary army captured Shawan, Fozi'ao, Yonghu, Baimanghua, Benggang, Sanduozhu etc. and mauled Qing army heavily. On October 22, because the lack of food and ammunitions, the insurrectionary army had to dismissed. Huizhou Uprising was the first armed uprising led formally by China's bourgeois revolutionary partisans to fight against Qing Dynasty. This is Huizhou Uprising situation map (from *The Revolution of 1911 History Atlas*).

▼ 92

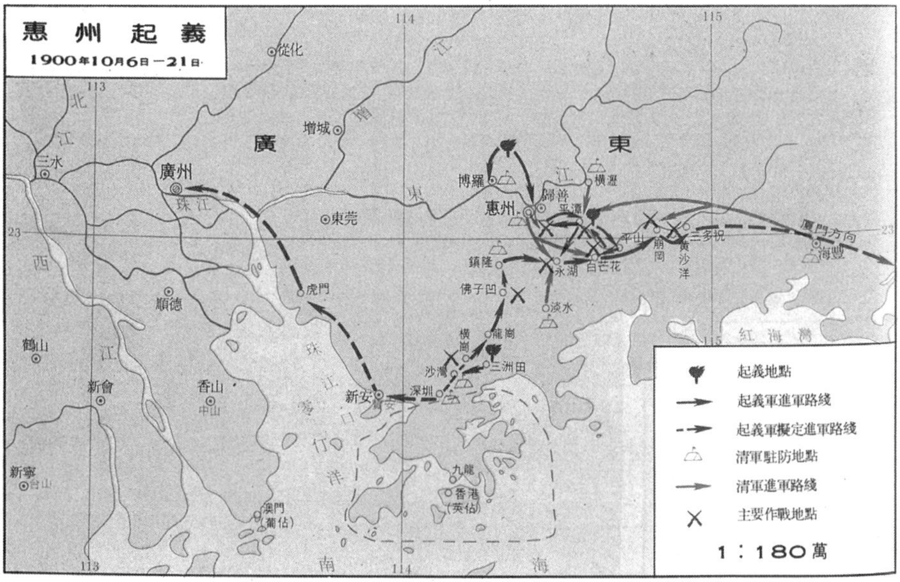

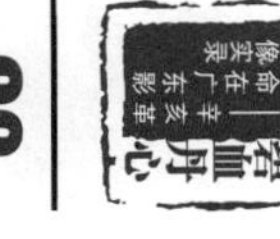

93

93. 1900年10月《中国旬报》27期刊载的惠州起义消息。

Zhongguo Xunbao (*China Ten-Day Report*), Issue No.27, in October of 1900, reported Huizhou Uprising.

94. 参与领导惠州起义的义军中路统兵司令、新安籍兴中会会员江恭喜。

Jiang Gongxi (from Xin'an County), commander-general of Central Army in Huizhou Uprising and member of Revive China Society.

95. 受孙中山委托前往惠州三多祝前线传达作战命令而牺牲的日本友人山田良政。

Yamata Yoshimasa, a Japanese, who went to Huizhou front to pass the fighting order of Sun Yat-sen and died in Huizhou Uprising.

96. 为便于领导和指挥起义，1900年9月，孙中山从日本抵台湾，在台北设立惠州起义指挥中心。图为孙中山在台北的住所。

In order to be easy to lead and command the uprising, in September 1900, Sun Yat-sen reached Taiwan from Japan and set up in Taibei the commanding centre for Huizhou Uprising. This is Sun Yat-sen's residence in Taibei.

94

95

96

奏為廣東惠州會匪被外匪句結起事派營勦辦
獲勝並仍飭搜捕餘匪情形恭摺具陳仰祈
聖鑒事竊照惠州會匪肆擾欽奉電
旨垂詢經岑將康孫各逆句結土匪起事及咨飭水
陸各軍勦辦情形於閏八月十八日先行電奏
二十三日欽奉電
旨此起土匪仍著督飭何長清等各營合力痛勦迅
速撲滅毋任蔓延欽此欽遵嚴督勦辦嗣據該丈
武先後稟報屢次接仗獲勝大股匪類業已撲
滅等情續經岑於九月初七日電奏十一日欽
奉電
旨惠州土匪辦理尚為迅速仍著嚴飭搜捕毋留餘
孽欽此又經恭錄轉行並嚴催各營欽遵辦理在
案茲將該土匪句結起事及調營勦辦詳細情
形謹縷晰陳之查廣東惠州府屬民情强悍聚
眾拜會械鬭搶擄習為故常近海之歸善海豐
等縣尤多洋盜鹽梟以故嘯聚甚易動輒滋事
即歸善一屬十餘年來稔山會匪黃亞春煙墩
會匪黃狂成拒敵官軍搶劫墟市屢經派營勦
散迄未淨絕根株本年閏八月初間岑訪聞歸
善縣屬三洲田地方有孫康逆黨句結土匪起
事並在外洋私運軍火至隱僻海汊轉入內地
當以逆黨主謀意圖大舉實非尋常土匪可比
且查三洲田地方山深林密路徑紆迴南抵新
安緊偪九龍租界西北與東莞縣接壤北通府
縣二城均可竄出東江直達省會東與海豐毗
連亦係會匪出沒之處非多派營勇兩面顧到
難期迅速撲滅爰咨水師提督何長清抽撥新
舊靖勇及各臺礮勇共足一千五百餘人先由
新安之深圳墟向北兜截直搗三洲老巢防擾
租界復派大小兵輪在洋面遊弋斷其接濟西
北一路派介勇一營駐紮歸善東莞交界要隘
又派總兵黃金福所統信勇一營提督刁經明
所帶廣安水軍一營分扼東江水陸防竄江面
東路為海豐陸豐二縣原派都司吳祥達帶哲
勇左營駐紮即飭回顧歸善並移潮州信勇一
營填紮海豐三面兜截而以惠州府歸善縣二
城為進兵之路陸路提督鄧萬林原統哲字中
左右三營練兵正副兩營廣毅軍一營分赴惠
州十屬辦理緝捕在歸善者僅哲勇練兵數哨
一聞匪警各屬震動不能抽回岑先派補用副
將莫善積管帶喜勇一營由省馳往會勦一面
咨令鄧萬林添募一營名曰立捷軍又派北海
鎮總兵劉邦盛另募一營名曰靜字營均由府
城直攻巢穴莫善積喜勇於閏八月初十日馳
抵歸善維時匪黨未齊猝聞兵到遂定於十三
日豎旗起事先以數百人猛撲新安沙灣墟欲
擾租界幸何長清靖勇已抵深圳乃回攻橫岡
進踞龍岡喜哲各勇連次接戰互有勝負兇燄
益張警報日至岑以總兵黃金福所統信勇已
撥兩營分駐東西兩路因令再帶一營由府城
進勦並令記名總兵陳維熊帶熊勇兩營繼進
以壯聲援此岑添調營勇分投防勦之情形也
逆首孫汶伏處香港暗施詭計而三洲田匪巢
則以鄭士良劉運滐等充偽軍師蔡景福陳亞
怡等充偽先鋒何崇飄黃盲幅黃耀廷等充偽
元帥黃揚充偽副元帥旗幟偽書大秦國及日
月等悖逆字樣各匪頭纏紅巾身穿白布鑲紅
號褂甫於閏八月初八九日聚集既踞龍岡四
出焚搶附會日眾總兵劉邦盛新募靜勇威軍
惠州府知府沈傳義募土勇二百名委歸善縣
縣丞杜鳳梧管帶二十二日會同喜哲各軍奔
赴前敵行至距城十餘里之平潭地方賊隊麕
至莫善積奮勇當先陣斬偽先鋒蔡亞生陳亞
幅等并匪數十名正期得手詎附近匪鄉糾約
千餘人各帶快搶牌刀齊來助匪分路包抄我
軍被困陣亡勇丁數十人縣丞杜鳳梧被擄府
縣兩城同時戒嚴幸是日都司吳祥達帶哲字
左營由海豐來鄧萬林所招立捷新軍亦同時
抵惠橫瀝森柏洞圍練適又誘獲偽副元帥黃
揚訊明正法兵氣稍振連日匪竄附城之梁化
雷公嶺意圖直出東江各軍力扼其前不得上
竄此閏八月二十六日以前歸善匪勢猖獗之
情形也匪既不得竄出江面乃折而向東欲與
海豐陸豐股匪聯為一氣三多祝者歸善著名
匪鄉與海豐交界之要隘也先派哲勇練兵擦
防句結二十六日匪攻三多祝相近之黃沙洋

97（1）

▲97（2）

97. 1900年11月5日，两广总督德寿奏报清军平定惠州起义经过。

On November 5, 1900, De Shou, governor general of Guangdong and Guangxi Provinces, presented a memorial to the emperor, relating how Qing army put down Huizhou Uprising.

98

98. 1900年10月21日，孙中山在台北写给日本友人犬养毅叙述军事行动进展，并请游说日本政府予以支持的信。

On October 21, 1900, in Taibei, Sun Yat-sen, wrote to his Japanese friend—Inugai Tsuyoshi about the progress of the military operation. This is the letter asking his friend to persuade Japanese government to support him.

99. 为配合惠州起义，兴中会会员宋少东（南海人）、黄大汉（南海人）、磻溪和尚（清远人）、陈瑞芝（高要人）等与史坚如在广州设立秘密机关，运动会党、绿林，密谋在广州起事配合。

In order to support Huizhou Uprising, members of Revive China Society: Song Shaodong (from Nanhai County), Huang Dahan (from Nanhai County), Panxi Buhdda (from Qingyuan County), Chen Ruizhi (from Gaoyao County),etc. together with Shi Jianru, set up a secret office in Guangzhou and contacted the greenwood outlaws and the secret societies to start the uprising.

宋少东

黄大汉

磻溪和尚

陈瑞芝

99

100. 史坚如、邓荫南等兴中会会员聘英国军事家摩根为军事顾问。图为摩根与邓掖廷（三水人）、原口闻一（日本人）、练达成（新兴人）在黄埔水陆师学堂。

Shi Jianru and Deng Yinnan,etc. members of Revive China Society, invited British military strategist—Morgan as a military adviser. They are Morgan, Deng Yeting (from Sanshui County), Haraguchi Bunnyichi (Japanese), Lian Dacheng (from Xinxing County,) at Huangpu land army and navy school.

100

101

101. 停泊在广州沙面一带的杏花紫洞艇，为史坚如、邓荫南、黄大汉等兴中会会员与英国顾问摩根联络办事的秘密据点。

The boat anchored off Shamian, Guangzhou, was a secret post where Shi Jianru, Deng Yinnan, Huang Dahan,etc. kept liaison with Morgan, the British military adviser.

102. 黄大汉带领邓荫南、摩根等在广州城四处侦探，并拍摄城楼、衙署及黄埔水闸、船坞、炮台等要隘的照片，以备起义时使用。图为他们拍摄的长洲炮台（上）、黄埔鱼雷局（中）、黄埔船坞（下）照片。

Huang Dahan led Deng Yinnan, Morgan,etc. in detecting everywhere in the city of Guangzhou and photographed the city gate tower, government administration and sluice, dock, fort,etc, of Huangpu's strategic pass in order to use while rise in revolt. These are pictures of Changzhou fort(upper), Huangpu torpedo office(middle), Huangpu dock (lower)which they photographed.

103. 1900年10月28日，史坚如在广州谋炸广东巡抚兼署两广总督德寿，事败被捕，备受酷刑，11月9日就义。兴中会在广州起事的计划也告流产。图为史坚如烈士（番禺人）。

On October 28,1900, in Guangzhou Shi Jianru bombed De Shou, governor general of Guangdong and Guangxi provinces, concurrently grand coordinator of Guangdong, and failed. He was arrested and cruelly tortured, died a martyr on November 9. The plan of Guangzhou Uprising by Society to Restore China's Prosperity was abortive, too. The picture of martyr Shi Jianru (from Panyu County).

102

103

▲104

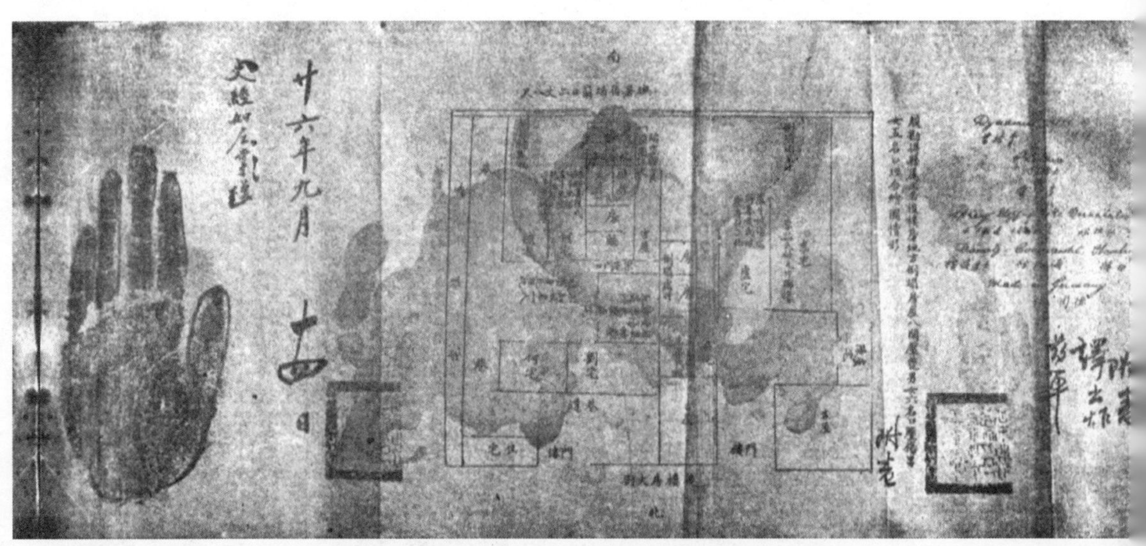

▲105

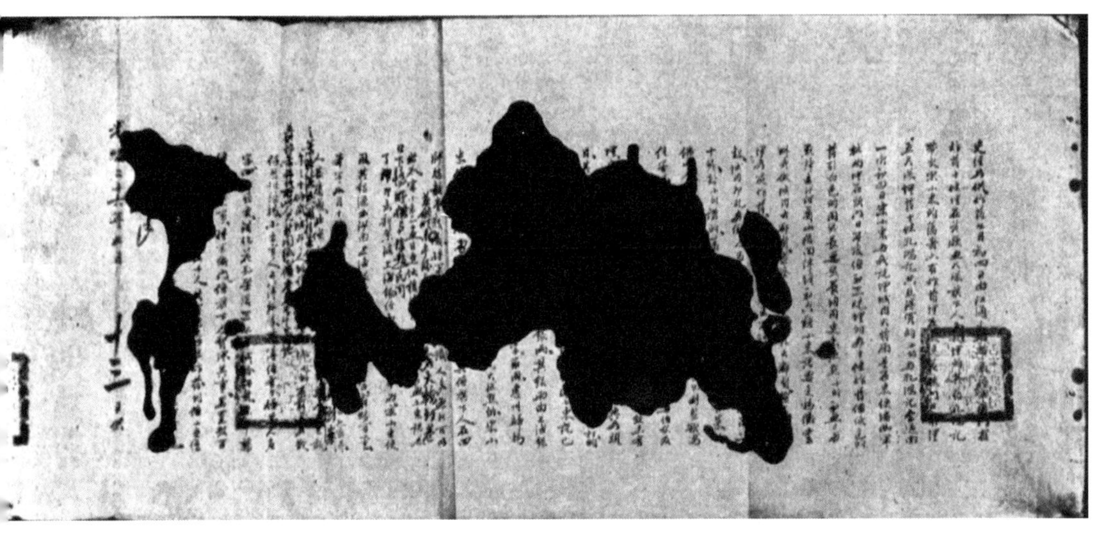

106

104. 清广东巡抚官署。

Administration office of Guangdong governor of Qing Dynasty.

105. 广州清吏审讯史坚如烈士的档卷。左为史坚如的手模。

The file of Qing official in Guangzhou questioning martyr—Shi Jianru. On the left is the palm-print of Shi Jianru.

106. 史坚如烈士的供词。纸面有被墨污之处，据说是由于内容过于激烈，清吏恐怕送达清廷，慈禧会赫然震怒，降下不测之祸，所以故意泼墨弄污，谎称为史坚如自己所为。

The confession of martyr Shi Jianru. On some parts of the paper had been blacken. It was said that because of the fierce contents, the Qing official was probably afraid Ci Xi, a feudal ruler, would be furious intensely and misfortune would fall onto his head. So he blackened it on purpose, lying that it was done by Shi Jianru himself.

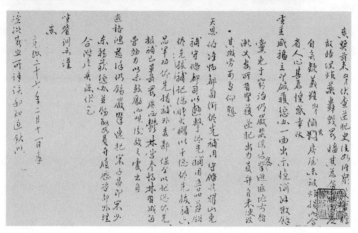

107

107. 1901年3月30日，两广总督德寿为缉获史坚如出力员弁请奖折。

The memorial to the throne, written on March 30,1901, by De Shou, governor of Guangdong and Guangxi Provinces, asking for an award for his officers' capture of Shi Jianru.

108

109

108. 1901年9月，香港兴中会会员谢缵泰、李纪堂与洪全福联络会党，密谋在广州举行武装起义，定国号为"大明顺天国"，经过一年多的准备，拟于1903年1月28日除夕夜在广州发难，但因事泄失败。图为起义领导人谢缵泰（左）、李纪堂（中，新会人）和洪全福（右，花县人）。

In September 1901, Xie Zuantai, Li Jitang and Hong Quanfu got in touch with the secret societies, planned secretly in Guangzhou to hold armed uprising, naming the state "Grand Ming Shuntian Kingdom". After more than one year's preparation, they planned to launch the uprising, but failed because the news was let out. The photos are Xie Zuantai (left), Li Jitang (middle,from Xinhui County) and Hong Quanfu (right, from Huaxian County), leaders of the uprising.

109. 起义前预制的《大明顺天国讨伐清朝檄》。

Call for Qing Dynasty by Grand Ming Shuntian Kingdom produced in advance before rise in revolt.

大明順天國南粵興漢大將軍天 賜

公理既明漢裔可興

安民告示 爾眾宜知
清朝無道 官吏貪私
荼毒天下 加稅加釐
捐柚重疊 竭盡民脂
爰動公憤 特舉義旗
除滿興漢 大公無私
保商保教 立太平基
弔民伐罪 順天應時
凡爾士庶 相安勿疑

大明國 元年 月 日

110

110. “大明顺天国”安民告示。

A notice of reassure the public by “Grand Ming Shuntian Kingdom”.

111. “大明顺天国”晓谕官绅军民应遵纪律的告示。

A notice of “Grand Ming Shuntian Kingdom” giving explicit instructions to officials, merchants, officers and people to observe disciplines.

111

▲112

112. 1903年5月21日，两广总督德寿向清廷报告镇压“大明顺天国”起义经过的奏折。

On May 21, 1903, governor general of Guangdong and Guangxi Provinces De Shou presented a memorial to the emperor, relating how Qing army put down the uprising of “Grand Ming Shuntian Kingdom”.

碧血丹心——辛亥革命在广东影像实录

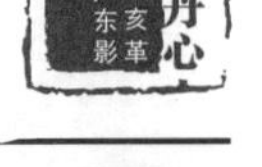

羣智社同人甲辰撮影

113

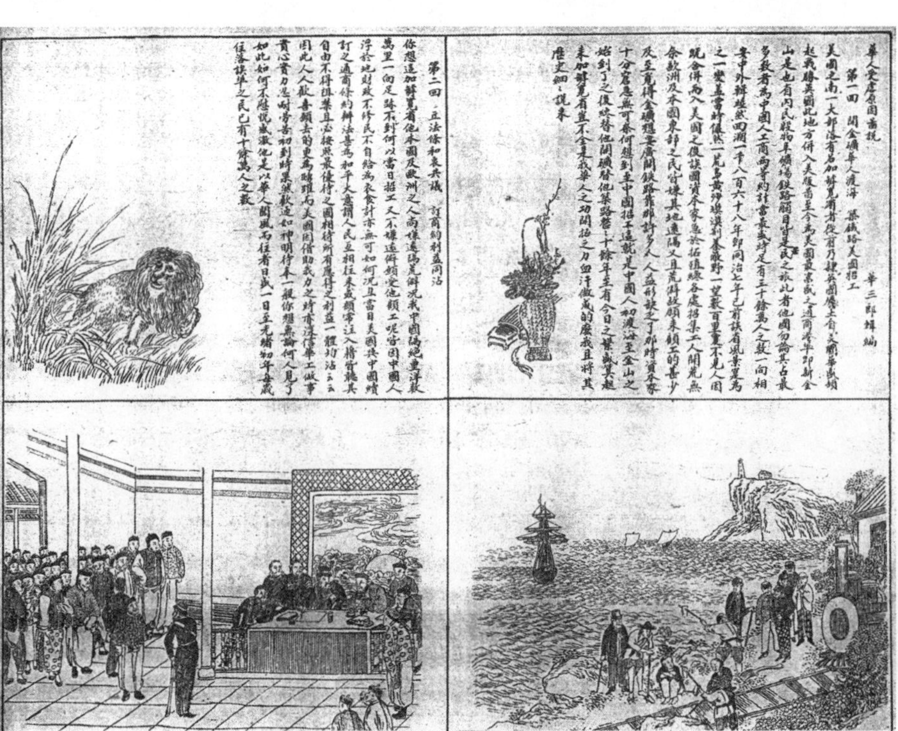

華人受虐原因畫說　　華三郎輯編

第一回　開金礦華人渡海　築鐵路美國招工

美國之南一大部落有名加鮮寬省從前乃隸英國屬土自美國華盛頓起義勝英國此地方併入美版圖至今為美國最富盛之道商港即新金山是也有內民殺狗羊礦場鐵路頗目皆是民之旅此者他國勿論其占最多數者為中國人工商兩等約計當最盛時足有三十餘萬人之數一向相安中外輯睦然回溯一千八百六十八年即同治七年已前該省風景宜為之一變其當時係然一荒島黃沙瑣漠荆蓁蔽野一望數百里裏不見人因既合併而入美國之後該國資本家急於拓殖乃各處招集工人開荒無奈歐洲及本國東部之民皆嫌其地遠隔又且荒僻故願來傭工的甚少及至覓得金礦想要廣闢鐵路需那許多人人益形缺乏了那時資本家十分窘急無可奈何想到去中國招工這就是中國人初渡海至金山之始到了之後替他開礦替他築路整整十餘年至有今日之繁盛其對未加鮮寬省豈不全是我華人之功開拓之力血汗做成的麼我且將其歷史細細說來

第二回　立法條和衷共議　訂商約利益同沾

你想這加鮮寬省他本國及歐洲之人尚嫌遙隔荒僻況我中國隔絕重洋數萬里一向足跡不到何以當日招工又不嫌遠僻頗受他傭工呢皆因中國人浮於地財政不修民不自給為衣食計亦無可如何況且當日美國與中國續訂之通商條約辦法甚為和平大意謂人民互相往來或願常住入籍皆聽其自由不得攔禁且必按照最優待之國相待所有應得之利益一體均沾云云因此人人散去頗去的更為踴躍而美國因借助我力之時亦待華工做事賣心賣力忍耐勞苦初到時果然歡迎如神明待奉一般你想無論何人見了如此如何不感恩戴德他是以華人聞風而往者日盛一日至光緒初年每歲往澇謀生之民已有十餘萬人之數

114

113. 1902年，汪兆铭、朱执信、古应芬等在广州组织群智社，探讨社会新思潮，阅读西方资产阶级名著和在国外发行的革命刊物。图为1904年群智社同人合影。后排左一为古应芬（番禺人）、左二为朱执信（番禺人）、左三为汪兆铭（即汪精卫，番禺人）。

In 1902, Wang Zhaoming, Zhu Zhixin and Gu Yingfen,etc. in Guangzhou organized Intelligent Group Society, probed into social new ideological trend, read the masterpieces of western bourgeois class and issued revolutionary publications abroad. The picture is a group photo of members of the society, taken in 1904. The first from left in back row is Gu Yingfen (from Panyu County), the second from left, Zhu Zhixin (from Panyu County); the third from left, Wang Zhaoming (namely Wang Jingwei, from Panyu County).

114. 1905年，为反对美国胁逼清政府续订限制华工赴美、驱逐华工的《中美会订华工条约》，上海、广东等地掀起拒约反美运动。这场爱国运动，对唤起民众的民族意识，促进民族资产阶级革命派力量的集结，起着积极的作用。图为广州《时事画报》刊登的《华人受虐原因图说》。

In 1905, in order to object USA forcing Qing Government to re-sign restriction of Chinese workmen to *America—China and the United State Re-sign Treaty of Chinese workers* which intended to expel Chinese workmen, Shanghai and Guangdong started a movement against USA and refusal of the renewal of the treaty. This patriotic campaign aroused people's national consciousness, promoted the gathering of strength of revolutionary group of national bourgeois, and played a positive role. *The Cause of Chinese Workmen Being Cruelly Treated with Pictures* was published in Guangzhou's *Pictorial of Current Affairs.*

115

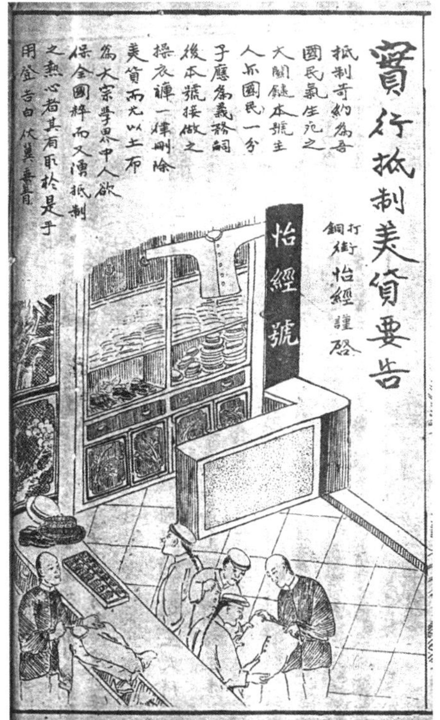

115.《时事画报》刊登的广州打铜街怡经号抵制美货要告。

An important notice about Yijing Firm at Datong Street in Guangzhou boycotting American goods, published in *Pictorial of Current Affairs.*

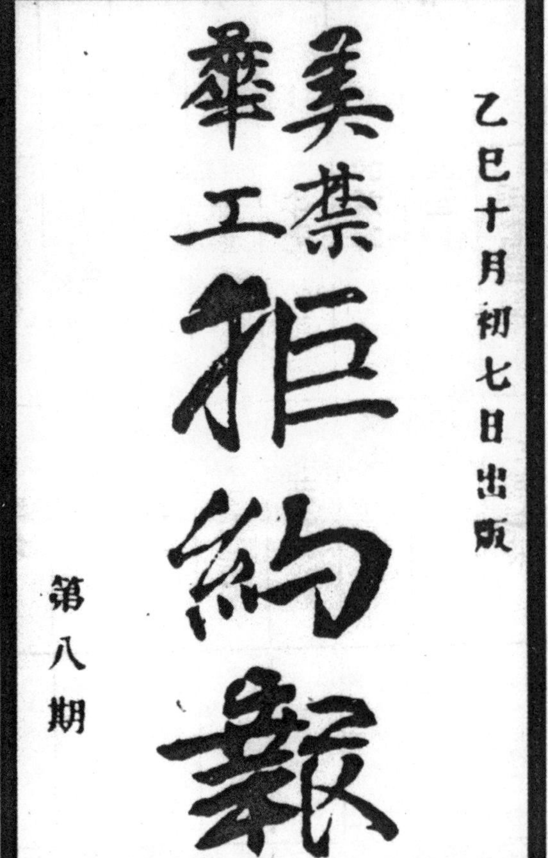

美禁華工拒約報

乙巳十月初七日出版

第八期

▲116

乙巳年七月十八日禮拜五　英一千九百零五年八月十八號　新聞紙四百十九號

廣東日報

"THE CANTON TIMES"

言論界

▲117

116. 广州出版的《美禁华工拒约报》。

Refusal of Renewal of USA Repelling Chinese Workmen Treaty, published in Guangzhou.

117.《广东日报》刊登的抨击清政府破坏反美拒约运动的评论。

Condemnation of Qing Government's sabotage the movement against USA and refusal of the renewal of the treaty, published in *The Canton Times*.

叁

THREE

同盟会在广东领导的反清斗争与广东的光复

Anti-Qing Dynasty Struggles Led by the Chinese Revolutionary Alliance in Guangdong and Restoration of Guangdong

1905年8月20日，孙中山、黄兴等在日本东京联合兴中会、华兴会、光复会等革命团体，组织成立中国第一个资产阶级政党——中国同盟会，提出“驱除鞑虏，恢复中华，创立民国，平均地权”的革命纲领。随后，孙中山委派冯自由、李自重往香港等地，联络同志，扩大组织，先后在香港、澳门、广州、番禺、花县、化州、肇庆等地设立同盟会的分支机构，广东成为同盟会活动的重点地区。

随着广东各地同盟会机关的成立，革命党人纷纷利用报刊阵地，批判康、梁保皇派的政治主张，鼓吹民主革命，扩大革命派的思想影响，使广东成为国内革命舆论宣传的中心。

广东同盟会组织在进行革命舆论宣传的同时，也积极策划武装起义，先后发动1907年潮州黄冈起义、惠州七女湖起义、钦廉防城起义，1908年钦廉上思起义，1910年广州新军起义，1911年广州黄花岗起义。起义次数之多，为各省之冠。历次武装起义，予清朝在广东的统治以沉重的打击，为辛亥广东光复奠定了基础。

1911年10月10日，武昌起义后，广东革命党人积极组织和发动各属民军起义，打击和孤立顽固势力，争取中间势力，促使省咨议局绅商倡行和平独立。1911年11月9日，广东宣告共和独立。

On August 20,1905, at Tokyo, Japan, Sun Yat-sen and Huang Xing, etc. united revolutionary groups—Revive China Society, Society of Chinese Revival, and Society of Restoration,etc.to found the first Chinese bourgeois party—the Chinese Revolutionary Alliance,with the revolutionary guiding principle: “Driving the Qing rulers out, reviving the Chinese nation, founding a republic, equalizing land rights”. After that, Sun Yat-sen sent Feng Ziyou and Li Zizhong to Hong Kong to get in touch with comrades, to expand the organization. They established branches of the Chinese Revolutionary Alliance in Hong Kong, Macao,Guangzhou, Panyu, Huaxian,Huazhou and Zhaoqing, etc., which made Guangdong become the important region of activities of the Chinese Revolutionary Alliance.

With the establishment of the regional offices of the Chinese Revolutionary Alliance in Guangdong, the revolutionary partisans utilized the newspapers and periodicals one after another to criticize the royalists to Qing Dynasty—Kang Youwei and Liang Qichao's political opinions, advocated democratic revolution, expanded the influence of thoughts of the revolutionary group, made Guangdong the centre of the domestic revolutionary public opinion propaganda.

While propagating revolution, the organizations of the Chinese Revolutionary Alliance in Guangdong planned armed uprisings actively. They launched Chaozhou Huanggang Uprising, Huizhou Seven-lady Lake Uprising and Qin-Lian Fangcheng Uprising in 1907, Qin-Lian Shangsi Uprising in 1908, Uprising of Guangzhou New Army in 1910, Yellow Flower Hill Uprising in 1911 successively. Every armed uprising struck Qing governance in Guangdong with heavy blows and laid the foundation for Guangdong restoration.

On October 11, 1911, after the Wuchang Uprising, Guangdong revolutionary partisans organized and started militia uprisings actively to attack and isolate the obstinate forces, and won over the middle force, impel province consultation and gentry of traders to advocate and practise peaceful independence. On November 9, 1911, Guangdong declared the republican independence.

▲ 118

118. 1905年8月20日，孙中山、黄兴等在日本东京，联合兴中会、华兴会、光复会等革命团体，组织成立中国第一个资产阶级政党——中国同盟会，提出“驱除鞑虏，恢复中华，创立民国，平均地权”的革命纲领。图为中国同盟会总理孙中山。

On August 20, 1905, in Tokyo, Japan, Sun Yat-sen and Huang Xing, etc. united revolutionary groups—Revive China Society, Society of Chinese Revival, and Society of Restoration, etc. to found the first Chinese bourgeois party—the Chinese Revolutionary Alliance, which put forward the revolutionary guiding principle: “Driving the Qing rulers out, reviving the Chinese nation, founding a republic, equalizing land rights”. This is Premier of the Chinese Revolutionary Alliance—Sun Yat-sen.

▼ 119

120

121

119. 一批广东籍留日学生参与同盟会的筹备工作，并担任有关领导职务。图为同盟会评议部评议长汪精卫（左）、同盟会评议员胡汉民（右,番禺人）和最早同盟会会员之一胡毅生（中,番禺人）在日本的合影。

A contingent of Guangdong students studying in Japan participated in the preparation to establish the Chinese Revolutionary Alliance and took the relative leading posts. In this group photo taken in Japan,are Wang Jingwei(left), speaker of consulation department of the Chinese Revolutionary Alliance; Hu Hanmin (right, from Panyu County), prolocutor of the Chinese Revolutionary Alliance and Hu Yisheng (middle, from Panyu County), one of the earliest members of the Chinese Revolutionary Alliance.

120. 同盟会评议部评议员兼书记朱执信。

Zhu Zhixin, prolocutor of consulation department and secretary of the Chinese Revolutionary Alliance.

121. 1905年底任同盟会执行部外务科职员的廖仲恺（归善人）。

Liao Zhongkai(from Guishan County), the accountant in External Affairs Section of Executive Department of the Chinese Revolutionary Alliance by the end of 1905.

▲ 122

122. 同盟会早期女盟员何香凝（南海人）。

He Xiangning (from Nanhai County), the early woman member of the Chinese Revolutionary Alliance.

123. 1905年9月8日，孙中山委派冯自由、李自重往香港、广州、澳门，联络同志，扩大组织。图为孙中山签署的委任状。

On September 8,1905, Sun Yat-sen sent Feng Ziyou, Li Zizhong to Hong Kong, Guangzhou and Macao to get in touch with comrades and to expand the organization. This is the letter of attorney signed by Sun Yat-sen.

▼ 123

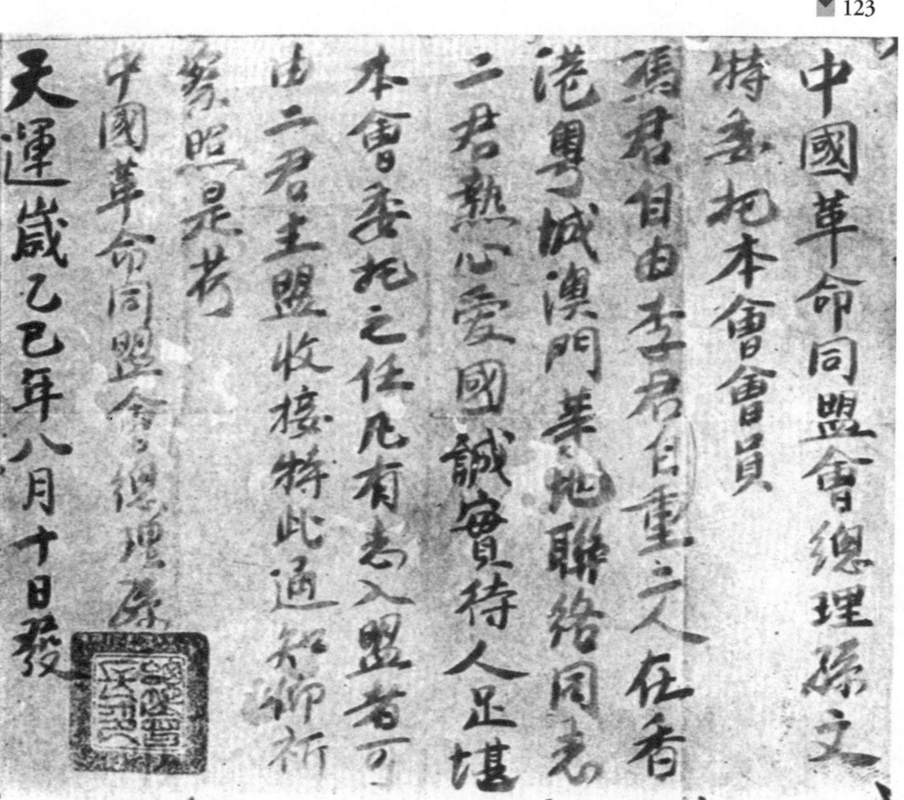

中國革命同盟會總理孫文
特委托本會會員
馮君自由李君自重二人在香
港粵城澳門等地聯絡同志
二君熱心愛國誠實待人足堪
本會委托之任凡有志入盟者可
由二君主盟收據特此通知仰祈
察照是荷
中國革命同盟會總理孫
天運歲乙巳年八月十日發

▲124

▲125

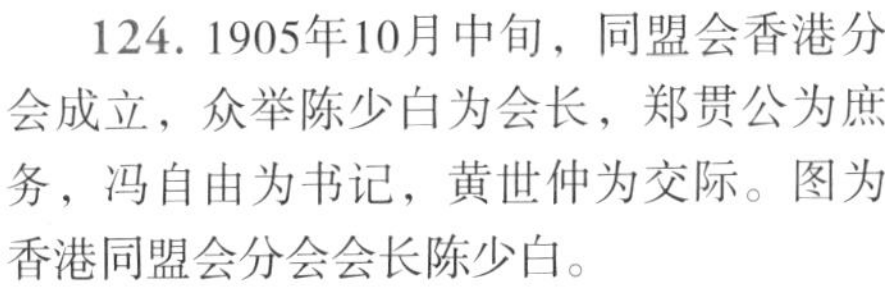

124. 1905年10月中旬，同盟会香港分会成立，众举陈少白为会长，郑贯公为庶务，冯自由为书记，黄世仲为交际。图为香港同盟会分会会长陈少白。

In mid-October of 1905, Hong Kong Branch of the Chinese Revolutionary Alliance was established with Chen Shaobai as president, Zheng Guangong as head of general affairs, Feng Ziyou as secretary, Huang Shizhong for communication. This is Chen Shaobai, the president.

125. 同盟会香港分会书记冯自由（后任会长，南海人）。

Feng Ziyou, secretary of Hong Kong Branch of the Chinese Revolutionary Alliance (later became president, from Nanhai County).

▲126

126. 同盟会香港分会主要组织者之一、李煜堂之子李自重（新宁人）。

Li Zizhong(from Xinning County), one of the leading organizers of Hong Kong Branch of the Chinese Revolutionary Alliance and the son of Li Yutang.

▲127　　▼128

127. 早期同盟会会员、香港爱国富商李煜堂（新宁人）。曾出资承办《中国日报》，多次捐巨资支持革命。

Li Yutang(from Xinning County), an early member of the Chinese Revolutionary Alliance and a patriotic rich businessman, provided funds for the *China Daily* and donated a large sum of money several times for the revolution.

128. 同盟会香港分会招待所之一——普庆坊原址。

One of the rest houses of Hong Kong Branch of the Chinese Revolutionary Alliance—Original site in Pu Qing Fang.

▲ 129

129. 同盟会香港分会经常集会的德辅道致发号（四楼）原址。

The former site of Zhifa Firm (the fourth floor) in Des Voeux Road where Hong Kong Branch of the Chinese Revolutionary Alliance often put their heads together.

130. 1909年10月，同盟会香港分会会员以各地党势日盛、任务繁杂，建议在香港分会之外，添设南方支部，负责西南各省的党务、军务，并推举胡汉民为支部长、汪精卫为书记、林直勉为会计，会所设在香港黄泥涌道。图为在香港参与组建同盟会南方支部的林直勉。

In October 1909, members of Hong Kong Branch of the Chinese Revolutionary Alliance suggested founding South Branch additionally, as the party growing up and the tasks increasing, to take charge of party affairs and military affairs of southwest provinces. They recommended Hu Hanmin as the branch head, Wang Jingwei as the branch secretary and Lin Zhimian as the accountant. The branch office was set in Wong Nai Chung Road in Hong Kong. The picture shows Lin Zhimian, who was taking part in founding the South Branch of the Chinese Revolutionary Alliance.

131. 1909年冬，同盟会澳门分会成立，由设在香港的同盟会南方支部领导，首任会长由同盟会香港分会会长谢英伯兼任。图为澳门同盟分会的组织领导者谢英伯（嘉应人）。

In the winter of 1909, Macao Branch of the Chinese Revolutionary Alliance was founded and led by the Chinese Revolutionary Alliance's southern branch in Hong Kong, its first president—Xie Yingbo who was president of Hong Kong Branch of the Chinese Revolutionary Alliance. This is Xie Yingbo(from Jiaying County), the organizer and leader of Macao branch.

130

131

132

133

132. 位于澳门南湾街41号同盟会澳门分会原址。

The former site of Macao Branch of the Chinese Revolutionary Alliance in No. 41 Nanwan Street of Macao.

133. 1909年底，同盟会广州分会成立，由高剑父、潘达微、徐宗汉负责。图为同盟会广州分会主要负责人高剑父（番禺人）。

At the end of 1909, Guangzhou Branch of the Chinese Revolutionary Alliance was established, which was in the charge of Gao Jianfu, Pan Dawei and Xu Zhonghan. This is Gao Jianfu(from Panyu County), chief leader of Guangzhou Branch of the Chinese Revolutionary Alliance.

 134

135

134. 同盟会广东分会主盟人之一胡毅生（番禺人）。

Hu Yisheng(from Panyu County), one of the leaders of Guangdong branch of the Chinese Revolutionary Alliance.

135. 1906年，奉孙中山命回国发展同盟会员，创办汕头《中华新报》，策划武装起义的嘉应籍岭东同盟会骨干谢逸桥。

Xie Yiqiao (from Jiaying County), a backbone of Lingdong Branch of the Chinese Revolutionary Alliance, in 1906, was sent by Sun Yat-sen back to Shantou to develop members, to establish *China New Paper* and to plan armed uprising.

136. 同盟会入会盟书。

The oath paper of the Chinese Revolutionary Alliance.

137. 同盟会党员执照。

Member certificate of the Chinese Revolutionary Alliance.

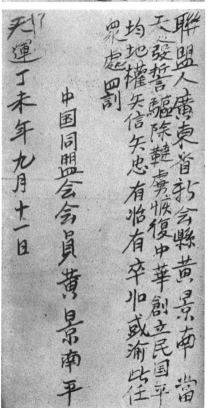

▼ 136

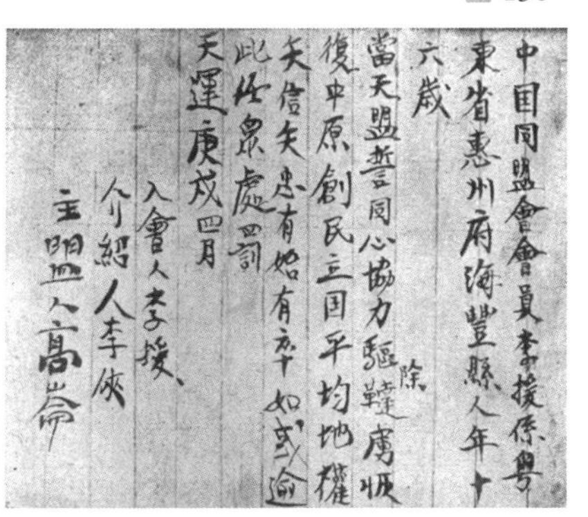

中国同盟會會員李援係粵東省惠州府海豐縣人年十六歲

當天盟誓同心協力驅除韃虜恢復中原創民主国平均地權

矢信矢忠有始有卒如或渝此任衆處罰

天運庚戌四月

入會人李援

介紹人李俠

主盟人高崙

聯盟人廣東省新会縣黃景南 當天發誓驅除韃虜恢復中華創立民国平均地權矢信矢忠有始有卒如或渝此任衆處罰

中国同盟会会員黃景南平

天運丁未年九月十一日

▼ 137

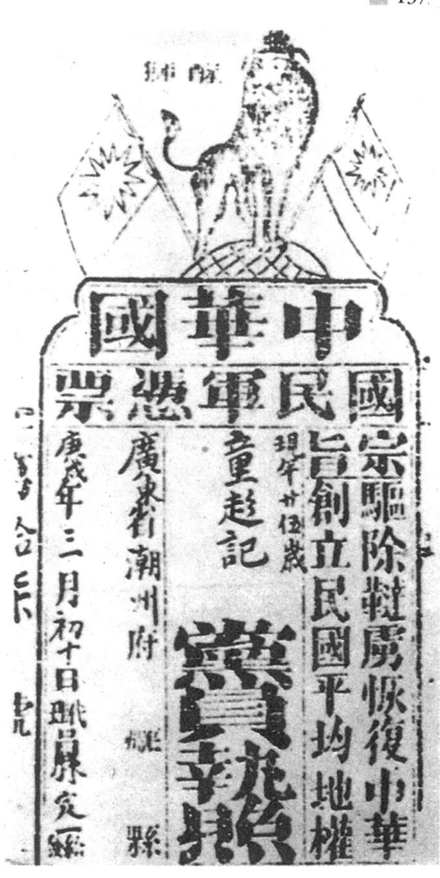

中華國

國民軍憑票

宗旨驅除韃虜恢復中華創立民國平均地權

現年廿伍歲

童趁記

廣東省潮州府 縣

寶號

庚戌年三月初十日

中國日報 丁未年十一月三十日禮拜五 西曆一千九百零八年正月三號 第柒頁

鼓吹錄

小說 幾道山恩仇記 中編

法國 亞歷山大仲馬著 中國 抱器室主譯

第三十一章 一百四十九續

二十九章自是夜為九月四日與五日之交句以下。當為三十章。是為上編。中編則自三十一章起。前報偶爾錯誤。特此更正。

佛連時自念尚有餘暑。且居停已得。無事張羅。乃納船長之議。船長見其已允。遂與同人竊議。語細不可辨。佛連時問曰。豈尚有事不易解決者乎。船長曰。否。惟有一事。須預告貴人者。此島蓋時出悖逆之事者也。佛連時曰。何哉。爾言余不解。船長曰。幾道山雖曰荒島。然時為海寇私販之巢穴。如知吾人一履其地。必為其囚繫六日。然後得歸力韓耳。佛連時曰。么魔可惡。此又當別論矣。且為時過久矣。船長曰。誰將以貴人曾至其地告人者。佛連時曰。余必不以此告人。衆水夫齊聲曰。吾人皆不為也。佛連時曰。然則吾往矣。船長下令。轉舵而發。直望幾道山而行。佛連時待諸事已妥。各帆飽張。四水夫。三居前。一居後。把舵不語。乃復以前事為問曰。爾曾幾道山為海寇之巢穴。然則待獲者與山羊大異其趣矣。船長曰。貴人之言然。佛連時曰。私販之流。余亦略有認識。惟自亞爾芝被獲之後。巢穴為之頓破。今日海寇之僅存者。亦惟有哥龍爾與船長馬耳辣小說中所載者耳。船長曰。貴人誤矣。其地固尚有海寇也。教皇利阿第十二自以為蕩平殆盡。不知羅馬京之發劫。則日有所聞。貴人之論海寇。得毋類是。六月前。法國公使為賊所掠。其地與皇宮相去。曾不及五百步之遙。貴人豈不聞乎。佛連時曰。然。余固聞之。船長曰。吾人日居力韓。每聞有某小船。或英國貨船。由某港來力韓。逾期不至。或竟爾失踪者亦有之。貴人想亦必有所聞耳。雖未有知其究竟者。然其遇礁而沒則無疑矣。惟聞此礁之形。既狹而長。由七八人負之而行。每當風雨月黑之夜。隱伏於荒島之側。若殺人越貨者。以快車待人於林木之間。時佛連時以衾裹身而臥。問曰。何以被劫者。總不聞有鳴諸法國沙的尼亞與度司加尼等政府者乎。船長微笑曰。貴人不知其故耶。佛連時曰。誠不能知之。船長曰。若輩既發來船。即將所有之物。苟能易賣者。攜諸己舟之內。以索繫船人之手足。每人項際。贅鉛二十斤。復將來船之底。穿一大洞。然後捨之去。 未完

趣評

保皇黨與妓女之比較

今日有最不容於醒眼人者厥惟二物。一曰保皇黨。一曰妓女。此二者之中。其人物雖不同。而其用心設計。則無不曾同也。其用心設計雖同。而其運動手段。則又各各不同也。或曰。保皇黨。一所謂政黨也。其人格固極高尚者也。妓女。一醜業婦也。其人格固極卑污者也。予以二者相比較。得毋水火乎。余曰。否。非也。今試比較之如下。則讀者將無辭矣。溫嶠燃犀。妖形畢現。斯文之作。其庶博閱者之一噱乎。保皇黨。著名揾丁者也。妓女。亦著名揾丁者也。保皇黨開口則稱仁慈聖主。藉光緒皇而揾丁。妓女開口則稱東家本錢父母世界。藉龜鴇而揾丁。保皇黨每於騙得錢財後。其交情必漸淡。妓女每於騙得白水後。其待客必變相。保皇黨出徵求而運動黃金。妓女出毛巾而運動白水。保皇黨最無廉恥。妓女亦最無廉恥。保皇黨揾丁之口舌最敏捷。妓女迷魂之舉動亦最速率。保皇黨揾丁濕走倉卒。妓女出局亦來往各酒樓。保皇黨每於演說時。即以如意油塗眼詐哭。妓女每於詐嬌時。亦以如意油塗眼詐哭。被保皇黨所迷者。如被催眠術。被妓女所迷者。亦如被催眠術。保皇黨捨揾丁外。最好嫖賭。妓女除出局外。亦最好打十五壺。保皇黨最好頂架子。妓女亦最好頂架子。某日又話演說。妓女某日又話出會。某日又話坐馬車。某日又話看戲。保皇黨一揾丁丁。即任意揮霍。妓女一開丁刀。亦任意揮霍。保皇黨被打。不敢聲張。妓女被打。亦惟有忍氣。保皇黨尚怕被人倒米。妓女最怕被客撻賬。保皇黨日日謡歸政。妓女日日想埋街。保皇黨一見亞丁。即加意逢迎。妓女一見闊佬。亦百般獻媚。保皇黨之奴隸性質甚深。妓女之老舉習氣極鄙。保皇黨有妖黨之名。妓女有鹹魚之號。曾中保皇毒者。一旦醒悟。必恨之切齒。曾受妓女迷者。一旦醒悟。亦必恨之切齒。保皇黨謂他人父。妓女人盡可夫。保皇黨之歸化革命者甚多。妓女之跟佬埋街者不少。噫。保皇黨耶。妓女耶。保皇黨耶。其一而二耶。其二而一耶。便一一比較之。吾恐書不勝書矣。嗚呼。保皇黨。嗚呼。妓女。嗚呼。保皇黨之妓女。嗚呼。妓女之保皇黨。嗚呼嗚呼。妓女妓女。嗚呼嗚呼。保皇黨保皇黨。

雜俎

新

▲ 138

▼ 139

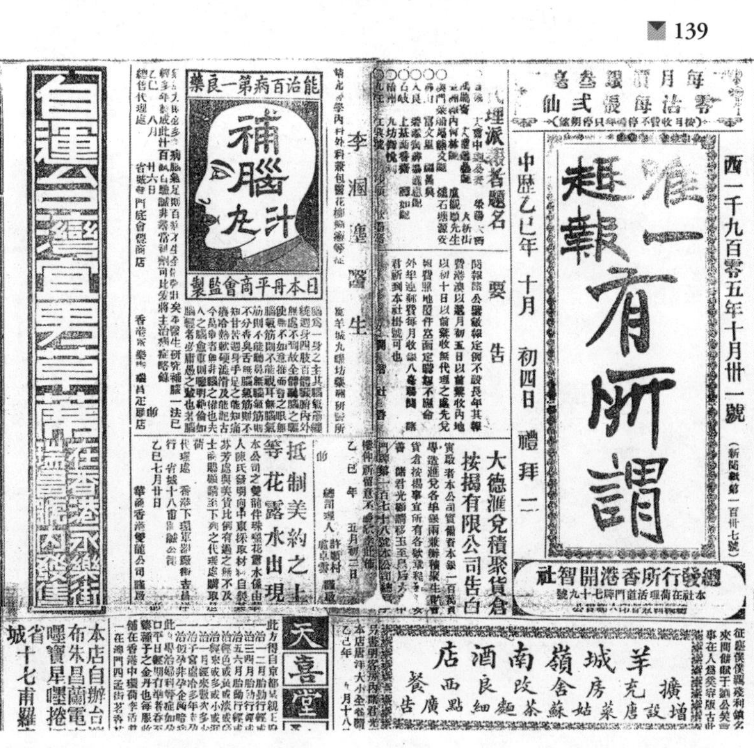
西一千九百零五年十月卅一號 (新聞紙第一百卅七號)

唯一趣報有所謂

中歷乙巳年 十月 初四日 禮拜二

每月價銀叁毫 零沽每張式仙 (按月收費不得停閱只停閱係)

總發行所香港開智社 本社在荷李活道門牌七十九號

要告

閱報諸公賜鑒敝報定例不設長年其報費港澳以逐月初五日以前照收內地以初十日以前照收無代理之處先兌報費照地設件為面定聯報不誤命外埠連郵費每月收銀八毫賜顧諸君新到本社掛號可也

埋派報者題名

大德滙兌積聚貨倉按揭有限公司告白

李澗廛醫生

補腦汁丸
能治百病第一良藥
日本丹平商會監製

抵制美約之上等花露水出現

自運台灣烏龍等茶

天喜堂

羊城嶺南酒店
擴充房舍改良西餐
增設唐菜姑蘇茶麵細點廣告

138. 随着广东各地同盟会机关的建立，革命党人纷纷利用报刊阵地，宣传民主革命，广东成了全国革命舆论宣传最为活跃的地区之一。图为1908年1月3日香港《中国日报》发表的“趣评”《保皇党与妓女之比较》，揭露保皇党政治娼妓的面目。

With the founding of the regional offices of the Chinese Revolutionary Alliance in Guangdong, the revolutionary partisans utilized the newspapers and periodicals as positions one after another, advocating the democratic revolution. Guangdong had become one of the most active areas of national democratic revolutionary public opinions and propaganda. This is "funny commentary"—*Comparing Royalists with Prostitutes* published in the *China Daily* on January 3, 1908, disclosing royalist's appearance of political prostitutes.

139. 《有所谓报》。1905年6月4日由郑贯公在香港创办，以通俗诙谐的文字，抨击清廷的黑暗和帝国主义的侵略，是最早用广东方言写作的报纸之一。

On June 4, 1905, Zheng Guangong established the *Yousuoweibao* in Hong Kong, which, with the popular and humorous writing, condemned the darkness of Qing court and the invasion of imperialism. It was one of the first newspapers written in Guangdong dialect.

◀ 140

140. 著名的香山籍革命报人郑贯公。曾任香港《中国日报》记者，创办《世界公益报》、《广东日报》和《有所谓报》等革命报刊。1906年因病而逝，年仅26岁。

Zheng Guangong, a famous revolutionary journalist and once a reporter of the *China Daily*, founded the revolutionary newspapers and periodicals—*World Commonweal*, *The Canton Times* and the *Yousuoweibao*, etc. He died of disease in 1906 at the young age of 26.

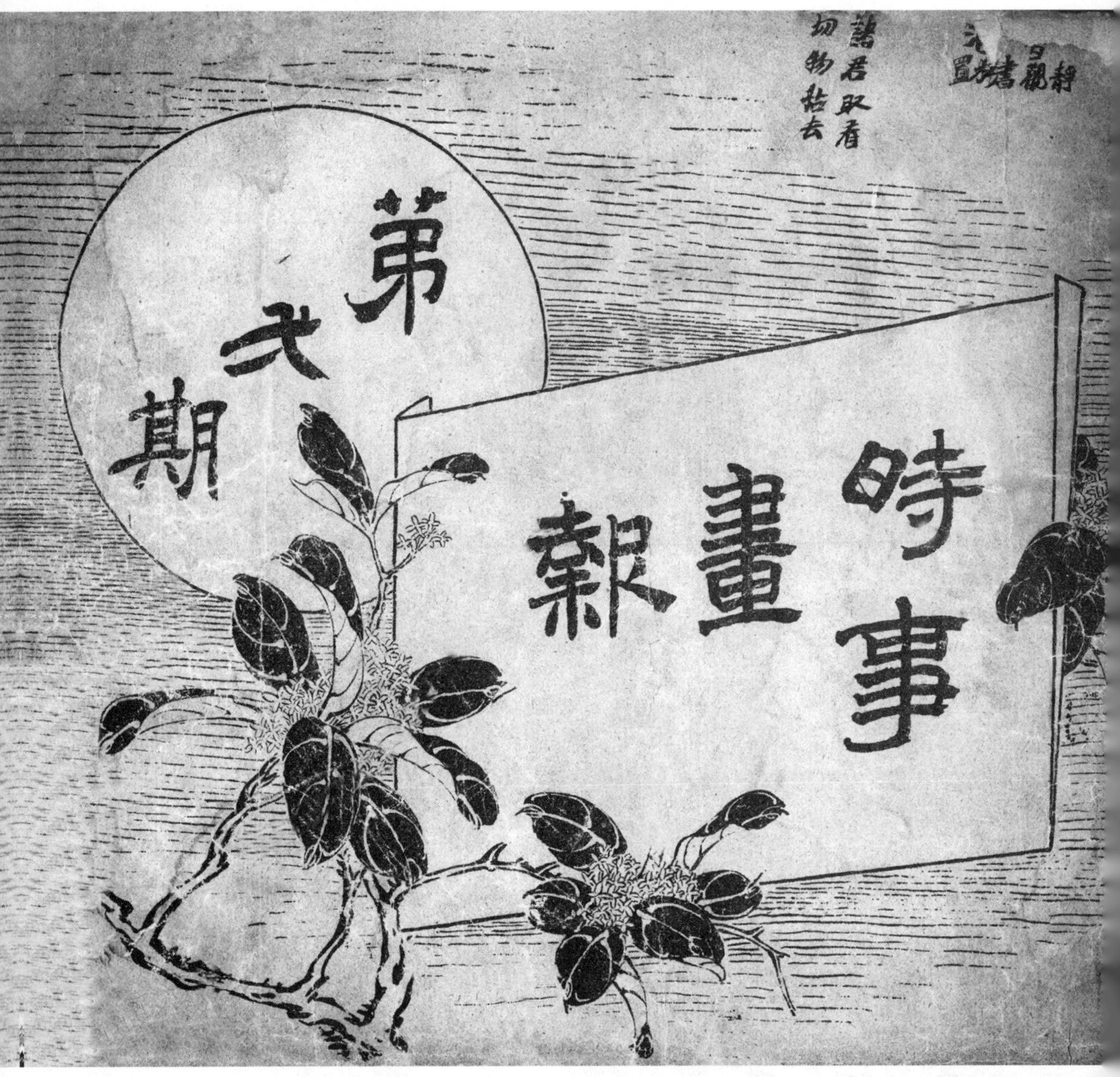

▲ 141

141.《时事画报》。1905年9月，高卓廷、潘达微、高剑父、何剑士、陈垣等在广州创办，以图文并茂的形式，进行民主革命的宣传，为广东最早的石印画报。

In September 1905, Gao Zhuoting, Pan Dawei, Gao Jianfu, He Jianshi and Chen Yuan,etc. established *Pictorial of Current Affairs* in Guangzhou, with excellent pictures and texts, propagating democratic revolution. It was the earliest lithographic printing pictorial in Guangdong.

按月收費

每月價銀三毫
零沽每張十五文

禮拜停派

西歷一千九百零六年五月二十號

（新聞紙第八十一號）

珠江鏡

中歷丙午年閏四月初八日禮拜三

（總發行所香港德輔道中門牌卅九號三樓）

看看看本報之特別廣告

要告

增聘訪員

周夢熊 大美國牙醫生

葉相廷醫生

請認良醫梁潤霖

代理一覽表

黃吉臣丈量畫則師

▲142

142.《珠江镜》。1906年春在广州创刊，总编辑兼督印人何言，宣传民族主义，抨击清政府的腐败。

In the spring of 1906, the *Pearl River Mirror* started publication in Guangzhou, with He Yan as its editor-in-chief and concurrently publishing supervisor. It propagated nationalism and condemned the corruption of the Qing Government.

143.《东方报》。1906年7月29日在香港创刊，前身是《有所谓报》。编辑及发行人谢英伯、陈树人、刘思复等，为资产阶级革命派在香港创办的报纸。

The *Eastern News* started publication on July 29, 1906. Its former name was the *Yousuoweibao*. Its editors and distributors were Xie Yingbo, Chen Shuren and Liu Sifu etc. This was a newspaper run by the bourgeois revolutionary partisans in Hong Kong.

144.《广东白话报》。1907年5月2日在广州创刊，撰述人黄世仲、欧博明、凤萍旧主等，是资产阶级革命派在广州创办的方言刊物。

On May 2, 1907, *Guangdong Dialect Paper* started publication in Guangzhou, and its writers included Huang Shizhong, Ou Boming and Fengpingjiuzhu, etc. It was the dialect publication that the revolutionary group of bourgeois class established in Guangzhou.

143

〔新聞紙第三號〕

每月銀四毫零沽每張三仙

西歷一千九百零六年七月 卅一號

東方報

EASTERN NEWS.

中歷丙午年 六月十一日 禮拜二

〔總發行所在香港德輔道中一百三十七號頂樓〕

逢禮拜一日停派

144

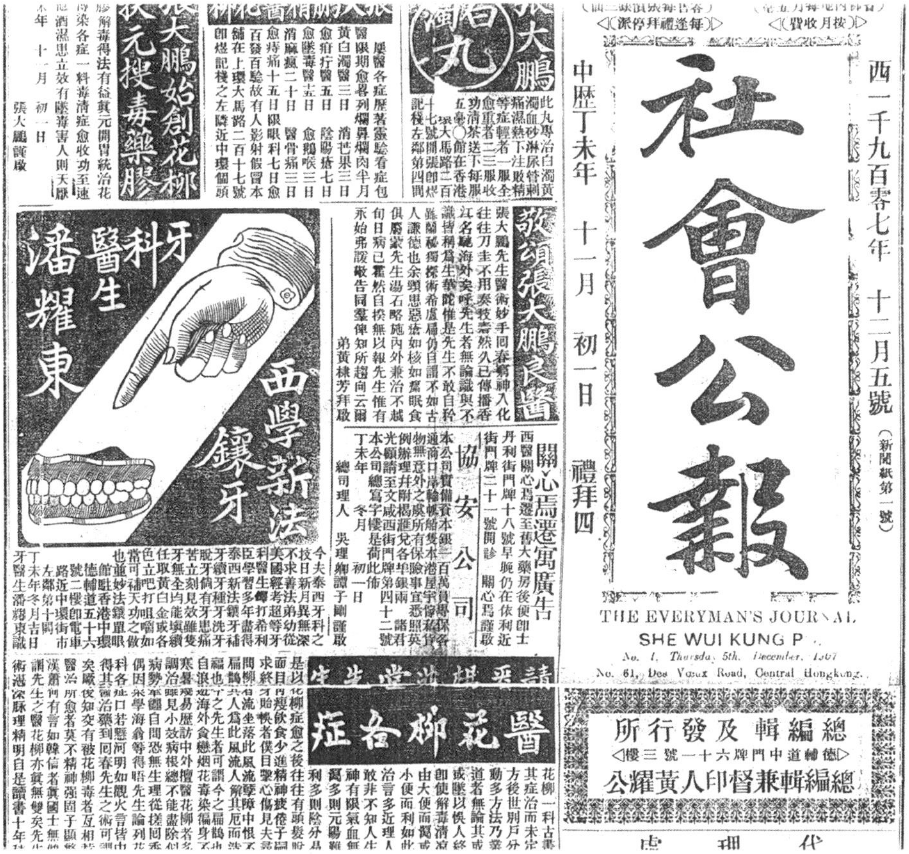

(禮拜每逢停派) (按月收費)

西一千九百零七年 十二月五號 (新聞紙第一號)

社會公報

中歷丁未年 十一月 初一日 禮拜四

THE EVERYMAN'S JOURNAL

SHE WUI KUNG PO

No. 1, Thursday 5th December, 1907

No. 61, Des Voeux Road, Central Hongkong.

總編輯及發行所

德輔道中門牌六十一號三樓

總編輯兼督印人黃耀公

牙科醫生潘耀東

西學新法鑲牙

醫花柳各症

敬頌張大鵬良醫

張大鵬始創花柳狀元搜毒藥膠

協安公司

關心焉遷寓廣告

145

146

145. 《社会公报》。1907年12月5日在香港创刊，总编辑兼督印人黄耀公，以宣传民主革命为主要内容。

The Everyman's Journal, which started publication in Hong Kong on December 5, 1907, whose editor-in-chief and concurrently printing supervisor was Huang Yaogong, propagated democratic revolution as its main contents.

146. 《岭南白话杂志》。1908年2月9日在广州创刊，撰稿人欧博明、黄耀公等，是宣传民主革命的方言刊物。

The Lingnan Dialect Magazine started publication on February 9, 1908, with its writers—Ou Boming, Huang Yaogong,etc. was the dialect publication which propagated democratic revolution.

147

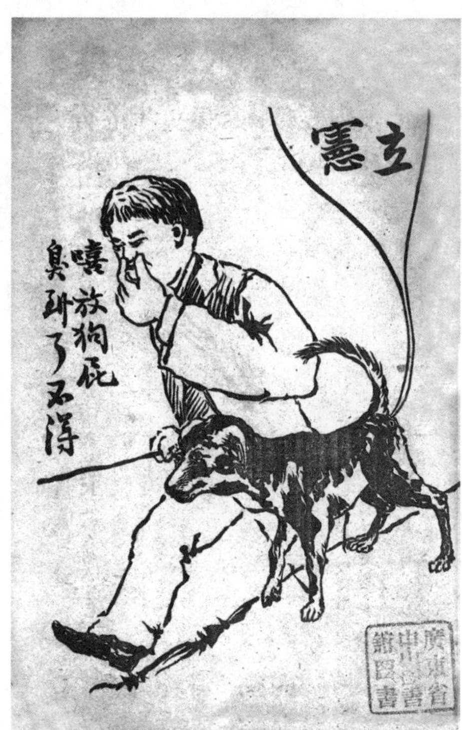

香山旬報

第玖期

戊申十一月初七日付印
戊申十一月十一日發行

每月三期逢一發行

148

147.《岭南白话杂志》刊登的政治讽刺漫画。

The political satirized caricatures published on *The Lingnan Dialect Magazine*.

148.《香山旬报》。1908年9月16日郑岸父在香山石岐创办，宣传反清爱国主张，风行省港澳以至南洋、美洲各地。

On September 16, 1908, in Shiqi (Now it is Zhongshan City.) Zheng Anfu established *Xiangshan Xunbao* (a ten-day publication) which propagated opinions of anti-Qing Dynasty and motherland-loving. The paper once prevailed in Hong Kong and Macao, Southeast Asia and all parts of America.

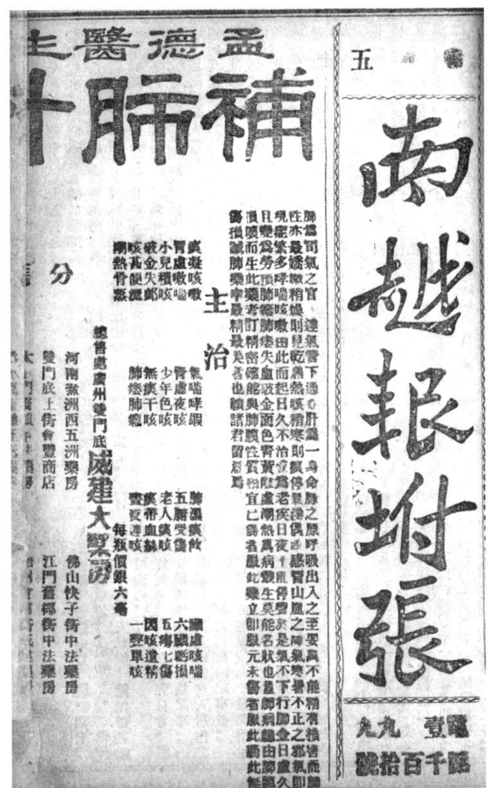

五

南越報附張

孟德醫生

補肺

主治

分

總售處廣州雙門底威建大藥房

每瓶價銀六毫

河南鰲洲西五洲藥房

雙門底上街會豐商店

佛山快子街中法藥房

江門舊郵街中法藥房

149.《南越报》。1909年6月22日在广州创刊，主编苏棱讽、卢博浪、李孟哲、杨计白等。该报报道、歌颂革命党人的起义斗争，揭露清政府昏庸无能的面目。

The *South China Paper* started publication in Guangzhou on June 22,1909, with Su Lingfeng, Lu Bolang, Li Mengzhe, Yang Jibai,etc. as its editors-in-chief. This paper reported and extolled uprising struggles of revolutionary partisans and ferreted out Qing Government's fatuous incompetent appearance.

150.《平民画报》。1911年7月16日在广州创刊，编辑兼发行人为邓警亚，撰述画师廖平子、冯百砺、何剑士、潘达微等，为资产阶级革命派在广州的机关刊物之一。

The *Populace Pictorial* started publication in Guangzhou on July 16, 1911, which was edited and concurrently issued by Deng Jingya, and whose pictures painted by painters Liao Pingzi, Feng Baili, He Jianshi and Pan Dawei. It was one of the official publication of bourgeois revolutionary group in Guangzhou.

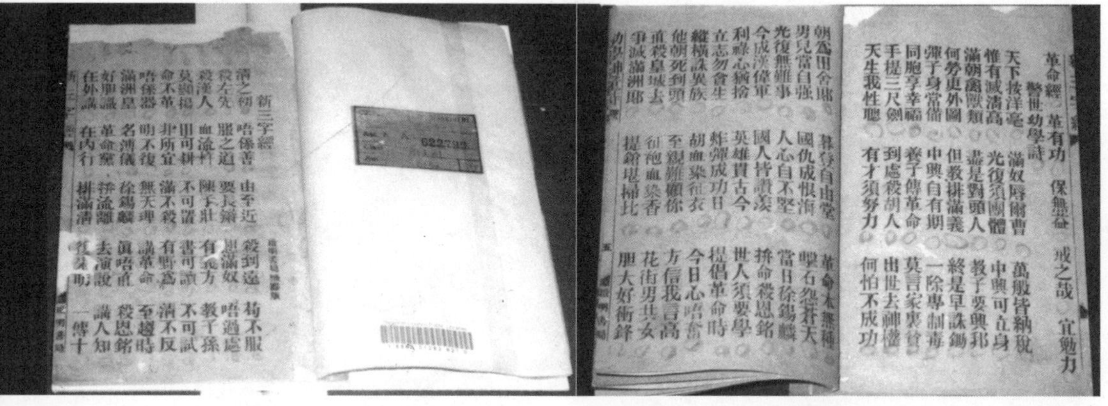

151

151. 流传粤港澳的反清蒙童课本《新三字经》、《幼学神童诗》。

The anti-Qing and enlightening children textbook—*New Three Characters Classic, Poems for Children and Young Genius* spread around Guangdong, Hong Kong and Macao.

152. 同盟会在进行革命舆论宣传的同时，也积极策划武装起义，使广东成为同盟会发动武装起义最多的省份。1906年，孙中山任命潮安籍新加坡侨商、同盟会会员许雪秋为“中华国民军东军都督”，回国伺机起事。1907年2月，许雪秋、余丑、陈涌波、余通等策划在潮州举义，以布置未就而中止。图为许雪秋。

While propagating revolutionary opinions,the Chinese Revolutionary Alliance actively planned armed uprisings, which made Guangdong become the province where the Chinese Revolutionary Alliance started armed uprisings the most. In 1906, Sun Yat-sen appointed Xu Xueqiu—Singaporean overseas Chinese businessman and member of the Chinese Revolutionary Alliance, commander-in-chief of “China National Army East” and sent him back to China, watching for a chance of uprising. In February 1907, Xu Xueqiu, Yu Chou, Chen Yongbo, Yu Tong,etc. planned in Chaozhou to launch an uprising, but discontinued because of bad arrangement. This is Xu Xueqiu.

152

153. 奉孙中山命入潮助许雪秋发动潮州起义的山西籍留英学生乔义生。

Qiao Yisheng, a student (from Shanxi Province),returned from England, went to Chaozhou to help Xu Xueqiu start the uprising at the order of Sun Yat-sen.

154. 广东潮安县庵埠官里乡迎祥里林受之故居，是最早策划潮汕一带革命运动的秘密机关之一。

Former residence of Lin Shouzhi, located in Ying Xiang Block, Guanli Village, Anbu Town, Chaoan County, Guangdong Province. It was one of the first secret organizations which started revolutions in the Chaoshan area.

153

154

▲155

155. 为便于领导武装起义，1907年3月，孙中山在越南河内设立指挥粤、桂、滇三省起义的领导机关。图为孙中山设于越南堤岸广东街办事处的旧址。

For being easy to lead armed uprising, in March 1907, in Hanoi, Vietnam, Sun Yat-sen set up a leading body commanding uprisings in Guangdong, Guangxi and Yunnan Provinces. This is the old site located in Guangdong Street, Vietnam.

156. 1907年3月，在越南河内时的孙中山。

Sun Yat-sen in Hanoi, Vietnam in March, 1907.

▶156

▲ 157

▼ 158

157. 1907年3月，孙中山派许雪秋负责策划潮州黄冈起义，并请日本人萱野长知等协助。图为许雪秋（右）与萱野长知（中）、汪精卫（左）合影。

In March 1907, Sun Yat-sen sent Xu Xueqiu to take charge of planning Huanggang Uprising in Chaozhou and asked the Japanese to help. This is a group photo of Xu Xueqiu (right), Kayano Nagatomo(middle) and Wang Jingwei (left).

158. 黄冈起义领导人之一陈涌波（饶平人）。

Chen Yongbo (from Raoping County), one of the leaders of Huanggang Uprising .

159

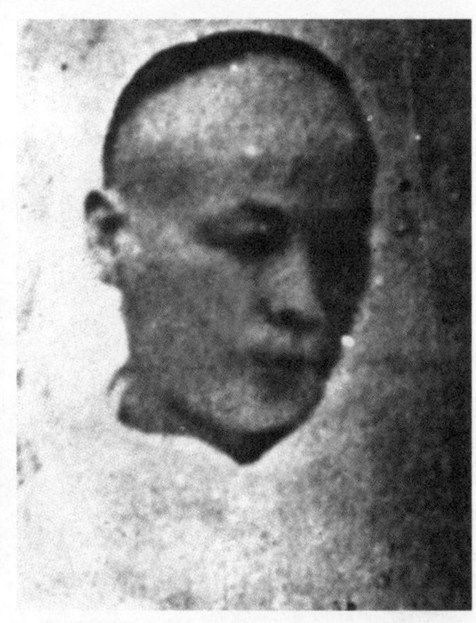

160

161

162

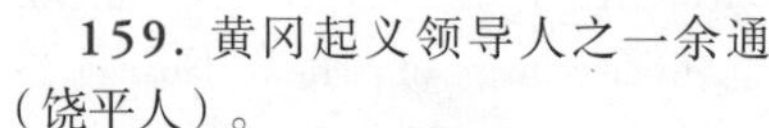

159. 黄冈起义领导人之一余通（饶平人）。

Yu Tong(from Raoping County), one of the leaders of Huanggang Uprising.

160. 黄冈起义领导人之一余丑（饶平人）。

Yu Chou(from Raoping County), one of the leaders of Huanggang Uprising.

161.黄冈起义领导人之一陈芸生（海阳人）。

Chen Yunsheng(from Haiyang County), one of the leaders of Huanggang Uprising.

162. 变卖家产，参加黄冈起义的同盟会会员、潮州籍新加坡侨商萧竹漪（海阳人）。

Xiao Zhuyi, a Businessman living in Singapore from Haiyang County, his native place was Chaozhou, and as a member of the Chinese Revolutionary Alliance, sold off his property to take part in Huanggang Uprising.

▲ 163

163. 黄冈起义的秘密机关——黄冈挑水巷泰兴杂货店。

Taixing Grocery in Tiaoshui Lane in Huanggang—the secret office of Huanggang Uprising.

164. 1907年5月22日，潮州饶平县黄冈三合会会众在首领、同盟会会员陈涌波、余丑、余通等领导下，发动起义，攻占黄冈等地，成立军政府，推陈涌波、余丑为革命军正、副司令。起义军与清军激战至27日，终因寡不敌众而失败。图为黄冈起义誓师的情景。

On May 22, 1907, Chen Yongbo, Yu Chou and Yu Tong, heads of the Triad and members of the Chinese Revolutionary Alliance, led the members of the Triad in Huanggang of Raoping County,Chaozhou, in starting the uprising, and captured Huanggang and set up a military government. Chen Yongbo was elected commander-in-chief of revolutionary army and Yu Chou, deputy commander-in-chief. The insurrectionary army fought fiercely with Qing Army until 27th and failed because of outnumber. This scene is the rally to pledge resolution before going to war in Huanggang.

▼ 164

165. 黄冈起义形势图（据《辛亥革命史地图集》）。

A map of Huanggang Uprising (from *The Revolution of 1911 History Atlas*).

166. 1907年11期《时事画报》刊载的黄冈起义激战场面。

Painting showing the fiercely fighting scene of Huanggang Uprising published in the *Pictorial of Current Affairs*.

167. 在黄冈起义中被焚毁的清廷协台衙门遗迹。

The remnant site of Qing County Administration building destroyed by fire during Huanggang Uprising.

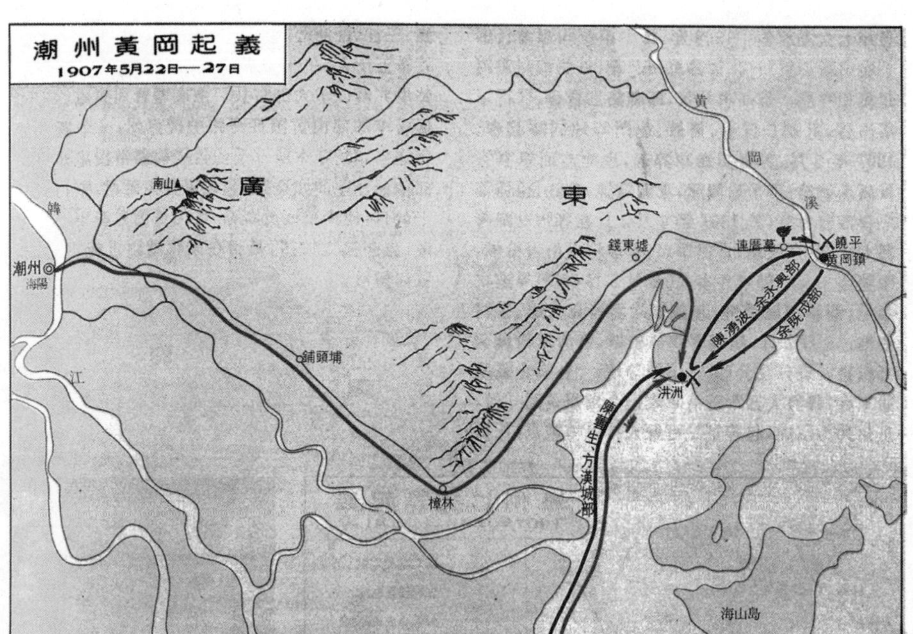

▲ 165

166

167

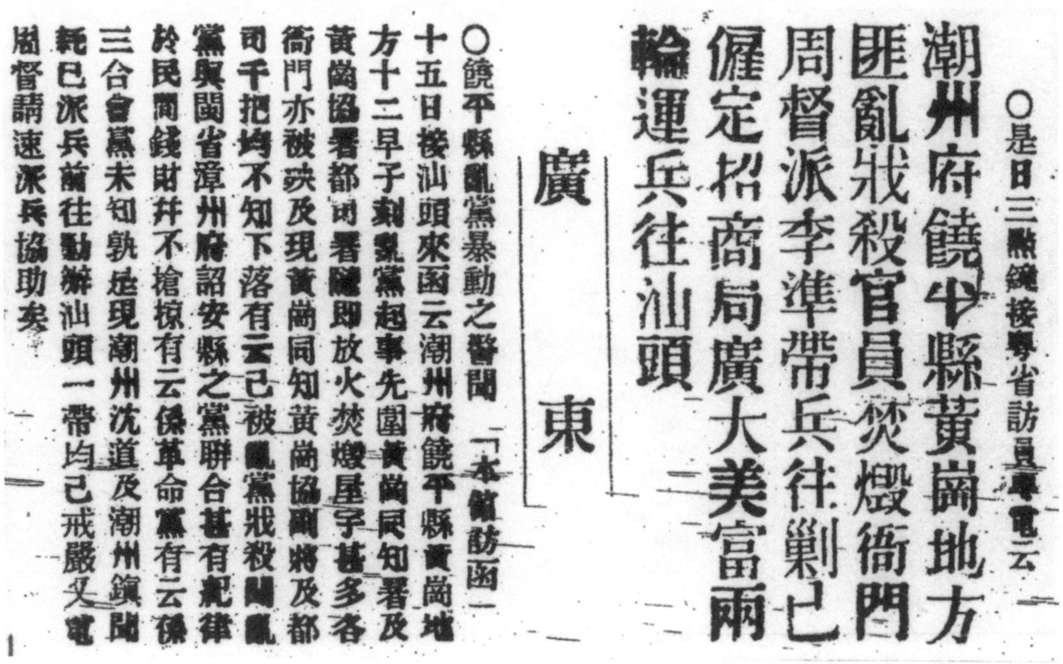

○是日三點鐘接粵省訪員專電云

潮州府饒平縣黃崗地方匪亂戕殺官員焚燬衙門周督派李準帶兵往剿已僱定招商局廣大美富兩輪運兵往汕頭

廣東

○饒平縣亂黨暴動之警聞「本館訪函」

十五日接汕頭來函云潮州府饒平縣黃崗地方十二早子刻亂黨起事先圍黃崗民知署及黃崗協署都司署隨即放火焚燬屋宇甚多各衙門亦被殃及現黃崗同知黃崗協副將及都司千把均不知下落有云已被亂黨戕殺聞亂黨與閩省漳州府詔安縣之黨聯合甚有紀律於民間錢財并不搶掠有云係革命黨有云係三合會黨未知孰是現潮州洗道及潮州鎮聞耗已派兵前往勦辦汕頭一帶均已戒嚴又電粵督請速派兵協助矣

168

168. 1907年5月27日《香港华字日报》刊载的黄冈起义消息。

News about Huanggang Uprising published in *the Hong Kong Chinese Mail* on May 27, 1907.

169. 1907年6月6日，两广总督周馥向清廷报告镇压黄冈起义经过的奏折。

On June 6, 1907, governor general of Guangdong and Guangxi Provinces —Zhou Fu presented a memorial to the emperor, relating how Qing army put down Huanggang Uprising.

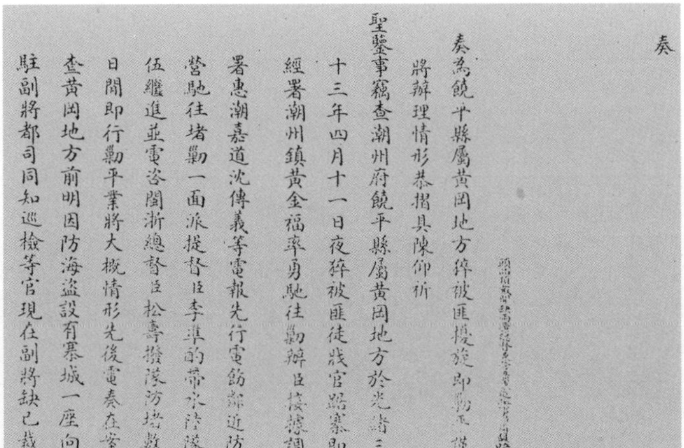

奏

奏為饒平縣屬黃岡地方猝被匪擾旋即剿平謹

將辦理情形恭摺具陳仰祈

聖鑒事竊查潮州府饒平縣屬黃岡地方於光緒三十三年四月十一日夜猝被匪徒戕官踞寨即經署潮州鎮黃金福率勇馳往剿辦臣接據調署惠潮嘉道沈傳義等電報先行電飭鄰近防營馳往堵剿一面派提督臣李準酌帶水陸隊伍繼進並電咨閩浙總督臣松壽撥隊防堵數日間即行剿平業將大概情形先後電奏在案查黃岡地方前明因防海盜設有寨城一座向駐副將都司同知巡檢等官現在副將缺已裁

169（1）

撤兵額亦減不免稍覺空虛該處距潮州府城並饒平縣城各九十里與福建詔安縣邊界素有三點會匪疊經嚴緝此拏彼竄迄未盡絕根株此次黃岡土匪起事變起倉猝據李準黃金福沈傳義等電稱係外匪陳芸生句結會匪首余丑即記成曾金全余錫天及福建詔安縣屬白石鄉匪首沈牛桑後嶺鄉匪首沈家塔等先在詔安縣屬烏山饒平縣屬浮山柘林等處拜會本年正月沈牛桑等帶來鷹球票布銀紙分給會黨刊刻偽示諭帖原圖搶劫已裁黃岡協署舊軍械起事因一時無隙可乘未敢蠢動適於四月十一日警兵拏獲匪夥邱倸張蟢二名會匪張添賜告知匪首余丑糾黨打奪經都司隆發巡防營哨弁蔡河宗率兵將犯押入協署匪衆圍攻弁勇堅禦至次日辰刻予礮用盡匪黨竄至焚攻益力兵勇傷斃者多力竭被困維時黃岡同知謝蘭馨城守把總許登科署柘林司巡檢王繩武各率兵差巡警抵禦奈賊衆兵寡援絕力盡把總巡檢登時被戕同知被擄各匪遂佔踞衙署焚拆關廠局所搶劫副將都司兩署舊械號召各路匪黨逼脅鄉民同叛外匪陳芸生等即於十四日乘機入寨將所刊偽示填寫四月妄稱大明軍政都督府孫等字樣豎旗起事分發偽諭勒索殷富銀米脅從頗衆下寮東窯各匪鄉皆濱海漁戶糾合外匪船載而來分為水陸兩黨水路踞古樓山後陸路踞寨此當日匪黨起事之情形也該管潮州府知府李象辰饒平縣知縣鄭世璜集團固守府縣城池分堵要隘署潮州鎮黃金福督兵馳往距黃岡三十里之井洲相機進剿惠潮嘉道沈傳義馳往汕頭保衛華洋商埠並電致福建漳州詔安府縣防堵十三日府城巡警營帶官外委邱焯五品軍功林清帶勇四名前敵偵探遇賊陣亡十四夜匪撲井洲黃金福率隊出戰小勝斃匪數十人是夜五鼓該匪大股數千分路包抄我軍分頭接仗傷斃賊匪百餘人賊勢少卻十五日黎明賊分五路水陸並進適巡防第九營管帶官趙祖澤繼至督弁徐士廉陳德等分路迎擊爭先衝殺陣斬悍匪百數十名奪獲旗幟馬匹槍械多件賊衆敗退三里外之大澳山腳佔住村房我兵追擊奪取大澳山賊衆且戰且卻我軍悉力猛攻相持至十五日戌刻該黨傷亡甚衆我軍亦陣亡十餘名受傷七名並在鏖戰之際大雨傾盆賊衆奔逃是夜五鼓我軍出其不意奪取踞寨數里之古樓山賊衆死守不出十六日夜該道沈傳義運開花礮子碼到營正在拔隊進逼賊衆棄寨潛逃當即分路追至東窯毀其巢穴直抵黃岡救出同知都司哨弁三員及勇丁二十一名查明槍械盡失並失去裁缺副將關防及同知關防各一顆並在賊巢搜出木質偽印及票布偽示板片軍火多件其偽檄偽示語多悖逆偽檄無姓名年月偽示有都督府孫字樣並無偽印據提督李準言訊各匪並不能指出孫姓係何人顯係匪首陳芸生等附和孫逆有意煽惑此十三至十六等日官兵擊平各匪救出被擄官兵之情形也當匪氛初起之際號召黨羽勢甚披猖嗣知大兵將臨海面並有兵輪堵截賊匪聞風膽落井洲戰敗古樓奪回棄械紛散奔逃十八日提督李準督軍到境聲威大振派兵會合追搜獲匪頗多各軍起獲槍械甚夥黃金福馳至分水關與福建軍官相見查得詔安縣並無股匪竄入居民安謐是役也官軍接仗七次殺傷賊匪五六百名自該匪起事以來六日之間即行撲滅未擾村鎮亦未擾及鄰境地方一律平靖戕官匪首余昇第擒獲正法曾金全業已陣斬在逃之陳芸生余丑余錫天等仍飭四路搜捕務絕根株查此次匪亂起事該管文武不能先事豫防致出戕官踞寨重案厥咎甚重相應請

旨將實任黃岡同知謝蘭馨署黃岡都司隆發調署饒平縣正任廣甯縣知縣鄭世璜巡防營哨弁督標候補千總蔡河宗一併革職署黃岡守備裁缺鎮標左營左哨千總黃其蕃先已另案革職尚未交卸此次復勦匪不力應請從重發往軍台効力贖罪該管鎮道府並不同城例得免議且一經聞報即行進兵撲滅辦理尚屬迅速擬懇

恩施免其議處至署柘林司巡檢王繩武存城把總許登科鎮標拔補外委邱焯五品軍功林清為匪所戕死事慘烈相應籲懇

天恩敕部從優議卹以慰忠魂一切善後事宜責成該道府等會同該鎮督率營縣妥辦並與福建文武議定稽查會哨之法以期永保治安遺失裁缺副將並同知各關防設法查起分別送銷換鑄除先另刊同知木質關防委員接署外所有饒平縣屬黃岡猝被會匪踞擾旋即勦平緣由理合恭摺具陳伏乞

皇太后

皇上聖鑒訓示謹

奏

著照所請該部知道

光緒三十三年四月 廿六 日

▲170

170. 1907年，孙中山与潮州黄冈起义的同志在新加坡晚晴园的合影。

The group photo of Sun Yat-sen and the comrades of Chaozhou Huanggang Uprising, taken in 1907 in the Wanqing Garden of Singapore.

171. 1906年，孙中山派同盟会会员邓子瑜（博罗人）由新加坡回国，策动惠州起义，与潮州黄冈起义相呼应。1907年6月2日，邓子瑜在惠州七女湖发动起义，攻占泰尾、三连、柏塘等圩镇，与清军激战十余日，终因孤立无援而失败。图为起义主要领导人邓子瑜。

In 1906, Sun Yat-sen sent Deng Ziyu (from Boluo County), a member of the Chinese Revolutionary Alliance, from Singapore to China to instigate Huizhou Uprising, in order to echoing Chaozhou Huanggang Uprising. On June 2, 1907, Deng Ziyu launched Seven-lady Lake Uprising, Huizhou and captured counties of Taiwei, Sanlian and Baitang,etc. They fought fiercely with Qing army for over ten days, but ended in failure because of being isolated and no support. This is the key leader—Deng Ziyu.

171

172. 惠州七女湖起义形势图（据《辛亥革命史地图集》）。

The situation map of Seven-lady Lake Uprising, Huizhou (from *The Revolution of 1911 History Atlas*).

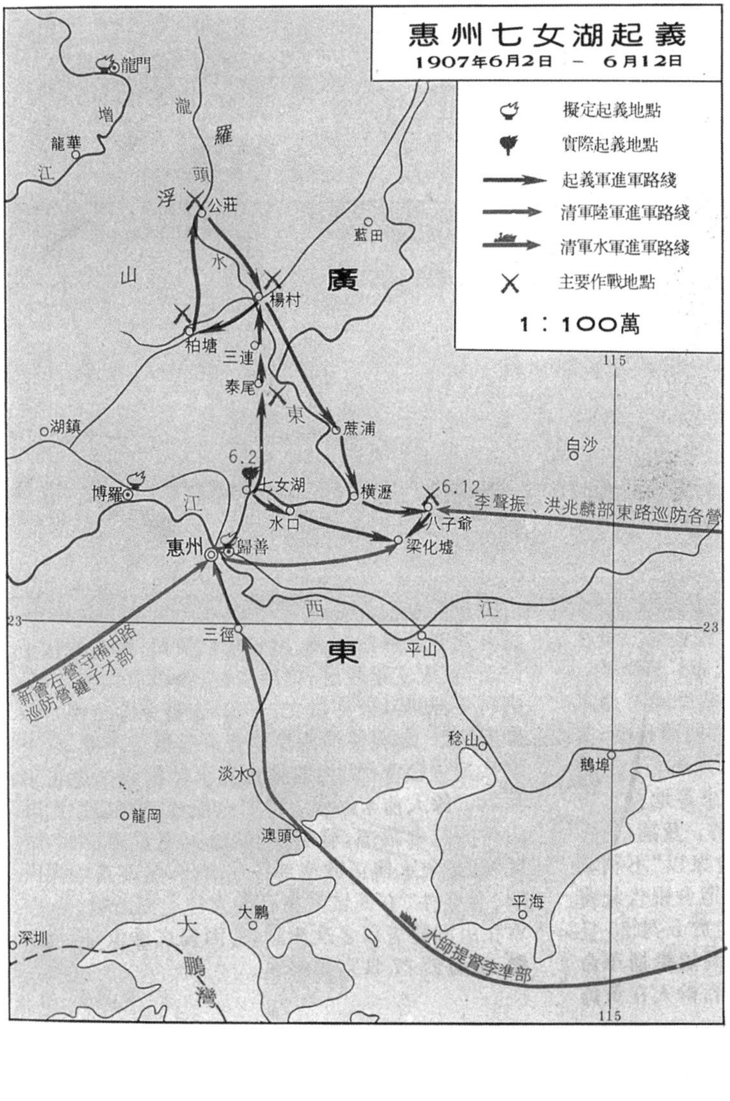

惠州七女湖起義
1907年6月2日 – 6月12日

擬定起義地點
實際起義地點
起義軍進軍路綫
清軍陸軍進軍路綫
清軍水軍進軍路綫
主要作戰地點
1：100萬

龍門
增
江
龍華
瀧
羅
浮
頭
山
公莊
水
藍田
廣
楊村
柏塘
三連
泰尾
東
蔗浦
湖鎮
白沙
6.2
七女湖
橫瀝
6.12
博羅
江
水口
八子爺
李聲振、洪兆麟部東路巡防各營
惠州
歸善
梁化墟
西
江
三徑
東
平山
新會右營守備中路巡防營鍾子才部
稔山
鵝埠
淡水
龍岡
澳頭
平海
大鵬
大
深圳
鵬
灣
水師提督李準部
115
23

172

○同日下午六點鐘接粵省訪員電云

惠州土匪揭竿倡亂勢甚披猖該處官吏有電至省速派兵赴援

○惠州七女湖匪勢之猖披　惠州離城三十餘里之七女湖地方時有土匪數聚其間廿三日巳刻忽有三百餘匪在該處發動將防營及水軍巡船登時派勇對壘衆寡不敵戰至未牌時候營勇被搶傷數名斃者數名未進哨弁被匪傷者一員刻即扛回縣城北門外稟報縣令及營務處惜城中營勇甚少除留守隊外無可添派屬令當即稟陳守電稟周督直至申刻該匪揚揚得意竟向泰尾而去

▲173

▼174

收兩廣總督周致外務部電

前接新嘉坡總領孫士鼎電探聞孫汶有回華作亂之謠當經電達大部現訪聞孫汶改洋裝住香港公益報館又有同黨鄧子瑜住香港旅安祥客棧前獲逆黨陳純供鄧子瑜為孫汶管外事現聞招集香港匪徒入內地勾引亂民滋亂前日黃岡戕官案即是逆黨昨日惠州府等獲十三匪亞法即供從香港來務求大部速密電商英使轉電英政府飭港督速將二逆逐出非此不足保護中外治安事關大局乞速酌奪馥二十四日

▲175

173. 1907年6月5日、7日《香港华字日报》刊载的惠州七女湖起义消息。

News about Huizhou Seven-lady Lake Uprising published in the *Hong Kong Chinese Mail* on June 5 and June 7, 1907.

174. 香港九龙青山红楼是李纪堂在青山农场建造的一座二层楼房。潮州黄冈起义及惠州七女湖起义败退下来的将士，曾转移到此，以避清吏缉捕。

The Red Building in Qingshan, Kowloon, Hong Kong, was a two-store house built up in Qing Shan Farm by Li Jitang. The generals retreated in defeat from Chaozhou Huanggang Uprising and Huizhou Seven-lady Lake Uprising ever moved here to keep away from being seized by Qing officials.

175. 1907年6月4日，两广总督周馥要求外务部与英国政府交涉，敦促港督驱逐孙中山、邓子瑜的电文。

The telegram sent on June 4, 1907, by Guangdong and Guangxi Provinces governor general—Zhou Fu, who required Department of Foreign Affairs to negotiate with the British government and to demand it to order the Governor of Hong Kong to expel Sun Yat-sen and Deng Ziyu.

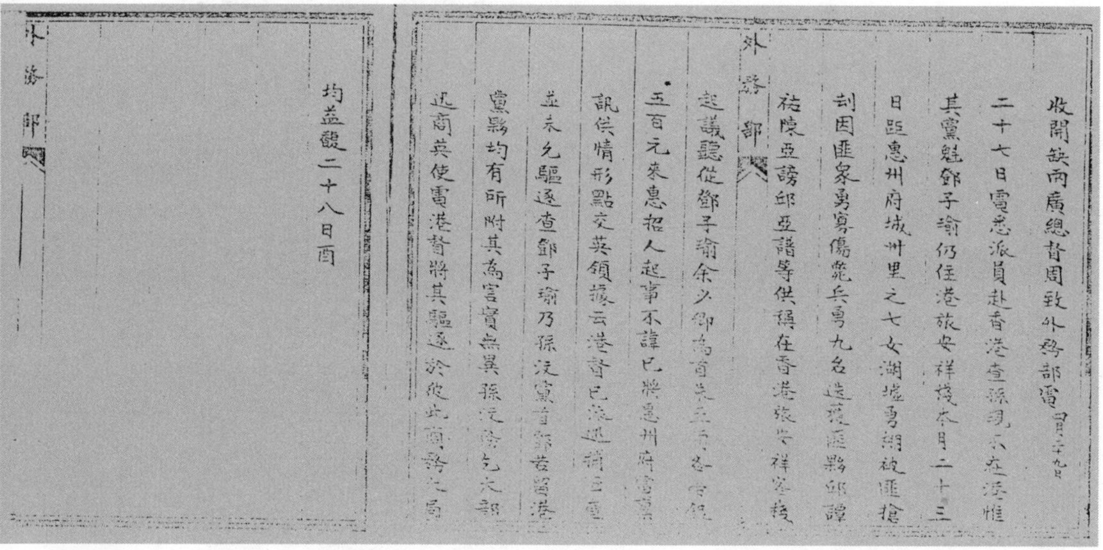

收閱鈔兩廣總督周致外務部電 四月廿九日

二十七日電悉派員赴香港查孫現不在港惟
其黨魁鄧子瑜仍住港旅安祥棧本月二十三
日距惠州府城卅里之七女湖塘勇哨被匪搶
劫因匪衆勇寡傷斃兵勇九名途獲匪黨邱譚
祐陳亞謗邱亞譜等供稱在香港旅安祥客棧
起議聽從鄧子瑜余少卿為首先三千各給
五百元來惠招人起事不諱已將惠州府電禀
訊供情形照交英領據云港督已派巡捕查覆
並未允驅逐查鄧子瑜乃孫汶黨首鄧若留港
黨黟均有所附其為害實無異孫汶務乞大部
迅商英使電港督將其驅逐於彼此商務之局
均益覆二十八日酉

外務部

176

177

176. 1907年6月8日，两广总督周馥再次要求外务部敦促港督驱逐邓子瑜的电文。

The telegram sent on June 8, 1907, by Guangdong and Guangxi Provinces governor—Zhou Fu, who again required Department of Foreign Affairs to urge the Governor of Hong Kong to expel Deng Ziyu.

177. 镇压潮州黄冈起义和惠州七女湖起义的两广总督周馥（左二）。

Zhou Fu(the second from the left), governor general of Guangdong and Guangxi Provinces who suppressed Huanggang Uprising, Chaozhou and Seven-lady Lake Uprising, Huizhou.

178

178. 1907年夏，孙中山委派同盟会会员王和顺为"中华国民军南军都督"，前往钦州等地联络抗捐群众，策划起义。9月1日，王和顺率200余人在钦州王光山起义，迅速占领防城。义军转战10余日，因饷械两缺而于17日失败。图为起义领导人王和顺（广西邕宁人）。

In the summer of 1907, Sun Yat-sen sent Wang Heshun, member of the Chinese Revolutionary Alliance, who was appointed commander-in-chief of National Army South to get in touch with the resist-donating masses in Qinzhou, etc. to plan the uprising. On September 1, Wang Heshun led more than 200 people in starting Wangguang Hill Uprising in Qinzhou and captured Fangcheng rapidly. The army fought in different parts for more than ten days, and failed on 17th because of lack of both food and ammunition. This is Wang Heshun, leader of the uprising(from Yongning County Guangxi Province).

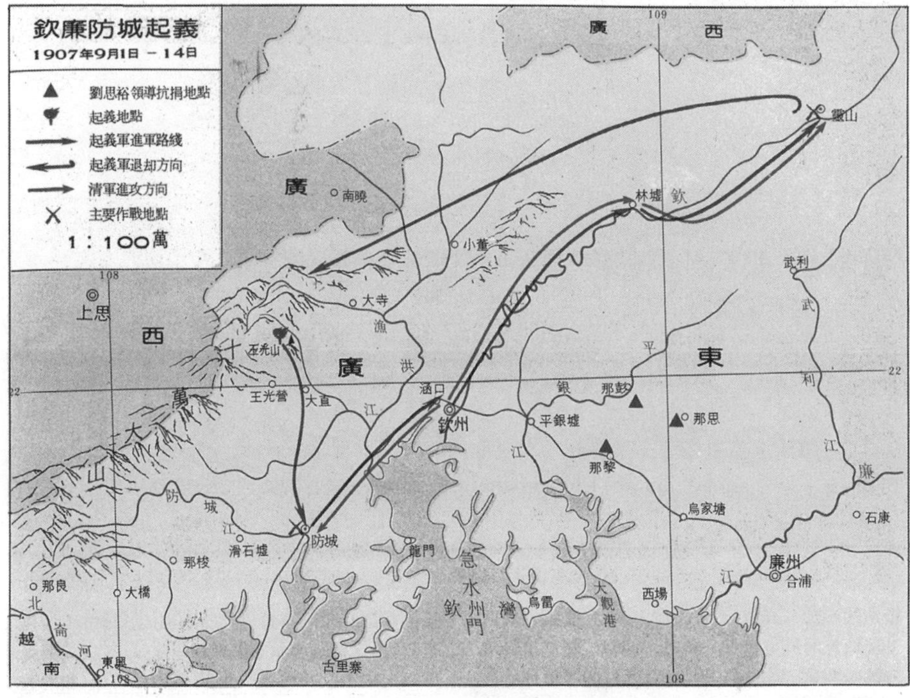

▲ 179

179. 钦廉防城起义形势图（据《辛亥革命史地图集》）。

A map showing Qin-Lian Fangcheng Uprising (from *The Revolution of 1911 History Atlas*).

180. 1907年9月5日，王和顺率起义军攻破防城，杀知县，开监狱。图为被革命军攻破的防城县署监狱。

On September 5, 1907,Wang Heshun led the insurrectionary army in breaking through Fangcheng, killed county magistrate and opened the prison. This is the Fangcheng County Prison broken by revolutionary army.

▲ 180

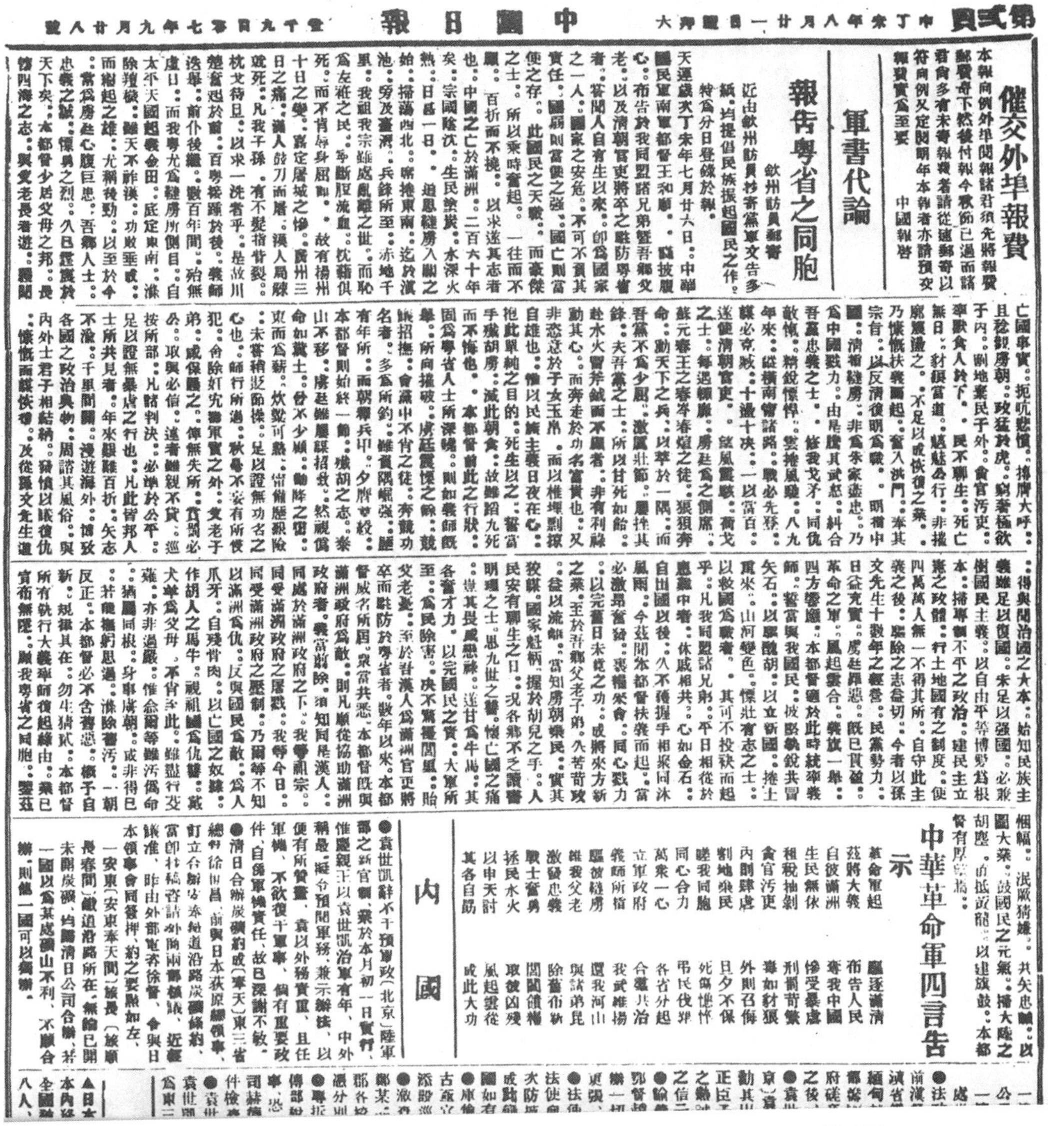

中國日報

催交外埠報費

軍書代論

報告粵省之同胞

中華革命軍四言告示

內國

181. 1907年9月28日《中国日报》刊载的王和顺于9月3日以“中华国民军南军都督”名义所发布的《报告粤省之同胞》和《中华革命军四言告示》，号召广东同胞在孙中山的领导下，奋力推翻清廷。

On September 28, 1907, the *China Daily* published Wang Heshun's *A Letter to Guangdong Compatriots* on September 3rd, and *Four Characters Notice of China National Army* in the name of commander-in-chief of South Army of China National Army, calling for the Guangdong compatriots to overthrow Qing Dynasty under the leadership of Sun Yat-sen.

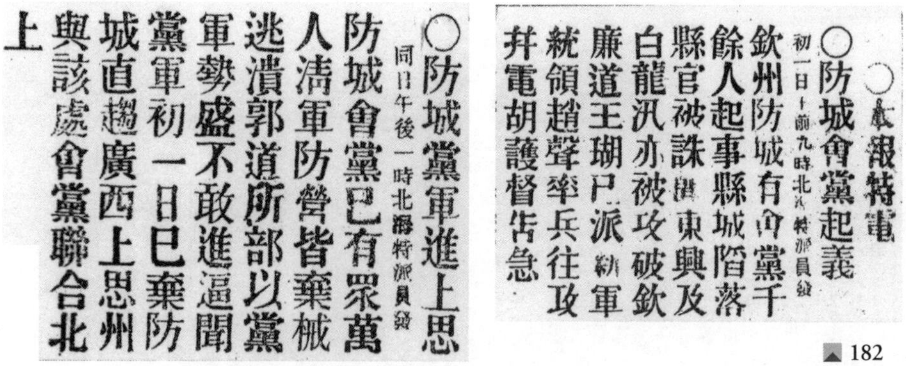

○本報特電
○防城會黨起義
初一日午前九時北海特派員發
欽州防城有會黨千餘人起事縣城陷落縣官被誅據東興及白龍汎亦被攻破欽廉道王瑚已派新軍統領趙聲率兵往攻幷電胡護督告急

○防城黨軍進上思
同日午後一時北海特派員發
防城會黨已有衆萬人清軍防營皆棄械逃潰郭道所部以黨軍勢盛不敢進逼聞黨軍初一日已棄防城直趨廣西上思州與該處會黨聯合北上

182

182. 1907年9月9日、12日《中国日报》登载的有关钦廉防城战事的消息。

The *China Daily* published the news regarding the battles of Qinzhou, Lianzhou and Fangcheng on September 9 and September 12, 1907.

183. 广西镇南关起义失败后，黄兴受孙中山命，从旅越华侨中挑选同盟会会员200余人，组成“中华国民军南军”，自任总司令。1908年3月27日，黄兴率部从越南芒街出发，发动钦廉上思起义。起义军转战粤桂边境40多天，后因后援不济、军心涣散而失败。图为3月19日起义军初战告捷的防城小峰乡。

After Zhennanguan Uprising of Guangxi failed, Huang Xing, at the order of Sun Yat-sen, selected over 200 members of the Chinese Revolutionary Alliance from overseas Chinese in Vietnam to form "South Branch of China's National Army", with himself as the commander-in-chief. On March 27, 1908, Huang Xing led the army, setting out from Mang street, Vietnam, and launching Qinzhou Uprising. The insurrectionary army fought in different parts on the borders of Guangdong and Guangxi for more than 40 days, afterwards failed because the backup was poor and the soldiers' morale was low. The picture is Xiaofengxiang, Fangcheng where the insurrectionary army won in the very first battle of March 19.

183

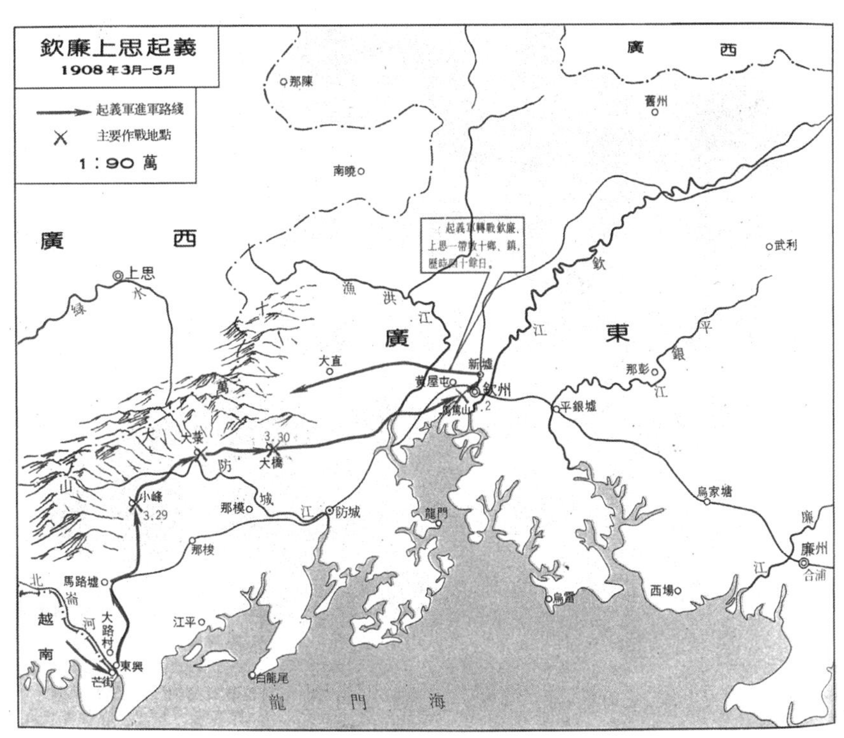

▲184

澤如同志仁兄鑒：刻接精衛、應培兩同志
函備述 足下熱心革命，力任籌餉，以濟軍
需，欽佩無極。現下我西路義師在欽廉連戰
大勝，聲勢大張。廣西邊防營勇之思反正以
為義師內應甚衆，今有數營已經定約，與我
廣西別軍同時起事，急需花紅並月餉萬元。
精衛來函謂 足下處力能籌五千，如此當
可克期集事，務望 足下早日籌便付來，以便
轉滙軍前。今立行事，若於此時廣西能大活
動，以為欽廉義師之聲援，則西路大局可
定，而東路惠潮亦可預備再舉矣。雲南之
局亦有布置，廣西得手，則雲南之師亦可
隨之而動，如此則兩廣雲貴可期恢復，而革命
軍之根本固矣。全局關鍵係於廣西邊防營
勇之響應，而響應之遲速又係於籌款之成
否。今得 足下力任一臂，事可無憂矣。惟機局
之來，難得而易失，今誠千載一時之機，若不致
遲延錯過，則南方基礎可定，而破竹之形成
矣。務為留意，幸甚。得款請滙星加坡張永福
君代收便妥。匪兄住址到下，此致，即候
義安。不一。
各同志統此問好，不另。弟孫文謹啓 西四月十七日

Mr. Teo Eng Hock
105 Beach Road
Singapore

184. 钦廉上思起义形势图（据《辛亥革命史地图集》）。

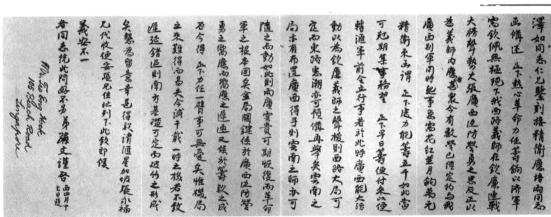

A map showing Qin-Lian Shangsi Uprising (from *The Revolution of 1911 History Atlas*).

185. 1908年4月17日，钦廉上思起义时，孙中山写给邓泽如告以两广边境革命形势，请筹款支持革命军行动的信。

On April 17, 1908, when rising in revolt in Qin-Lian Shangsi, Sun Yat-sen wrote to Deng Zeru, informing him about the revolutionary situation on the borders of Guangdong and Guangxi Provinces and asked him to raise money. This is the letter.

186. 1908年12月16日，两广总督张人骏奏报剿办钦廉两地革命活动情形的奏折。

On December 16, 1908, governor general of Guangdong and Guangxi Provinces Zhang Renjun presented a memorial to the emperor, reporting how he suppressed Qin-Lian's revolutionary activities.

▲186（1）

千餘里北接廣西南鄰越南中皆亂山叢箐逃
首孫文在該處起事旋進則可以牽動兩省退
則可以竄穴越南蓄謀尤為深遠且該逆在南
洋各埠斂錢甚多積資甚厚若事成固足
遂其大欲不成亦由藉此開銷欺詐仇官仇富為
名專以煽惑軍心殺戮我黔首一時人心
驚迷如欽州廉欽一帶該黨已編為革命虜
軍其所刊革命方略等偽書悖逆之言實不忍
寓目臣於軍旅之事向未之學幸遵
宸謨指示不致調度乖方惟此次亂事實與從前不同
兩省會剿辦之難約有數端論匪巢在越以逸
待勞彼能來而我不能往此進剿為難一也行
軍全恃偵探越境布滿華黨諜人前往屢遭
慘殺此偵探為難二也軍情瞬息萬變全恃消
息靈通匪黨每毀折電線電桿以擾我軍機
關此電報為難三也主客軍多至數十營餉械
為軍隊性命所關刻難久缺而廉欽距省二千餘
里水陸並進此轉運為難四也此次匪徒依界外人每
乘隙以要挾搆釁追匪稍不詳慎動生枝節
此交涉為難五也有此數難故用兵較久用
人較多幸賴
朝廷威福將士用命鄉團奮勇得有此肅清之一
日實為臣始初料所不及至屢綑先帥發生臣之不
知兵事而出力之文武員弁或剿匪於深箐深

山或搏命於槍林彈雨寒暑罹瘴冒險不辭實
未便沒其勞勤所有督飭之廣東陸路提督臣
秦炳直調度布置均合機宜前任廉欽兵備閩
粵南澳鎮總兵果勇巴圖魯現署廣東水師提
督臣李準統兵抗戎獨操勝算二品頂戴廣東
廉欽道龔心湛兼顧餉糈廉功最偉應如何從
優獎敘恭候
聖裁留粵補用道郭人漳始終其事勞苦功高擬請
賞給勇號並加二品頂戴開缺北海鎮總兵現署北
海鎮總兵黃英積保準廣東有缺全省二品頂
戴廣西補用道宋安樞力解城圍戰功卓著
請均
交部從優議敘三品銜四川候補知府夏文炳銜餘滔
陣廉戰甚勇擬請免補本班以道員留粵儘先
補用免交留省銀兩並
賞加二品頂戴廣東補用直隸州知州吳雷源擬請免
補本班以知府仍留原省補用免交留省銀兩候
選通判馮錫蔽擬請免選通判以直隸州知州
分省補用並加知府銜前署欽州直隸州知州候選
知縣夏[illegible]擬請免選本班以直隸州知州分省補
用通判職銜鄭國光陸世儒均擬請以通判分
省補用州同職銜吳福昌擬請以州同分省
補用並
賞加五品銜並銅五品頂戴附貢生嚴寶濱擬請以

府經歷分省補用新軍第二標統江南陸師學堂
畢業生趙[illegible]擬請以陸軍副參領記名補
授都司銜守備黃[illegible]守備廖大鍾均擬請
免補本班以都司儘先補用並
賞加遊擊銜千總杉基瑞擬請免補千總以守備
儘先補用並
賞加都司銜其餘在事出力文武各員紳謹分別異
常尋常共二百三十七員並將請獎各單員查
明被泰廉案均另繕清單恭呈
御覽以上人數合計雖多然用兵年餘大小數十戰
每次案請獎尚見其少臣已再三核減委無冒
濫合無仰懇
天恩俯准如請給獎以資鼓勵現派郭人漳擬辦
欽州邊防統欽新練軍駐紮東興兼充對汛
大員防備已臻周密仍當謹遵
諭旨廣佈偵探相機剿捕並慎選守令勤求撫輯各屬教養以期長治久安查邊前廉欽邊防每屆五年保獎一次今首情形不同籌邊更為吃緊四年改為三年保獎一次出自
逾格鴻施除將傷亡各員弁另摺請卹並將千總以下各弁咨部核獎暨飭取各員弁履歷送部外所有廣欽肅清請獎緣由理合恭摺具陳伏乞
皇上訓示謹
奏
光緒三十四年十二月二十三日奉
旨一俟該部議具奏單三件併發欽此

十二月二十三日

購拿革黨之賞格

欽匪亂後著名首要雖迭經大兵剿獲而漏網尙多茲得秦提龔道懸拿賞格照錄如下爲懸賞購拿事案准郭統領電開據稱報係汝去後將軍事交僞都督黃和順僞總司令官黃軫僞總參謀胡漢民汪精衛田相劉霖生譚人風等請懸賞分別購緝旋准兩廣總督部堂張電批黃軫准懸紅九千兩胡漢民懸紅四千元汪田劉譚四匪各懸紅二千元刊發賞格移行兩省文武一體購緝如能按名弋獲即照數給賞并予破格給獎等因除黃和順先已懸賞購緝外准電前因合行懸賞爲此示仰軍民諸色人等一體知悉如能拿獲後開各匪解案訊明即照格給賞並請破格保獎指引官兵拿獲或格殺後驗明確係正身亦即減半給賞酌予獎勵決不食言現聞越南竄回各匪後開之匪亦多在內挾帶貲財頗多如有拿獲一併悉數充賞云云

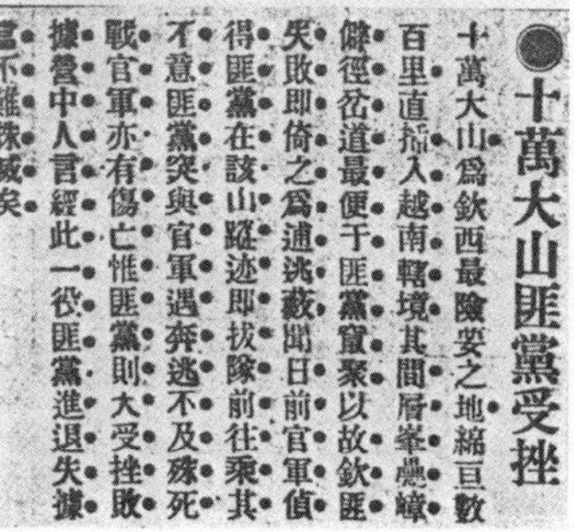

十萬大山匪黨受挫

十萬大山爲欽西最險要之地綿亘數百里直插入越南轄境其間層巒疊嶂僻徑岔道最便于匪黨竄聚以故欽匪失敗即倚之爲逋逃藪聞日前官軍偵得匪黨在該山蹤迹即拔隊前往乘其不意匪黨突與官軍遇奔逃不及殊死戰官軍亦有傷亡惟匪黨則大受挫敗據營中人言經此一役匪黨進退失據當不難誅滅矣

▲187

187. 孙中山在西南地区接连发动多次起义失败后，革命党人一部分前往南洋，一部分则潜入十万大山。图为当时的上海报纸刊载清廷悬赏缉拿革命党人的新闻。黄和顺应为王和顺，黄轸为黄兴，田相应为田桐，谭人风应为谭人凤。

After failures many times in succession in southwest China, Sun Yat-sen sent some of revolutionary partisans to Southeast Asia and some hid in big mountains in Guangxi. This is the news in Shanghai newspaper at that time about Qing court's awards for the wanted revolutionary partisans.

188. 孙中山和革命党人在潮、惠、钦、廉诸役中使用的电报密码。

The secret telegraphic codes which Sun Yat-sen and revolutionary partisans used in the battles of Chaozhou, Huizhou, Qinzhou and Lianzhou.

▼188

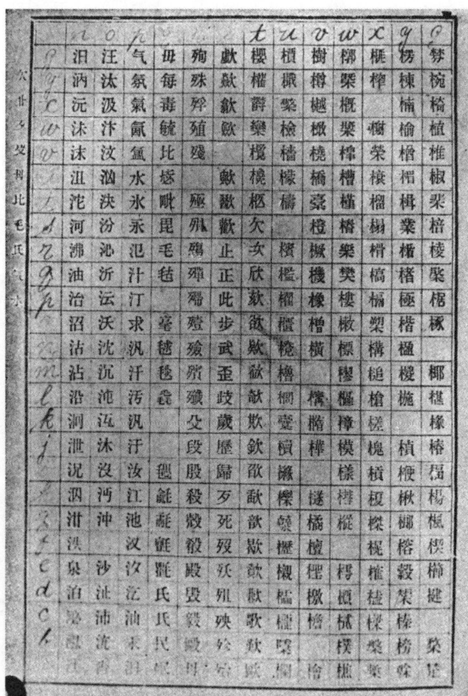

	n	o	p				t	u	v	w	x	y	
g	汩	汪	气	毋	殉	歔	櫻	樻	樹	欂	樜	榜	[illegible]
y	汭	汰	氛	每	殊	歑	櫂	檟	橧	櫱	榫	楝	椀
x	沅	汲	氣	毒	殍	歙	櫵	槷	樾	概		楠	椅
w	沫	汴	氤	毓	殖	歐	欒	檢	橄	槳	[illegible]	榆	植
v	沬	汶	氲	比	殘		欖	檣	橈	槔	榮	楢	椎
	沮	汹	水	毖		歜	欑	檬	橋	槽	槟	楣	椒
	沱	泱	氷	毗	殛	歠	櫪	檮	橐	槿	榴	楫	[illegible]
s	河	汾	永	毘	[illegible]	歡	欠		橙	橋	榭	業	棓
r	沸	沁	氾	毛	殤	止	次	檳	橛	樂	楷	楯	棱
q	油	沂	汁	毡	殫	正	欣	檻	機	樊	槁	楮	棨
p	治	沄	汀		殭	此	欵	檑	橡	樓	槅	極	棍
	沼	沃	求	毫	殪	步	欲	櫃	橧	樕	槊	楷	椽
	沽	沈	汎	毬	殮	武	欸	櫳	橫	標	構	楹	
m	沾	沉	汗	毯	殯	歪	欷	檮		樛	槌	楼	椰
l	沿	沌	污	毳	殲	歧	歆	檷	[illegible]	樞	槍	椸	椹
k	泂	沍	汛		殳	歲	欺	檯	橢	樟	槎		椽
j	泄	沐	汙		段	歷	欽	檳	樺	模	槐	楨	椿
	況	沒	汝	氊	股	歸	欿	檪		樣	槓	梗	[illegible]
	泅	沔	江	氈	殺	歹	歃	櫟	樣	樽	椴	楸	楊
	泔	沖	池	氄	殼	死	歆	檠	橘	樅	樑	椰	楓
	洪		汊	氅	殽	歿	歇	櫪	檀		榥	榕	楔
c	泉	沙	汶	氎	殿	[illegible]	歈	櫬	檉	樗	榷	穀	楠
d	泊	沚	汔	氏	毀	殂	歍	櫼	檄	樻	槤	桀	楗
e	泠	沛	汕	氐	穀	殃	歌	檯	檜	槭	樑	榛	
f	泓	流	汞	民	毅	殄	歉	檗		樸	槃	榜	槃
	[illegible]	[illegible]	[illegible]	[illegible]	[illegible]	[illegible]	[illegible]	[illegible]	檜	樵	槧	[illegible]	[illegible]

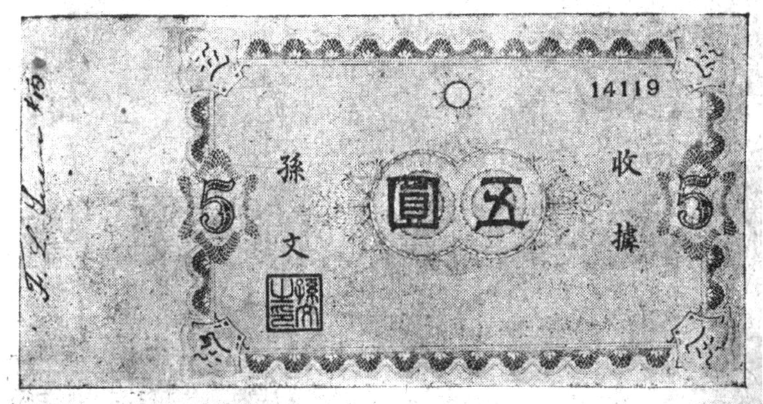

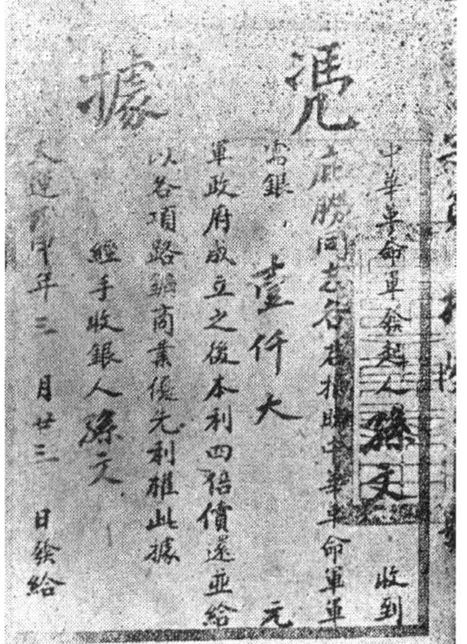

▲ 189

189. 孙中山领导同盟会发动的武装起义，得到南洋华侨的积极支持。图为孙中山签发的革命债券。

The armed uprisings launched by the Chinese Revolutionary Alliance led by Sun Yat-sen got the positive supports of the overseas Chinese in Southeast Asia. The picture is the revolutionary bond that Sun Yat-sen signed and issued.

▲ 190

190. 黄冈之役助饷最力的南洋华侨林受之。

Lin Shouzhi, an overseas Chinese of Southeast Asia, who contributed much money for Huanggang Uprising.

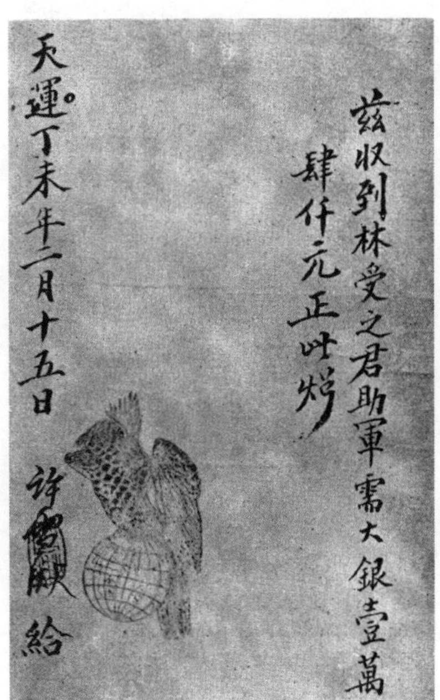
茲收到林受之君助軍需大銀壹萬肆仟元正此炤

天運丁未年二月十五日

許[illegible]給

▲191

▲192

▲193

191. 林受之支援黄冈起义的捐款收据。

The contribution receipt of Lin Shouzhi's donation for Huanggang Uprising.

192. 倾一生积蓄以供起义军需的越南西贡华侨小贩、同盟会会员黄景南（新会人）。

Huang Jingnan (from Xinhui County), a pedlar in Saigon, Vietnam and a member of the Chinese Revolutionary Alliance,who contributed all his savings of all his life for the support of the military supplies for the uprising.

193. 在越南参与运输、供应起义所需军饷、枪支弹药和粮食的越南华侨服装商、同盟会会员黄隆生（新宁人）。

Huang Longsheng (from Xinning County), a Vietnamese overseas Chinese, a clothing trader, and a member of the Chinese Revolutionary Alliance, who in Vietnam participated in transporting and supplying of necessary soldiers' pay and provisions, grain, medicine and cartridge.

時河口鎮南關之役失敗後撤在星洲蔡厝港地方開辦中興石山以安置各同志

戊申年（一九〇八年）

▲ 194

194. 1908年10月11日，孙中山给林义顺请速开设石山公司，以便安置流亡南洋的起义军的信。

This is the letter on October 11, 1908, written by Sun Yat-sen to Lin Yishun, which told him to set up a miniature stone mountain company rapidly in Southeast Asia in order to resettle of insurrectionary armymen in exile.

◀ 195

195. 在南洋积极设法安置粤、桂、滇起义军退居南洋后生计的新加坡侨商、同盟会会员林义顺（澄海人）。

Lin Yishun (from Chenghai County), a member of the Chinese revolutionary Alliance and Singaporean overseas Chinese merchant, who found room and livelihood in Southeast Asia for insurrectionary armymen retreated from Guangdong, Guangxi and Yunnan.

▲196

196. 为了抵制日益高涨的革命风潮，1906年9月，清政府宣布预备立宪，全国各地纷纷成立立宪团体。1907年底，广州同时成立两大立宪团体——粤商自治会和广东地方自治研究社。图为位于华林寺的粤商自治会旧址。

In order to resist the revolutionary tide, in September of 1906, the Qing Government claimed to prepare the constitutionalism. All parts of the country established constitution groups one after another. At the end of 1907, Guangzhou established, at the same time, two major constitution groups—Guangzhou Traders' Autonomy Society and Guangdong Local Autonomy Study Society. The picture is the old site of Guangdong Traders' Autonomy Society located in Hualin Temple.

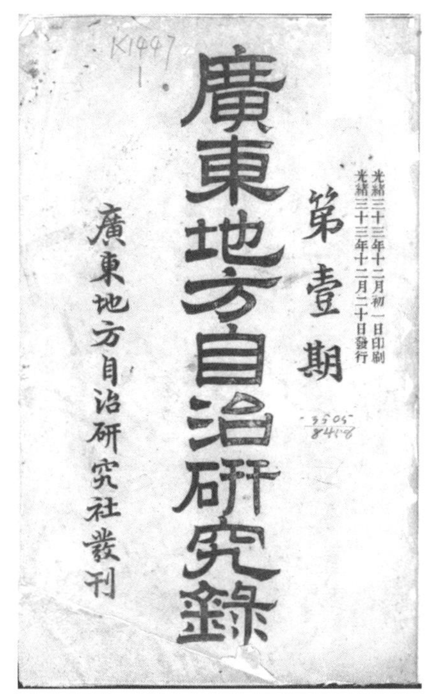
廣東地方自治研究錄

第壹期

光緒三十三年十二月初一日印刷
光緒三十三年十二月二十日發行

廣東地方自治研究社發刊

▲ 197

197. 广东地方自治研究社出版的《广东地方自治研究录》。

The Study Record of Guangdong Local Autonomy published by Guangdong Local Autonomy Study Press.

198. 为推进预备立宪，1908年，清廷批准《各省咨议局章程及议员选举章程》。1909年2月，两广总督张人骏成立广东咨议局筹备处，10月，正式成立。图为广东咨议局开幕纪念照。

For advancing constitutionalism preparation, in 1908, the Qing court approved *The Charter for Every Province Consultation Bureau and Senators Election*. In February 1909, Zhang Renjun, governor of Guangdong and Guangxi Provinces established Guangdong consultation preparatory department. In October Guangdong Consultation Bureau was founded formally. This is the commemorating photo of the opening ceremony.

▲ 198

199. 两广总督张人骏。

Zhang Renjun, governor general of Guangdong and Guangxi Provinces.

200. 广州大东门外广东咨议局会堂（今广东革命历史博物馆），建于1909年。

The Assembly Hall of Guangdong Consultation Bureau outside Dadongmen, Guangzhou, built in 1909 (today's Revolutionary History Museum of Guangdong).

▲199

▼200

201

202

201. 广东咨议局组织的禁赌大游行。

The great parade of gamble-banning organized by Guangdong Consultation Bureau.

202. 广州庆祝禁赌的盛况。

The grand occasion of celebrating gamble-banning in Guangzhou.

203

203. 1910年冬，孙中山在香港的同学关心焉等发起成立“剪发不易服会”，以示反清。图为该会成立纪念照。前排右起：胡礼垣、关元昌、王元琛、吴秋湘、温清溪、区凤墀。后排右二陈宝东、右三关心焉、右四黄江波、右五陈子裘、右六曹季彭、右八郭翼之。

In the winter of 1910, Guan Xinyan etc. , Sun Yat-sen's classmates in Hong Kong, organized the society of cutting pigtails but not changing clothes in order to show their resolution of anti-Qing Dynasty. This is the commemoration photo of the founding. Front row from the right: Hu Liyuan,Guan Yuanchang,Wang Yuanchen, Wu Qiuxiang, Wen Qingxi, Ou Fengchi; back row from the right: Chen Baodong (second),Guan Xinyan(third), Huang Jiangbo(fourth), Chen Ziqiu (fifth), Cao Jipeng (sixth), Guo Yizhi (eighth).

204

205

204. 为加强同盟会的领导力量，1909年10月，同盟会南方支部在香港成立。该组织在策划广州新军起义和广州黄花岗起义中发挥了重要作用。图为同盟会南方支部部长胡汉民。

In order to strengthen the leading force, in October 1910, the Southern Branch of the Chinese Revolutionary Alliance was founded in Hong Kong. This branch played an important role in planning the Guangzhou New Army Uprising and Yellow Flower Hill Uprising. This is Hu Hanmin, director of the branch.

205. 同盟会依靠会党在西南边境发动的一系列起义失败后，转而运动清廷的新军。同盟会南方支部在香港成立后，即着手筹划以新军为主体的广州起义。1910年2月12日，倪映典率新军近3 000人，在广州燕塘起义。起义因准备不周及寡不敌众而失败。图为新军起义司令官倪映典（安徽人）。

The Chinese Revolutionary Alliance depended on the secret societies launching a series of uprisings on southwest China borders, but failed. Then they turned to New Army of Qing Dynasty. After the Chinese Revolutionary Alliance's southern branch was established in Hong Kong, they set about preparing the Guangzhou Uprising, taking New Army as the main force. On February 12, 1910, Ni Yingdian led 3,000 soldiers of New Army in starting the uprising in Yantang, Guangzhou. The uprising failed because of the weak preparation and hopeless outnumber. This is Ni Yingdian (from Anhui Province), commander-in-chief of New Army.

206. 广州新军起义形势图（据《辛亥革命史地图集》）。

A map showing Guangzhou New Army Uprising (from *The Revolution of 1911 History Atlas*).

206

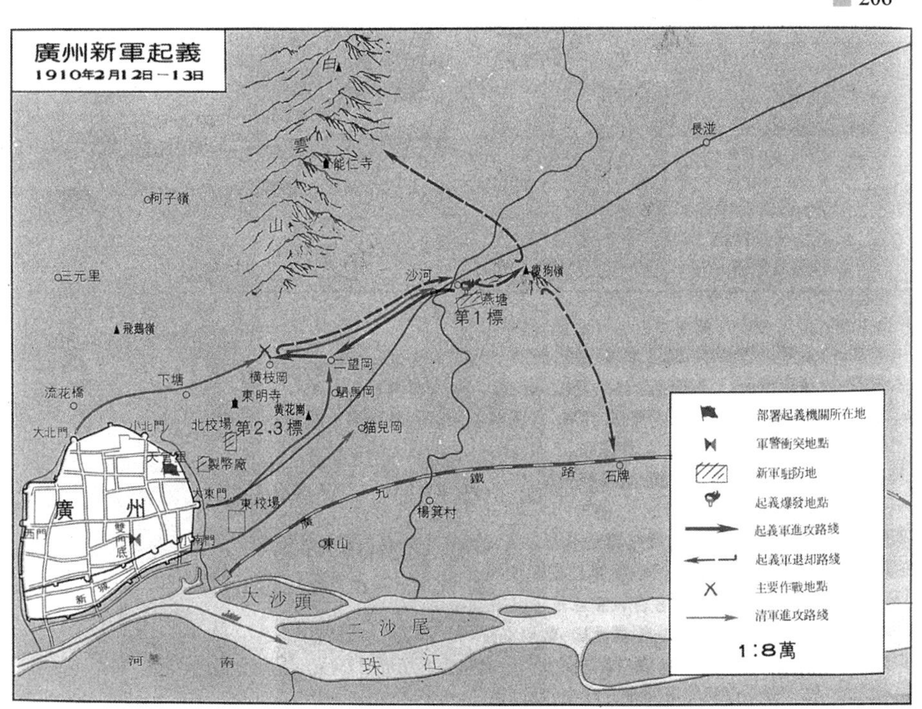

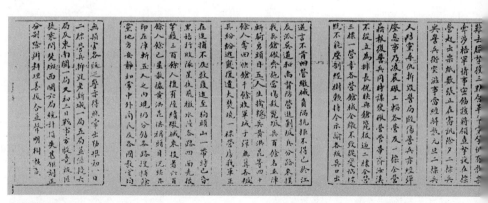

207

208

207.《神州画报》刊载的广州新军与清军激战的场面。

The fierce fighting scene between Guangzhou Uprising New Army and Qing troop published in the *China Pictorial*.

208. 1910年2月15日，两广总督袁树勋向民政部报告镇压广州新军起义的电文。

The telegram sent on February 15, 1910, by Guangdong and Guangxi Provinces governor general Yuan Shuxun, reporting to Ministry of the Civil Affairs about the suppression of Guangzhou New Army Uprising.

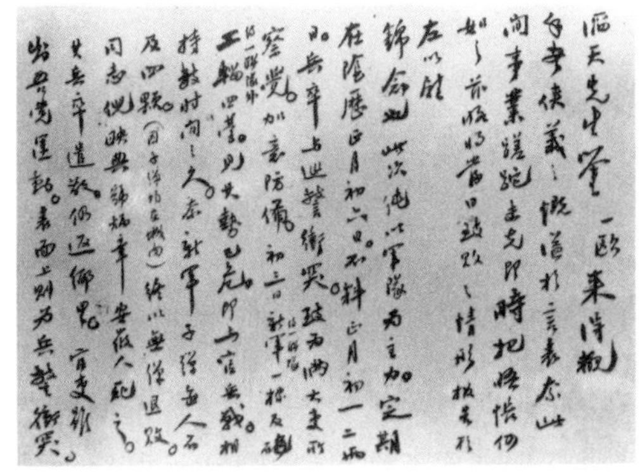

▲209

209. 1910年4月28日，黄兴为告知广州新军起义失败经过及今后革命计划致宫崎寅藏函。

It is a letter from Huang Xing to Miyazaki Torazou on 28 April 1910, telling the failure course of New Army Uprising in Guangzhou, as well as the revolution plan for the future.

210. 1910年秋，黄兴受孙中山之托，在霹雳（今属马来西亚）怡保决醒园召集各地同盟会会长举行会议，筹划广州起义。图为与会者合影。

In the autumn of 1910, entrusted by Sun Yat-sen, Huang Xing called a meeting of heads from different branches of the Chinese Revolutionary Alliance, in Yi Bao Jue Xing Garden, Pi Li (presently belongs to Malaysia), to prepare the Guangzhou Uprising. It is a picture of the meeting participants.

▲210

211. 1910年夏秋间，广东连州等地因官府编订门牌，勒收牌费，激起民变。图为1910年10月13日天津《大公报》关于连州编订门牌风潮的报道。

Between summer and autumn of 1910, the local authorities numbered the houses and extorted fees for house plates in Lianzhou of Guandong and others, this caused mass uprising. The picture shows the report of *Takungpao* about the storm of house plates in Lianzhou on October 13, 1910.

廣東

連州編訂門牌之大風潮○連州來函云該州城內現因調查戶籍編訂門牌州官談國政縱任收發家丁串同劣紳勒抽牌費州民不服以致激成衆怒勢甚洶洶將該州之中學堂小學堂屠捐公司甑捐公司及附近社學並某紳住宅盡行拆毀所有校具什物等一概焚燒州官徬徨無措飭令閉城兩日州民益形鼓噪衙署亦幾被拆去嗣由連陽游擊雷鎮穀極力彈壓始得無事

212. 1910年10月14日，孙中山致邓泽如等函，告国内因钉门牌，收粱税，人心不服，皆思反抗，机局大有可为，嘱筹款图大举。

Letter from Sun Yat-sen to Deng Zeru others and on October 14, 1910, telling that collecting tax for house plates in home caused bad popular feeling and thinking of resisting. It was a good opportunity for uprising. They should raise funds for actions on a large scale.

213. 1910年11月13日，孙中山在槟榔屿召集同盟会的重要骨干和南洋、国内东南各省代表举行秘密会议，黄兴、胡汉民、赵声、孙眉等同盟会骨干出席了会议。会议决定在广州再次策划起义。图为孙中山在槟榔屿的寓所。

On November 13, 1910, in Penang, Sun Yat-sen convened important backbones of the Chinese Revolutionary Alliance and representatives of the Chinese Revolutionary Alliance from Southeast Asia, provinces of southeast China to hold a secret meeting. Huang Xing, Hu Hanmin, Zhao Sheng, Sun Mei, etc., backbones of the Chinese Revolutionary Alliance attended the meeting. They decided to plan an uprising again in Guangzhou. The picture shows the residence of Sun Yat-sen in Penang.

澤如仁兄並列位同志大鑒：近日內地因釘門牌
收糧稅，各處人心不服，皆成反抗，杭州局大有可為，
吾黨不可不乘時圖大舉。惟弟所謀歐美之
路皆尚未成就，倘今有革命軍起，則事亦立
可成議也。且現時民心軍心皆變，本不須大款也。
可舉事者有十萬為事前之預備，使可
數籌畫而計成功矣。弟現已發函各埠詢問各
可担任錢幾何，若合各埠可以籌足此數固佳，否
則籌少亦可冒險一發也。貴埠能担任多少，並另
有何法向他處籌資以助成此舉，請為早知。
弟事務安頓後，當來與各位面商也。此致，即候
大安不一 弟孫文不一 西十月十五号

▲ 212

▼ 213

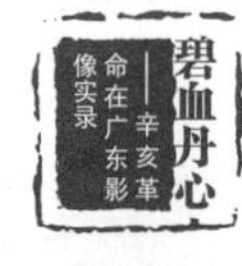

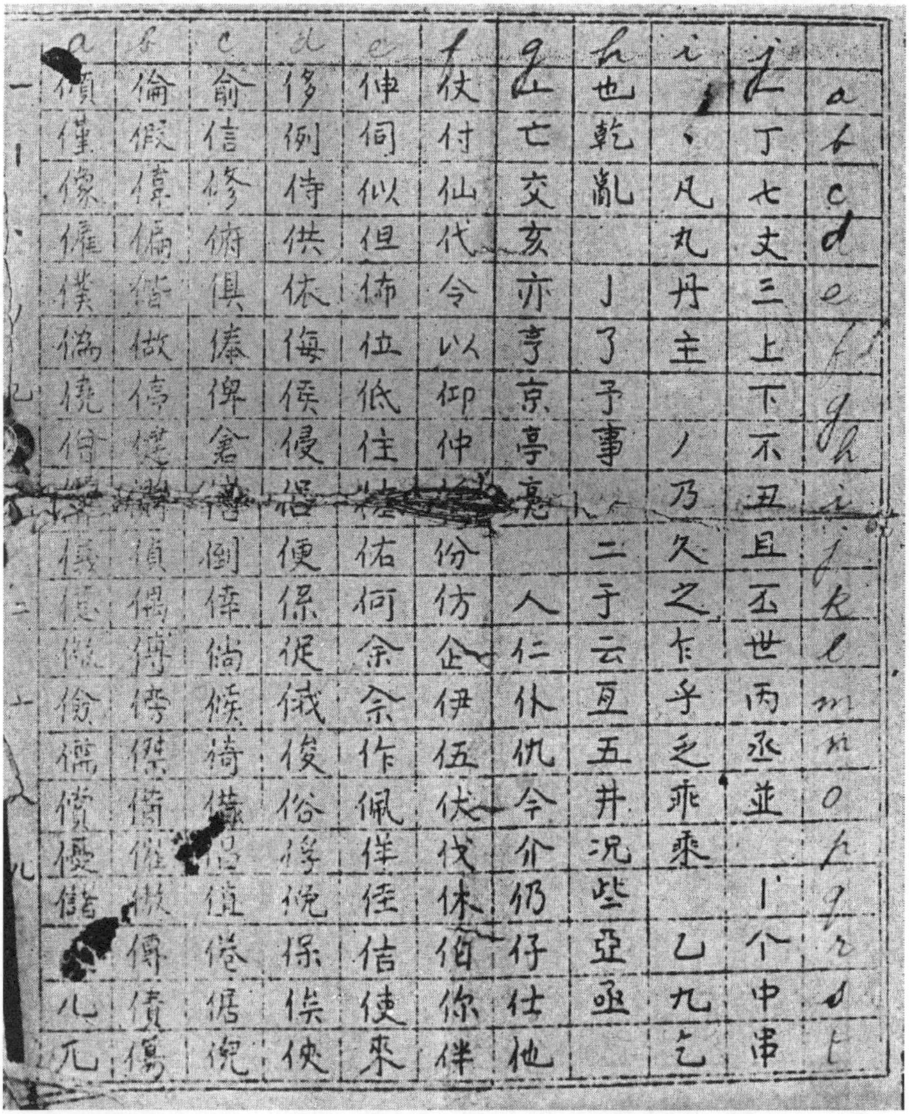

▲214

214. 策划黄花岗起义时，孙中山和革命党人使用的电报密码。

The secret telegraphic codes which Sun Yat-sen and revolutionary partisans used during Yellow Flower Hill Uprising.

215. 槟榔屿会议后，孙中山致力为广州起义筹款。图为发往各地的筹款通知。

After the meeting in Penang, Sun Yat-sen devoted himself to raising funds for the Guangzhou Uprising. The picture of the fund-raising notice mailed to all parts.

216. 1910年11月20日，孙中山致怡保同盟会副会长李源水的筹款函。

The letter of fund-raising written on November 20, 1910,by Sun Yat-sen to Li Yuanshui, deputy director of the Chinese Revolutionary Alliance in Ipoh, Malaysia.

耀垣列位盟長公鑒大事急矣冀諸公戮力全心籌欵速匯以應義舉茲將
孫先生書錄出呈覽
前函所云需十萬元乃能布置周到而實收成功之效者非待十萬到齊而後發刻下已開始陸續布置在在需欵矣此次之動乃因日俄協約時勢甚急岌岌不可終日而內地革命風潮亦已普及軍心民心皆同歸向加以吾黨久困奇窮不能稍待有此三者相迫而來不得不發故主動各人決意爲破斧沉舟之舉誓不反顧與虜一搏有十萬元爲事前之布置固起無之亦必冒險而起也況精位君已去吾輩何忍徒生若事不成則寧爲玉碎不爲瓦全也弟亦決意到時潛入內地親與其事故今日若得十萬元則出以安全不得十萬則必出以冒險耳此十萬元不過一安全冒險之問題非爲起不起之問題也今內地同志既有決死之心亦何暇計其安險但念海外同志必不忍內地同志獨出冒險而不一援手而拯之於安全之地也故欲各盡所能以相有濟內地同志捨命海外同志出財庶免內地同志有輕擲寶貴性命如精位君者則誠莫大之幸矣弟望美洲各埠同志各盡義務惟力是視能籌足十萬元固佳否則多少亦望速速電匯以應急需是爲至禱中國與亡在此一舉革命軍盡此一役也　此詢
義安　十一月　由南洋弟孫文謹啟　英蘇 [illegible] 同上

215

澤如[illegible]兄足下　啟者　[illegible]夢生[illegible]來
南洋之舉
兄於此次之計畫極力贊助並允出助
款為[illegible]深感
兄等既肯[illegible]苦計　弟敢不[illegible]
魯連之志以酬[illegible]等　[illegible]有進者此番
決心係由[illegible]力多同人默察時機已熟
咸願犧牲身命以與虜拚　軍界之人
更爲激烈　前歲土耳其之革命　上月葡萄
牙之成功　全賴軍力　皆原於此　我今既具有
此雄力　安忍聽其軀肉相搏　不爲欵備以
喪我志士　此擇[illegible]等所以發慈悲施
歛力以爲之者也　我
[illegible]洞明時局　切大義　知交既廣　[illegible]易
[illegible]必能設法籌措鉅欵　以成此破斧
沉舟之[illegible]　今[illegible]已[illegible]美[illegible]華
盛頓等處[illegible]各處[illegible]重[illegible]受
後世國民之[illegible]拜　豈不[illegible]當日之疆場
戰士耶　當知其中有破[illegible]財產以充
軍實[illegible]若[illegible]大[illegible]有[illegible]君[illegible]
捍衛社稷　不有[illegible]　今[illegible]等
爲行者[illegible]身當[illegible]劍收欵
兄等[illegible]若有以提攜之　則中國可大有
爲矣　千祈[illegible]力[illegible]埠之行[illegible]則
當再[illegible]辦[illegible]熱心黨事[illegible]與
兄交情[illegible]必可得其助力
特此先佈[illegible]請
大安
弟孫文謹啟　[illegible]十一月二十[illegible]

216

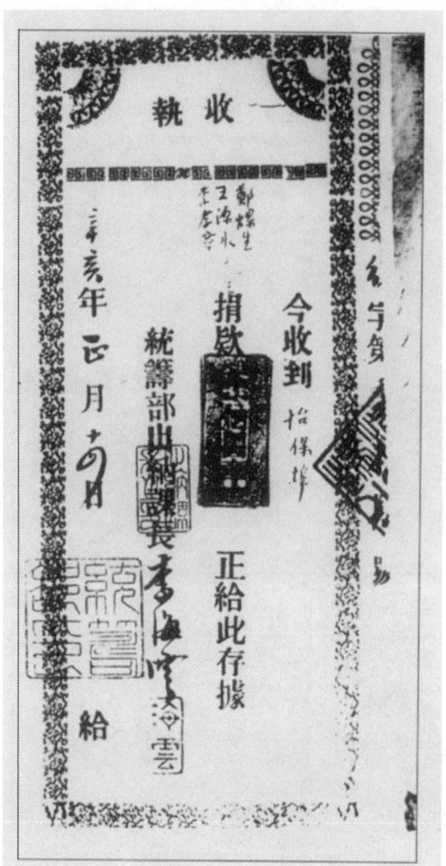

收執

今收到怡保埠 鄭螺生 王源水 李孝章
捐欵
正給此存據
統籌部出納課長 李海雲
辛亥年正月十四日 給

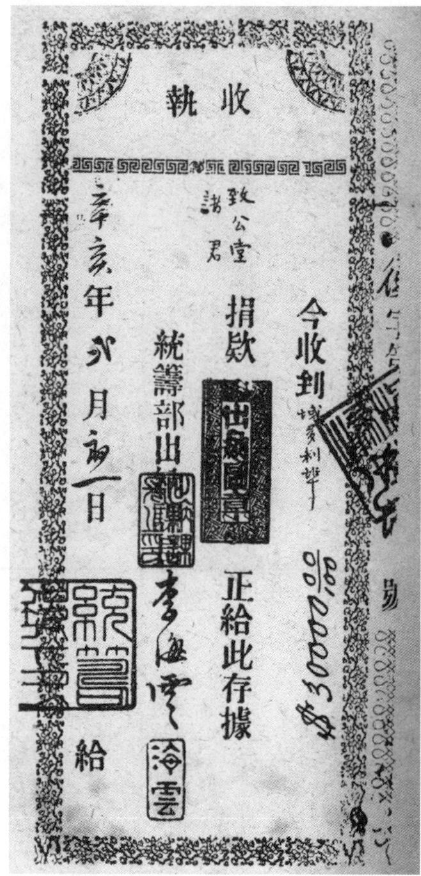

收執

今收到域多利埠致公堂諸君
捐欵
正給此存據
統籌部出納課長 李海雲
辛亥年弍月初一日 給

217. 南洋怡保埠华侨支援广州起义的捐款收据。

The contribution receipt in the support of Guangzhou Uprising by overseas Chinese of Ipoh in Malaysia.

218. 域多利致公堂支援广州起义的捐款收据。

The contribution receipt in the support of Guangzhou Uprising by Victoria Society.

219. 杜朗度致公堂支援广州起义的捐款收据。

The contribution receipt in the support of Guangzhou Uprising by Dulangdu Society.

220. 在南洋积极筹饷支援广州起义的同盟会会员、新会侨商邓泽如。

Deng Zeru, a member of the Chinese Revolutionary Alliance and overseas Chinese merchant from Xinhui County, who actively raised money in Southeast Asia to support Guangzhou Uprising.

221. 1911年，同盟会本部为筹集起义经费发行的中华革命军义饷凭单。

A pay voucher of Chinese Revolutionary Volunteer Army issued to raise funds for uprising by Head Office of the Chinese Revolutionary Alliance in 1911.

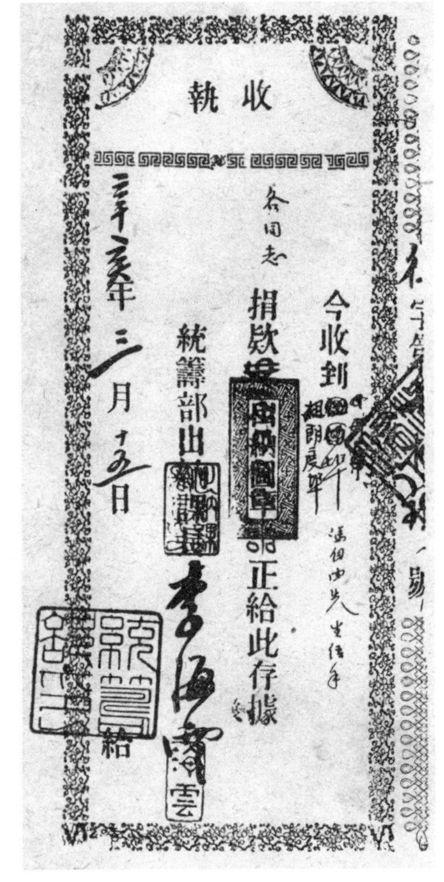

收執

今收到

捐欵

正給此存據

統籌部出給

▲ 219

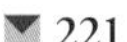

▼ 221

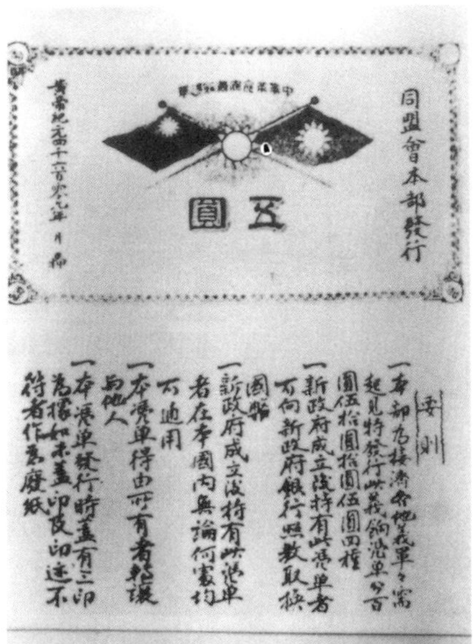

同盟會本部發行

五圓

▲ 220

▲ 222

222. 1911年1月18日，黄兴抵香港主持广州起义筹备工作，月底，在跑马地成立统筹部。图为统筹部部长、起义军副总司令黄兴。

On January 18, 1911, Huang Xing arrived in Hong Kong to take charge of the preparatory work of Guangzhou Uprising. At the end of the month, an overall planning group was founded in Happy Valley. This is Huang Xing, the minister and deputy commander-in-chief of insurrectionary army.

▲223

▲224

223. 1911年3月6日，黄兴与赵声、胡汉民为陈述广州起义筹划情况致孙中山函。

A letter to Sun Yat-sen from Huang Xing, Zhao Sheng and Hu Hanmin on March 6, 1911, stating situation of fundraising for Guangzhou Uprising.

224. 1911年4月18日，黄兴为广州起义筹款事致李源水等函。

A letter from Huang Xing to Li Yuanshui and others on April 18, 1911, telling fundraising for Guangzhou Uprising.

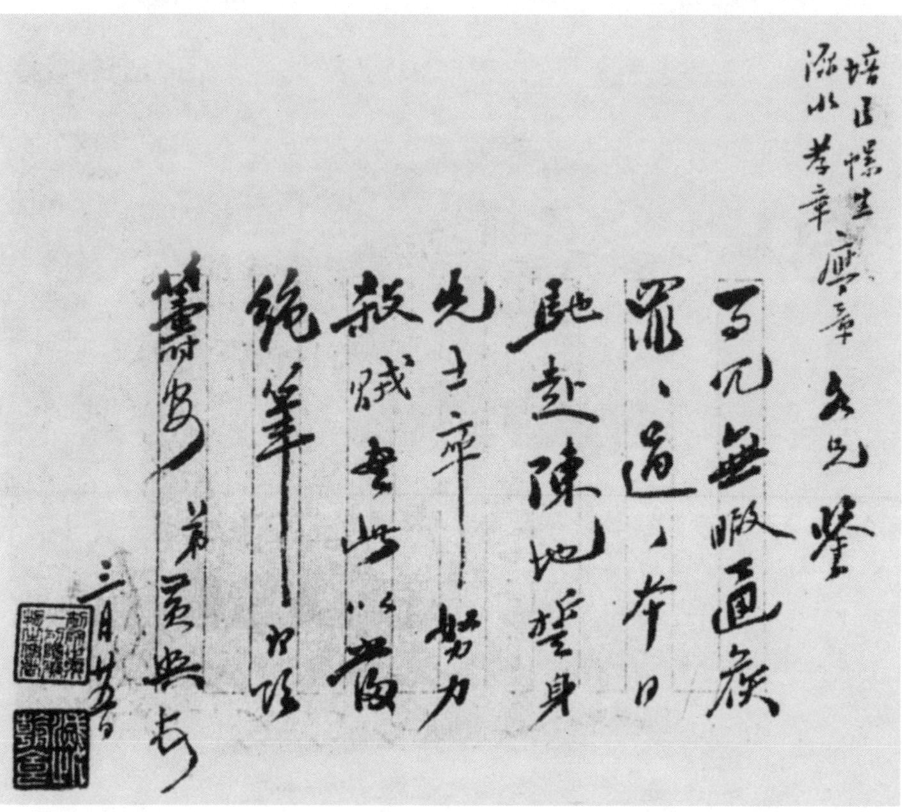

培正　惺生
添水　孝章　賡章　文兄鑒：

事冗無暇面敘，羅、羅、通、過、今日馳赴陳地，誓身先士卒，努力殺賊，書此以當絕筆。即頌

籌安

弟黃興上

三月廿五日

▲225

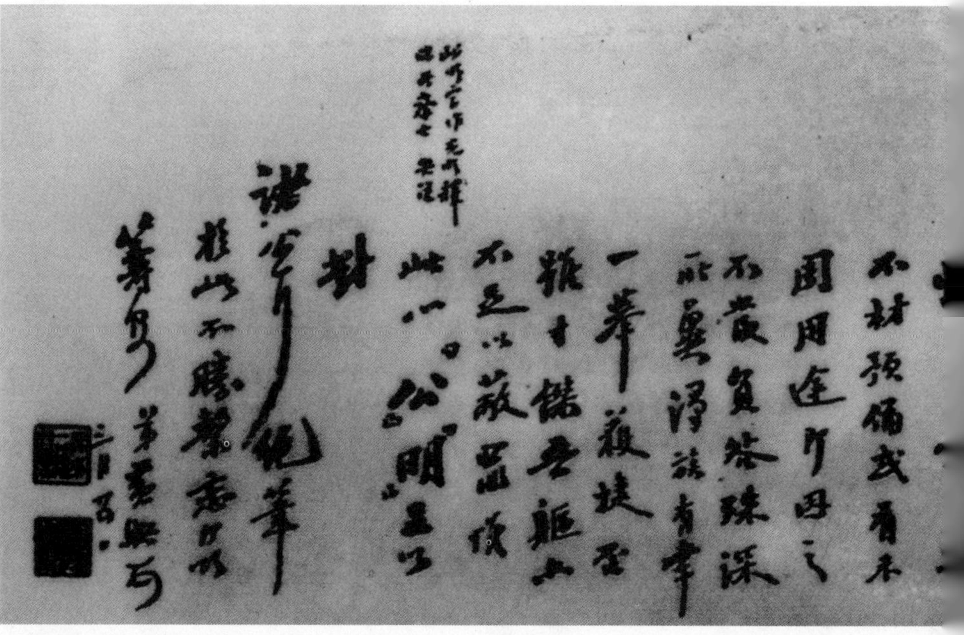

▲226

225. 起义前夕，黄兴写给南洋同志的绝笔书。

On the eve of the uprising, Huang Xing wrote his farewell letter to his comrades in Southeast Asia.

226. 黄兴致邓泽如绝笔书。

The farewell letter from Huang Xing to Deng Zeru.

227. 统筹部副部长、起义军总司令赵声（江苏丹徒人）。

Zhao Sheng (from Dantu County, Jiangsu Province), vice-minister of the overall planning group, commander-in-chief of insurrectionary army.

▲227

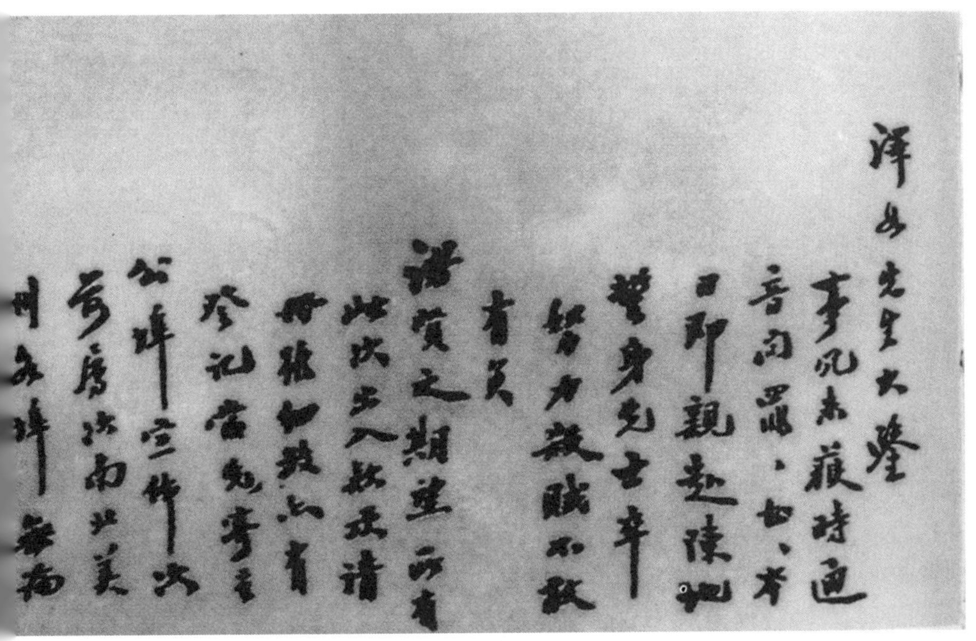

▶ 228

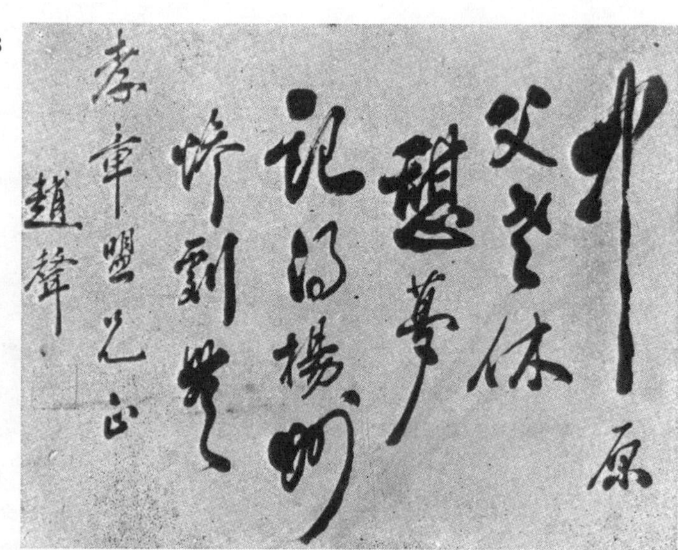

228. 赵声遗墨。
Zhao Sheng's handwriting.

229. 革命党人设在广州越华路小东营的起义指挥部。
The uprising commanding post at Xiaodongying in Yuehua Road, Guangzhou.

▼ 229

▲ 230

230. 1911年4月初，准备参加起义的福建籍同盟会会员林文等在起义前于香港合影留念。前排左起：李恢、高怡书、黄光弼、黄展云、施明；后排左起：陈杨鑣、林文、郑烈、王学文。

In early April 1911, Lin Wen and other members of the Chinese Revolutionary Alliance from Fujian, who were ready to take part in an uprising, had a group photo taken in Hong Kong before the uprising. From left in the front row: Li Hui, Gao Yishu, Huang Guangbi, Huang Zhanyun and Shi Ming. From left in the back row: Chen Yanglu, Lin Wen, Zheng Lie and Wang Xuewen.

231. 同盟会会员方声洞由日本归国参加起义前与妻儿诀别。

Fang Shengdong, a member of the Chinese Revolutionary Alliance, bided farewell with his wife and child before he took part in the uprising after his homecoming from Japan.

▶ 231

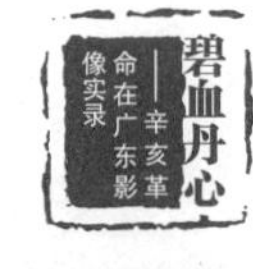

▲232

232. 1911年4月27日（农历三月二十九日）下午5时，黄兴率领先锋队约130人攻打两广总督署和督练公所，两广总督张鸣岐落荒而逃。起义军又兵分三路在龙王庙、小北门、大南门等处与清军展开激烈巷战。图为1911年7月出版的《平民画报》刊载的“焚攻督署”图。

On 5 o'clock pm, April 27, 1911 (Chinese lunar calendar March 29), Huang Xing led a vanguards of about 130 to attack Guangdong and Guangxi Provinces governor general's office. Zhang Mingqi, Guangdong and Guangxi Provinces governor general fled in panic. The insurrectionary army soldiers, divided into three teams, fought a fierce street battles with Qing troop in Dragon King Temple, Xiaobeimen and Dananmen, etc. This is the picture of the insurrectionary army's attacking and burning of government office building published in the *Populace Pictorials* in July of 1911.

233. 黄花岗起义形势图（据《辛亥革命史地图集》）。

A map showing Yellow Flower Hill Uprising (from *The Revolution of 1911 History Atlas*).

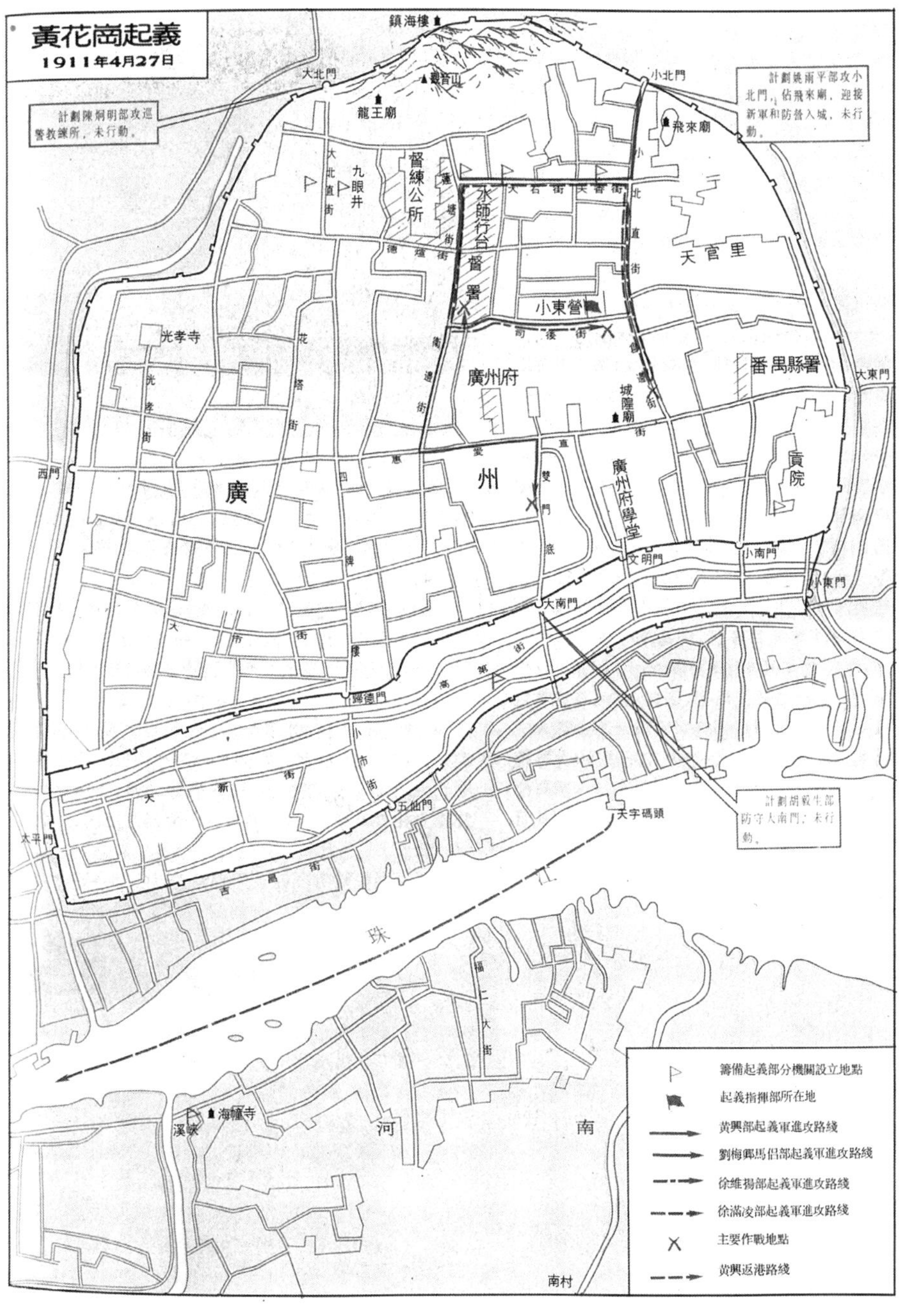

黃花崗起義
1911年4月27日
計劃陳炯明部攻巡警教鍊所，未行動。
計劃姚雨平部攻小北門，佔飛來廟，迎接新軍和防營入城，未行動。
計劃胡毅生部防守大南門，未行動。
鎮海樓
觀音山
龍王廟
大北門
小北門
飛來廟
九眼井
大北直街
督練公所
水師行台
督署
小東營
廣州府
番禺縣署
天官里
光孝寺
光孝街
城隍廟
貢院
廣州府學堂
西門
大東門
小南門
文明門
大南門
小東門
歸德門
五仙門
太平門
天字碼頭
廣
州
大市街
大新街
小市街
高第街
吉祥街
珠
江
河
南
海幢寺
溪峽
南村
福仁大街
籌備起義部分機關設立地點
起義指揮部所在地
黃興部起義軍進攻路线
劉梅卿馬侶部起義軍進攻路线
徐維揚部起義軍進攻路线
徐滿凌部起義軍進攻路线
主要作戰地點
黃興返港路线

THREE 叁 147

234

235

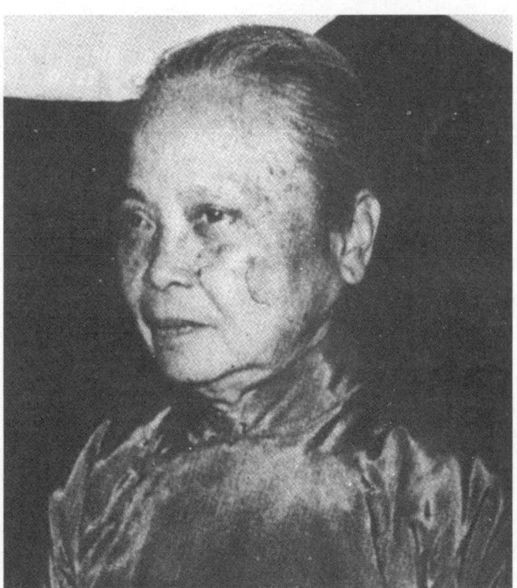

236

234. 清两广总督署。

The government building of Guangdong and Guangxi Provinces governor general of Qing Dynasty.

▲ 237

▲ 238

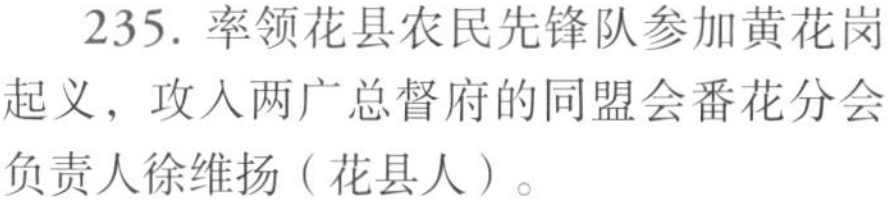

235. 率领花县农民先锋队参加黄花岗起义，攻入两广总督府的同盟会番花分会负责人徐维扬（花县人）。

Xu Weiyang (from Huaxian County), a director of Panyu-Huaxian County branch of the Chinese Revolutionary Alliance, who led a vanguards of peasants in capturing the government building while participating in Yellow Flower Hill Uprising.

236. 巧扮新娘掩护装有炸弹的花轿入广州城的“革命新娘”卓国华（香山人）。

Zhuo Guohua (from Xiangshan County), who skillfully played the part of “revolutionary bride” to shield bombs with bridal sedan chair to enter the city of Guangzhou.

237. 起义中运输武器的少女罗谏（左）、罗四妹（右）。

Luo Jian (left) and Luo Simei (right) were the girls who transported weapons in the uprising.

238. 参加黄花岗起义的先锋队第三队队长莫纪彭（东莞人）。

Mo Jipeng (from Dongguan County), a team leader of No.3 vanguards participated in Yellow Flower Hill Uprising.

239. 镇压起义的清两广总督张鸣岐。

Zhang Mingqi, Guangdong and Guangxi Provinces governor general, who suppressed the uprising.

240. 镇压起义的清广东水师提督李准。

Li Zhun, commander of Guangdong navy division, who suppressed the uprising.

239

240

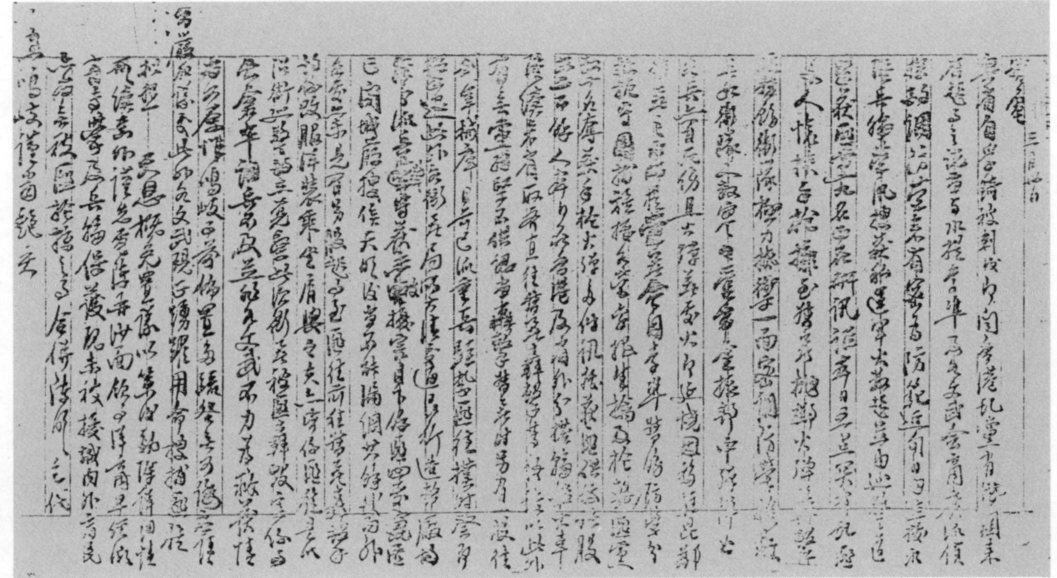

241

241. 1911年4月28日，两广总督张鸣岐向清廷报告黄兴等革命党人起义情形的电报。

The telegram sent on April 28, 1911, by governor general of Guangdong and Guangxi Provinces—Zhang Mingqi, reporting to Qing court about Huang Xing and other revolutionary partisans' uprising.

242. 由于敌我力量悬殊，黄花岗起义很快失败，大批革命党人被捕牺牲。是役战死者57人，被捕后就义者29人，共为86人。图为被捕的部分黄花岗起义义士。

Because of a great disparity in strength, Yellow Flower Hill Uprising failed quickly. A large number of revolutionary partisans were arrested and died: 57 people died in the battle, 29 died a martyr after arrest, 86 altogether. They are the martyrs arrested in Yellow Flower Hill Uprising.

▼ 242

▶ 243

243. 黄花岗起义战士惨遭清政府的血腥屠杀。图为黄花岗起义部分烈士忠骸。

The soldiers of Yellow Flower Hill Uprising massacred by Qing Government. These are parts of the martyr's bodies in Yellow Flower Hill Uprising.

▲ 244

244. 起义后英勇就义的南海籍安南机器工人罗遇坤（左）、嘉应籍教员饶辅廷（中）和南海籍越南华侨罗联（右）。

Luo Yukun (left), a worker from Nanhai County, Rao Futing(middle), a teacher from Jiaying County, Luo Lian (right, from Nanhai County), a Vietnamese overseas Chinese, who died a heroic death after the uprising.

245. 在起义中阵亡的南海籍南洋华侨余东雄（左）和增城籍南洋华侨郭继枚（右）。

Yu Dongxiong (left), an overseas Chinese from Nanhai County and Guo Jimei (right), an overseas Chinese from Zengcheng County, killed in action in uprising.

▲ 245

246. 起义前夕，余东雄、郭继枚写给怡保同志的绝命书。

The last letter written by Yu Dongxiong and Guo Jimei to his comrades in Ipoh before the uprising.

▼ 246

螺生 孝章 源水先生 暨列位同志鑒
啓者握別後安抵香江克強展堂伯先諸君均藉
會晤黨中健者集中香港東南洋所回同志均與焉
弟察同志熱誠大堪嘉敬惜舉動頗不秘密時南旋
黨人裴東咸穿黃白斜紋衣裳不啻表示洋客而且
三五不等結隊遊市計省港相隔一水吾人一舉一動
無不被奸探偵悉尤可慮者最近道路傳述非曰今
日攻城則云明宵破省風声鶴唳幾於草木皆兵致令
省垣商民遷港遷澳竄不盡恐慌形狀弟不過將種
種聞見錄述尊前非畏死亦非反對弟之生命早已
置諸度外林君時爽及閩省三數同志義腸俠膽
流露於談吐舉止間弟一見便崇拜不置異日奮身
殺賊當推為先鋒弟既屬克強君指揮無論如何猛
進一往向前誓無返顧倘目的能達與公等羊垣
握手或有其時否則敵眾我寡萬一失敗雖戰勝我
繼妹東雄二人或受千鋸百創手無寸鐵猶必奮臂
殺賊死而後已溫先烈生財之俠舉弟殊崇敬溫
公為國先死弟亦何敢偷生前仆後繼方顯吾黨
中大有人在視死如歸弟之素志但求馬革裹尸
以為榮耳從此或與先生長別此函請作最後之
永訣觀可也先生倘以弟言為可採以之留示吾
黨後起弟雖死猶生矣此頌
公安
弟 余東雄 郭繼枚 仝上言
叁月廿五日

▲ 247

▲ 248

▲ 249

247. 起义中阵亡的南海籍南洋机器工人杜凤书、黄鹤鸣，越南华侨陈才、游寿，南洋华侨周华（从上至下）。

Du Fengshu, Huang Heming(both from Nanhai County), workers of machinery in Southeast Asia; Chen Cai, You Shou, Vietnamese overseas Chinese; Zhou Hua(from upper to lower), overseas Chinese in Southeast Asia, killed in action during the uprising.

248. 起义后英勇牺牲的南海籍越南华侨陈春（上）、罗坤（中）、罗遇坤（下）。

Chen Chun(upper), Luo Kun(middle),Luo Yukun (lower), Vietnamese overseas Chinese from Nanhai County, died a heroic death after the uprising.

249. 起义后英勇就义的花县农民徐松根（上）、徐满凌（下）。

Xu Songgen(upper) and Xu Manling(lower), peasants from Huaxian County, died a heroic death after the uprising.

250

251

252

250. 起义中阵亡的花县农民徐日培。
Xu Ripei, a peasant from Huaxian County, killed in action during the uprising.

251. 起义中阵亡的开平籍《星洲晨报》记者劳培。
Lao Pei (from Kaiping County), a journalist of *Singapore Morning*, killed in action during the uprising.

252. 起义后英勇就义的开平籍南洋华侨李雁南。
Li Yannan (from Kaiping County), an overseas Chinese in Southeast Asia, died a heroic death after the uprising.

253

254

255

253. 起义中阵亡的番禺籍越南华侨马侣。
Ma Lü (from Panyu County), a Vietnamese overseas Chinese, killed in action during the uprising.

254. 起义后英勇就义的东莞籍香港《中国日报》经理李文甫。
Li Wenfu (from Dongguan County), manager of Hong Kong's *China Daily*, died a heroic death after the uprising.

255. 起义中阵亡的清远籍《星洲日报》印刷工人李文楷。
Li Wenkai (from Qingyuan County), a printer of *Singapore Daily*, killed in action during the uprising.

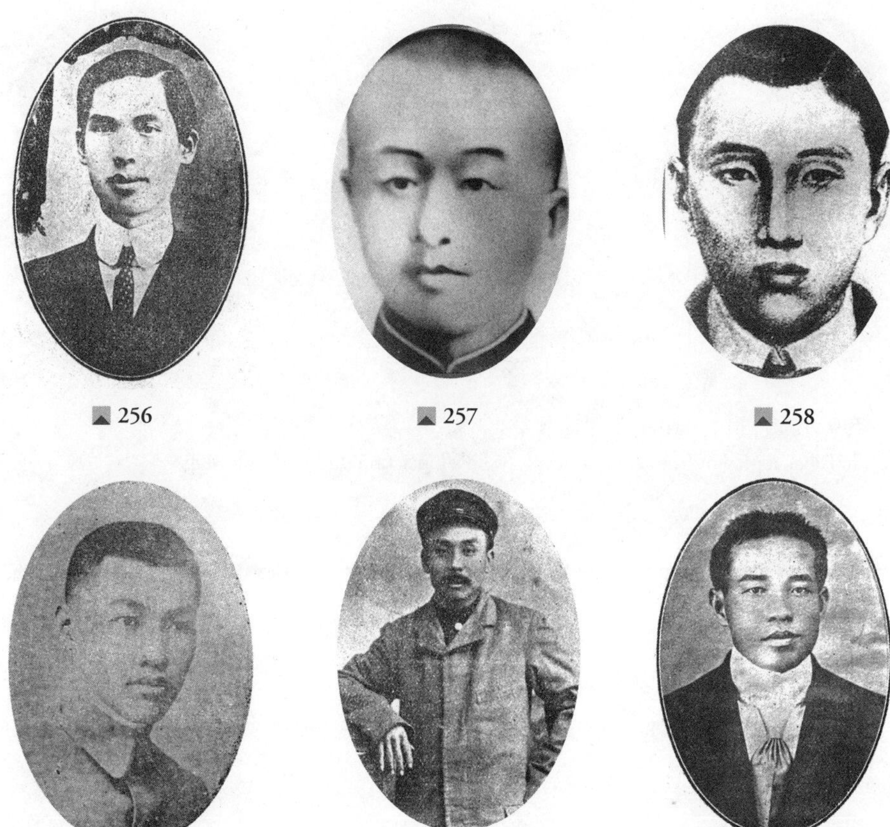

256 257 258

259 260 261

256. 起义后英勇就义的惠阳籍南洋教员罗仲霍。

Luo Zhonghuo (from Huiyang County), a teacher in Southeast Asia, died a heroic death after the uprising.

257. 起义中阵亡的海丰农民陈潮。

Chen Chao, a peasant from Haifeng County, killed in action during the uprising.

258. 起义后英勇就义的兴宁籍南洋华侨陈甫仁。

Chen Furen(from Xingning County), an overseas Chinese in Southeast Asia, died a heroic death after the uprising.

259. 起义中阵亡的蕉岭籍梅县松口公学教员林修明。

Lin Xiuming (from Jiaoling County), a teacher of Song Kou School in Meixian County, fell death in battle.

260. 起义中阵亡的大埔籍南洋华侨陈文褒。

Chen Wenbao (from Dabu County), an overseas Chinese in Southeast Asia, killed in action during the uprising.

261. 起义中阵亡的云浮籍南洋华侨李晚。

Li Wan (from Yunfu County), an overseas Chinese in Southeast Asia, killed in action during the uprising.

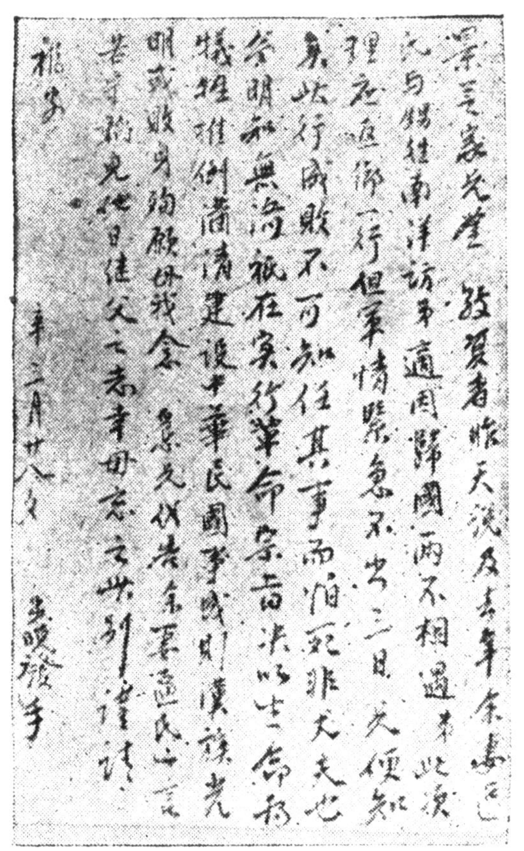

鏡兄家兄座 敬覆者 昨天談及去年余毒已
決與錫桂南洋訪弟 適因歸國 兩不相遇 弟此次
理應返鄉一行 但軍情緊急 不出二日 大便知
矣 此行成敗不可知 任其事而怕死 非丈夫也
余明知無濟 祇在實行革命宗旨 決以生命爲
犧牲 推倒滿清 建設中華民國 事成則漢族光
明 或敗身殉 願毋我念 惟兄代告余眾親友之言
若事敗 兄他日繼父之志 幸毋忘之 此別 謹請
福安
辛三月廿八夕 弟晚頓手

▲262

262. 起义前夕李晚烈士写给其兄的绝命书。

The last letter written by Li Wan, a martyr, to his elder brother on the eve of the uprising.

263. 起义中阵亡的封川籍南洋教士李炳辉。

Li Binghui (from Fengchuan County), a priest in Southeast Asia, killed in action during the uprising.

264. 起义后英勇就义的吴川籍新军士兵庞雄。

Pang Xiong (from Wuchuan County), soldier of New Army, died a heroic death after the uprising.

▲263

▲264

▲265

265. 起义中阵亡的福建籍日本留学生方声洞（上左）、南洋水师学校学生冯超骧（上中）、南台消防会会长刘钟群（上右）、日本大学学生林文（下左）、日本第一高等学校学生林尹民（下右）。

Fang Shengdong(upper left), a returned Chinese student from Japan, Feng Chaoxiang (upper middle), a student of navy school in Southeast Asia, Liu Zhongqun(upper right), president of Nantai Fire-Fighting Society, Lin Wen(lower left), a Japan University student, Lin Yinmin(lower right), a student of Japan No.1 High School. They all came from Fujian Province, killed in action during the

266. 起义后英勇就义的福建籍日本正则学校学生陈可钧、福建讲武堂学生刘锋烈、福建长门炮术学校毕业生陈更新、日本早稻田大学留学生陈与燊（从左至右）。

Chen Kejun, a student of Japan Seisoku School; Liu Fenglie, a student from Fujian Military School; Chen Gengxin, a graduate from Fujian Changmen Artillery School; Chen Yushen, a student of Japan Waseda University (from left to right). They all came from Fujian Praina, died a heroic death after the uprising.

266

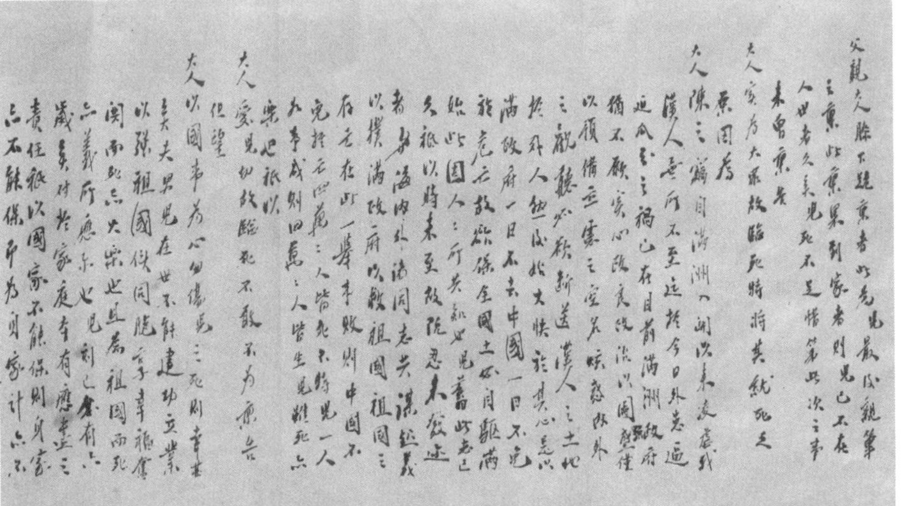

父親大人膝下：跪稟者，此為兒最後親筆之稟，此稟果到家者，則兒已不在人世者久矣。兒死不足惜，第此次之事未曾稟告
大人，實為大罪，故臨死時將其就死之原因為
大人陳之。竊自滿洲入關以來，凌虐我漢人無所不至，迨於今日，外患逼迫，瓜分之禍已在目前，滿洲政府猶不顧，實心改良政治，以圖強盛；僅以預備立憲之空名，惑內外之觀聽，必欲斷送漢人之土地於外人，然後始快其心。是以滿政府一日不去，中國一日不免於危亡，故欲保全國土，必自驅滿始，此固人人所共知也。兒蓄此志已久，祗以時未至，故隱忍未發。邇者與海內外諸同志共謀起義，以撲滿政府，以救祖國。祖國之存亡在此一舉，事敗則中國不免於亡，四萬萬人皆死，不特兒一人；如事成則四萬萬人皆生，兒雖死亦樂也。祗以
大人愛兒切，故臨死不敢不為稟告，但望
大人以國事為心，勿傷兒之死，則幸甚矣。夫男兒在世，不能建功立業，以強祖國，使同胞享幸福，奮鬥而死，亦大樂也，且為祖國而死，亦義所應爾也。兒刻已廿有六歲矣，對於家庭本有應盡之責任，祗以國家不能保，則身家亦不能保，即為身家計，亦不

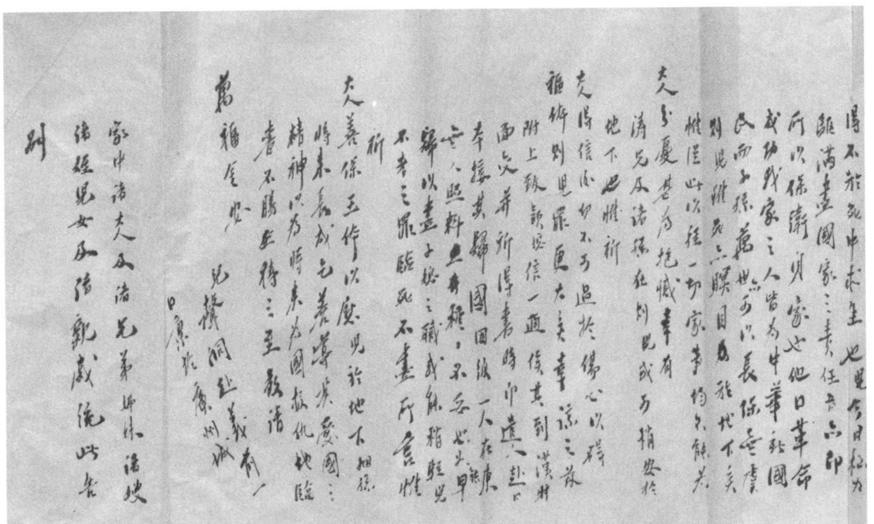

得不於死中求生也。兒今日極力驅滿，盡國家之責任，亦即所以保衛身家也。他日革命成功，我家之人皆為中華新國民，而子孫萬世亦可以長保無虞，則兒雖死亦瞑目矣。兒才不能侍奉
大人，惟從此以往，一切家事均不能為
大人分憂，甚為抱憾。幸有
滿兄及諸孫在側，兒或可稍安於地下。惟祈
大人得信後，切不可過於傷心，以傷
福體，則兒罪更大矣。幸諒之。茲附上致穎媖信一函，俟其到漢時面交。并祈本擬其歸國，因彼一人在東，無人照料，且有孕，不妥，兒早歸以盡子媳之職，或能稍贖兒不孝之罪。臨死不盡所言，惟祈
大人善保玉體，以慰兒於地下。賢媖將來長成，乞善導其愛國之精神，以為將來為國復仇也。臨書不勝悲痛之至。敬請
萬福金安

兒 聲洞 赴義前一日稟於廣州城

家中諸大人及諸兄弟姊妹諸嫂、諸姪兒女及諸親戚統此告
別

▲ 267

267. 起义前夕，方声洞写下的禀父书。

A letter written by Fang Shengdong to his father before the uprising.

268

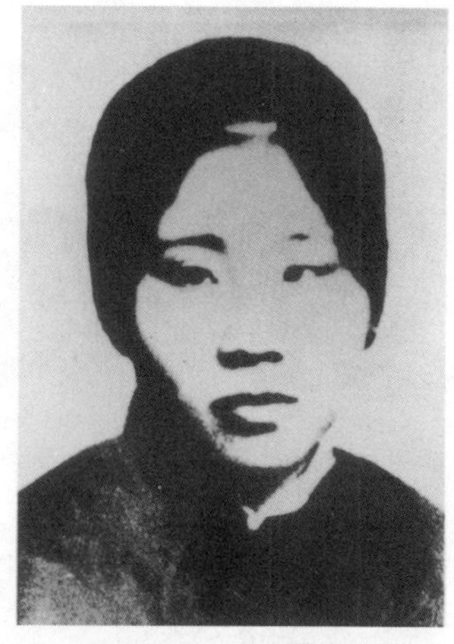

269

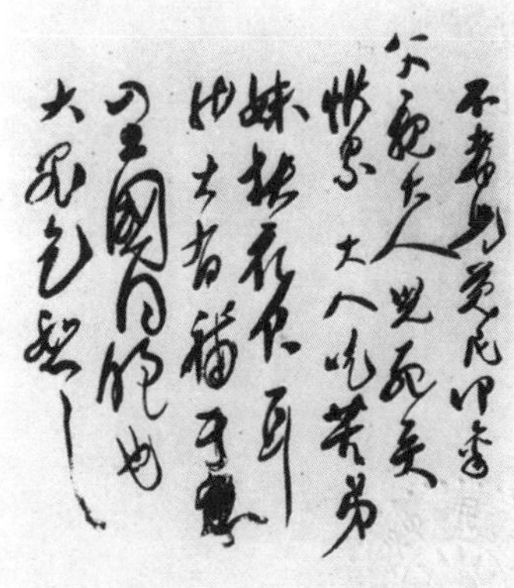

不孝儿觉民叩禀
父亲大人
儿死矣
惟累大人吃苦
弟妹缺衣食耳
然大有补于全国同胞也
大罪乞恕之

270

268. 起义后英勇就义的福建籍日本庆应大学学生林觉民。

Lin Juemin(from Fujian Province), a Japan Keiou University student, died a heroic death after the uprising.

269. 林觉民妻陈意映（福建闽县人）。

Chen Yiying, wife of Lin Juemin (from Min County in Fujian Province).

270. 林觉民写给父亲、妻子的诀别书。

The last farewell letters Lin Juemin wrote to his father and wife.

271. 起义后英勇就义的四川籍日本千叶医学校学生喻培伦（左）、四川陆军速成学校毕业生饶国梁（右）。

Yu Peilun (left),from Sichuan Province, a student of Japan Chiba Medical School, and Rao Guoliang(right), a graduate of Ground Force Accelerated School, Sichuan, died a heroic death after the uprising.

272

273

272. 起义中阵亡的四川籍新军军官秦炳。

Qin Bing (from Sichuan Province), an officer of New Army, killed in action during the uprising.

273. 起义中阵亡的安徽籍日本警监学校学生石德宽。

Shi Dekuan (from Anhui Province), a student of Japan police supervisal school, killed in action during the uprising.

274. 起义后英勇就义的安徽籍新军军官宋玉琳（左）、陆军小学教官程良（右）。

Song Yulin(left, from Anhui Province), an officer of New Army, Cheng Liang(right),a teacher of primary school of ground force,died a heroic death after the uprising.

274

275. 起义后英勇就义的广西籍新军军官韦云卿（左）、龙岸民团管带李德山（右）。

Wei Yunqing(left), an officer of New Army from Guangxi Province, and Li Deshan(right), a brigade commander of Long'an militia, died a heroic death after the uprising.

275

276

277

276. 参加起义的女同盟会会员徐宗汉（香山人）。起义失败后护送黄兴到香港，后与黄兴结为夫妻。

Xu Zonghan (from Xiangshan County), a woman member of the Chinese Revolutionary Alliance, who participated in the uprising, escorted Huang Xing to Hong Kong after failure and became a couple with Huang Xing later.

277. 与徐宗汉一起护送黄兴到香港的女同盟会会员、医师张竹君（番禺人）。

Zhang Zhujun (from Panyu County), a doctor and woman member of the Chinese Revolutionary Alliance, escorted Huang Xing to Hong Kong together with Xu Zonghan.

278. 黄花岗起义中的革命夫妻——潘达微和陈伟庄。他们不仅于起义前参与弹药运输工作，而且于起义失败后，冒死收殓72具烈士遗骸，安葬于黄花岗。

Pan Dawei and Chen Weizhuang, a revolutionary couple in Yellow Flower Hill Uprising. participated in ammunition transport work before the uprising. At the risk of life, they collected the remains of 72 martyrs in coffins, and buried them in Yellow Flower Hill after the failure.

起報　禮拜三　副張第壹頁

近說小事 五日風聲（著者世次郎）（三十）

先是黨人復分一隊於順德一方面。并欲起一路於梧州。若順德一路。則視事機何如。以爲行止。蓋羊垣各部苟已得手。則西上以窺梧州。不然。則率其黨羽以應羊城也。時有陸陵者。亦綠林巨魁。曾赴外洋。聞革命之說。欣然附從。且自悔其爲盜之非。乃欲率其黨羽。以從革黨之後。自謂能招集黨徒至千人。蓋順德黨爲盜藪。各立堂號。以收取行水。每堂或數百人。或數千人。各踞一處。以橫行鄉曲。而陸陵之意。則欲合集各堂以爲一隊。則聲勢必大也。果也。招集近千人。乃計其所自有之槍械若干。不足則僱運以資其應用。故順德一路之所運入者。槍枝爲少。彈子爲多。以槍枝多爲該處人所自有也。

查順德盜黨。最盛者爲大黃埔。而樂從附近次之。黨人即借樂從一帶爲駐點。以該處離佛山不遠。而赴城較易也。初黨人之至樂從也。先沿途向人叢中演說。皆言革命之理。土人多信之。不特不爲告發。且以彼爲捨身爲國也。頌之弗衰。設黨人亦與土人無忤。故運動益靈。中有練局焉。黨人向其主任者言曰。吾輩非爲盜劫而來。汝輩毋恐。但局中軍械。須爲吾等用矣。且汝輩勿驚。吾輩此次不論事之成敗。苟有禍患。惟自當之。斷不爲汝樂從禍也。復以此意告知坊人。始則坊人見黨人已至。盜黨亦同來。有閉門而避者。及黨人告慰之。并告以昔之盜徒。其至此亦改盜性而爲革命。不再搶掠也。不然則豈閉門所能避耶。因而坊人安之。絕有驚懼者焉。（仍未完）

俠義小說 義犬復仇（卅九）（劍士）

竊思此娘。君亦佔一分子。若李君長此沈迷。君與彼又形骸隔閡。何法將其勸止。我若聽其濫支濫用。即又無以對故友。若不聽其支用。君不定遭疏遠。處此數難。惜哉。吾故能發一言以取決之也。天乎。吾故友一生之銖積。竟喪於一婦人之手乎。蘇達聞語。若不省者。倔然臥睡椅上。兩目若開若合。恍如宮翁適當休息時。不暇招荅賓客形像。彼既穿人衣。又作此怪狀。蠢利幾乎忍俊不禁。意謂此犬知識亦不尋。與語無益於事。初欲坐待李回。詎時已入黑。猶未返。枵腹雷鳴。勢不可復留此。心內尋思一會。連連歎氣。時又作恨恨聲。卒乃懷中取出記事冊。撕去一紙。以鉛筆作數行短札。壓於桌上。其示意蘇達曰。吾今者店戶有事。不暇候李君回寓。留此一札。請汝代達之。即起以巾拂拭其帽。出門立定。略一躊躇。俯首緩步向東而去。蠢去未久。而此怪形之蘇達亦外出。（仍未完）

279. 1911年5月份起，广州《南越报》连载黄世仲撰写的《五日风声》，记述黄花岗起义的过程，为中国最早的报告文学作品。

From May 1911, *South China Paper* serialized *Five Day's Storm and Thunder* written by Huang Shizhong about the course of Yellow Flower Hill Uprising, which was China's earliest literary reportage.

280. 在同盟会组织武装起义的同时，部分同盟会会员也将暗杀清朝大吏作为一项重要的斗争手段。1907年6月11日，同盟会会员刘师复为谋炸广东水师提督李准，在广州旧仓巷凤翔书院装配炸弹，不慎炸弹突然爆炸，刘左手及面部受伤。刘被岗警捕获后判解回原籍香山县监押。图为刘师复（香山人）。

While organizing the armed uprising, some members of the Chinese Revolutionary Alliance, regarded it as an important means of struggle to assassinate the high-ranking officials, too. On June 11, 1907, Liu Shifu, member the Chinese Revolutionary Alliance, planned to bomb Li Zhun, the Guangdong Navy Commander. While assembling a bomb in Fengxiang Academy, at Jiucang Lane, Guangzhou, the bomb was unexpectedly exploded. His face and left hand were injured. He was arrested by policeman on duty and sentenced to imprisonment in the native place—Xiangshan County. The picture is Liu Shifu.

281. 1911年4月8日，嘉应籍南洋霹雳埠同盟会会员温生才在广州东门外开枪击毙副都统兼署广州将军孚琦，在逃避途中被捕；4月15日从容就义。图为就义前的温生才。

On April 8,1911, Wen Shengcai (from Jiaying County), a member of the Chinese Revolutionary Alliance in Southeast Asia, shot Fu Qi, Guangzhou general, outside East Gate of Guangzhou and was arrested while escaping. On April 15, he died a martyr calmly. The picture is Wen Shengcai before dying a martyr.

▼ 280

▼ 281

孝章
源水 三志兄鉴 弟别後返省城在朋
螺生
友处暂住想欲先寻头路棲身
然後緩图心事看满贱种太无
人道恨火焚心時刻不能忍自從
徐汪二君事失敗後繼起無人
弟思欲步二君後塵回手無
寸鐵亦無鬼炮莫奈何暫忍
能得手有鬼炮時一定有好
戲看 弟心已決死之日即生
之年從此永别矣望 君等
尽力進行達目的而後止勿學
我温某誤事有头無尾也
順請
侠安
弟温生才顿手
温生才吉東

▲ 282

282. 1911年3月底，温生才写给南洋同志李孝章、李源水、郑螺生的绝命书。

The last letter written by Wen Shengcai, to Li Xiaozhang, Li Yuanshui, Zheng Luosheng, his comrades in Southeast Asia at the end of March 1911.

▲ 283

283. 清副都统兼署广州将军孚琦。
Fu Qi, Guangzhou general.

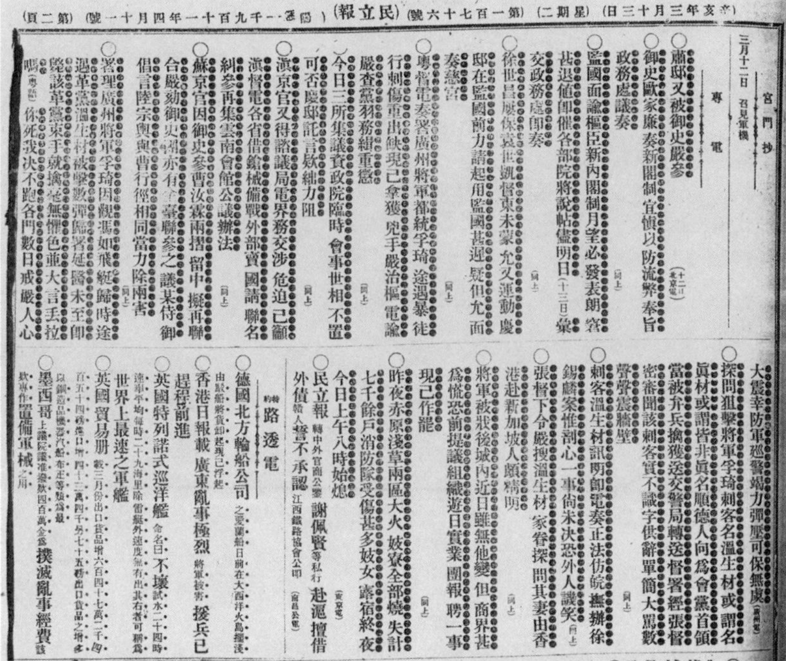

辛亥年三月十三日（星期二）（第一百七十六號）（民立報）（陽曆一千九百十一年四月十一號）（第二頁）

宮門抄

三月十二日 召見軍機

專電

○肅邸又被御史嚴參（十二日北京電）

○御史歐家廉奏新閣制宜慎以防流弊奉旨政務處議奏（同上）

○監國面諭樞臣新內閣制月望必發表朗窰甚退值即催各部院將說帖儘明日（十三日）彙交政務處即奏（同上）

○徐世昌屢保袁世凱督東未蒙允又運動慶邸在監國前力請起用監國甚遲疑但允面奏慈宮（同上）

○粵督電奏署廣州將軍都統孚琦途遇暴徒行刺傷重出缺現已拿獲兇手嚴治樞電諭嚴查黨羽務緝重懲（同上）

○今日三所集議資政院臨時會事世相不置可否慶邸託言欵絀力阻（同上）

○滇京官又得諮議局電界務交涉危迫已籲滇督電各省借鎗械備戰外部實國請聯名糾參再集雲南會館公議辦法（同上）

○蘇京官因御史參曹汝霖兩摺留中擬再聯合嚴劾御史溫肅亦有全臺聯參之議某侍御倡言陸宗輿與曹行徑相同當力除兩害（同上）

○署理廣州將軍孚琦因觀馮如飛艇歸時途過革黨溫生材被擊數彈臨署延醫未至即斃該革黨束手就擒毫無懼色並大言丟拉嗎（粵語）你死我決不跑各門數日戒嚴人心大震幸防軍巡警竭力彈壓可保無虞（廣州電）

○探問狙擊將軍孚琦刺客名溫生材或謂名眞材或謂皆非眞名順德人向爲會黨首領當被弁兵擒獲送交警局轉送督署經張督密審聞該刺客實不識字供辭單簡大罵數聲聲震牆壁（同上）

○刺客溫生材訊明即電奏正法仿皖撫辦徐錫麟案惟剖心一事尚未決恐外人譏笑（同上）

○張督下令嚴搜溫生材家眷探問其妻由香港赴新加坡人頗精明（同上）

○將軍被戕後城內近日雖無他變但商界甚爲慌恐前提議組織遊日實業團報聘一事現已作罷（同上）

○昨夜赤原淺草兩區大火妓寮全部燒失計七千餘戶消防隊受傷甚多妓女露宿終夜今日上午八時始熄（東京電）

○民立報轉中外官商公鑒謝佩賢等私行赴滬擅借外債贛人誓不承認 江西鐵路協會公叩（南昌公電）

路透電 特約

○德國北方輪船公司之愛蘭船日前在大西洋火島擱淺由該船將貨卸起現已浮起

○香港日報載廣東亂事極烈將軍被害援兵已趕程前進

○英國特列諾式巡洋艦命名曰不壞試水二十四時速率平均每時二十九海里除雷艇外速度無有出其右者可稱爲世界上最速之軍艦

○英國貿易册載三月份出口貨品增六百四十七萬二千四百五十四磅進口增四十二萬四千另七十五磅出口貨品之增多以鋼造品機器汽船布疋等類爲最

○墨西哥上議院議准發款四百萬金磅撲滅亂事經費該款專作置備軍械之用

▼284

284. 1911年4月11日《民立报》刊登温生才刺杀孚琦的消息。

The news that Wen Shengcai assassinated Fu Qi, published in *Minlibao* on April 11, 1911.

▲285

285. 1911年8月3日，同盟会会员、支那暗杀团成员陈敬岳（嘉应人）、林冠慈（归善人）在广州双门底炸伤广东水师提督李准。林冠慈当场牺牲，陈敬岳在逃避途中被捕，11月7日英勇就义。图为林冠慈。

On August 3,1911, Chen Jingyue (from Jiaying County) and Lin Guanci (from Guishan County), both members of the Chinese Revolutionary Alliance and members of Indo-China assassinating regiment bombed and wounded Li Zhun, Guangdong Navy Commander, at Shuangmendi, Guangzhou. Lin Guanci died on the spot and Chen Jingyue was arrested while escaping. On November 7, he died a heroic death. The picture is Lin Guanci.

286

286. 被捕后的陈敬岳。

Chen Jingyue, after arrested.

287. 陈敬岳写给李孝章的绝命书。

The last letter Chen Jingyue wrote to Li Xiaozhang.

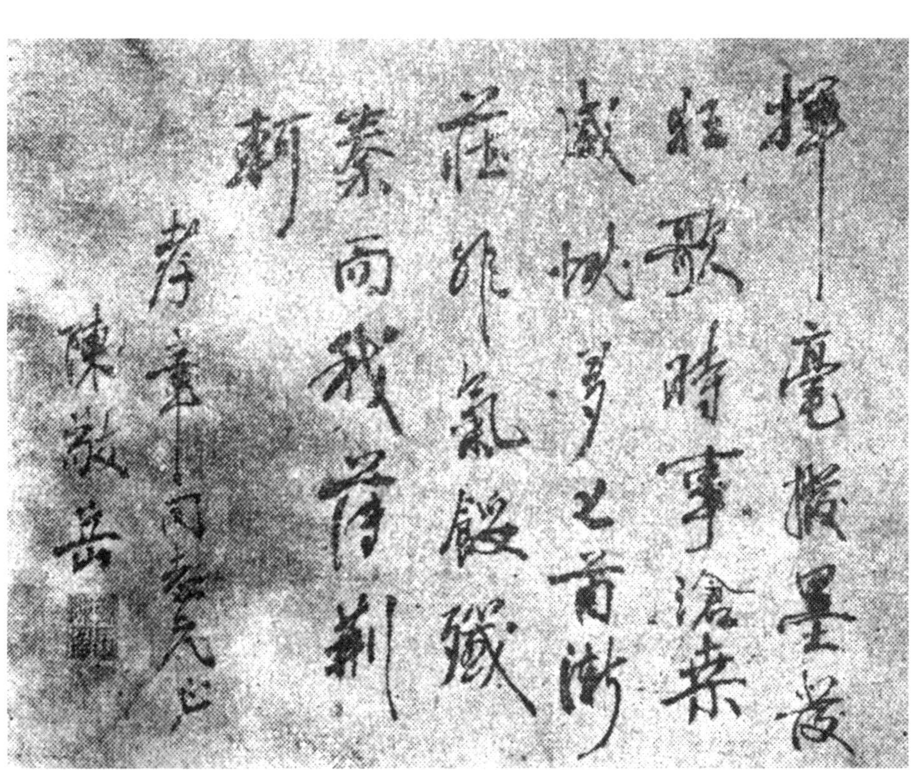

287

▲ 288

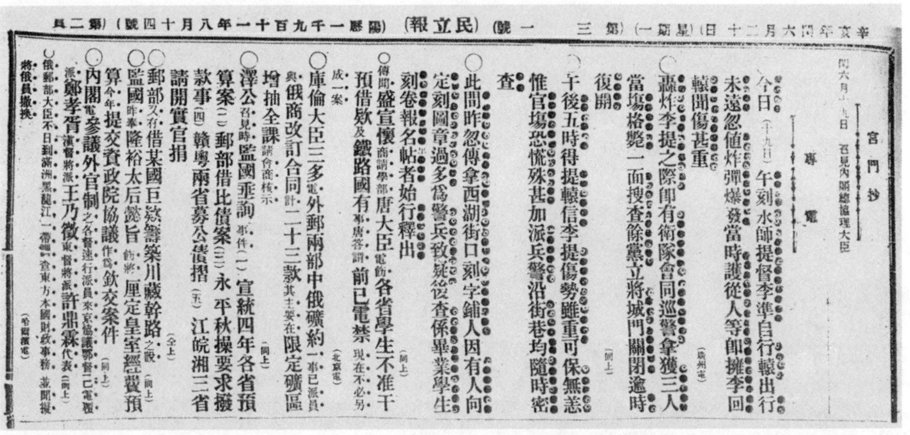

辛亥年閏六月二十日（星期一）第三 一號（民立報）（陽歷一千九百十一年八月十四號）第二頁

宮門抄

閏六月十九日 召見內閣總協理大臣

專電

今日（十九日）午刻水師提督李準自行轅出行，未遠忽值炸彈爆發，當時護從人等即擁李回轅，聞傷甚重。（廣州電）

轟炸李提之際，即有衛隊會同巡警拿獲三人，當場格斃一，面搜查餘黨，立將城門關閉，逾時復開。（同上）

午後五時得提轅信，李提傷勢雖重，可保無恙，惟官場恐慌殊甚，加派兵警沿街巷均隨時密查。

此間昨忽傳拿西湖街口刻字鋪人，因有人向定刻圖章過多，為警兵致疑，後查係畢業學生刻卷報名帖者，始行釋出。（同上）

傳聞盛宣懷商請學部唐大臣電飭各省學生不准干預借欵及鐵路國有事，唐答謂前已電禁，現在不必另成一案。（北京電）

庫倫大臣三多電外郵兩部，中俄礦約一事已派員與俄商改訂合同，計二十三款，其主要在限定礦區增抽全課，請會商核示。（同上）

澤公召見時，監國垂詢事件：（一）宣統四年各省預算案，（二）郵部借比債案，（三）永平秋操要求撥款事，（四）贛粵兩省募公債摺，（五）江皖湘三省請開實官捐。（同上）

郵部又有借某國巨欵籌築川藏幹路之說。（全上）

監國昨奉隆裕太后懿旨，飭將釐定皇室經費預算，今年提交資政院協議，作為欽交案件。（同上）

內閣電參議外官制之各督速行派員來京協議，鄂督已電派鄭孝胥，滇督將派王乃徵，東督將派許鼎霖代表。（同上）

俄郵部大臣不日到滿洲黑龍江一帶，查東方本國財政事務，並聞擬將俄員撤換。（哈爾濱電）

▲ 289

288. 两广总督张鸣岐关于清水师提督李准被刺及革命党人陈敬岳被镇压情形致内阁海陆军部的代奏电。

The telegram sent by Zhang Mingqi, governor general of Guangdong and Guangxi Provinces, to Ministry of Army and Navy in cabinet, about how Li Zhun, provincial navy commander was assassinated and Chen Jingyue, a revolutionary partisan, was executed.

289. 1911年8月14日上海《民立报》刊登陈敬岳、林冠慈谋刺李准的消息。

On August 14,1911, *Minlibao* published news that Chen Jingyue and Lin Guanci assassinated Li Zhun.

▲290

290. 1911年10月25日，支那暗杀团成员李沛基在广州南门炸死新任广州将军凤山，事成后从容脱险到香港。图为李沛基（番禺人）。

On October 25, 1911, Li Peiji, a member of Indo-China assassinating regiment, in south gate blasted the newly-appointed general of Guangzhou Fengshan to death. After that, he escaped from danger to Hong Kong. This is Li Peiji (from Panyu County).

291

291. 清广州将军凤山。

Fengshan, a Guzngzhou general of Qing Dynasty.

292. 凤山被炸现场。

The spot site where Fengshan was blasted to dead.

293. 1911年10月31日上海《民立报》刊载的《凤山被诛记》，详记凤山被炸情形。

On October 31, 1911, Shanghai's *Minlibao* published *Fengshan Put to Death* relating the detailed course about how Fengshan was blasted to dead.

294. 1911年5月3日，孙中山在美国芝加哥召集会议，商讨广州起义失败后的善后及再图大举等问题。图为孙中山和与会同志合影。

Sun Yat-sen called a meeting in Chicago, USA on May 3, 1911, to deal with matters after the failure of Guangzhou Uprising and to issue of actions on a large scale. It is a picture of Sun Yat-sen with others on the meeting.

 292

▲滿莛被封 臨時警察傳辦處近查得滿人札某寶某裕某三家產業。約可值數十萬金。派員調查發封充公。諸云多藏厚亡。不信然歟。

▲滿人肆虐 蘄昌三十日派馬隊兵二十名至黃陂縣署。勒令助米五百石洋五百元。並出僞示一道煽惑愚民。縣令曹元鼎因兵力單薄。莫敢與抗。特飭[illegible]商會。商會即與馬隊爲難。馬隊云爾等若不助餉。即送爾等歸[illegible]頭之國。後經職商劉鼎芬等籌辦米二百石洋二百元。含糊了事。是亦出於不得已也。

▲節婦助捐 有節婦胡氏。家道小康。稍有蓄積。在都督府前願報効千金。以助軍餉。噫婦人尙知大義。人民復漢之心可見矣。

▲木商捐助 漢陽鸚鵡洲五府十八幫木商邀集至兩湖公所會議。以鄂軍起義。秋毫不犯。保護商民不遺餘力。議定共捐軍餉三十萬。俟收迄即稟呈軍政府繳納云。

▲駐軍橋口 黎都督飭軍隊將橋口一帶棚戶盡行折毀。即派軍在該處駐紮。防範北軍由襄河襲入之虞。

▲英雄新面目 孫君武。初名葆仁。字堯卿。亦字搖清。此次義舉之主動力也。數年來秘密運動。多方經營。鄂省軍隊始有革命思想之傳播。八月十八日午下一句鐘。在俄租界寶善里第十四號裝自製炸彈。因管心有未淨之磺強[illegible]與炸藥[illegible]登時爆烈。君面部及兩手均受重傷。當由同志數人送至口口醫院調養。君於途[illegible]同志諸人曰。傷勢絕無大危險。但此處機關既破。同志之被逮捕者必多。轉相株連。漢族將無噍類矣。非火速舉事不可。當即擬十八夜暾爲號。嗣滿人稍知風聲。是夜防備最嚴。各營同志皆未敢動。反至小朝街八十五號逮余及同志多人。君於病中聞之。大叫氣絕。十九日不顧病勢。規畫一切。命人赴各標營傳達命令。謂無論如何。皆宜作破釜沉舟之計。寧可玉碎。勿圖瓦全。十九夜所以能克復武昌。驅走僞督。固由我軍舉同志熱心毅力。勇往直前所致。而得力於君之平時結以德義。臨時授以方略。究屬不少也。迨二十後大局既定。君之傷部亦因過勞而增劇。同志多人恐再加勞瘁。傷勢必難驟好。婉言勸其靜養。請暫勿勞心。軍事近日由醫士蝦力醫治。漸就痊愈。[illegible]各傷有小部未從[illegible]瞿耳。前日(初一)同志以日來軍事方面需君勞畫者甚夥。已由漢口接回武昌。駐都督府附近。以便籌商一切。所有面部瘡痂均皆脫去。換出一副新面目。同志與都督商議。已公推爲軍務部部長。不日即可履新。新中華之新人物。宜乎有此新面目。以振新舊日河山也。

◉鳳山被誅記

▲東三區稟報 昨奉憲台電論。本月初四日將軍憲由天字馬頭上船。即令妥爲保護等因。當經遵照辦理。並電請撥派特務巡警暨教練所學生赴區調遣在案。乃初四早八點一十五分鐘。軍憲由寶璧兵輪登岸。行至倉前直街。突有一人在廣興草席店南生鐘錶店附近瓦面。猛將炸彈擲下。轟然一聲。區官督同長警排列將軍衛隊之[illegible]聞聲立即回頭搜尋。其地正與區所距離不遠。除由區官飭令長警飛登瓦面跟追。當時[illegible]匪徒一人由瓦面縱身跌下。正在搜尋餘黨之際。其廣興店已因被炸起火延燒。火勢猛烈。與常居民均惶恐奔走。餘匪遂得以乘機雜集逃逸。未能悉數擒拿。是役旗營衛隊新軍及隨從人等受傷者一十五人。已由區所分別送往拾字會醫院等處醫治。並在火場瓦礫之內挖起尸身二十六具。內有一具係在爛碎綠呢大轎之旁。身穿行裝。腰束腰帶。并有鼻烟壺等件。面貌焦黑。四肢不全。惟察其情形。似係鳳將軍憲。其由瓦面跌落之匪亦已燒得焦頭爛額。辨認不清。計鋪戶共燒去六間。折毀二間。至九點五十分鐘。始行漸漸撲滅。[illegible]聞軍憲之夫人乘輿在後。聞變不敢進前。行即由游擊隊巡官梁永存帶同長警護送至水師公所暫駐。事後檢得旗兵所遺無煙槍三桿。並飭管五檢驗匪徒者。保甲班巡長嚴北願三級巡警梁昌張雄安三名。至用去槍子若干及傷斃之人是何姓名。容後再行詳報。除拾得槍枝另文稟解外。所有鳳將軍憲被炸大概情形。理合稟陳。區官事前防範未周。實難辭咎。應如何懲處之處。伏候憲裁。

▲保安營審訊 是役據區官稟報。則云槍斃兇手一人。惟現在尙不知姓名。且死者身中亦未有還兇確據。而又謂當場拿獲三人。即押交李世桂之保安營審訊。惟此人傷得太重。不能言語。經李總[illegible]屢次審[illegible]欲知其姓氏亦不可得。現由紅十字會醫治。俟醫愈後方能再審云。則是眞兇[illegible]否。今尙未悉也。

◉革命聲中之京報

京報有關時事者。轉載如下。

▲西安兵變。其協統某逃至潼關。有電到京云。西安城門已閉。惟有一門可以出入。並有革黨守之。城中官吏存亡莫卜。

▲廣西巡撫沈秉堃電告政府。革黨所宣布之檄文。湖南都督爲焦姓。

▲聞成都現已爲革黨所據。趙督被戕。並聞趙督因下命屠城。該處人民憤極。奔赴新津雙流。與虜黨人會集。久不應消。成都倡亂舊兵與新軍均與黨人聯絡大舉。成都以陷。

▲又端方所帶赴川之兵中途生變。端方帶數人逃遁。

▲[illegible]

蔡廷幹[illegible]

▲又聞通永道近亦有電致民政部。謂通州一帶發見定期起事匿名揭帖。民部即飭內外兩廳嚴密防範。現總廳已於各站崗添派警弁。並飭每夜不准脫衣就寢云。

▲此次北兵南下。異常匆促。鋪帳等件或尙須趕造。或久已[illegible]敗。或不及備帶。兵士十卅有在車上住宿。不可以致與車守時有爭論。

▲前軍十有將軍守綱禁南段。有一二站人員紛紛逃避。京漢路局諸事[illegible]

293

294

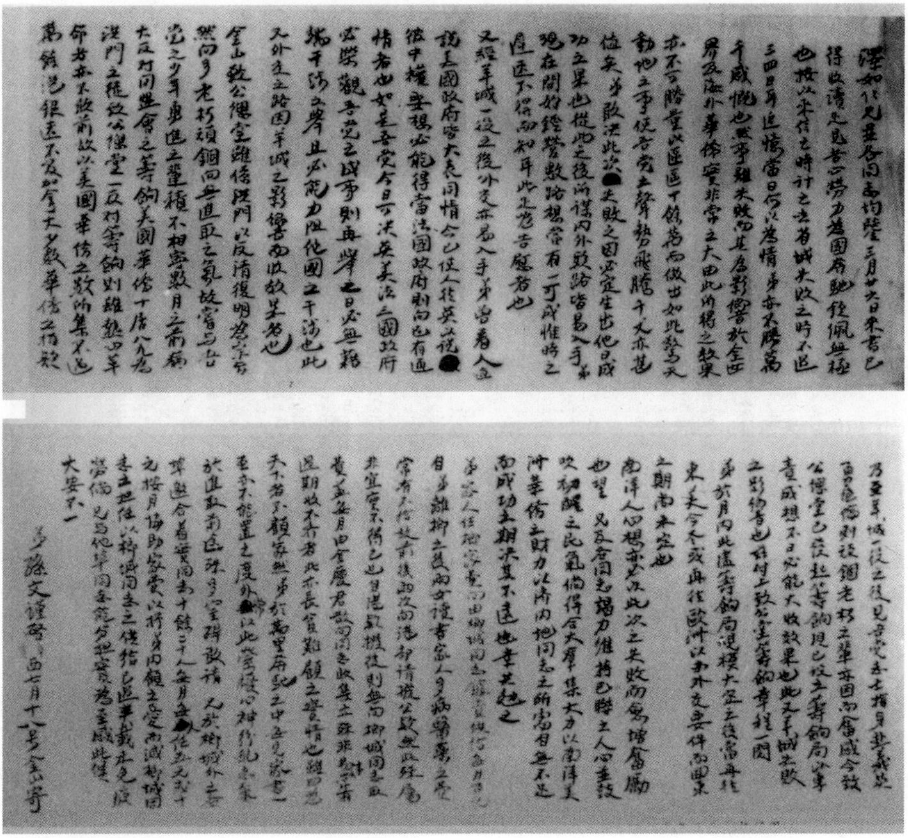

295

295. 1911年7月18日，孙中山复邓泽如函，告广州起义已产生巨大影响，并促筹款支援国内图谋再起。

A letter from Sun Yat-sen to Deng Zeru on July 18, 1911, answering that Guangzhou Uprising had brought huge influence, and urging fundraising to support launching domestic actions.

296. 1911年5月，清政府借“铁路国有”的名义，强行把商办粤汉、川汉铁路的主权出卖给帝国主义国家，激起粤、湘、鄂、川四省人民的反对，掀起了保路运动。图为1911年6月12日上海《民立报》刊登广东粤汉铁路公司举行股东大会。

In May 1911, in the name of nationalization of railways, Qing Government sold to the imperialist countries by force the sovereignty of Guangdong-Hankou Railway and Sichuan-Hankou Railway run by Chinese traders, which evoked opposition of the people of Guangdong, Hunan, Hubei, Sichuan Provinces. They started the movement to protect the railway. On June 12, 1911, Shanghai's *Minlibao* published the report that Guangdong-Hankou Railway Company hold shareholder's meeting to protest Qing Government's policy of railway nationalization.

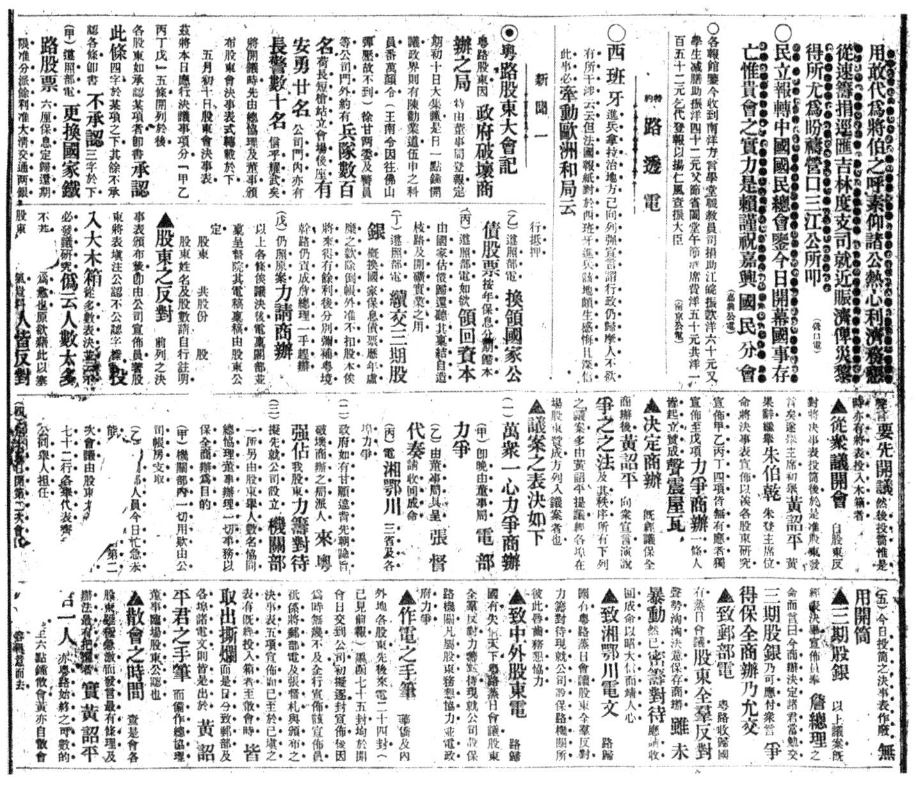

用敢代為將伯之呼素仰諸公熱心利濟務懇從速籌捐逕匯吉林度支司就近賑濟俾災黎得所尤為盼禱營口三江公所叩（營口電）

○民立報轉中國國民總會鑒今日開幕國事存亡惟貴會之實力是賴謹祝嘉興國民分會（嘉興公電）

○各報館鑒今收到南洋方言學堂職教員司捐助江皖振款洋六十元又學生減膳助振洋四十二元又節省圖堂午節酒席費洋五十元共洋一百五十二元乞代登報以揚仁風查振大臣（南京公電）

特約路透電

○西班牙進兵拿拉治地方已向列強宣言謂行政仍歸摩人不欲有所干涉云云但法國報紙對於西班牙進兵該地頗生感悔且深信此事必牽動歐洲和局云

新聞一

◉粵路股東大會記

粵路股東因政府破壞商辦之局　特由董事局登報定期初十日大集議是日一點鐘開議政界則有陳勸業道伍中之科員番禺顧令（王南令因往佛山彈壓故不到）徐廿兩委及警員等公司門外約有兵隊數百名荷長短槍站立會場後座有安勇廿名公司門內亦有長警數十名　儼乎耀武矣　將開議時先由總協理及董事預布股東會決事表式轉載於下

五月初十日股東會決事表

茲將本日應行決議事項分「甲乙丙丁戊」五條開列於後　各股東如承認某項者即書承認四字於某項之下其餘不承認各條即書不承認三字於下

(甲)遵照部電更換國家鐵路股票　六厘保息定歸還期限准分派餘利准大清交通兩銀行抵押

(乙)遵照部電換領國家公債股票按年保息分期償本

(丙)遵照部電如欲領回資本由國家估價歸還聽其棄結自造枝路及開礦實業之用

(丁)遵照部電繳交三期股銀　概換國家保息債票應年應[illegible]之欵除倒帳外准不扣股本俟將來得有餘利後分別彌補粵境幹路仍責成舟總理一手經辦

(戊)仍照原案力請商辦

以上各條俟議決後電稟關部並稟呈督院其電稿稟稿由股東公定

股東　共股份　股

股東姓名及股數請自行註明

▲股東之反對　前列之決事表須布發即由公司宣佈員奮股東將表填注公認不公認字樣投入大木箱從多數表決[illegible]必發議研究偽云人數太多[illegible]焉愈也原欵辦此以塞[illegible]股東氣量料人皆反對

發言要先開議然後投簡惟是時亦有將表投入木箱者

▲從衆議開會　自股東反對將決事表投簡後於是准股東發言矣遂舉主席初衆舉黃詔平　黃果辭遂舉朱伯乾　朱登主席位命將決事表宣佈以俟各股東研究宣佈甲乙丙丁四項皆無有應者獨宣佈至戊項力爭商辦一條人皆起立贊成聲震屋瓦

▲決定商辦　既經議保全商辦後黃詔平　向衆宣言演說爭之之法及其秩序所有下列之議案多由黃詔平提議邦各埠在場股東贊成方列入議案者也

▲議案之表決如下

(一)萬衆一心力爭商辦

(甲)即晚由董事局電部力爭

(乙)由董事局具呈張督代奏請收回成命

(丙)電湘鄂川三省及各埠力爭

(二)政府如有甘願違背先朝諭旨破壞商辦之局派人來粵強佔我股東力籌對待

(三)擬先就公司設立機關部一所另由股東舉人數名協同總協理董事辦理一切事務以保全商辦為目的

(甲)機關部內一切用欵由公司帳房支取

(乙)[illegible]部人員今日忙急未能[illegible]第二次會議由股東[illegible]七十二行各舉代表齊[illegible]公同衆人担任

(四)[illegible]開第二次會[illegible]

(五)今日投簡之決事表作廢無用開筒

▲三期股銀　以上議案既經衆決舉宣佈員奉詹總理之命而宣曰今爾辦決定諸君當勉交三期股銀乃可應付衆管爭得保全商辦乃允交

▲致郵部電　粵路收歸國有蒸日會議股東全羣反對聲勢洶洶決意保存商辦雖未暴動然已密籌對待應請收回成命以昭大信而靖人心

▲致湘鄂川電文　路歸國有蒸日會議股東全羣反對力籌對待現就公司為保路機關所彼此唇齒務懇協力

▲致中外股東電　路歸國有失信天下粵路蒸日會議股東全羣反對力籌對待現就公司設保路機關凡屬股東務懇協力並電政府力爭

▲作電之手筆　華僑及內外地各股東先後來電二十四封（已見前報）黑函七十五封均於開會日交到公司初擬遂封宣佈後因為時無幾不及全行宣佈該宣佈員祇係將郵部電及張督札與預布之決事表五項宣佈已至於已壞之表有既經投入箱者至散會時皆取出撕爛　而是日分致郵部及各埠諸電文則皆是出於黃詔平君之手筆　而備作總協理董事臨場股東公認也

▲散會之時間　查是會各股東雖極憤激而發言最有條理及辦法最有把握者實黃詔平一人　亦粵路始終之可數的[illegible]六點鐘散會黃亦自散會[illegible]而去

296

297

297. 揭露清政府出卖国家主权和外国列强掠夺中国铁路的漫画。

The caricature which disclosed Qing Government sold national sovereignty and foreign powers robbed China of railway.

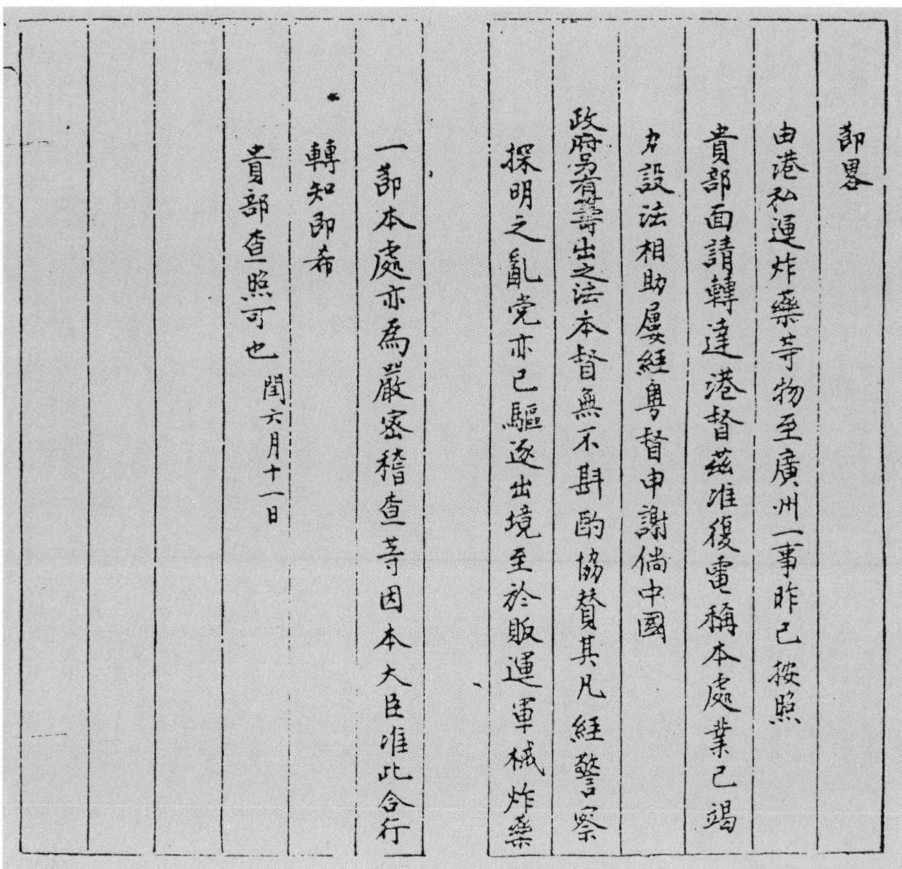

部畧
由港私運炸藥等物至廣州一事昨已按照
貴部函請轉達港督茲准復電稱本處業已竭
力設法相助屢經粵督申謝倘中國
政府另有籌出之法本督無不斟酌協贊其凡經警察
探明之亂党亦已驅逐出境至於販運軍械炸藥
一節本處亦為嚴密稽查等因本大臣准此合行
轉知即希
貴部查照可也　閏六月十一日

298

298. 英国香港当局长期阻挠革命党人在香港的革命活动。图为1911年8月5日英国大使朱尔典给清廷外务部的文书。

The British Hong Kong authorities had prevented revolutionary partisan's revolutionary activity in Hong Kong for a long time. On August 5, 1911, the British ambassador John N.Jordan presented document to Ministry of Foreign Affairs of Qing Dynasty.

299. 广州黄花岗起义和川、粤、湘、鄂等省的保路运动，激起了资产阶级民主革命潮流的高涨。1911年10月10日晚，湖北革命党人在武昌发动起义，血战一夜，占领武昌。10月11日，组建了第一个资产阶级革命政权——中华民国湖北军政府。图为革命军把起义旗帜插在占领的湖北咨议局门前。

Yellow Flower Hill Uprising and the movement to protect the railways in Sichuan, Guangdong, Hunan and Hubei Provinces aroused the upsurge of bourgeois revolutionary trend. On October 10,1911, the revolutionary partisans in Hubei launched the Wuchang Uprising, fought the sanguinary battle one night, captured Wuchang. On October 11, the first bourgeois revolution regime—Hubei Military Government of the Republic of China was set up. In the photo the revolutionary armymen hang the uprising flags in front of Hubei Consultation Office.

299

公啓者：

武昌已於本月十九日光復，義聲所播，國人莫不額手相慶，而虜運行將告終。本會謹擇於二十四日開預祝中華民國成立大會，仰各界僑胞屆期踴躍齊臨慶祝，以壯聲威，有厚望焉。

此佈。

天運辛亥年八月二十二日

芝加古同盟會啓

300

300. 1911年10月12日，孙中山在美国科罗拉多州丹佛城获悉武昌光复的消息，并启程赴纽约，10月13日抵达芝加哥。这是他为芝加哥同盟会代拟的召开预祝中华民国成立大会的通告。

On October 12, 1911, Sun Yat-sen received the message of Wuchang's restoration in Denver City, Colorado, USA. He started a journey to New York and arrived in Chicago on October 13. It is an announcement Sun Yat-sen drafted out for the Chinese Revolutionary Alliance Chicago, which would hold a meeting to congratulate beforehand the founding of the Republic of China.

301. 武昌起义后，孙中山赴欧洲，为建立民国进行外交活动。1911年12月21日，孙中山自欧洲归国途中，在香港船上与日本友人山田纯三郎的合影。

After Wuchang Uprising, Sun Yat-sen went to Europe to develop diplomatic activities for the fourding of Republic of China. Sun Yat-sen took a picture on board in Hong Kong with Japanese friend Yamada Junzaburo on his homecoming way from Europe on December 21, 1911.

301

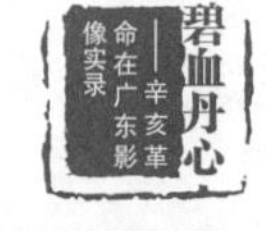

302

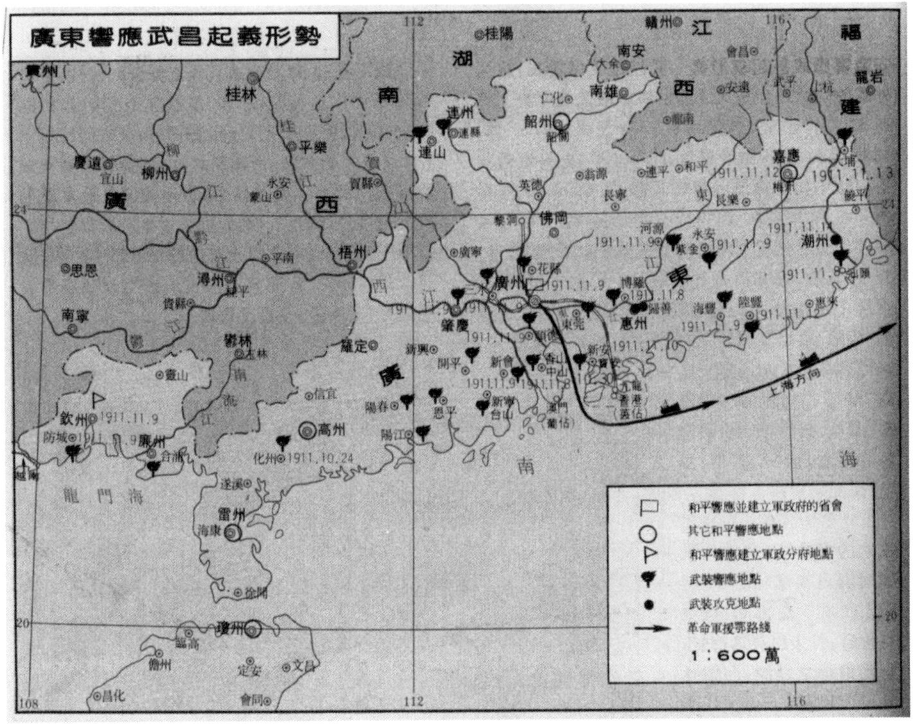

303

302. 1911年12月21日，孙中山自欧洲归国途经香港时，在船上与欢迎者合影。前排左起：荷马李、山田纯三郎、胡汉民、孙中山、陈少白、何天炯；第二排右起廖仲恺、第六为宫崎寅藏。同年12月25日，孙中山返抵上海。

A picture Sun Yat-sen with gladhanders on board in Hong Kong on his homecoming way on December 21, 1911. The front row from left: Homer Lea, Yamada Junzaburo, Hu Hanmin, Sun Yat-sen, Chen Shaobai, He Tianjiong; the second row first person from right was Liao Zhongkai, the sixth person was Miyazaki Torazō. Sun Yat-sen arrived in Shanghai on December 25.

303. 武昌首义的胜利震动了全国。广东革命党人制定了四路发动、合攻广州的计划，组织各地绿林、会党，发动一系列武装起义。图为广东响应武昌起义形势图（据《辛亥革命史地图集》）。

The victory of the Wuchang Uprising had shaken the whole country. Guangdong revolutionary partisans pressed on Guangzhou from 4 directions jointly, organized the greenwood outlaws and the secret societies in all parts, launched a series of armed uprisings. The map showing the situation responded by Guangdong to support the Wuchang Uprising (from *The Revolution of 1911 History Atlas*).

304

304. 1911年11月1日，同盟会会员陈炯明、邓铿等在惠州淡水率众起义，组织循军。陈炯明任总司令，林激真任参谋长，邓铿任西江司令，尹德明任东江司令，丘耀西任博罗司令。10日，清提督秦炳直投降，民军占领惠州城。图为惠州城。

On November 1, 1911, Chen Jiongming and Deng Keng, members of the Chinese Revolutionary Alliance, at Dan Shui, Huizhou led masses in revolt, forming the Xunjun (the Xunzhou army). Chen Jiongming acted as commander-in-chief while Lin Jizhen as chief of staff, Deng Keng as Xijiang commandant, Yin Deming as Dongjiang commandant, Qiu Yaoxi as Boluo commandant. On 10th, Qing provincial military commander Qin Bingzhi surrendered. The militia captured Huizhou directly. The photo is Huizhou.

305

306

305. 循军西江司令邓铿（即邓仲元，嘉应人）。

Deng Keng (namely Deng Zhongyuan, from Jiaying County), Xijiang commandant of Xunjun(the Xunzhou army).

306. 驻扎香港，负责筹措军械军需，接应光复广东各路起义人员的同盟会会员邹鲁（大埔人）。

Zou Lu （from Dabu County）, a member of the Chinese Revolutionary Alliance, lived in Hong Kong, took the responsibility to raise funds for the armament and military supplies, coordinated with people taking part in uprisings of Guangdong's restoration.

307. 1911年11月5日、10日，上海《民立报》有关广东各地纷纷光复的报道。

The report about the restoration of all parts of Guangdong one after another published in Shanghai's *Minlibao* on November 5 and 10, 1911.

307

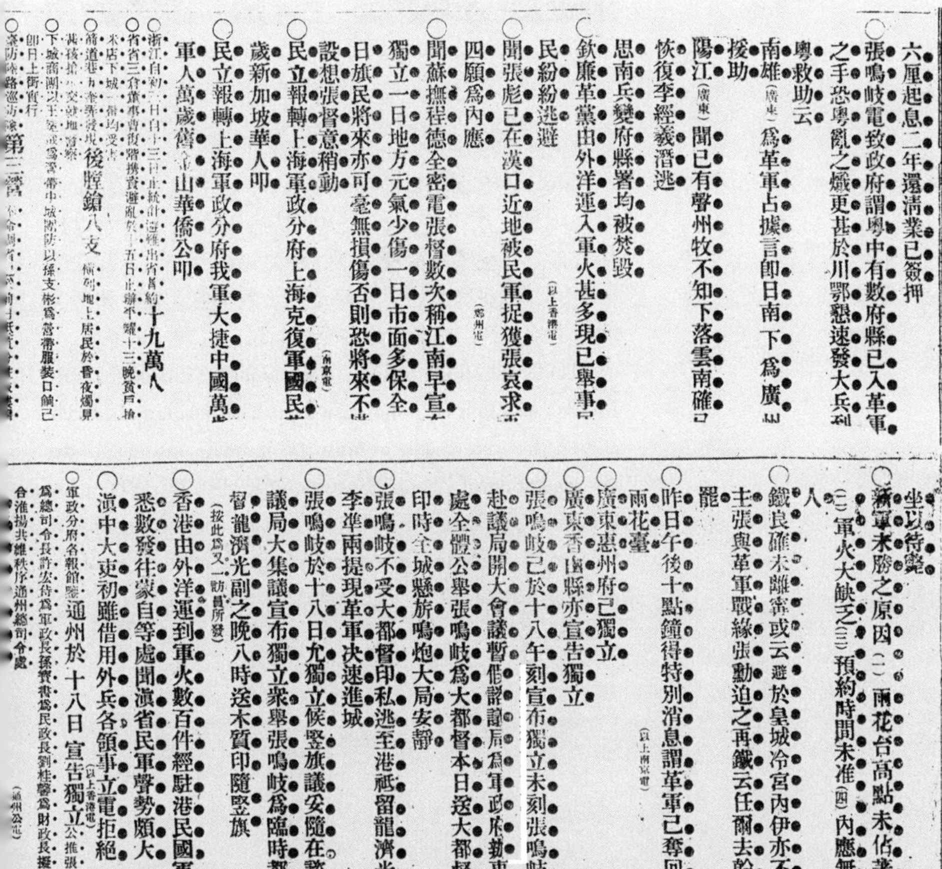

六厘起息二年還清業已簽押

○張鳴岐電致政府謂粵中有數府縣已入革軍之手恐粵亂之熾更甚於川鄂懇速發大兵到粵救助云

○南雄（廣東）爲革軍占據言卽日南下爲廣[illegible]援助

陽江（廣東）聞已有聲州牧不知下落雲南確[illegible]恢復李經羲潛逃

思南兵變府縣署均被焚毀

○欽廉革黨由外洋運入軍火甚多現已舉事[illegible]民紛紛逃避（以上香港電）

○聞張彪已在漢口近地被民軍捉獲張哀求[illegible]四願爲內應（鄭州電）

○聞蘇撫程德全密電張督數次稱江南早宣[illegible]獨立一日地方元氣少傷一日市面多保全[illegible]日旗民將來亦可毫無損傷否則恐將來不[illegible]設想張督意稍動（南京電）

○民立報轉上海軍政分府上海克復軍國民[illegible]歲新加坡華人叩

○民立報轉上海軍政分府我軍大捷中國萬[illegible]軍人萬歲舊金山華僑公叩

○浙江自初三日自十三日止統計避難出省者約十九萬人

○省省三倉[illegible]携資避亂於十五日止[illegible]十三晚貧戶搶米店下城一帶均受害

○[illegible]後膛鎗八支橫列地上居民於晝夜燭見[illegible]

○下城商闆以[illegible]帶中城[illegible]防以孫支彬爲營帶服裝口餉已

○[illegible]防陸路巡防隊第三營[illegible]

即日上街實行

坐以待斃

○新軍未勝之原因（一）雨花台高點未佔著（二）軍火大缺乏（三）預約時間未准（四）內應無人

○鐵良確未離甯或云避於皇城冷宮內伊亦不主張與革軍戰緣張勳迫之再鐵云任爾去幹罷

○昨日午後十點鐘得特別消息謂革軍已奪回雨花臺（以上南京電）

○廣東惠州府已獨立

○廣東香山縣亦宣告獨立

○張鳴岐已於十八午刻宣布獨立未刻張鳴岐赴議局開大會議暫借諮議局爲軍政府辦事處全體公舉張鳴岐爲大都督本日送大都督印時全城懸旂鳴炮大局安靜

○張鳴岐不受大都督印私逃至港祗留龍濟光李準兩提現革軍決速進城

○張鳴岐於十八日允獨立候豎旗議妥隨在諮議局大集議宣布獨立衆舉張鳴岐爲臨時都督龍濟光副之晚八時送木質印隨豎旗（按此爲又一訪員所發）

○香港由外洋運到軍火數百件經駐港民國軍悉數發往蒙自等處聞滇省民軍聲勢頗大

○滇中大吏初雖借用外兵各領事立電拒絕（以上香港電）

○軍政分府各報館鑒通州於十八日宣告獨立公推張謇爲總司令長許宏待爲軍政長孫寶書爲民政長劉桂馨爲財政長擬聯合淮揚共維秩序通州總司令處（通州公電）

308

308. 在革命形势的强大压力下，曾经凶残镇压革命的张鸣岐、李准等人再无力坚持顽固立场，有意以反正自保。在张鸣岐的授意下，1911年10月25日，江孔殷（左）、邓华熙（中）、梁鼎芬（右）等人在广州西关文澜书院召开广东各界维持公安会议，宣布“自保”。

Under the strong pressure of revolutionary situation, Zhang Mingqi, Li Zhun etc. who once suppressed revolution fiercely and cruelly, were unable to insist the obstinate position. Under the suggestion of Zhang Mingqi, on October 25, 1911, Jiang Kongyin (left), Deng Huaxi (middle), Liang Dingfen (right) were holding Guangdong public security meeting of all walks of life at Wenlan Academy in Xiguan, Guangzhou, announcing “self-protection”.

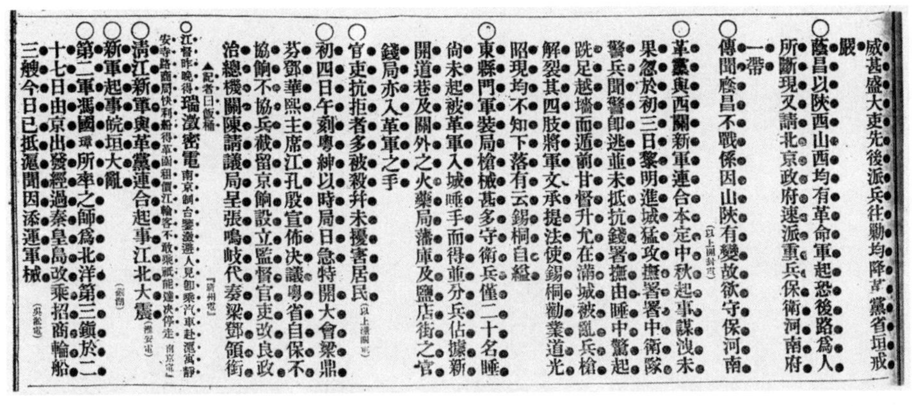

威甚盛大吏先後派兵往勦均降革黨省垣戒嚴

○蔭昌以陝西山西均有革命軍起恐後路為人所斷現又請北京政府速派重兵保衛河南府一帶

○傳聞蔭昌不戰係因山陝有變故欲守保河南 (以上國聞電)

○革黨與西關新軍連合本定中秋起事謀洩未果忽於初三日黎明進城猛攻撫署署中衛隊警兵聞警即逃並未抵抗錢署撫由睡中驚起跣足越牆而遁前甘督升允在滿城被亂兵槍解裂其四肢將軍文承提法使錫桐勸業道光照現均不知下落有云錫桐自縊

○東縣門軍裝局槍械甚多守衛兵僅二十名睡尚未起被革軍入城唾手而得並分兵佔據新開道巷及關外之火藥局藩庫及鹽店街之官錢局亦入革軍之手

○官吏抗拒者多被殺并未擾害居民 (以上滬關電)

○初四日午刻粵紳以時局日急特開大會梁鼎芬鄧華熙主席江孔殷宣佈決議粵省自保不協餉不協兵截留京餉設立監督官吏改良政治總機關陳請議局呈張鳴岐代奏梁鄧領銜 (廣州電)

▲記者日飯稿

○江督昨晚得瑞澂密電南京制台警遊人見即乘汽車赴滬寓靜安寺路商局快利船得革函租價江輪客不敢乘祇能達決停走 (南京電)

○清江新軍與革黨連合起事江北大震 (淮安電)

○新軍起事皖垣大亂 (安慶)

○第二軍馮國璋所率之師為北洋第三鎮於二十七日由京出發經過秦皇島改乘招商輪船三艘今日已抵滬聞因添運軍械 (吳淞電)

309

309. 1911年10月27日，上海《民立报》刊登的文澜书院召开广东各界维持公安会议的消息。

Shanghai's *Minlibao* published the news of Guangdong public security meeting of all walks of life, at Wenlan Academy on October 27, 1911.

310

310. 张鸣岐策划的“反正自保”根本没有提到脱离清政府，赞成共和，因此，引起商界、学界和舆论的反对。图为1911年11月1日上海《民立报》以“广东之滑头自保”为标题，披露“反正”真相。

When Zhang Mingqi planned “come-over and self-protecting”, he didn't mention at all breaking away from the Qing Government and did not agree to republicanism, which caused the opposition of the business circles, education circles and public opinion. On November 1, 1911, an article in Shanghai's *Minlibao* revealed the true fact of “come-over” with Sly self-protecting safe of Guangdong as its title.

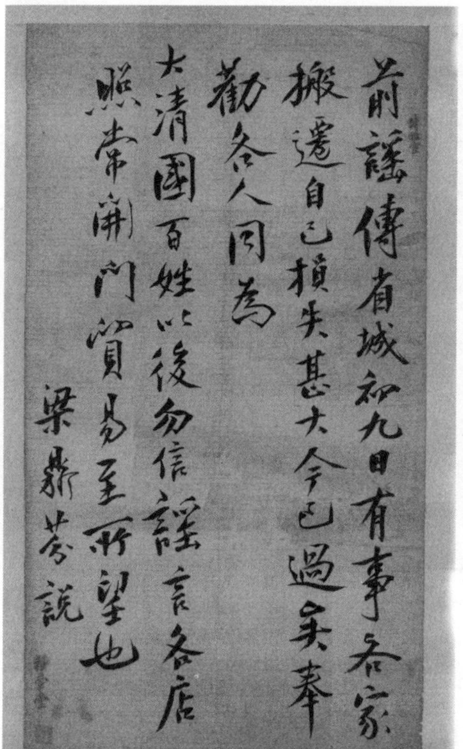

前謠傳省城初九日有事各家
搬遷自己損失甚大今已過矣奉
勸各人同為
大清國百姓以後勿信謠言各店
照常開門貿易至所望也
梁鼎芬說

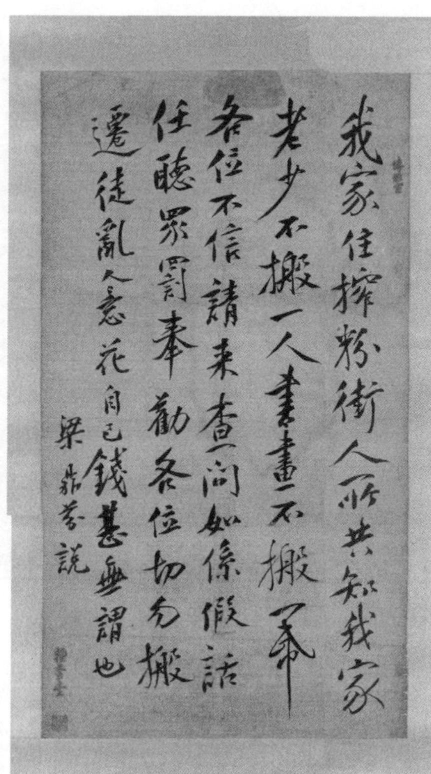

我家住搾粉街人所共知我家
老少不搬一人書畫不搬幷
各位不信請來查問如係假話
任聽衆罰奉勸各位切勿搬
遷徒亂人意花自己錢甚無謂也
梁鼎芬說

311

311. 广东光复前夕，广东宣慰使梁鼎芬为安定人心而发布的文告。

A statement issued by Liang Dingfen, the Pacification Commissioner of Guangdong, before the restoration of Guangdong, in order to settle popular feeling.

312

313

312. 1911年10月29日，粤商自治会会长陈惠普等召集广州九大善堂、七十二行商总商会各团体集议于广州爱育善堂，议决承认共和政府，举代表用正式公文“呈知”督院，并派人前往香港与革命党人接洽。图为陈惠普。

On October 29, 1911, Chen Huipu, president of Guangdong Society of Traders Autonomy, convened nine charitable halls, general chamber of commerce of all trades and other groups in Aiyu Church, Guangzhou and discussed to admit republic government after deliberation. They elected representatives to inform the superintend institute with formal official document and went to Hong Kong to make contact with revolutionary partisans. This picture is Chen Huipu.

313. 武昌起义后，力排众议，在广州策动清广东水师提督李准反正，推动广东光复的嘉应籍同盟会会员谢良牧。

Xie Liangmu (from Jiaying County), member of the Chinese Revolutionary Alliance. After the Wuchang Uprising, he prevailed over all dissenting views, in Guangzhou instigated Li Zhun, Guangdong provincial navy commander of Qing Government to come over from the Qing's side, which promoted Guangdong's restoration.

314. 谢良牧促李准反正的信函。

The lettter in which Xie Liangmu urged Li Zhun to come over from Qing's side.

314

專聲責某督之罪。二策行其一。皆可令某督授首。百粵景從。如是則爲民國立大功勳。某提之名位。當不在黎元洪下。前茲與黨人之惡感。亦渙然冰釋。其道至正。其勢至順。某提何惑而不出此耶。良牧炯明非有愛於某提。而愛我桑梓。不欲多流血而定。至轉禍爲福。爲某提計。則更無愈此者。今某督方且効趙爾豐之故智。若某提又必欲步張彪之後塵。則事勢至於不容已時。用力多寡。非所再計。良牧等亦可告無過於鄉人矣。區區之意。非楮墨所盡。惟執事鑒之。

九月十三日

謝良牧等來書

直繩足下。今者滿洲政府已亡。中華各省。大都已告光復。惟兩粵尚懸而未定。僕等不願桑梓糜爛。知足下亦必不願爲已亡之滿清。効無益之死。故敢進一言。釋足下之疑慮。若足下能即反正。取粵省之抗拒民軍若張鳴岐龍濟光之屬而誅之。斷絕清政府。服從民國。則足下與兩粵俱安。前茲國民對於足下之惡感。俱可渙然冰釋。足下値此時會。當審明哲保身之義。須知豪傑作事。貴於見識。榮辱生死。祇在轉機一髮之間。僕等更不必爲刼持之言。惟足下善自擇之。粗舉數事。爲約如左。且企鑒行。

一以兵據省城殺張鳴岐龍濟光江孔殷李世桂等以謝粵人。

二樹國民軍旗。通告各國領事。

三約束旗滿人。不使生反抗力。

四布告全粵以舉兵反正事。布告文中須表明斷絕清政府關係服從民國新政府命令。並誓守民族民權民生三大主義。

315

315. 1911年11月9日，广州各界代表在咨议局举行大会，在同盟会会员陈景华、邓慕韩等人的主持下，宣布广东共和独立。图为广东咨议局大楼。

On November 9,1911, people from all walks of life in Guangzhou held a conference in Consultation Bureau, presided by members of the Chinese Revolutionary Alliance—Chen Jinghua and Deng Muhan,etc.announcing the republican independence of Guangdong. This is the building of Guangdong Consultation Bureau.

316

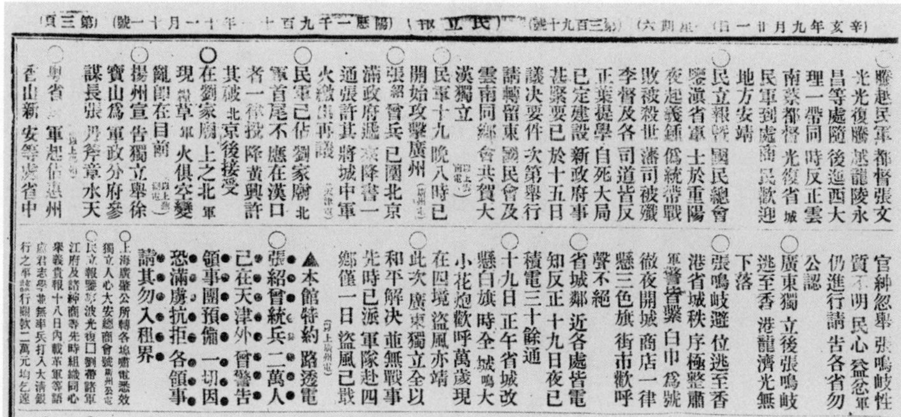

（辛亥年九月廿一日）（星期六）（第三百九十號）民立報（陽歷一千九百十一年十一月十一號）（第三頁）

○騰越民軍都督張文光光復騰越龍陵永昌等處隨後進西大理一帶同時反正雲南蔡都督光復省城民軍到處商民歡迎地方安靖

○民立報轉國民總會鑒滇省軍士於重陽夜起義鍾偽統帶戰敗被殺世藩司被殲李督及各司道皆反正葉提學自死大局已定建設新政府事甚緊要已於十五日議決要件次第舉行請轉留東國民會及雲南同鄉會共賀大漢獨立（以上雲南電）

○民軍十九晚八時已開始攻擊廣州（廣州電）

○張紹曾兵已圍北京滿政府遞表降書一通張許其將城中軍火繳出再議（天津電）

○民軍已佔劉家廟北軍首尾不應在漢口者一律投降黃興許其破北京後接受

○在劉家廟上之北軍現糧草軍火俱空變亂即在目前（以上漢口電）

○揚州宣告獨立舉徐寶山為軍政分府參謀長張丹斧章水天（以上揚州電）

○粵省民軍起佔惠州香山新安等處省中官紳忽舉張鳴岐性質不明民心益忿軍仍進行請告各省勿公認

○廣東獨立後張鳴岐逃至香港龍濟光無下落

○張鳴岐避位逃至香港省城秩序極整肅軍警皆繫白巾爲號徹夜開城商店一律懸三色旗街市歡呼聲不絕

○省城鄉近各處皆電知反正十九日夜已積電三十餘通

○十九日正午省城改懸白旗時全城鳴大小花炮歡呼萬歲現在四境盜風亦靖

○此次廣東獨立全以和平解決並無戰事先時已派軍隊赴四鄉僅一日盜風已戢（均上廣州電）

▲本館特約路透電

○張紹曾統兵二萬人已在天津外晉警告領事團預備一切因恐滿虜抗拒各領事請其勿入租界

○上海廣肇公所轉各埠肅電悉效獨立人心大安總商會號廣州公電

○民立報鑒寧波光復口劉帶諸軍江府及諸紳商等先時組織同心舉義貴報十八日內載革軍等語應君志學並無率兵打入大清銀行之事請行劃款二萬元均乞速

317

316. 1911年11月11日上海《民立报》报道广东光复的消息。

Shanghai's *Minlibao* reported the news of Guangdong's restoration on November 11, 1911.

317. 1911年11月10日，同盟会会员张醁村、孙丹崖、梁金鳌等率民军光复汕头。接着澄海、潮阳、普宁、揭阳等县亦次第光复。12日，张醁村等率民军攻入潮州，诛清知府陈兆棠，光复潮州。图为潮州民军预备进攻府署。

On November 10,1911, Zhang Lucun, Sun Danya and Liang Jin'ao, members of the Chinese Revolutionary Alliance, led militia in recovering Shantou, then took counties, such as Chenghai, Chaoyang, Puning, Jieyang,etc. On 12th, leading militia, Zhang Lucun entered Chaozhou, put to death Chen Zhaotang, prefect of a superior prefecture, and recovered Chaozhou. In the picture the militia in Chaozhou were planning to attack the administration office.

318

318. 被民军攻毁的潮州府署。

The administration office of Chaozhou destroyed by the militia.

319

320

319. 与革命党人共同策动汕头独立的汕头商会会长高绳之（澄海人）。

Gao Shengzhi (from Chenghai County),president of the Commerce Chamber of Shantou, who instigated Shangtou independence, together with revolutionary partisans.

320. 1911年11月12日，率民军在高雷起义的信宜籍同盟会会员林云陔。

Lin Yungai (from Xinyi County), member of the Chinese Revolutionary Alliance, on November 12, 1911, led militia in rising in revolt in Gaolei.

321

322

321. 组织光复高州的叶举（归善人）。

Ye Jü (from Guishan County), Who organized Gaozhou County of the recovery.

322. 1911年11月16日，同盟会会员黄明堂率会党、绿林组成的“明字顺军”在杜阮墟起义，旋光复江门。19日，黄明堂率民军乘胜光复新会。图为黄明堂（钦州人）。

On November 16, 1911, leading army formed by the secret societies and the greenwood outlaws, Huang Mingtang, member of the Chinese Revolutionary Alliance,launched uprising in Duruanxu, then recovered Jiangmen. On 19th, the militia led by Huang Mingtang, captured Xinhui on the crest of the victory. This is Huang Mingtang (from Qinzhou County).

323

323. 武昌起义后，率部与各路民军入驻广州的“仁字军”首领关仁甫（广西上思人）。

Guan Renfu(from Shangsi County of Guangxi Province), head of “benevolence army”, after the Wuchang Uprising, led the army and the militia in entering Guangzhou and stationed there.

324

324. 武昌起义后，组织炸弹队、敢死队进攻海口府城的文昌籍同盟会会员陈策。

Chen Ce (from Wenchang County), member of the Chinese Revolutionary Alliance, after the Wuchang Uprising, organized bomb team and dare-to-die corps to attack prefecture office of Haikou.

325. 1911年11月16日，上海《民立报》刊载的《香港光复记》。

Shanghai's *Minlibao* published report about Hong Kong's Restoration on November 16, 1911.

告各國書稿一通今日當外交者所當引爲依據也譯錄如下

我等中華之國民也憤滿政府之殘戾用是特起雄師與學種職務新推翻惡劣之政府驅除暴戾而建立共和國與各友邦共結厚誼使世界享和平之幸福而人類躋於太平之境域此余等日孜孜以求之者今佈宣告徵意如下

(一)滿政府於我軍起事以前與各國所有之條約皆作爲有效至該政府傾覆之時爲止

(二)於我軍未起事以前滿政府所借之外債一概承認償還決無改議將來以海關稅款抵賠

(三)滿政府於我軍未起事以前圖與各國之租界一律保全

(四)居留中國之外人及其財產担任切實保護

(五)滿政府於我軍起事以後與各國所訂開之條約租界及借款一概永不承認

(六)各國如有助滿政府以攻我軍者即視同敵人

(七)各國如有以軍械供給滿政府一經查獲即行充公

◎香港光復記

十六晚七點鐘後港中各報得接上海訪員來電京城已破傳單一出擧埠如雷後合港人民無遠無近均燃砲竹其聲隆隆不絕於耳比之元旦一日尤爲熱鬧該炮竹之聲至十二點鐘後乃止而砲竹遂成絕市沿途電車人山人海皆脫帽搖巾喧聲載道車上有標貼漢族萬歲字樣者有標貼漢族光明字樣者車費亦收給不暇並有手執新式旗幟沿路歡呼各商店高懸新式之旗亦指不勝屈各國西人睹此情形無不脫帽搖巾致敬無線電車一時租賃已盡車上亦插新式旗雪廠街之某大酒店燃燒爆仗多至數萬先施公司多多福及各商店同時燃燒者已逾數百人艷芳影相館懸件高拾大旗中有新漢萬歲四字爲之先導次則高拾放大相二面其一爲孫汶肖像其一爲黎元洪肖像巡遊各街歷路行人及居民商店莫不歡迎德輔道南北行街口等處見有手車數輛乘坐者皆外國人前驅的高搖籃底日旗在後之車則燃放爆仗並見沿途中西士女均搖巾脫帽無限歡欣其平日堅持保皇主義之商報亦燃爆竪旗途人聚衆門外嬉笑怒罵無所不有甚至好事者紛紛擲石玻璃門扇大鐘電燈等物均被毀破英差印差上前干涉即拘執四人(想係太惡作劇者)俟衆姑靜追該報高懸漢字白旗後即見門外標貼紙條云此報館已升認罪旗同胞各守文明即可免外人干涉所拘之人經已釋放云此香港十六晚熱鬧之情形也

◎東京之革命潮

▲馬扁去　革命事起梁啓超初則稱病不出繼竟稱請日本新聞記者宣布意見陽歷十一月四日北京來一密電促其回京梁得電後已於六日午前十時携同其寶淫女令嫻乘坐二等汽車由須磨出發直赴北京又哀求須磨醫察署長送至姬路乘船而行又恐爲人識破自穿淺黃色之中國裝頭垂長辮其形蹤怪奇如此臨行時由南洋寄

325

326

326. 1911年11月英文《今日世界》上发表的标题为“是大清王朝还是革命的共和国？”的大幅插图。图片背景为民主革命策源地广州的珠江江畔，右上头像为湖广总督袁世凯，左下人像为总理大臣庆亲王奕劻。

A large illustration in an article titled “Is it Qing Dynasty or a Republic?” which was published on the *World Today* in November, 1911. The picture on the background was bank of the Pearl River, where the democratic revolution was origirated. The upright head portrait was Yuan Shikai, the Viceroy of Huguang; the bottom left head portrait was Yi Kuang, the Prime Minister Prince Qing.

327

327．1911年12月29日，在南京举行十七省代表会议，选举孙中山为中华民国临时大总统。图为会议代表合影。

On December 29, 1911, representatives from the seventeen provinces gathered in Nanjing to elect Sun Yat-sen as the Provisional Grand President. It is a group photo of the representatives.

328．当选为临时大总统的孙中山。

Sun Yat-sen was elected as the Provisional Grand President.

328

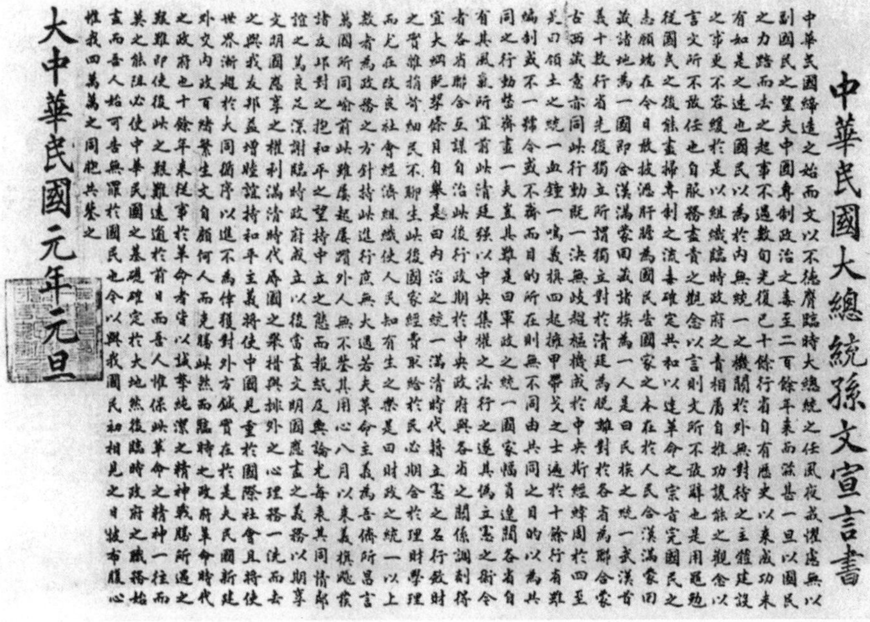

中華民國大總統孫文宣言書

中華民國締造之始而文以不德膺臨時大總統之任夙夜戒懼慮無以副國民之望夫中國專制政治之毒至二百餘年來而滋甚一旦以國民之力踣而去之起事不過數旬光復已十餘行省自有歷史以來成功未有如是之速也國民以為於內無統一之機關於外無對待之主體建設之事更不容緩於是以組織臨時政府之責相屬自推功讓能之觀念以言文所不敢任也自服務盡責之觀念以言則文所不敢辭也是用黽勉從國民之後能盡掃專制之流毒確定共和以達革命之宗旨完國民之志願端在今日敢披瀝肝膽為國民告國家之本在於人民合漢滿蒙回藏諸地為一國即合漢滿蒙回藏諸族為一人是曰民族之統一武漢首義十數行省先後獨立所謂獨立對於清廷為脫離對於各省為聯合蒙古西藏意亦同此行動既一決無歧趨樞機成於中央斯經緯周於四至是曰領土之統一血鐘一鳴義旗四起擁甲帶戈之士遍於十餘行省雖編制或不一號令或不齊而目的所在則無不同由共同之目的以為共同之行動整齊畫一夫豈其難是曰軍政之統一國家幅員遼闊各省自有其風氣所宜前此清廷強以中央集權之法行之遂其偽立憲之術今者各省聯合互謀自治此後行政期於中央政府與各省之關係調劑得宜大綱既挈條目自舉是曰內治之統一滿清時代藉立憲之名行斂財之實雜捐苛細民不聊生此後國家經費取給於民必期合於理財學理而尤在改良社會經濟組織使人民知有生之樂是曰財政之統一以上數者為政務之方針持此進行庶無大過若夫革命主義為吾儕所昌言萬國所同喻前此雖屢起屢躓外人無不鑒其用心八月以來義旗飆發諸友邦對之抱和平之望持中立之態而報紙及輿論尤每表其同情鄰誼之篤良足深謝臨時政府成立以後當盡文明國應盡之義務以期享文明國應享之權利滿清時代辱國之舉措與排外之心理務一洗而去之與我友邦益增睦誼持和平主義將使中國見重於國際社會且將使世界漸趨於大同循序以進不為倖獲對外方針實在於是夫民國新建外交內政百緒繁生文自顧何人而克勝此然而臨時之政府革命時代之政府也十餘年來從事於革命者皆以誠摯純潔之精神戰勝所遇之艱難即使後此之艱難遠逾於前日而吾人惟保此革命之精神一往而莫之能阻必使中華民國之基礎確定於大地然後臨時政府之職務始盡而吾人始可告無罪於國民也今以與我國民初相見之日披布腹心惟我四萬萬之同胞共鑒之

大中華民國元年元旦

329

329. 1912年1月1日，孙中山在南京宣誓就任中华民国临时大总统，宣告中华民国临时政府成立，从而结束了统治中国两千多年的封建帝制，创立了中国历史上第一个共和国。图为中华民国临时大总统孙中山发布的就职宣言书。

On January 1, 1912, Sun Yat-sen was sworn in as the Provisional Grand President of the Republic of China. He declared the founding of the government of the Republic of China, thus ending the rule of feudal monarchy, which lasted over 2, 000 yeas in China. The first Republic in the history of China was born. The photo shows The Manifesto of Sun Wen promulgated by Sun Yat-sen, the Provisional Grand President of the Republic of China.

肆 FOUR

广东军政府的施政方略与二次革命在广东的失败

The Policies and Strategies of Guangdong Military Government and the Failure of the Second Revolution in Guangdong

1911年11月12日，广东军政府成立，胡汉民、陈炯明出任正、副都督。为支援长江下游各省的革命斗争，广东军政府响应孙中山北伐的号召，组织北伐军，出师沪宁，屡创围攻南京的清兵，有力地捍卫南京革命政府的安全。与此同时，广东军政府实行澄清吏治、加强政权建设，整治军队、严肃军纪，改革司法制度，建立临时省议会，废除苛捐杂税、实行地价税契和赋税改革，推动市政建设，兴办文化教育事业，整顿治安、改良社会风气等系列革命措施，显示新生革命政权的生机，为执行孙中山在南京临时政府所颁布的施政方针，把广东建设成“模范省”做出可贵的努力。

1913年3月，窃取辛亥革命果实的袁世凯，为扫除建立封建专制独裁统治的障碍，派人暗杀将在国会选举中可能获胜的国民党领袖宋教仁，公然向国民党人发起明目张胆的挑战。为维护共和的旗帜，孙中山发起了反袁的“二次革命”。7月18日，广东都督陈炯明宣布广东独立，加入反袁武装斗争的行列。但由于大批军官受袁世凯收买，纷纷倒戈。8月11日，龙济光率部进驻广州，广东“二次革命”失败。

On November 12, 1911, Guangdong Military Government was founded. Hu Hanmin took the post of Provincial Military Governor and Chen Jiongming, deputy Provincial Military Governor. In order to support the revolutionary struggles of the provinces of low reaches of Changjiang River, Guangdong Military Government answered the call of Sun Yat-sen's Northern Expedition, organized Northern Expedition Troops and sent them to Shanghai and Nanjing. They beat repeatedly the Qing troops who were besieging Nanjing, and defended Nanjing Revolutionary Government effectively. Meanwhile, Guangdong Military Government implemented a series of revolutionary measures, clarified the administration of local officials, strengthened regime construction, renovated the army, enforced military disciplines, reformed the judicial systems, set up Provisional Senate, abolished exorbitant taxes and levies, implemented reform of price of land tax, contract and levy, promoted the urban construction, initiated the cultural and education undertakings, rectified the public security, improved social conduct, etc. which showed the vitality of newly-born revolutionary regime. They made valuable efforts to carry out the administrative policy which Sun Yat-sen put forward in the Provisional Government of Nanjing, to build Guangdong into a model province.

In March 1913, in order to steal the fruit of the Revolution of 1911 and clear away the obstacles of setting up feudal autocratic ruling, Yuan Shikai sent an assassin to gun down Song Jiaoren, leader of Kuomintang(the National Party) who was about to win in the Congress election. He initiated the out-and-out challenge to Kuomintang openly. To defend the flag of republicanism, Sun Yat-sen staged the Second Revolution against Yuan. On July 18, Chen Jiongming, Guangdong Provincial Military Governor, declared Guangdong independence and joined the ranks of armed struggle against Yuan. But, because a large number of the officers were brought over with bribery by Yuan Shikai, they changed sides one after another. On August 11, Long Jiguang's troop came and pressed on Guangzhou. Guangdong's Second Revolution failed.

330. 1911年11月12日，广东军政府成立。图为位于越华路前清两广总督署的军政府旧址。

On November 12,1911, Guangdong Military Government was founded. This is the old site in the former building of Guangdong and Guangxi Provincial Government of Qing Dynasty, in Yuehua Road.

330

331 332 333

334 335 336

337 338 339

331. 广东军政府临时都督、军事部长蒋尊簋（浙江诸暨人）。

Jiang Zungui (from Zhuji County of Zhejiang Province), interim Provincial Military Governor and military minister of Guangdong Military Government.

332. 广东军政府都督胡汉民。

Hu Hanmin, Provincial Military Governor of Guangdong Military Government.

333. 广东军政府副都督陈炯明（海丰人）。

Chen Jiongming (from Haifeng County), deputy Provincial

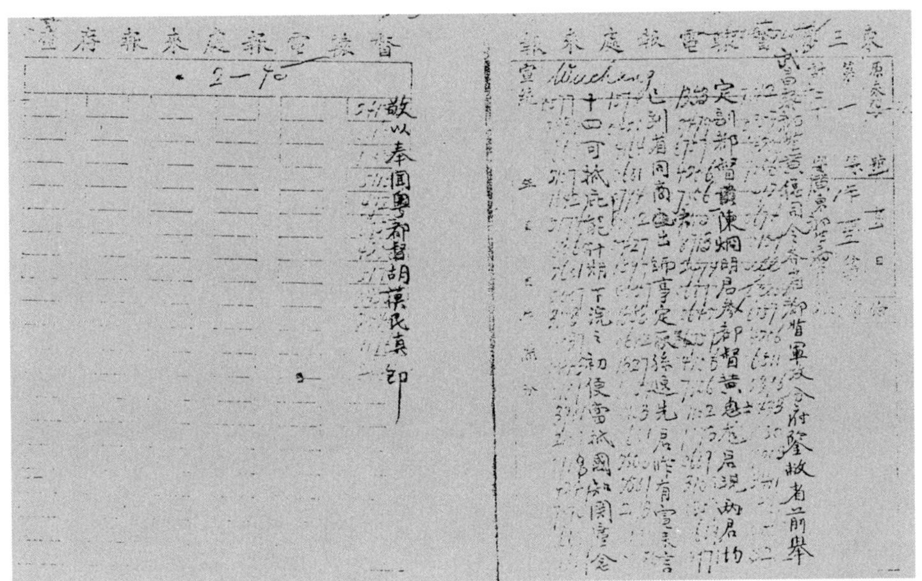
敬以奉聞粵都督胡漢民真印

340

Military Governor of Guangdong Military Government.

334. 广东军政府参都督黄士龙（花县人）。

Huang Shilong (from Huaxian County), assistant Provincial Military Governor of Guangdong Military Government.

335. 广东军政府总参议、枢密处负责人、核计院院长朱执信。

Zhu Zhixin, General Adviser, Head of Bureau of Military Affairs, Director of Accounting Institute, of Guangdong Military Government

336. 广东军政府陆军司司长邓铿。

Deng Keng, chief of Ground Force Department of Guangdong Military Government.

337. 历任广东军政府参议、教育部和司法部长的叶夏声（番禺人）。

Ye Xiasheng (from Panyu County), had served successively as the Senator of Guangdong Military Government, Education Minister and Justice Minister.

338. 广东军政府军务处长胡毅生。

Hu Yisheng, Director of Military Affairs Division of Guangdong Military Government.

339. 广东军政府交通司司长李纪堂（新会人）。

Li Jitang (from Xinhui County), Director of Traffic Department of Guangdong Military Government.

340. 1911年12月1日，广东都督胡汉民致电武昌黄兴等，报告副都督陈炯明等已到省商决出师事的电报。

On December 1, 1911, Hu Hanmin, Guangdong provincial military governor sent a telegram to Huang Xing,etc. in Wuchang, reporting Chen Jiongming, deputy provincial military governor had come to the capital city to talk over sending out troops to battle.

▲341

341.辛亥革命后，同盟会由秘密转向公开。图为同盟会广东支部会所。

After the Revolution of 1911, the Chinese Revolutionary Alliance made public from the secret. The picture is the office of Guangdong Branch.

342. 1911年12月24日，广东临时议会在广州成立。黄锡铨为议长，卢信、谢已原为副议长。女同盟会会员邓惠芳等10名妇女当选代议士。当时妇女出任议员，在中国和远东堪称创举。图为邓惠芳（东莞人）。

On December 24, 1911, the Provisional Senate of Guangdong was established in Guangzhou with Huang Xiquan as the speaker, Lu Xin, Xie Yiyuan as vice speakers. 10 women in all were elected senators, such as Deng Huifang, a woman member of the Chinese Revolutionary Alliance. It was the first time in China and the Far East that women took the posts of the Senators. The picture of Deng Huifang (from Dongguan County).

▶342

▶343

曐之濟大當司帖給領否則一律充公決不寬貸仰即知照

▲十一月初一日廣東臨時議會開幕

日廣東臨時會議協商則當衆表決(二)代議士席次以抽籤定之(三)星期日休會倘遇緊急事件可由議長之意見或會議之決議臨時開會(三)議事時各稱其職名惟代議士須兼稱席次(四)議案及報告書等議長當先一日令該入員印刷以備分送代議士但緊急議案不在此限(五)發言討論除訴陳處語俱可自由惟以國語發言爲主須由書記譯爲廣語以廣語發言者須由書記譯爲國語總以簡要爲主如有偏漏由代議士於譯時得促書記更正之(六)通常會議自午後一時起至五時止不得遲誤但仍由議長之意見或會議之決議臨時更變其時間(七)會議開始時議長臨席報告出席人數及一切書函然後宣告開議(八)記畢於議事日表之事件議移無論歸數何時均可散會倘事未議終已至午後五時得以延會唯緊急事件不在此限(九)議事爭執至於騷動時議長當搖鈴制息無效則暫行宣告中止(十)議事未終不得退席但遇緊急事當告知議長乃可退席(十一)開會散會延會中止均由議長宣告之其開會以鈴爲號(十二)代議士出席按照定額未及半數應由議長宣告延會(十三)議長未宣告開會以前及宣告散會延會中止之後無論何人不得有關於議事之發言(十四)欲發言須向議長報明席次驗名議長按報名之先後爲發言之先後如同時報名者由議長決其發言之先後(十五)提議既經甲說未終乙說不得攙雜尤不許互相嘲笑(十六)議場內地非有證票不許擅進入場者一律免冠毋得吸食烟草及涕唾於地

▲十一月初二日一點鐘議長搖鈴開會出席代議士六十六人書記長宣佈本日提議擬議各種規則一旁聽規則二議長權限三審查分股辦事章程四書記辦事章程五警察守衛章程及補議議事規宣佈畢議長發言本日代議士所到人數未及過半按照簡章不能開議請衆表決應否開議十一號[illegible]賓向起言以鄙見而論本日所議各事不過關於內部組織似宜開議為是三十四號楊永泰五十二號周孔博均和議隨議決先行派定擔任起草人五位爲起草員衆贊成議長請定起草期限由衆議決初三日上午十一時即將草案議定發交全體研究表決一俟議決通過各審查員分股辦事後即於初四日開議交[illegible]

344

343. 1911年12月29日，上海《申报》刊登的《广东临时议会开幕》。

Opening Ceremony of the Provisional Senate of Guangdong published in Shanghai's *Shenbao* on December 29,1911.

344. 广东光复后，广大商民踊跃捐款，支持军政府克服财政困难。岭南学堂师生组织“协助军政府筹饷队”，积极为军政府筹饷。图为该队队员的合影。

After the restoration of Guangdong, the masses and merchants contributed money enthusiastically to support the military government to overcome the financial difficulty. The teachers and students of Lingnan School organized fund-raising team for the military government. This is a group photo of the team members.

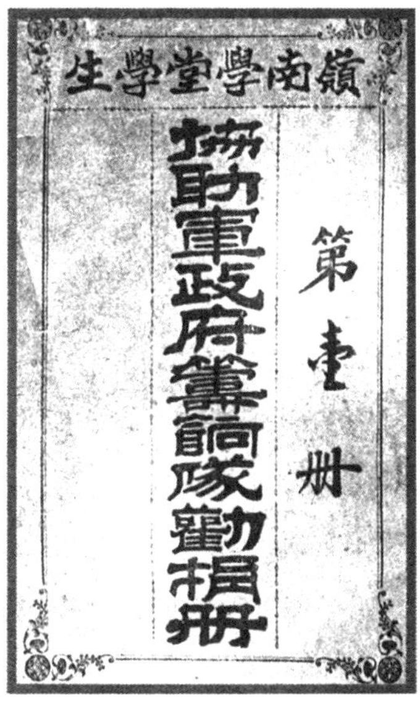

345

345.《岭南学堂学生协助军政府筹饷队劝捐册》。

The Donating Advice Volume of Lingnan School's Fund-raising Team.

嶺南學堂學生勸捐軍需啓

我諸父昆弟乎。邦人諸友乎。亦知今日爲我[illegible]之[illegible]乎。[illegible]立之地位爲萬分險惡乎。[illegible]存亡。生生死死。[illegible]於此[illegible]之間。[illegible]。滿奴之强横不叠再否。漢奸之[illegible]可恕否。外人之[illegible]不[illegible]否。[illegible]之[illegible]者子遺否。諺曰。打亦死。不打亦死。與其不打而坐死。[illegible]打去。以[illegible]一不死。且從前我[illegible]之死。死其身耳。今日若死。[illegible]之子[illegible]死[illegible]。[illegible]及此。能不寒心。能不[illegible]。今已有[illegible]打[illegible]死者出矣。[illegible]出[illegible]者。[illegible]現[illegible]。雖有死心。終無死所。然則人出頭。我出手。人流血。我流汗。人捐命。我捐錢。亦何爲而不可。且[illegible]身[illegible]南之[illegible]。人所以[illegible]許[illegible]。[illegible]亡後多妻子。[illegible]多財産者。[illegible]我等生命財産計。而我等乃[illegible]一方。[illegible]金玉。纍妻子。[illegible]食。[illegible]敗。豈復有人心乎。吾以知諸父兄弟邦人諸友之必不然也。生等[illegible]此。身不[illegible]。[illegible]不[illegible]。父兄之教不暇[illegible]。[illegible]之[illegible]不暇[illegible]。[illegible]軍。共[illegible]督府。請得命令。承[illegible]軍需。分[illegible]四出。[illegible]奔走。以哀求我諸父昆弟邦人諸友之前。[illegible]。共急公義。多者捐多。少者捐少。[illegible]。推數[illegible]。以[illegible]軍實。是亦爲我諸父昆友所樂爲者。古人有出財佐軍。且[illegible]矣。豈我諸父昆友。[illegible]乎。小子末學。言多不文。[illegible]有本其至誠至[illegible]直者以言之。我諸父昆友。[illegible]其[illegible]。[illegible]其苦而[illegible]助之。使吾粵軍餉。立有所需。晉漢民族。必存光復之一日。不然噫其危矣。

代收捐款各號如左

省城 [illegible]西三[illegible]本[illegible]事所　十三行[illegible]　[illegible]　新城天平街十五號　一八甫[illegible]公司　[illegible]七約大[illegible]號

香港 大道中[illegible]新公司[illegible]　大道中[illegible]街口三十五號二樓　石塘咀[illegible]酒樓　[illegible]

澳門 [illegible]

總辦事所在[illegible]西三[illegible]門牌第十號

346

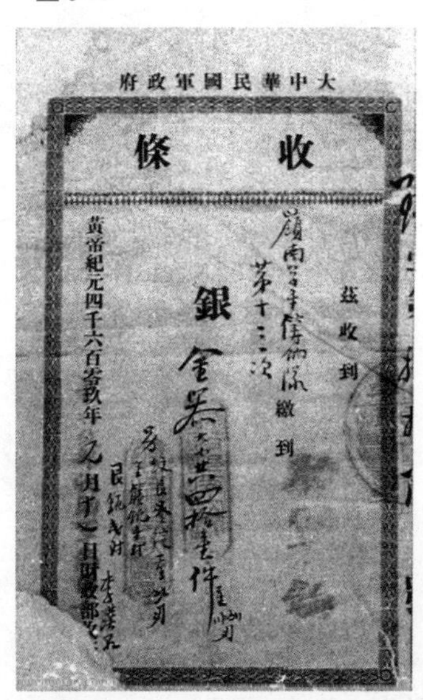

347

346. 岭南学堂印发的《岭南学堂学生劝捐军需启》。

The Military Supplies-donating Advice printed and distributed by students of Lingnan School.

347. 广东军政府发给岭南学堂学生筹饷队缴款的收条。

The receipt of donation which Guangdong Military Government gave to the students of Lingnan School.

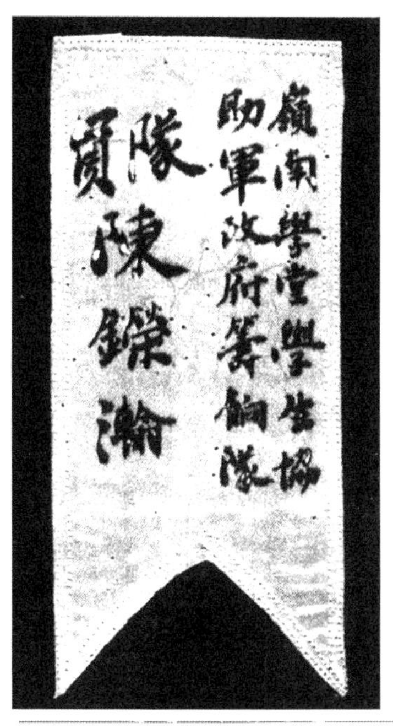
嶺南學堂學生協助軍政府籌餉隊
隊員陳鑅瀚

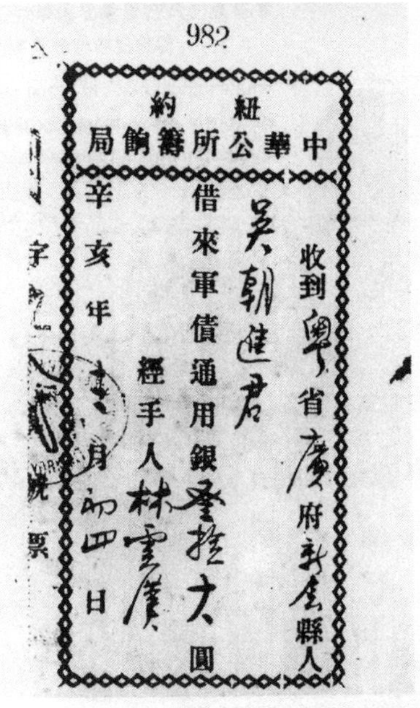
982
紐約中華公所籌餉局
收到粵省廣府新会縣人
吳朝進君
借來軍債通用銀叁拾大圓
經手人林雲廣
辛亥年[illegible]月初四日

348

證書
中華民國粵省軍政府大都督 為
發送証書事案照粵省自舊歷辛亥九
月十九日反正惟時人心無主庫儲一
空幸得港商將袂至省會同省城各界
公舉臨時都督以定大局即以籌餉為
已任不半日而集鉅款大觀俾輪船解省
以應餉需報紙宣傳虜廷變色而各同
胞亦聞風響應踴躍捐輸卒能推翻專
制同享共和雖是人心所趨實賴諸
公於光復之日在諮議局參議大計人
心藉以安靖軍餉藉以維持本都督對
於諸公熱誠萬謳應代國民公認殊
勳除照當日詳情即向本省政府存案
永留紀念外亟應製備頭等壹級勳章
隨同證書發送以獎勳勞而資觀感
為係存須至證書者右送
香港籌款局局員

349

348. 岭南学堂学生筹饷队队员标志（左）和纽约中华公所筹饷局代广东军政府筹饷的收据（右）。

The emblem of team member of Lingnan School's Fundraising Team (left). The receipt of donation issued by Fundraising Bureau of China Guild of New York City for Guangdong Military Government (right).

349. 广东军政府颁发的褒扬香港同胞筹饷支持广东光复的证书。

The certificate issued by Guangdong Military Government to Hong Kong compatriots who donated money to support Guangdong restoration.

廣東財政部收入報告冊 柒

港商籌款部	十月初三日	五千一百一十七圓	
工商公所	同上	三萬九千六百零七圓	
	同上	一十九圓三毫五仙	港紙補紙水
	同上	三千一百九十三圓	
酒樓西家行慎餘堂	十月初九日	五百圓	
九八行商業公所	十月十二日	一十萬零五千八百圓	港紙
金銀業行	十月十三日	二萬零二百圓	同上
南北行	同上	六萬零七百零二圓	內港紙陸萬零零陸拾叁元
小呂宋庄東福公司	十月十四日	一萬圓	
上海庄	十月十五日	一萬圓	港紙
聯益保險公司	十月十五日	八千圓	港紙
疋頭行	同上	四萬一千圓	
綢緞行綿綸堂	同上	一萬圓	港紙
南海九江商務局	十月十六日	二萬零二百圓	同上
八邑公所	同上	四萬圓	此款交官錢局收已入來往數計
鹹魚鹹蛋店	十月十七日	一千二百圓	廣紙
中華酒店	十月十八日	五百圓	
金山庄華安公司	同上	六萬八千二百五十圓	港紙
綢緞庄	十月十九日	一萬圓	同上
鄧仲澤	十月二十一日	三萬九千五百一十二圓	內港紙叁萬捌千八百七拾六元

廣東財政部收入報告冊 捌

	鹹魚行聯益社	同上	一萬圓	港紙
	魚翅行	同上	四千零五十圓	
	銅鐵行	十月二十六日	二萬九千九百一十五圓	內港紙貳萬玖千伍百壹拾元
	公白行	十月二十七日	七千圓	
	港商許遠昀	十月二十八日	二百圓	港紙
	鄧仲澤等	九月二十一日	二十二萬二千一百九十五圓	同上
	各商團	同上	四百四十二圓	
	港商團	同上	二十二萬九千一百五十圓	港紙
香港商團	李煜堂	九月二十五日	一萬五千圓	
	寶璧	同上	二萬圓	
	寶璧	九月二十六日	三萬圓	
	同上	同上	一百一十一圓一毫一仙	
	同上	九月二十七日	一千圓	
		九月二十八日	六萬圓	
		同上	一萬五千圓	
	先施新廣合泰益萬益生	同上	三萬三千一百七十九圓六毫	
	李煜堂	十月初一日	一千圓	港紙
	李星衢	同上	三萬圓	同上
	港團	十月初九日	一萬七千圓	同上
	港商團銀業聯安堂	十月十二日	五萬零五百圓	同上

350（1）

廣東財政部收入報告冊

	十月初七日	一千五百七十五圓	
	十月初九日	五千九百一十圓	
	十月初十日	六千三百四十圓	
	同上	一萬六千一百五十圓	
	十月十一日	二萬八千九百二十圓	
	十月十二日	一萬四千一百三十五圓	
	十月十三日	一萬八千九百二十五圓	
	十月十四日	六千四百四十五圓	
	十月十五日	五千六百圓	內港紙貳千元
	十月十六日	四千二百八十圓	
	十月十七日	一萬一千零三十圓	
	十月二十七日	一萬九千九百二十九圓五毫八仙	內港紙陸百捌拾捌元
	十月二十八日	四千零六十圓	
	十月二十九日	六千七百六十五圓	
香港 李自重	九月二十三日	六千圓	
李星衢	同上	二萬圓	
李自重	同上	三千圓	
同上	九月二十四日	三千圓	
同上	九月二十六日	一萬圓	
同上	十月初一日	三千圓	

港

▲350（2）

350. 港澳及海外各界人士资助广东革命政府捐借款项记录。

Records of donation and loan from Hong Kong, Macao and oversea for the Guangdong Revolutionary Government.

351. 1912年，广东军政府颁发的“革命军功牌”，表彰广东光复有功人士。

In 1912, Guangdong Military Government issued “revolutionary military exploit brand” in praise of the meritorious personages for Guangdong restoration.

▲351

▲352

352. 1911年12月8日，广东军政府响应孙中山北伐的号召，组织北伐军从广州出发，北上沪宁，屡创围攻南京的清兵，拱卫南京。图为广东北伐决死队全体队员合影。

On December 8,1911, Guangdong Military Government in conformity with the request of Sun Yat-sen's Northern Expedition, organized Northern Expeditionary Army and set out from Guangzhou to protect Shanghai and Nanjing. This is the group photo of all members of dare-to-die corps of Guangdong Northern Expeditionary Army.

▼353

▲354

▲355

▼356

353. 广东北伐决死队部分队员合影。

The group photo of some members of dare-to-die corps of Guangdong Northern Expeditionary Army.

354. 率军进驻南京的广东北伐军总司令姚雨平。

Yao Yuping, commander-in-chief of Guangdong Northern Expeditionary Army, had troops stationed on Nanjing.

355. 广东北伐炸弹队。中坐者队长徐宗汉，后立者队员右起李应生、卓国兴、李沛基。

The bomb squad of Northern Expeditionary Army. Sitting in the middle is Xu Zonghan, team leader. Standing at back row are team members, (from right) Li Yingsheng, Zhuo Guoxing and Li Peiji.

356. 广东北伐军红十字队。

Guangdong Northern Expeditionary Army's Red Cross Squad.

357

358

359

360

361

357. 广东北伐军在广州郊外瘦狗岭演习。

Guangdong Northern Expeditionary Army are rehearing manoeuvre at Shougouling, outskirts of Guangzhou.

358. 广东北伐军在瘦狗岭演放地雷。

Guangdong Northern Expeditionary Army are practising laying mines at Shougouling.

359. 潮州北伐军在会操。

Chaozhou Northern Expeditionary Army are holding a joint drill exercise.

360. 潮州北伐军在操练。

Chaozhou Northern Expeditionary Army are drilling.

361. 潮州北伐军军官合影。

The group photo of officers of Chaozhou Northern Expeditionary Army.

362

363

364

365

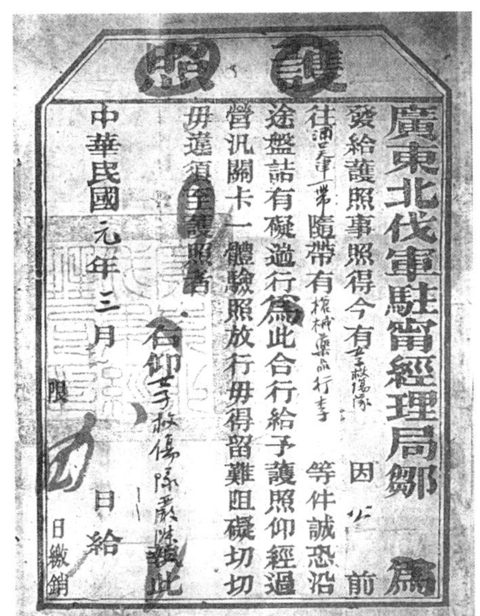

護照

廣東北伐軍駐甯經理局鄒　為
發給護照事照得今有[illegible]　因公前
往[illegible]隨帶有[illegible]等件誠恐沿
途盤詰有礙遄行爲此合行給予護照仰經過
營汛關卡一體驗照放行毋得留難阻礙切切
毋違須至護照者
右仰[illegible]准此
中華民國元年三月　日給
限　日繳銷

366

362. 潮州北伐军集中在汕头会操。

Chaozhou Northern Expeditionary Army are holding a joint drill exercise in Shantou.

363. 广东北伐军乘船抵达上海的情形。

Guangdong Northern Expeditionary Army reach Shanghai by ship.

364. 驻扎南京的广东北伐军。

Guangdong Northern Expeditionary Army stationed in Nanjing.

365. 广东北伐军机关枪队在南京演习的情形。

Guangdong Northern Expeditionary Army's machine-gun squad were rehearsing manoeuvre in Nanjing.

366. 广东北伐军护照。

Guangdong Northern Expeditionary Army's certificate.

▲ 367

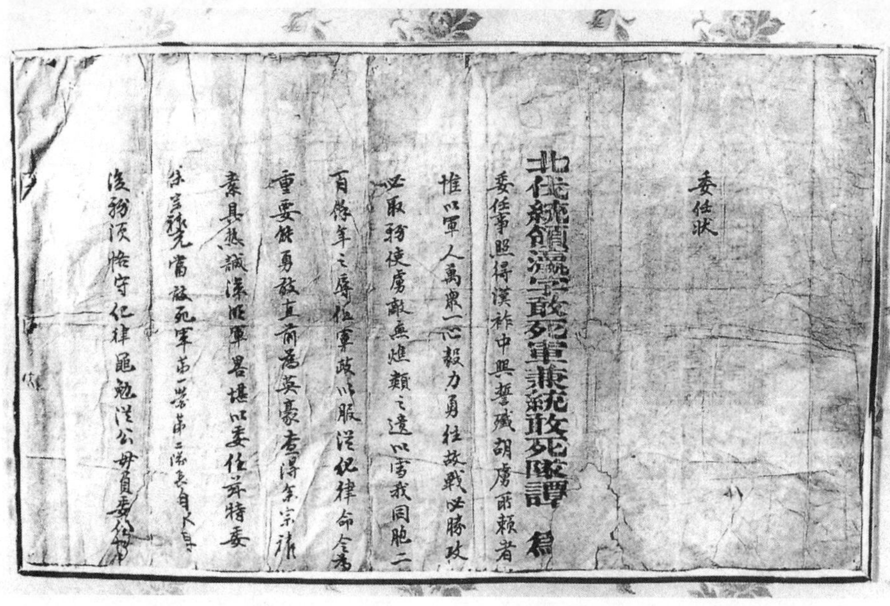

委任狀

北伐統領瀛字敢死軍兼統敢死隊譚　為

委任事照得漢祚中興誓殲胡虜所賴者

惟以軍人萬衆一心毅力勇往故戰必勝攻

必取務使虜敵無噍類之遺以雪我同胞二

百餘年之辱但軍政以服從紀律命令為

重要能勇敢直前為英豪查得朱宗祿

素具熱誠深明軍略堪以委任為特委

朱宗祿充當敢死軍第一營第二隊長自[illegible]

後務須恪守紀律黽勉從公毋負委任

▲ 368

367. 南京追悼广东北伐军殉难诸烈士的场面。

Nanjing people were mourning martyrs of Guangdong Northern Expeditionary Army.

368. 参加光复广州的民军首领谭瀛组织瀛字敢死军，准备参加第二批北伐。图为广东军政府颁发的委任状。

Tan Ying, leader of Guangzhou militia, who participated in Guangdong restoration, organized dare-to-die corps and prepared to participate in second Northern Expedition. This is the letter of attorney issued by Guangdong Military Government.

369. 广东北伐学生军。1911年11月16日，由广东军政府批准成立，两广方言学堂、广东农林讲习所、南武公学、育才书社等校学生496人参加。原定1912年2月出发，后因南北和议达成而解散。

The student troops of Guangdong Northern Expeditionary Army were founded by 496 students of Dialect School of Guangdong and Guangxi Provinces, Guangdong Institute for Training Peasants, Nanwu Public School, Yucai College, on November 16, 1911, approved by Guangdong Military Government. They were set up originally in February of 1912, afterwards were dismissed because the peace talks between the north and south reached an agreement.

▲ 369

370. 广东北伐学生军在野外训练后休息的情形。

The student troops of Guangdong Northern Expeditionary Army were having a rest in the open air after training.

▼ 370

興漢紀念廣東獨立全案　　五四

(三)海面之情形　是日省河大小兵輪暨水巡船。均一律改懸民國軍旂。各兵輪且懸萬國旗以誌慶典。其餘大小商船。亦一律懸竪民國軍旂。并紛紛燃串炮及鳴鑼鼓樂。永安輪船碼頭。亦高懸通識旗以誌慶。種種歡欣情形。誠令見者精神爲之大振。

(四)剪辮之踴躍　實行反正之議既决。無論老弱少壯之男子以及士農工商兵。罔不爭先恐後。紛將天然鐵鍊剪去。是日堤岸一帶之剪辮店。自朝至暮。擠擁非常。操此業者。幾致食亦無暇。到車衣店定購公裝衣服者。亦紛至沓來。統計是日剪辮者。儘有二十餘萬人。

(五)商界之休業　是日午後。各街店舖均閉門休業。并設筵慶叙痛飲。

(六)保皇報之投降　國事報固保皇黨之機關也。其與港之商報通同一氣。甘作虎倀。頃該報有鑒於商報之覆轍。十九日特書字招二張。分貼於門之左右。如對聯然。該字招云。廣東現已獨立。快看國事報投降。(可憐可憐)并懸漢族光明旗幟。及燃放串炮。人見其已知悔。故亦不爲已甚。然

371

372

373

371. 广东军政府成立后，颁布改元剪发令，民众群情激昂，纷纷剪去民族歧视的标志——辫子。图为当时出版的《兴汉纪念广东独立全案》记载广州民众剪辫的盛况。

After Guangdong Military Government was established, it issued an order to cut the hair-pigtails, which made people's feeling very high and cut one after another their pigtails—a sign of race discrimination. This is *The whole case of revitalizing China and commemorating Guangdong's independence* published then, recording the grand occasion of Guangzhou people cutting their pigtails.

372. 1911年底，剪去辫子、服式趋新的广州中学生。

The middle school students in Guangzhou who cut their pigtails in new-fashion clothes at the end of 1911.

373. 广东光复后，香港街头流行新发式和新服饰的人群。

The crowds with new hairdo and new dress in Hong Kong streets after Guangdong's restoration.

374

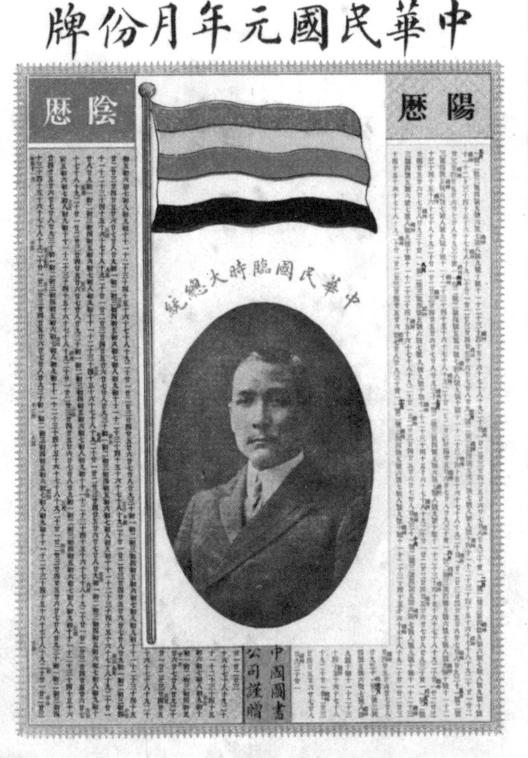

374. 中华民国元年月份牌。

The calendar of the first year of the Republic of China.

375

附錄

粵省選用官吏及勸懲暫行簡章

第一條　具左列資格之一者得選爲官吏

一政治學識

（甲）東西洋及中國法政學堂畢業者

（乙）講求政治學確有建白或經衆推舉者

一政治閱歷

（子）無論本省外省人曾入仕途政績卓著者

（丑）新舊政府各署局佐治員之有成績者

（寅）向充幕友佐理政務之有經驗者

第二條　具左列事項之一者不得選用爲官吏

一反對共和政體者（以有事實及著作行世者爲斷）

一有精神病者

一輿情不洽者（以經衆指控案據確鑿者爲斷）

一失財產上之信用者

一吸食鴉片未戒斷者

第三條　缺分等級　舊制分繁中簡缺三級現擬改爲一等二等三等稱職者以次遞升才力不及者遞降

第四條　任用期限　一年爲試用期三年爲實任期

一年期滿有成績者應即加狀改爲實任三年期滿有成績者得連任或量移一二等缺不稱職者立罷

第五條　激勸之種類　論奬　存記　實任　右遷（量移一二等缺）

第六條　懲戒之種類　申飭　記過　罰薪　轉職（量移左職）　撤任

376

377

378

375. 为澄清吏治，军政府颁布《粤省选用官吏及劝惩暂行简章》。

In order to improve administration of local officials, the military government issued *A Brief Charter of Provisional Regulation about Election and Punishment of Guangdong Government Officials*.

376. 各地民军的起义，对促进广东光复起着积极作用。图为进驻广州的民军首领刘永福、王和顺、黄明堂、关仁甫、杨万夫等在广州东园合影。

Regional uprisings played an active role in promoting Guangdong restoration. Liu Yongfu, Wang Heshun, Huang Mingtang, Guan Renfu and Yang Wanfu, heads of the militia stationed in Guangzhou. This is their group photo in East Garden, Guangzhou.

377. 1911年11月中下旬，广东军政府成立“民团督办处”，以总摄各路民军。图为民团总长刘永福。

In the later part of November, 1911, Guangdong Military Government established the “Militia Supervision Department” to supervise different militia troops. This is the picture of Liu Yongfu, commander-in-chief of militia.

378. 1911年12月，黄世仲接任广东民团总长，提出“裁弱留强”的主张。次年4月9日，黄世仲被代理都督陈炯明扣押，5月1日被都督胡汉民以索贿等罪名，冤杀于广州观音山（今越秀山）五层楼下。图为黄世仲的尸棺。

In December 1911, Huang Shizhong took over the post of commander-general of Guangdong Alliance and proposed the opinion of “dismissing the weak and keeping the strong”. On April 9 next year, Huang Shizhong was detained by Chen Jiongming, acting provincial military governor. On May 1, he was wrongly executed by Hu Hanmin, provincial military governor, on the charge of demanding bribery etc., on the ground of Five-Story Tower in Guanyin Hill (today’s Yuexiu Hill) in Guangzhou. This is Huang Shizhong’s coffin.

▲379

工務部通告

工務部爲通告事現因軍政府需建營房棚廠以備民軍駐紮之所業由本部遴派課員工程師分往四城郊外測量擇地建搭合行通告凡有本部擇定之地址係屬民業及興工後有傷及前後左右之桑園菜圃者隨時來部報明自必派員驗勘明確分別給租賠償爲此通告其各安心幸毋懷疑是爲至要此佈

中華民國元年五月二日工務部長程天斗

▲380

379. 1912年5月，参加致祭黄花岗烈士的民军队伍。

The militia procession participating in a memorial ceremony for martyrs of Yellow Flower Hill in May 1912.

380. 广东军政府工务部为建营房安置民军所颁发的通告。

A notice issued by department of construction affairs of Guangdong Military Government about building barracks for the militia soldiers.

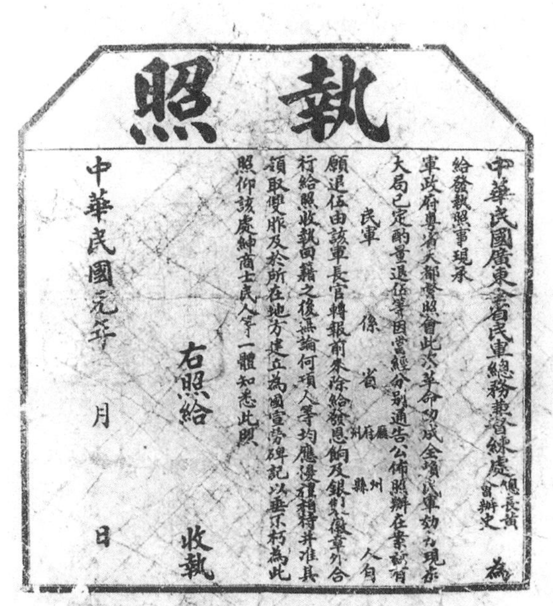

執照

中華民國廣東全省民軍總務兼督練處總長黃 會辦史　爲
給發執照事現承
軍政府粵省大都督照會此次革命功成全頼民軍効力現在
大局已定酌量退伍等因當經分別通告公佈照辦在案茲有
民軍　係　省　府廳州縣　人自
願退伍由該軍長官轉報前來除給發恩餉及銀[illegible]徽章外合
行給照收執回籍之後無論何項人等均應優禮相待并准其
領取[illegible]及於所在地方建立爲國宣勞碑記以垂不朽爲此
照仰該處紳商士民人等一體知悉此照
右照給　收執
中華民國元年　月　日

▲381

第二次執照

中華民國粵省軍政府都督胡　爲
發給執照事茲准第二次委任借欵局報告
陸耀　繳到認借軍債　港紙銀伍拾元
按照美洲華僑軍債票辦法借銀壹圓還銀壹員伍
毫以二年爲限至期發還請發給執照以昭大信等
情前來准此特發回執照并蓋關防交陸耀
收執存據此照
財政部總長廖仲愷　簽押
中華民國元年二月初五日　發給

▲382

381. 为减轻财政压力，维持省城社会治安，军政府决定遣散民军回籍。图为民军回籍执照。

In order to lighten financial pressure and keep provincial capital's social security in good order, Guangdong Military Government determined to disband the militia and sent them to their home villages. This is a return certificate.

382. 为改善广东的财政困境，军政府采取整顿税收、发行公债、改进货币流通、更换土地契约等措施，使收支得以平衡。图为廖仲恺签押的广东军政府华侨军债执照。

In order to improve financial predicament of Guangdong, Guangdong Military Government took measures to rectify tax revenue,to issue public bond, to improve money flow, to change land contracts and to make revenue and expenditure balanced. This is the military bond certificate of overseas Chinese of Guangdong Military Government signed by Liao Zhongkai.

383. 广东军政府发行的中华民国广东全省地方劝业有奖公债。

Guangdong provincial prize-bonds of the Republic of China issued by Guangdong Military Government.

384. 广东军政府发行的中华民国粤省军政府通用银票。

Current notes of Guangdong Military Government of the Republic of China issued by the Guangdong Military Government.

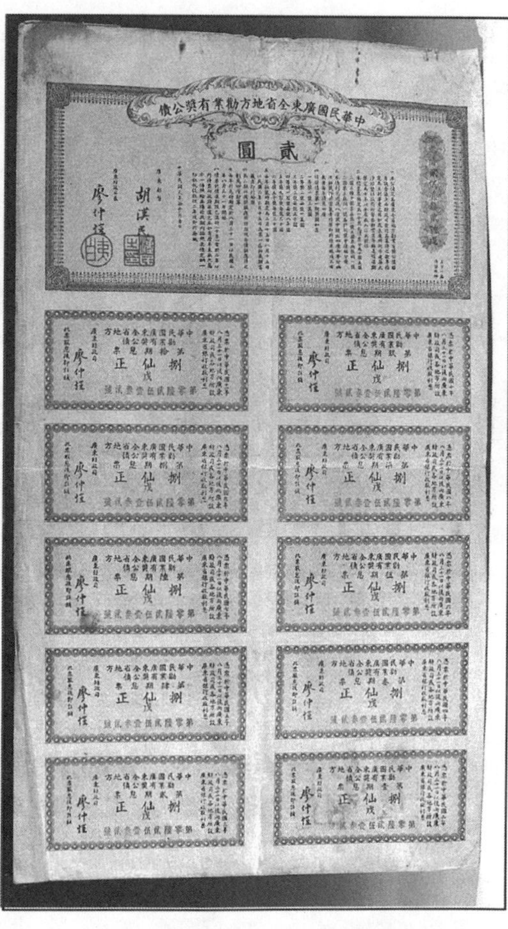

▶ 383

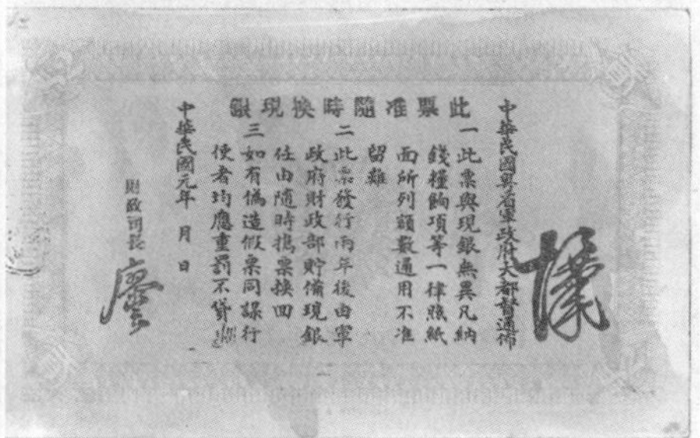

▲ 384

385. 广东军政府财政部副部长、财政司司长廖仲恺。

Liao Zhongkai, vice-minister of Ministry of Finance, chief of Financial Department of Guangdong Military Government.

386. 1912年6月底7月初，广东省议会通过了廖仲恺制定的广东地价税契法案《广东税契简章》，这是当时全国各省以法令形式来实行孙中山“平均地权”革命纲领的最早的也是唯一的尝试。图为1912年6月24日广州《民生日报》的有关报道。

From the beginning of June to the end of July 1912, Guangdong Provisional Senate passed Guangdong land tax and contract bill-*A Brief Charter of Guangdong Tax and Contract*, mapped out by Liao Zhongkai. It was the only and earliest valuable trial for practising the creed equal land right by laws in China. The photo of the relevant reports in *People's Livelihood Daily* in Guangzhou, dated June 24 , 1912.

385

第五頁　中華民國元年六月廿四日　（民生日報）　舊曆壬子年五月初十日　禮拜一

新聞二

386

工務部通告　工務部通告

工務部佈告

▲ 387

▲ 388

387. 广东军政府成立后，关注城市建设，设工务部专管市政建设事宜。图为工务部颁发的有关整治马路、疏通渠道、拆毁城墙的通告。

After Guangdong Military Government was established, it paid close attention to urban construction, too, setting up department of construction affairs in charge of urban construction. This is the notice issued by the department to renovate roads, to dredge the underground drainage and to demolish the city wall.

388. 广东军政府工务部部长程天斗。

Cheng Tiandou, head of department of construction affairs of Guangdong Military Government.

389. 为疏畅城市马路交通，1912年3月，广东军政府下令拆卸城墙。图为大北门附近城基拆卸后的情形。

In order to smooth the city traffics, in March 1912, Guangdong Military Government ordered to dismantle the city wall. This is the view near Dabeimen after dismantling the city wall foundation.

▲ 389

390. 拆城墙之前的广州大北门城楼。
The city gate tower at Dabeimen, Guangzhou, before the city wall was dismantled.

▼ 390

▲391

▲392

391. 1912年的广州城外沿江马路。

Yanjiang Road outside the city of Guangzhou in 1912.

392. 广东军政府教育司厉行教育改革，推动新式教育。图为教育司司长钟荣光。

The Education Department of Guangdong Military Government strictly enforced the education reform and promoted new-type education. This is Zhong Rongguang, chief of Education Department.

393. 1912年7月1日，广州《民生日报》刊登教育司对7岁以上学龄儿童实行强制义务教育的消息。

On July 1, 1912, *People's Livelihood Daily* published the news that Education Department implemented school-agers (above 7 years old) compulsory education.

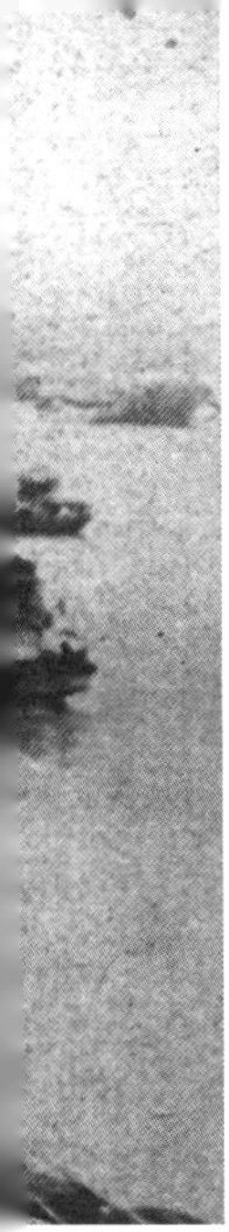

第五頁　中華民國元年七月一日　（民生日報）　舊曆壬子年五月十七日　禮拜一

新聞二

▲▲本省之聞

394

394. 1912年2月成立的广东高等师范学校，为民国初年广东唯一的高等学校。

In February 1912, Guangdong Higher Normal School was founded, which was the only higher learning institute in Guangdong in the early years of Republic of China.

395

396

395. 1912年10月，广东高等学校改为广东省立第一中学，实行高中三年、初中三年新学制，为广东学校试行新学制之始。图为省立一中校园。

In October 1912, Guangdong Senior High School was changed its name into The Provincial No.1 Middle School. The new school systems of three-year's senior and three year's junior were implemented. This was the start of new system tried out in Guangdong high schools. This is the campus of The Provincial No.1 Middle School.

396. 1912年10月10日，教育司组织广东男女学生大运动会。图为女学生浣衣竞走的场面。

On October 10,1912, Education Department organized Guangdong university sports meet of men and women students. This is the school-girls participating in heel-and-toe walking race.

397. 广东军政府民政司司长、警察厅厅长陈景华（香山人）。任内整顿警政,查禁烟赌,清除盗匪，革除旧俗，推行新政，创办女子教育院。

Chen Jinghua (from Xiangshan County), civil administration chief and police chief of Guangdong Military Government, rectified police policy,banned opium-smoking and gambling, removed bandits, expelled old customs, pursued new policies and established women education institute during his term of office.

▲397

廣東公報　命令　八月二日第二號　五

命令（本省）

都督令

都督令各屬購閱廣東公報文

廣東大都督令　旣開辦廣東公報以爲宣佈各項法令之用先經通告各級官廳知照在案查公報發行簡章第七條各官廳有購閱該報之義務爲此令仰俟該報發行後照章購閱預將應納全年報費送交該報印刷處收納准在公費內作正開銷並仰轉飭所屬一體遵照辦理毋得延忽此令　七月三十日發

都督諭廣陽綏靖處不准擅許娼寮營業文

廣東大都督諭　照得娼妓營業旣不正當際此地方未靖藏匿匪徒酗酒打架滋生事端尤屬在在堪虞前經前督陳諭令停止開設各縣令有地方之責應如何恪遵辦理乃訪聞南海縣令在佛山地方順德縣令在陳村地方有准許娼寮復業情事殊屬荒謬已極應即迅令取銷除分諭各該縣令凜遵辦理外合行諭飭貴綏靖處嗣後如查有未經稟准擅令開設娼寮者仰即將該准許開業官長嚴拿懲辦以肅官紀而靖地方此諭　七月三十日發

廣東公報　命令　八月十三日第十一號　八

經畧陳炯明
會辦龍濟光

總綏靖處通諭各督辦各縣令限期禁絕賭博文

爲通飭事照得粵省賭博之風爲害最烈久已懸爲厲禁經本處劃入軍事範圍歸督辦理獲犯得以軍法從事前已三令五申嚴加督飭禁例森嚴原期尅日肅清以絕盜源而安良善乃近日訪聞各縣賭風仍未少息豈督縣耳目有所不及抑故爲庇縱耶該督辦及各縣令等責無旁貸必當振刷精神設法嚴拿禁絕何得仍令披猖毫無察覺茲特嚴申禁令限至本年九月初十日以前務將所屬賭博一律禁絕凡有開設賭廠賭館嚴行查封或加焚拆其庇賭收規及出財開賭之犯獲訊明確由各綏靖處核准即行槍斃以昭炯戒如蠻鄉巨族有敢庇賭抗捕者格殺勿論自此次通飭之後各屬務必如限禁絕不准怠玩倘限後尚有賭博發見一經查出定惟該督縣是問治以弛禁縱賭之罪該督辦及各縣令等宜各凜遵愼勿違玩干咎切切特諭

經畧陳炯明
會辦龍濟光

廣東公報　命令　正月二十二日第一百四十五號　二十

再行發去刷印規則計四十本請貴司分交所屬各審判檢察廳及未設審檢廳地方之各受理訴訟衙門俾日後表式大小可歸一律等由到司爲此令仰該〇即便查照辦理此令　一月十八日發

警察廳佈告

佈告人民勿再干犯烟禁致罹罪罰文

二年一月一號以後凡吸烟及藏有烟具者必嚴重懲罰早經通佈乃因此被逮者日尚數十起本廳長不忍國民罹於罪罰爲此苦口瀆告有烟癮者切勿吸烟有烟具者速行銷燬萬勿玩視特再佈告　一月十八日發

▲ 398

398. 广东军政府颁布的禁烟、禁赌、禁娼文告。

The proclamation on prohibition of opium-smoking, gambling and prostitutes issued by Guangdong Military Government.

399.1912年6月11日，广州《民生日报》有关广东军政府禁烟、禁赌、禁娼的报道。

The news about Guangdong Military Government's prohibition of opium-smoking, gambling and prostitute published in the *People's Livelihood Daily* on June 11, 1912.

400. 1912年，广东地方检察厅判决惯盗周昌处以绞刑。图为在广州监狱内被执行绞刑的周昌。此为广东施行绞刑之第一次。

Guangdong Local Procuratorial Bureau sentenced Zhou Chang, a habitual thief, to hanging. This is Zhou Chang, who is being hanged in Guangzhou Prison. This was the first hanging in Guangdong.

第五頁　中華民國元年六月十一日　（民生日報）　舊歷壬子年四月廿六日　禮拜二

新聞二

▲▲本省之續

▲▲煙精又叫苦

胡都督示、查禁烟一事、前經警察廳擬定禁吸期限、以本年十二月三十一爲期、宣布在案、惟禁烟必先禁運、尤在禁種禁吸、方能杜絕本源、剷除積弊、合再出示嚴禁、爲此示仰一體遵知、嗣後如再有私種、應以文到日、即行禁絕、其私吸不遵限期戒斷者、一經查出、立予嚴懲、不稍寬貸特示、

▲▲蠶市悲盜

容奇桂州兩鄉、近因盜劫頻頻、各蠶市均皆休業、昨年風潮、順德蠶絲損失數十萬、幸本年頭造桑大豐、絲綢消路頗旺、故各農工皆有些活動、已稍漸恢復、今因被劫者、日有數起、故多有開張而仍閉者、不知政界諸公、有何術以去此爲生大害也、

▲▲烟怪現形

禁烟事務、自歸警察辦理後、經飭行各區署嚴密查拿、連日計起獲私開煙燈者數十人、城廂內外、私燈爲之一絕、日昨警察在九如坊拘捕烟人二名、併烟槍烟斗等項、該烟人骨瘦如柴、兩肩高聳、口涎旁滴、噴唾交流、途觀者均謂民國頭等廢人、均推此二君矣、

▲▲拿獲妓婦數十名

邇來省垣寮寨、實爲警廳取締、各區均已歇業、惟陳塘一帶、仍有私娼聚集、引動匪人、不料昨晚八時、爲巡警偵悉、當場拿獲妓婦數十名、解交第九區署、未知如何懲辦也、

▲▲侯廣賓之催命符

廣軍標統侯廣賓、近日因案拘留於法務局中、昨有清遠何維範、復以伊私將營中鎗械藥彈、賣與李文軒、又私購鎗枝、運回清遠、居心實不可問等情、控諸都督、現飭法務局併案查明、噫、侯之被控如確、候補打靶人員、又添一個矣、

▲▲嚴辦抗阻開礦者

都督批、羅定縣呈報杜姓抗阻黃膽礦命礦情形由、批、曾耀新承辦黃膽礦、該杜姓人等、竟敢糾衆抗

399

400

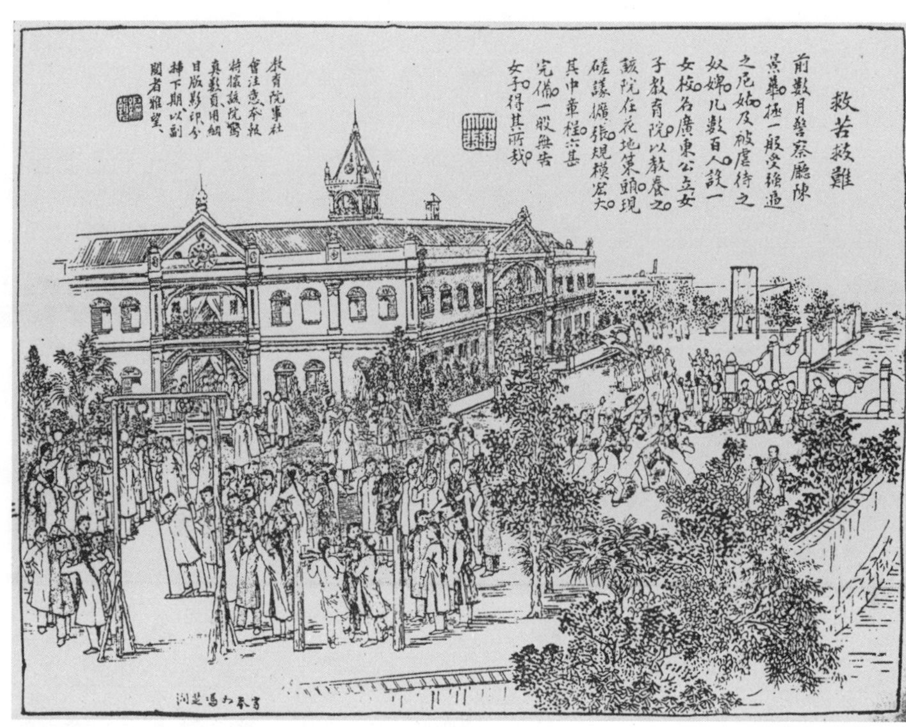
救苦救難
前數月警察廳陳景華極一般受稀造之厄姤及被虐待之奴婢凡數百人設一女校名廣東公立女子教育院以教養之該院在花地策頭現硅議擴張規模宏大其中章程亦甚完備一般無告女子得其所哉
教育院事社會注意本報特據該院寫真數頁用銅目版影印今特下期以副閱者雅望

401

碧血丹心
——辛亥革命在广东影像实录

402

▲403

401. 1912年10月，陈景华、潘达微在广州花地创办广东公立女子教育院，专门收容受虐待的婢妾、雏妓、幼尼等受苦女子。

In October 1912, Chen Jinghua and Pan Dawei established Guangdong Public Woman Education Institute in Huadi, Guangzhou, specially accommodating suffering women, such as abused slave girls, concubines, young prostitutes, young nuns, etc.

402. 1912年3月5日，孙中山在南京出席粤中倡义死事诸烈士追悼会。

On March 5, 1912, Sun Yat-sen presented at the memorial meeting in Nanjing, to mourn for martyrs in all previous uprisings in Guangdong.

403. 1912年2月，孙中山辞去临时大总统职，任全国铁路督办。4月1日，孙中山莅临临时参议院举行临时大总统解职典礼后与代表合影。

Sun Yat-sen resigned the Provisional Grand President's duty and acted as the National Railway Supervisor in February 1912. On April 1, Sun Yat-sen took a group picture with participants after presented the resignation ceremony of Provisional Grand President held by the Provisional Senate.

▲404

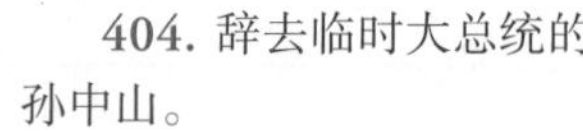

404. 辞去临时大总统的孙中山。

Sun Yat-sen resigned the Provisional Grand President' duty.

▼405

廣東陸軍全體歡迎第一期大總統中山孫先生回粵撮影圖

▲ 406

405. 1912年4月25日，孙中山抵广州视察，26日，孙中山出席广东陆军在广州德宣街陆军司令部举行的欢迎会，并发表演说。图为在欢迎会上合影。

On April 25, 1912, Sun Yat-sen arrived in Guangzhou for inspection. On 26, he attended the welcoming reception held by headquarters of Land Army at Dexuan Street in Guangzhou and delivered a speech. The picture is a group photo at the welcoming reception.

406. 1912年5月2日，上海《民立报》刊登《孙中山先生抵粤记》，报道孙中山抵粤的盛况以及孙中山向广东陆军所作的演说。

On May 2,1912, Shanghai's *Minlibao* published *Mr. Sun Yat-sen's Arriving in Guangdong*, reporting the grand occasion and Sun Yat-sen's speech for the ground force of Guangdong.

407

408

▲ 409

407. 1912年4月29日，孙中山出席广东同盟模范军欢迎会的合影。

On April 29, 1912, Sun Yat-sen attended the welcoming meeting of Guangdong Allied Model Troop and took a group photo.

408. 1912年5月4日，孙中山出席广州报界在东园举行的欢迎会，并作关于平均地权具体方法的演说。图为在欢迎会上合影。

On May 4, 1912, Sun Yat-sen attended the welcoming reception by Guangzhou press at Dongyuan and made a speech about the concrete methods in equalization of land right. This is a group photo at the welcoming reception.

409. 1912年5月12日，上海《民立报》发表孙中山在广州报界欢迎会上所作的关于平均地权具体方法的演说。

On May 12, 1912, Shanghai's *Minlibao* published Sun Yat-sen's speech about the concrete methods in equalization of land rights at the welcoming reception by Guangzhou press.

▲410

▲411

▲412

410. 1912年5月7日，孙中山出席岭南学堂的欢迎会，并在马丁堂向员生作“非学问无以建设”的演讲。图为在欢迎会上合影。

On May 7,1912, Sun Yat-sen attended the welcoming reception of Lingnan School and delivered a speech of *No Knowledge, No Construction* at Martin Hall. The picture is a group photo at the welcoming reception.

411. 1912年5月9日，孙中山出席母校广州博济医院欢迎大会合影。

On May 9, 1912, Sun Yat-sen attended the welcoming reception of his Alma Mater—Guangzhou (Boji) Hospital Medical College. This is a group photo.

412. 1912年5月9日下午，孙中山出席在广东军政府卫生司举行的医学共进会欢迎会，并被推为该会名誉会长。图为在欢迎会上合影。前排右四为孙中山、右三为孙中山次女孙婉、右五为宋霭龄。

On the afternoon of May 9, 1912, Sun Yat-sen attended the welcoming reception by Health and Medical Department of Guangdong Military Government and was elected the honorary chairman. The picture is a group photo at the reception. From right in front row, the fourth is Sun Tat-sen, the third is Sun Wan, Sun Yat-sen's second daughter, the fifth is Song Ailing.

413

414

415

413. 1912年5月11日下午，孙中山出席于广州大石街萧公馆举行的孙族恳亲会时合影。

On the afternoon of May 11, 1912, Sun Yat-sen attended a meeting of Sun Clan at Hall of Lord Xiao in Dashi Street, Guangzhou. This is a group photo of the meeting.

414. 1912年5月12日，孙中山等与留广州的日本人士合影。二排右起：廖仲恺、孙婉、孙中山、宋霭龄。

Sun Yat-sen with friends from Japan in a picture taken on Guangzhou on May 12, 1912. Second row from right: Liao Zhongkai, Sun Wan, Sun Yat-sen and Song Ailing.

415. 1912年5月13日，孙中山在广州巡视广东黄埔海军学堂后与师生合影。

Sun Yat-sen took a group photo with teachers and students after an inspection tour of Guangdong Huangpu Navy School in Guangzhou on May 13, 1912.

▲416

▲417

416. 1912年5月17日下午，孙中山出席商办粤路公司欢迎会时合影。前排右一为著名铁路工程师詹天佑。

On the afternoon of May 17,1912, Sun Yat-sen attended the welcoming reception of Guangdong Railway Company run by traders and took a group photo. The first from right in the front is Zhan Tianyou, the famous railway engineer.

417. 1912年5月17日，孙中山偕夫人卢慕贞及子女出席广东佛教总会于广州六榕寺召开的欢迎会时合影。

On May 17, 1912, Sun Yat-sen, together with his wife—Lu Muzhen and children, attended the welcoming reception by Guangdong General Society of Buddhism in Six Banyan Temple in Guangzhou and took a group photo.

418. 1912年5月18日，孙中山抵香港。图为孙中山下榻的香港大酒店。

Sun Yat-sen arrived in Hong Kong on May 18, 1912. It is a picture of Hong Kong Hotel Sun Yat-sen stayed.

▼ 418

419

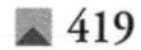

420

▲421

419. 1912年5月下旬，孙中山与家人自香港取道澳门访问家乡香山翠亨村。5月22日，抵澳门。5月24日，孙中山在卢园（今卢廉若公园）与各界人士合影。

In the latter part of May, 1912, Sun Yat-sen and his family visited his hometown Cuiheng Village of Xiangshan County from Hong Kong, passing through Macao. On May 22, they arrived in Macao. On May 24, Sun Yat-sen took a photo with people from all circles in Lu Garden (presently the Lu Lianruo Garden).

420. 1912年5月24日，孙中山与澳葡总督、主教及绅商名流等在卢园合影。

On May 24, 1912, Sun Yat-sen was together with Macau's Governor, bishop, gentlemen, businessmen, celebrities and others in the Lu Garden in Macau.

421. 1912年5月24日，孙中山视察香山香洲时，与欢迎者合影。

Sun Yat-sen with gladhander when he visited Xiangzhou of Xiangshan County on May 24, 1912.

碧血丹心
——辛亥革命在广东影像实录

▲422

恭都公立小學
中華民國元年五月二十五日
孫總理遜位臨時總統由南京回粵時蒞臨前山首次躬親行抵前山中山亭
美基與禮本區各界人士開歡迎大會於恭都公立小學堂合照
劉希明誌

▲423

▲424

422. 1912年5月25日，孙中山访问早年从医的澳门镜湖医院。图为孙中山与镜湖医院值理在卢园春草堂门廊前合影。右五为孙中山，右六为孙婉，右一为卢园主人卢廉若。

On May 25, 1912, Sun Yat-sen visited Jinghu Hospital, where he practiced medicine in early years. The picture shows Sun Yat-sen with Director of Jinghu Hospital in front of the porch of Chuncao Hall in Lu Garden. The fifth from right was Sun Yat-sen, the sixth from right was Sun Wan, and the first from right was Lu Lianruo, owner of the Lu Garden.

423. 1912年5月25日，孙中山应邀到香山恭都前山（今属珠海市）参加中山亭奠基仪式。图为孙中山与欢迎者合影。

On May 25, 1912, Sun Yat-sen was invited to Gongdu Qianshan of Xiangshan County (presently belongs to Zhuhai) to attend the foundation ceremony of Zhongshan Pavilion. The picture shows Sun Yat-sen together with gladhander.

424. 1921年5月27日，孙中山自澳门抵翠亨村，在家乡仅3天，即于5月30日晨至广州，旋赴上海，再为国事奔走。图为孙中山抵翠亨村与当地天主教教士握手时的情景。

On May 27, 1912, Sun Yat-sen reached Cuiheng Village from Macau. He stayed in hometown only three days then arrived in Guangzhou on morning of May 30, and continued to Shanghai for the national affairs. It is a picture Sun Yat-sen in Cuiheng Village, shaking hands with a Catholicism clergyman.

425

425. 1912年5月27日，孙中山在家乡住室前与家人合影。左起：孙中山次女孙婉、秘书宋霭龄、夫人卢慕贞、孙中山、孙眉、孙眉夫人，右一为孙中山长女孙娫。

On May 27, 1912, Sun Yat-sen took a picture with family in front of the room in hometown. From left: Sun Wan, the second daughter of Sun Yat-sen; Song Ailing, the secretary; Lu Muzhen, Sun Yat-sen's wife; Sun Yat-sen; Sun Mei; Sun Mei's wife. The first from right is Sun Yan, the oldest daughter of Sun Yat-sen.

426

▲427

▲428

426. 1912年5月28日，孙中山在香山县左埗乡与宗亲在孙氏宗祠前合影。

A group photo of Sun Yat-sen with his relatives taken in front of Sun Clan's Ancestral Hall at Zuobu Village in Xiangshan County on May 28, 1912.

427. 1912年5月，孙中山与家人在广州合影。前排左起：卢慕贞、孙中山；后排左起：孙娫、孙科、秘书宋霭龄、孙婉。

In May 1912, Sun Yat-sen and family took a group photo in Guangzhou. The front row from the left: Lu Muzhen, Sun Yat-sen; the back row from left: Sun Yan, Sun Ke, Song Ailing(secretary), Sun Wan.

428. 袁世凯窃取国家政权后，梦想建立封建专制独裁统治。1913年3月20日，袁世凯派人在上海暗杀国民党代理理事长宋教仁。图为被刺身亡的宋教仁。

After Yuan Shikai stole the state power, dreaming of resuming feudal autocratic rule, on March 20, 1913, Yuan Shikai sent a killer to assassinate Song Jiaoren, Kuomintang's acting president in Shanghai. The Picture shows dead Song Jiaoren after assassinated.

▲429

429. 1913年6月中旬，为策动陈炯明宣布广东独立讨袁，孙中山由沪乘船往香港、澳门。图为孙中山在赴粤途中与同志合影。

In the mid of June 1913, Sun Yat-sen left Shanghai for Hong Kong and Macao by ship to persuade Chen Jiongming declaring to suppress Yuan Shikai independently in Guangdong. It is a photo Sun Yat-sen together with comrades on the way to Guangdong.

430. 为反击袁世凯的倒行逆施，捍卫共和制度，1913年7月，孙中山发动反袁的“二次革命”。图为孙中山于7月22日在上海《民立报》发表的讨袁宣言。

In July 1913, Sun Yat-sen launched the Second Revolution against Yuan Shikai's retroaction in order to defend republic system. This is Sun Yat-sen's statement of condemning Yuan published in Shanghai's *Minlibao* on July 22.

(西曆一九一三年……) 民立報 (第九百九十二號) (陰曆癸丑年六月十九日) (第二頁)

言論之部

孫中山先生宣言

當南北統一之際：僕推薦袁世凱於參議院：原望其開誠布公：盡忠民國：以慰四萬萬人之望：自是以來：僕於權利所在：則爲引避：危疑之交：則爲襄助：雖激昂之士：對於袁氏：時有責言：僕之初衷：未嘗少易：不意宋案發生：袁氏陰謀：一旦盡揭：僕於當時：已將反對袁氏之心：宣布天下：使袁氏果知公義自在：輿論難誣：爾時即應辭職：以謝國民：何圖袁氏專爲私謀：倒行不已：以致東南人民：荷戈而逐：旬日之內：相連並發：大勢如此：國家安危：人民生死：胥繫於袁氏一人之去留：爲公僕者：不以國利民福爲懷：反欲犧牲國家與人民：以爭一己之位置：中華民國豈容開此先例：願全體國民一致主張令袁氏辭職：以息戰禍：庶可以挽國危而慰民望：無任翹企之至：

敬告全國同胞

（蔡）子民

兵凶戰危：吾儕安分良民：對於不正當之戰爭：決無有贊成之者：其正當之戰爭：爲保護吾儕安全幸福之間接作用：則吾儕不特不肯反對：且相率而助成之：其或吾儕雖不必加入戰爭：而確於戰爭以外：尚有可以致力之處：使吾儕之安全幸福：由此而保存：而且使間接作用之戰爭：由此而截止：則尤吾儕所當引以爲己任者矣：

一年以來：政府之失德：雖吾儕摯愛之者：決不能爲之諱：至於恣行暗殺：擅借外欵：不復留吾儕以承認政府之餘地：吾儕中之一部份所謂民黨也者：攻擊政府爲激烈之主張：何嘗不公認爲必不得已之舉：徒以兵亂初經：瘡痍未復：苟於平和解決一方面：尚有幾希之望：則終告誡民黨：而强抑制之：雖然政府之播惡也：乃變本而加厲：且以是爲鋤除民黨之機會：而日日與之挑戰：於斯時也：吾儕而稍稍移其注視民黨之目光：而靜觀政府：得民黨所以不能不激昂之故：糾政府而去其疾：未嘗不可以達保持和平之希望：不幸吾儕大多數見未及此：徒日日監視民黨：責以不許妄動：而轉使政府益放其縱惡挑戰之手段：旣民黨忍無可忍：而爲武力解決之宣告：反之於吾儕往日希望平和之美意：誠不能不謂之失望：然吾儕於歸咎政府之餘：又不能不自省縱容政府之過：而深自引咎也：

今者戰端開矣：猶未至全國糜爛之境也：往者不諫：來者可追：吾儕而坐視其孰勝孰負：若秦越人之觀肥瘠：則亦已耳：若惕於戰禍之延長：而爲迅

▲430

431

431. 1913年7月18日，广东都督陈炯明宣布广东独立，加入反袁武装斗争的行列。图为陈炯明。

On July 18,1913,Chen Jiongming, Guangdong provincial military governor,declared independence of Guangdong and joined in the struggle against Yuan. This is Chen Jiongming.

432. 1913年7月19日广州《民生日报》发表陈炯明以广东大都督兼讨袁军总司令名义发布的讨袁布告。

The Proclamation of Condemning Yuan issued by Chen Jiongming in the name of Guangdong provincial military governor and commander-in-chief of the punitive expedition army against Yuan published in *People's Livelihood Daily* on July 19,1913.

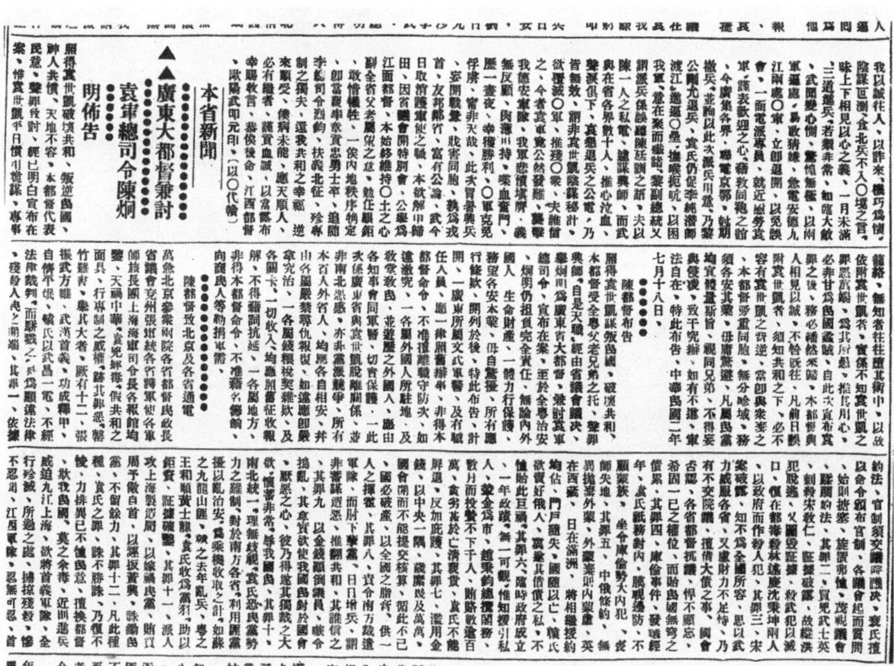

本省新聞

廣東大都督兼討袁軍總司令陳炯明佈告

432

▲433

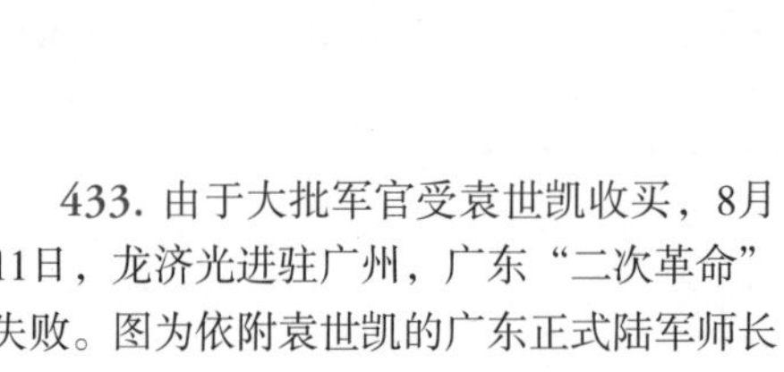

433. 由于大批军官受袁世凯收买，8月11日，龙济光进驻广州，广东“二次革命”失败。图为依附袁世凯的广东正式陆军师长钟鼎基。

Because a large number of officers were bought over with bribery by Yuan Shikai. On August 11, Long Jiguang entered and stationed in Guangzhou. The Second Revolution in Guangdong failed. The picture is Zhong Dingji, division commander of regular ground force of Guangdong, who attached himself to Yuan Shikai.

▲434

434. 1913年8月3日，袁世凯任命龙济光为广东都督兼署民政长，并授为陆军上将。广东进入了军阀龙济光的统治时期。图为龙济光。

On August 3, 1913, Yuan Shikai appointed Long Jiguang as Guangdong provincial governor and director of Civil Affairs, and awarded him General of Land Army. Guangdong entered the ruling period of warlord—Long Jiguang. This is Long Jiguang.

伍 FIVE

永恒的纪念

Eternal Commemoration

轰轰烈烈的辛亥革命运动虽然以失败告终，但是以孙中山为首的中国资产阶级革命民主派领导的这场革命运动，是中国近代旧民主革命的高峰，具有划时代的历史意义。这次革命推翻了清朝的统治，结束了中国延续两千多年的封建君主专制制度，创立了中华民国，广泛传播了民主共和思想，为以后的革命运动开辟道路，促进中华民族历史的发展。

广东作为辛亥革命的主要策源地和重要战场，在辛亥革命史上占有重要的历史地位。在这片热土上，一代南粤儿女为挽救民族危亡，追求祖国的独立、统一、民主、富强，前赴后继，英勇奋斗，谱写出可歌可泣的光辉篇章。孙中山和广东革命党人在这场革命运动中所建立的不朽功业和表现出来的崇高爱国主义精神，永垂青史，值得后人永恒纪念。

Though the dynamic Revolution of 1911 ended in failure, the revolutionary movement led by Chinese bourgeois revolution democratic group headed by Sun Yat-sen was a peak of China's modern old democratic revolution, which is of the epoch-making historic significance. This revolution had overthrown the governance of Qing Dynasty, and put an end to China's feudal autocratic monarchy systems which extended more than 2,000 years in succession and founded the Republic of China, propagated the democratic republicanism thought extensively, opened up the road for the revolutionary movement for the future, and promoted the development of Chinese nation's history.

Guangdong occupied the important historical position in the Revolution of 1911, as the main base and important battle fields. On this stretch of hot soil, a generation of sons and daughters of Guangdong, who pursued the independent, united, democratic, prosperous and strong motherland, advanced wave upon wave in order to save the nation at stake and struggled bravely, which had composed the heroic and moving, glorious chapter. Sun Yat-sen and Guangdong revolutionary Partisan's immortal exploits and sublime patriotic spirit shown in this revolutionary movement, will be forever remembered in the annals of history, and deserve descendants' eternal commemoration.

▲435

435. 为纪念辛亥革命的胜利，中华民国临时政府1912年9月28日公布以武昌首义日（即10月10日）为国庆日。1912年10月10日，广东都督府举行隆重的国庆庆祝活动。图为广东都督胡汉民、副都督陈炯明赴广州东郊检阅军队情形。

In order to commemorate the victory of the Revolution of 1911, on September 28, 1912, the Provisional Government of the Republic of China announced the date (October 10th) on which the Wuchang Uprising broke out as the National Day. On October 10, 1912, Guangdong government held a grand celebration of National Day. Hu Hanmin, Guangdong provincial military governor, and Chen Jiongming, deputy provincial military governor, were going to inspect troops in the eastern suburbs of Guangzhou.

436

436. 在国庆日接受检阅的军队。
The troops being inspected on National Day.

437. 国庆日的香港海滨。
The seashore of Hong Kong on National Day.

437

▲ 438

438. 国庆日的香港街道。

The Hong Kong streets on National Day.

439. 广东中山市翠亨村孙中山故居纪念馆大门。

The gate of memorial museum of Sun Yat-sen's former residence at Cuiheng Village in Zhongshan City of Guangdong Province.

▼ 439

440

441

440. 孙中山故居正面图。1892年孙中山设计建造。

The main building of Sun Yat-sen's former residence,designed by Sun Yat-sen in 1892.

441. 1935年11月2日，孙中山早年学医的博济医院改名为孙逸仙博士纪念医院并竖立纪念碑。

On November 2, 1935, Guangzhou (Boji) Hospital, where Sun Yat-sen studied medicine in early years, renamed as Dr. Sun Yat-sen Memorial Hospital and set up a monument.

▲ 442

442. 广州先烈南路青龙坊的兴中会坟场。1923年兴建。

The tomb field of China Revival Society at Qinglongfang, Xianlie Road South, Guangzhou, built in 1923.

443. 中华民国成立后，在潮州西湖边建立的黄冈起义纪念塔。

After the Republic of China was founded, the Monument Tower of Huanggang Uprising (1907) was set up beside the West Lake of Chaozhou.

▼ 443

▲ 444

▼ 445

444. 1934年建立的黄冈丁未（1907）革命纪念亭。

Huanggang Uprising (1907) Revolutionary Memorial Pavilion set up in 1934.

445. 广州沙河先烈路庚戌新军起义烈士墓。

The martyrs' tombs of New Army Uprising (1910) at Xianlie Road, Guangzhou.

446. 1912年5月15日，孙中山率广州各界人士十余万人至广州黄花岗，主持公祭黄花岗起义烈士。

On May 15,1912, Sun Yat-sen led more than 100,000 people from all walks of life in Guangzhou to Yellow Flower Hill and presided the public memorial ceremony of martyrs.

446

447

447. 1912年5月15日，广东海军致祭黄花岗起义烈士的场面。

The scene of mourning martyrs of Yellow Flower Hill Uprising by the soldiers of Guangdong Navy on May 15,1912.

448

449

450

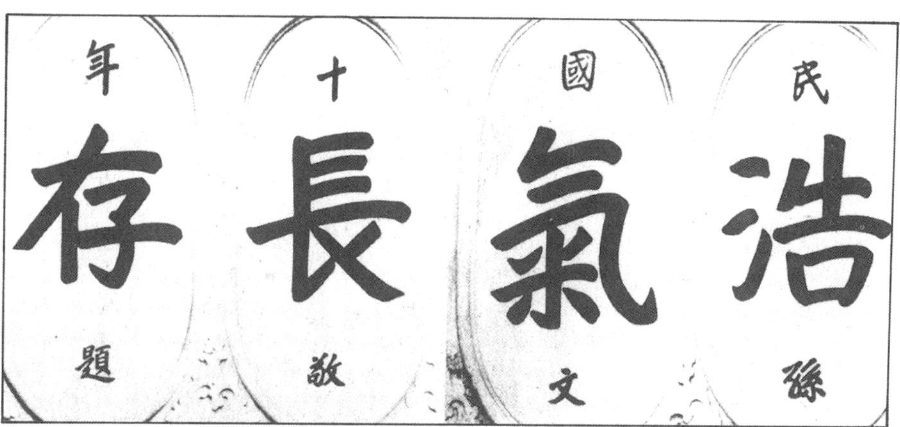

451

黃花岡七十二烈士之碑

448. 1919—1920年间，广州各界公祭黄花岗七十二烈士墓。

Between 1919 and 1920, all circles in Guangzhou held a public memorial ceremony at the Mausoleum of 72 Martyrs of Yellow Flower Hill Uprising.

449. 广州黄花岗七十二烈士墓。

Mausoleum of 72 Martyrs of Yellow Flower Hill Uprising.

450. 孙中山为黄花岗七十二烈士墓的题词。

The tomb epigraph of 72 Martyrs of Yellow Flower Hill Uprising, written by Sun Yat-sen.

451. 黄花岗七十二烈士之碑。

The tablets of 72 Martyrs of Yellow Flower Hill Uprising.

452. 1911年11月，各界改葬林冠慈于红花岗（即今黄花岗），并举行追悼礼的场面。

In November 1911, The scene of mourning Lin Guanci by all walks of life while changing his burial ground to Red Flower Hill (today's Yellow Flower Hill).

453. 1918年兴建的安葬温生才、林冠慈、陈敬岳和钟明光的红花岗四烈士墓。

The four martyrs'tombs of Wen Shengcai, Lin Guanci, Chen Jingyue and Zhong Mingguang, in Red Flower Hill, build in 1918.

▲ 452

▼ 453

454. 红花岗四烈士墓道。

The tomb-tablet of four Martyrs in Red Flower Hill.

455. 越秀山广东光复纪念碑，建于1929年，表彰香港同胞捐资支持广东光复的伟大功绩。1938年遭日寇毁灭。

Guangdong Memorial Pavilion for Restoration in Yuexiu Hill, built in 1929, in praise of the great contribution of Hong Kong compatriot's donation and support for restoration of Guangdong. In 1938, it was destroyed by Japanese invaders.

454

455

▲456

▲457

458

459

456. 越秀山广东光复纪念亭。建于1948年。
Guangdong Memorial Pavilion for Restoration in Yuexiu Hill, built in 1948.

457. 广东中山市翠亨村的陆皓东烈士坟场。
The tomb field of Lu Haodong at Cuiheng Village of Zhongshan City in Guangdong Province.

458. 广州先烈南路青菜岗的史坚如墓。1913年兴建。
Shi Jianru's tomb at Qingcaigang in Xianlie Road South, Guangzhou, built in 1913.

459. 广州先烈南路青龙坊的邓荫南墓。1929年兴建。
Deng Yinnan's tomb at Qinglongfang, Xianlie Road South, Guangzhou, built in 1929.

▲ 460

◀ 461

460. 黄花岗七十二烈士墓东侧的潘达微墓。1951年兴建。

Pan Dawei's tomb at the east side of 72 Martyrs Tomb of Yellow Flower Hill, built in 1951.

461. 广州先烈东路驷马岗的朱执信墓。

Zhu Zhixin's tomb at Simagang in Xianlie Road East, Guangzhou.

▲ 462

▼ 463

462. 广州先烈东路黄花岗公园内的邓仲元墓。1924年兴建。

Deng Zhongyuan's tomb inside Mausoleum of 72 Martyrs of Yellow Flower Hill in Xianlie Road East, Guangzhou, built in 1924.

463. 广州仲恺农学院的廖仲恺先生纪念碑。1978年重建。

The monument to Mr. Liao Zhongkai inside Zhongkai College of Agriculture, Guangzhou, rebuilt in 1978.

▲464

▼465

464. 广州市龙眼洞的胡汉民墓。1936年兴建，后毁。1985年重建。

Tomb of Hu Hanmin in Longyandong in Guangzhou, originally built in 1936, destroyed later and rebuilt in 1985.

465. 广东惠州西湖紫微山东麓的陈炯明墓。1934年兴建。

Tomb of Chen Jiongming in East foot of Ziwei Mountain near West Lake in Huizhou City, Guangdong Province, built in 1934.

466. 广东中山市翠亨村北犁头尖山的孙眉墓。1934年兴建。

Tomb of Sun Mei in north Litoujian Mountain, Cuiheng Village, Zhongshan City, Guangdong Province, built in 1934.

467. 广东中山市翠亨村金槟榔山的杨鹤龄墓。1934年兴建。

Tomb of Yang Heling in Jinbinlang Mountain, Cuiheng Village, Zhongshan City, Guangdong Province, built in 1934.

466

467

468

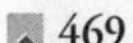
469

470

468. 广东江门市外海茶庵后山的陈少白墓。1935年兴建。

Tomb of Chen Shaobai in back Cha'an Mountain, Waihai Town, Jiangmen City, Guangdong Province, built in 1935.

469. 广东珠海市前山的中山纪念亭。1912年孙中山亲自奠基兴建，1928年重修。

The memorial pavilion of Sun Yat-sen at Qianshan in Zhuhai City of Guangdong Province. Sun Yat-sen laid a foundation personally in 1912, rebuilt in 1928.

470. 越秀山中山纪念碑。1929年兴建。

The Monument Stele of Sun Yat-sen in Yuexiu Hill, built in 1929.

471. 澳门国父纪念馆。1918兴建，1930年因军队火药库爆炸被毁，1933年由孙科重建。

The Memorial Museum of Father of Republic in Macao, built in 1918, destroyed by the explosion of the army's ammunition warehouse and rebuilt in 1933 by Sun Ke.

▼ 471

▲ 472

▼ 473

472. 中山大学。1926年8月17日，为纪念孙中山，将原广东大学改名为中山大学。

Sun Yat-sen University. On August 17, 1926, in memory of Dr. Sun Yat-sen, the former University of Guangdong was renamed Sun Yat-sen University.

473. 广州中山纪念堂。1931年落成。

Guangzhou Sun Yat-sen Memorial Hall, built in 1931.

474. 广州市立中山图书馆。1933年落成开馆。

The Municipal Sun Yat-sen library, Guangzhou, opened in 1933.

474

后记 POSTSCRIPT

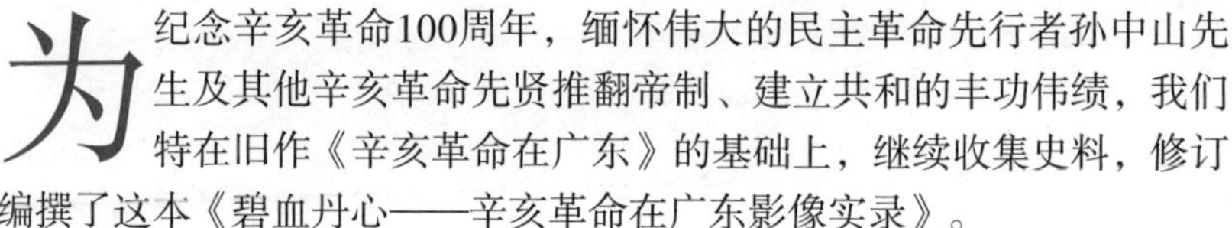

为纪念辛亥革命100周年，缅怀伟大的民主革命先行者孙中山先生及其他辛亥革命先贤推翻帝制、建立共和的丰功伟绩，我们特在旧作《辛亥革命在广东》的基础上，继续收集史料，修订编撰了这本《碧血丹心——辛亥革命在广东影像实录》。

编撰者在广泛搜集有关广东辛亥革命历史资料的基础上，力求比较全面和客观地反映广东辛亥革命的历史过程。在编纂过程中，得到中山大学历史系段云章老师、余齐昭老师、吴义雄老师的热情帮助，广东省立中山图书馆黄群庆研究馆员协助翻译70余幅图片的英文说明，并校对英文书稿，郭超强先生协助全书图片的扫描，在此谨致以诚挚的感谢！

限于编撰者的学识水平，本书可能存在某些疏漏和错误，期待广大读者批评指正。

倪俊明

2011年6月1日

In order to commemorate the 100th anniversary of the Revolution of 1911 and to recall the great achievement of Mr.Sun Yat-sen, the great democratic revolution forerunner, and of other sages of the Revolution of 1911, who overthrew the autocratic monarchy and founded a republic, we revised and compiled this album: Righteous Blood and Red Heart—Recording The Revolution of 1911 in Guangdong Through Camera Lens, at the basis of the previous work, The Revolution of 1911 in Guangdong, after continuous search for historical pictures.

On the basis of extensive collecting the historical materials about the Revolution of 1911 in Guangdong, we make every effort to reflect the historical course of the Revolution of 1911 in Guangdong objectively and in an all-round way. In the course of compiling, we got enthusiastic helps from Prof. Duan Yunzhang, Prof. Yu Qizhao and Wu Yixiong from History Department of Sun Yat-sen University. Also, Huang Qunqing, professorial librarian in Sun Yat-sen Library of Guangdong

Province assists translating the captions into English for about 70 pictures and proofreading the manuscript in English. And Mr. Guo Chaoqiang assists scanning all the pictures in this album. We express sincere thanks to them here!

Since our knowledge is limited, our album may have some careless omissions and weakness, we welcome any comments and suggestions from readers.

Ni Junming
June 1, 2011